THE OXFORD BOOK OF
Spy Stories

THE OXFORD BOOK OF

Spy Stories

Edited by

Michael Cox

Oxford   New York

OXFORD UNIVERSITY PRESS

1996

Oxford University Press, Walton Street, Oxford OX2 6DP
Oxford New York
Athens Auckland Bangkok Bombay
Calcutta Cape Town Dar es Salaam Delhi
Florence Hong Kong Istanbul Karachi
Kuala Lumpur Madras Madrid Melbourne
Mexico City Nairobi Paris Singapore
Taipei Tokyo Toronto
and associated companies in
Berlin Ibadan

Oxford is a trade mark of Oxford University Press

British Library Cataloguing in Publication Data
Data available

Library of Congress Cataloging in Publication Data
The Oxford book of spy stories / edited by Michael Cox.
p.   cm.
1. Spy stories, English.   I. Cox, Michael, 1948–
PR1309.S7094   1996   823'.087208—dc20   95–15519
ISBN 0–19–214242–9

10 9 8 7 6 5 4 3 2 1

Typeset by Graphicraft Typesetters Ltd., Hong Kong
Printed in Great Britain
on acid-free paper by
The Bath Press Ltd
Bath, Avon

For Harry and Eleanor

ACKNOWLEDGEMENTS

I am grateful to the following individuals and institutions for help and assistance of various kinds received during the course of compiling this anthology: Jack Adrian; Rosemary Herbert; Edward D. Hoch; Dr Rhodri Jeffreys Jones; John McLaughlin; Jean Sanderson; Professor John Sutherland; Professor David Trotter; the staff of the Bodleian Library, Oxford; the staff of the University Library, Cambridge. I must thank particularly Professor Robin W. Winks at Yale for his advice and good offices regarding American authors and stories, and, above all, Owen Dudley Edwards for his unfailing helpfulness.

CONTENTS

x · *Contents*

INTRODUCTION

'I wonder if a man is less a traitor when he is twice a traitor?'

G. K. Chesterton, 'The Fairy Tale of Father Brown'

The world of the spy story is, by definition, founded on deception, betrayal, and duplicity. But at the same time it is also one in which patriotism, duty, and selfless sacrifice supply the springs of action. It is a genre replete with dualities. The spy story can present itself as a plain no-nonsense thriller, or cloak itself in shifting ambiguities; celebrate cynical manipulation as much as honourable enterprise; tell it like it is, or how it never was. Read it one way and it can be filed under adventure, pure and simple; read it another, and it becomes propaganda, or even a potent philosophical metaphor; sometimes it is all three at once.

Operating in the macrocosm of political ideologies and national loyalties, many spy stories concurrently focus on individual predicaments— moral choices, questions of identity and perception, the price of loyalty. In a genre in which there are few true absolutes, viewpoint is paramount. '"You have employed spies to dog me?"' cries the villain in a story by E. Phillips Oppenheim, included in this collection: '"We don't call the officers of the American Intelligence Department spies," Mr Cray observed coldly.' Yet morally dubious, even criminal, activities are routinely sanctioned in spy fiction. The national interest being the supreme neutralizer of iniquity, however, it becomes a simple matter for those engaged in espionage to assume, like Mr Cray, that their side—which, in fiction, is almost invariably 'our' side—operates from a position of moral superiority. As James Bond says to 'M' in *For Your Eyes Only* (1960), '"I suppose I assume that when I'm given an unpleasant job in the Service the cause is a just one.' And so it is that throughout spy fiction, from its imperial beginnings in the late nineteenth century to the bleak fantasies of the late twentieth, runs the black thread of the double standard: *They* are spies; *We* act secretly. *They* pursue unprincipled ends; *We* have God on our side. There is only one moral law in espionage, whether fictional or real: justification by results.

The spy—mostly he, sometimes she—is one of the great icons of the twentieth century. Born in an era of imperial decline, the spy in fiction has reflected the shifting currents of national and international politics for a century and more. Yet though it exists in relationship to historical realities, spy fiction is essentially the expression of a mythology. It has never been an implicit literature of record as some of its practitioners would have us believe. But it does have—it must have—reference to activities of which most of us are unaware but which are necessary to the business of government and international diplomacy, in peace as much as in war. As in other forms of fantasy, spy stories routinely blur the boundaries between fact and fiction. Because of the necessary secrecy of real espionage, its fictional counterpart has often assumed an aura of authenticity by default, and much of the appeal of spy fiction lies in its exploitation of this apparent realism and the creation of alternative or counter-histories which assume the garb of truth. So powerful have been some of these fictions that life has sometimes undoubtedly imitated art. Spying can even become a metaphor for the act of writing: 'he watches,' says Graham Greene of the novelist in *A Sort of Life*, 'he overhears, he seeks motives and analyses character, and in his attempt to serve literature he is unscrupulous.' Somewhere in this nexus of possibilities—between the real and the imagined, the adventure and the metaphor—lies the continuing appeal of spy fiction.

At its most basic, the spy story is one in which at least one of the central characters is actively involved in politically directed intelligence work. The emphasis in many stories is on sheer incident and the result is a form of thriller literature. In its more introspective manifestations, spy fiction uses the context of espionage to explore themes concerned with the moral, political, or psychological consequences of intelligence work. Throughout the last hundred years, powerful cultural anxieties have helped shape a genre that, more than any other, resonates with the temper of the century. 'If the finished canvas is often lurid,' writes David Stafford, 'this is hardly because the artist has used synthetic materials. War, revolution, subversion, terror, genocide, and the threat of nuclear obliteration are the authentic experience of twentieth-century man. None of us is safe, wherever we are . . . Since the spy novel emerged at the beginning of this century, it has provided a barometer for measuring the fragility of our world.'[1]

---

[1] David Stafford, *The Silent Game: The Real World of Imaginary Spies* (1988), 3.

Amongst the older professions, spying cannot be much younger than prostitution, and when Moses—clearly no fool in these matters—sent men into the land of Canaan 'to spy out the land' he was only doing what prudent military commanders and political leaders have done throughout history. However, there is little spy *fiction* worthy of the name before the early years of the twentieth century—or, with some latitude of definition, before the last decade of the nineteenth. Fenimore Cooper's unambiguously titled *The Spy* (1821), set during the American War of Independence, has some claim to be the first spy novel in English. The central character, Harvey Birch, 'the spy of the neutral ground', is suspected by the Americans of spying for the British but turns out to be working for Washington. Crude in many ways, Cooper's novel was none the less one of the first attempts to analyse the professional exercise of duplicity during a time when national loyalties were fiercely, often tragically, divided. Despite a general feeling that American democratic culture was antithetical to the kinds of covert activity sponsored by the old European powers (a feeling which persisted well into the twentieth century), *The Spy* spawned a host of story-paper and dime-novel imitations. It was, however, in the corrupt Old World—in imperial Britain—that spy fiction proper had its genesis, and to a large extent it has remained a peculiarly British tradition.

At the end of the nineteenth century Britain, along with other major European governments, became increasingly committed to officially sponsored espionage as a function of international diplomacy. Together with growing military rivalry amongst the major industrial powers, this encouraged a climate of clandestinity that offered fertile possibilities for writers of fiction. The beginnings of modern spy fiction can be traced in stories of diplomatic intrigue—such as Allen Upward's *Secrets of the Courts of Europe* (1897)—that were presented for popular consumption as illustrating what Conan Doyle later called 'that secret history of a nation which is often so much more intimate and interesting than its public chronicles' ('The Bruce-Partington Plans', *Strand Magazine*, December 1908). In Britain one of the catalysts for the further development of fiction concerned with this 'secret history' was an increasing sense of national insecurity and imperial rivalry throughout the 1890s and into the first decade of the new century. As early as 1885 the *Pall Mall Gazette* was complaining that 'At every turn we are confronted with the gunboats, the sea lairs, or the colonies of jealous and eager rivals . . . The world is filling up around us.' Twenty years later, in 'The Second Stain', Lord Bellinger tells Sherlock Holmes that 'The whole of Europe is an armed camp', and by the eve of the First World War the threat to the British way of life had become starkly palpable: ' "Did you ever reflect, Mr Leithen," ' asks Lumley in John Buchan's *The Power-House* (1913), ' "how precarious is the tenure of the civilization we boast about?" ' Politically motivated (as well as purely criminal) acts of terrorism brought home to the British public that the established order was threatened from within as well as from without. The violent activities of anarchists, Fenians, nihilists, and other terrorists—often assumed, rightly or wrongly, to be in the pay of foreign powers—produced a flood of sensational fiction throughout the 1880s. Added to the overt belligerence of continental rivals, terrorism produced the vivid sense, in the words of Henry James in *The Princess Casamassima* (1886), 'that the forces secretly arrayed against the present social order were pervasive and universal, in the air one breathed, in the ground one trod, in the hand of an acquaintance that one might touch or the eye of a stranger that might rest a moment on one's own'. Anxieties about national security were nothing new: they had been voiced frequently throughout the Napoleonic period, and after the Franco-Prussian War of 1870 such fears produced the curious sub-genre of invasion fiction— most famously, George Chesney's *The Battle of Dorking* (1871), in which Britain is invaded by Germany; but during the 1890s the sense of apprehension grew more insistent. 'The nineteenth century', said an article in *Pearson's Magazine* for September 1898, 'is closing with a clouded sky, and with a troubled sea over which the British Lion stands gazing.'

The traditional enemy had been France, but at the turn of the century the focus of distrust began to shift decisively towards Germany. In the first great modern spy novel, *The Riddle of the Sands* (1903) by Erskine Childers, Carruthers speaks of Germany as being 'our great naval rival of the future': 'she grows and strengthens and waits, an ever more formidable factor in the future of our delicate network of Empire'. The arch-popularizer of anti-German sentiment was William Le Queux, whose novel *The Invasion of 1910* (1905) sold over a million copies in book form. Le Queux's *Spies of the Kaiser* (1909) had an even greater impact on public opinion, and following its publication its author received many letters from readers denouncing people for being German spies (often for the most trivial of reasons) which were passed on to the Secret Service Bureau and were used to bring about government acceptance of the 'fact' of German espionage activity in England. Again, the notion of a 'secret history' in international relations provides the context for Le Queux's xenophobic fantasies:

I was playing a deep game . . . During the years I had been endeavouring to prove the peril to which England was exposed from foreign invasion, I had never been nearer failure than now . . . Little does the average Englishman dream of the work of the secret agent, or how his success or failure is reflected in our diplomatic negotiations with the Powers. Ambassadors and ministers may wear smart uniforms with glittering decorations, and move in their splendid embassies surrounded by their brilliant staffs; attachés may flirt, and first secretaries may take tea with duchesses, yet to the spy is left the real work of diplomacy, for, after all, it is upon the knowledge he obtains that His Excellency the Ambassador frames his despatch to his Government, or the Minister for Foreign Affairs presents a 'Note' to the Powers. (*Spies of the Kaiser*)

The equally popular stories of E. Phillips Oppenheim drove home similar warnings against British complacency in the face of German militarism. Both Le Queux and Oppenheim provided thrills aplenty for their many readers, their entertainment value only increasing the propaganda potential of their fiction. As a result, the figure of the dastardly foreign spy became frantically ubiquitous—on bookstalls and in bookshops, in newspapers and magazines, on the stage, and eventually in films. Edgar Wallace even found a way of playing the convention for laughs in *The Adventures of Heine* (1919), which describe the risible exploits of an incompetent German spy operating in England.

It was no coincidence that between 1900 and the outbreak of the First World War both British spy fiction and the British Secret Service were effectively created. But though State-directed espionage was placed on a new professional footing with the establishment of the Secret Service Bureau in 1909, it acted largely on old and inaccurate assumptions—for example the perceived threat of a German invasion—that popular fiction did much to encourage and perpetuate. As David Trotter has observed, 'The British Secret Service, like the British spy novel, invested in fantasy'; indeed, as Trotter goes on to say, it was essentially the same fantasy.[2] The dominant figure in spy fiction during the First World War and the decade following was John Buchan, whose second 'shocker', *The Thirty-Nine Steps* (1915) was an immediate bestseller. Buchan's Richard Hannay became one of the most influential fictional exemplars of the British secret agent—not a spy (a term of opprobrium reserved for unprincipled foreigners), but a gentleman patriot with a taste for adventure (like Sherlock Holmes in another sphere, the first generation of fictional spies played the game for the game's own sake). At a stroke, Buchan created the

---

[2] 'The Politics of Adventure in the Early British Spy Novel', in Wesley K. Wark (ed.), *Spy Fiction, Spy Films and Real Intelligence* (1991).

heroic mode of the spy story and an image of the spy that has proved remarkably resilient, and those who wrote in the romantic Buchanesque mould perpetuated the notion of secret service work as a species of invigorating adventure for gentlemen. The spirit of Robert Baden-Powell, who described intelligence work as 'a great recuperator for the man tired of life', lived on well into the twentieth century.

The break with the romantic tradition of spy fiction began in 1928 with the publication of *Ashenden; or, The British Agent* by W. Somerset Maugham. Like Buchan, Maugham had had wartime experience of intelligence work, but in him it produced disenchantment. Though there remained a strong patriotic undertone to Maugham's stories, and though a distinction was still asserted between spying for one's own country and spying for the enemy (which Ashenden himself describes as 'a base and dishonourable calling'), these stories rejected the heroic trappings of much pre-war spy fiction, and the effect on the moral atmosphere of Maugham's stories was a powerful one. For the first time there is an acknowledgement that the efficient prosecution of intelligence operations is, by its nature, a dirty business. Gone is the sense of cleansing, redemptive adventure for the man tired of life; in its place is dull routine, hypocrisy, evasiveness, and the ruthless completion of the task in hand, at whatever human cost. 'Never before', said *The Times Literary Supplement* of *Ashenden*, 'has it been so categorically demonstrated that counter-intelligence work consists of morally indefensible jobs not to be undertaken by the squeamish or conscience-stricken.' The move away from Buchanesque romanticism continued in the work of Eric Ambler, in whose fiction the spy became marginalized, both socially and in terms of his anti-establishment sympathies. Ambler soon began to give his stories a leftist dynamic: manipulative international capitalism, rather than political or ideological aggression, became the precipitator of crisis. In Ambler, the spy story as adventure was deliberately abandoned in favour of narratives that explored the psychological landscape of betrayal and conflicting commitments.

The same process of deromanticization characterizes the early 'entertainments' of Graham Greene (yet another writer who had been directly involved in intelligence operations). Greene was a lifelong admirer of Buchan, but he recognized the increasing irrelevance of the Buchanesque tradition to the modern world. 'Patriotism', he wrote, 'had lost its appeal, even for a schoolboy, at Passchendaele . . . while it was difficult, during the years of the Depression, to believe in the high purposes of the City of London or of the British Constitution . . . It was no longer a Buchan world.' The menace of Fascism, rootlessness (symbolized by frontiers, passports, and train journeys), the conspiracy within, are some of the dominant themes of 1930s spy fiction as typified by Ambler and Greene.

During the Second World War patriotism naturally revived. As in the previous world conflict, writers of detective fiction diverted their heroes away from private iniquities and towards national salvation. To some extent, such hybridizations arrested the development of the mainstream spy story. Ironically, the renaissance of spy fiction after the war was largely accomplished by a return to the heroic mode, though transformed to reflect the temper of the times. *Casino Royale* (1953), the first James Bond novel by Ian Fleming, was essentially a contemporary reworking of earlier models. Bond is a patriot and man of action, but he is also a killer whose sexual proclivities are definitely not in the Buchan tradition. After the sensational advent of James Bond there were many variations of Fleming's version of heroic spy fantasy, with devilish master criminals, international conspiracies, weapons of mass destruction, conspicuous consumerism, and of course sex. It also gave rise to sub-genres such as the assassination thriller—pre-eminently Frederick Forsyth's *The Day of the Jackal* (1971)—and terrorist thrillers such as Tom Harris's *Black Sunday* (1975) which signalled a growing fragmentation of the simple spy story form.

A decade after *Casino Royale*, and just a year after the release of the first James Bond film, John Le Carré's *The Spy Who Came in From the Cold* (1963) established yet another profoundly influential development. The spy as swashbuckler is replaced by the salaried and world-weary bureaucrat. Espionage is no longer a great game but a necessary, and grubby, business, cynically justified by the old distinction between Us and Them. As 'Control' says to Leaman in *The Spy Who Came in From the Cold*,

'We do disagreeable things so that ordinary people here and elsewhere can sleep safely in their beds at night . . . Of course, we occasionally do very wicked things . . . And in weighing up the moralities, we rather go in for dishonest comparisons; after all, you can't compare the ideals of one side with the methods of the other, can you, now?'

Le Carré's George Smiley is still a patriot, but the rules of the game have changed in a profound and unsettling way. Who is the enemy? As Smiley himself puts it in *The Honourable Schoolboy* (1977), 'Today, all I know is that I have learned to interpret the whole of life in terms of conspiracy.'

Since the Second World War spy fiction has moved steadily away from its narrowly genrist origins with its clear distinctions between right and wrong, hero and adversary. The focus has been on the mole, the double-agent, the traitor within. Real-life treachery has often reinforced fiction: Kim Philby, for instance, appears as himself in both Alan Williams's *Gentleman Traitor* (1974) and Frederick Forsyth's *The Fourth Protocol* (1984). With the ending of the Cold War, fictitious espionage has continued to fragment, reflecting the many fronts on which national intelligence agencies now operate.

The impact of espionage activities on mass culture has been predominantly through novels and films; but many of its central preoccupations and stock situations emerge also in the short story form. The field of the short spy story in its purest form, however, is not as extensive as that of, say, the short detective story. It is a common cry amongst anthologists of spy fiction that the number of good short stories of quality is severely limited. That may be true, though the definition of a spy story can occasionally be extended legitimately to include fiction in which espionage becomes yet another arena for criminous behaviour. Spy fiction, when all is said and done, is part of that protean genre we call thriller literature—mystery stories, tales of crime and detection, and so on—and little purpose is served by trying to make the sub-genres of this form artificially exclusive.

In this selection I have been deliberately catholic in my judgement of what constitutes a spy story. There are pure forms as well as mixed types (for example, detective stories in which espionage provides a central plot element); superior thrillers and stories that make use of espionage and its imperatives to explore character; stories that represent the heroic mode of early spy fiction, others that take a more cynical view or that utilize the metaphoric potential of spying. And there are one or two in which fantasy is the predominant mode—most notably, a gloriously daft story from Lord Dunsany. I have also tried to select a range of settings: spying in peacetime as well as in the heat of war; and stories set in the past as well as in the fictive present.

Unlike most previous anthologies of the genre, everything reprinted here was conceived and written as a self-contained short story. There are no extracts from longer works. Finally, as the contents inescapably reinforce, the short spy story (somewhat like spy fiction as a whole) is a predominantly British phenomenon. Despite strenuous attempts, it has proved difficult to increase the representation of American writers of espionage fiction who have written with consistent success in the short-story form.

And is there continuing life for the spy story in the post-Cold War world? The prognostication must be favourable, for, like war and taxes, espionage is a perennial human activity. Economic espionage, counter terrorism, the narcotics war, covert activities directed against new potential enemies: clandestine operations in these and other spheres of operation are now intrinsic to all political systems, and the human dramas they set in train will certainly continue to supply writers of fiction with an abundance of material. Even friends have secrets that they would rather keep to themselves, and political allies are no different. There may no longer be a single, starkly defined opponent; but governments still have enemies —actual or potential, external or internal. Information remains to be traded, and treachery will always have its price. Nor is the old enemy yet consigned to the annals of espionage history, as the Aldrich Ames case has shown. For writers, the great game is still there to be played.

MICHAEL COX

Parker Adderson, Philosopher

'Prisoner, what is your name?'

'As I am to lose it at daylight tomorrow morning, it is hardly worth concealing. Parker Adderson.'

'Your rank?'

'A somewhat humble one; commissioned officers are too precious to be risked in the perilous business of a spy. I am a sergeant.'

'Of what regiment?'

'You must excuse me; if I answered that it might, for anything I know, give you an idea of whose forces are in your front. Such knowledge as that is what I came into your lines to obtain, not to impart.'

'You are not without wit.'

'If you have the patience to wait, you will find me dull enough tomorrow.'

'How do you know that you are to die tomorrow morning?'

'Among spies captured by night that is the custom. It is one of the nice observances of the profession.'

The General so far laid aside the dignity appropriate to a Confederate officer of high rank and wide renown as to smile. But no one in his power and out of his favour would have drawn any happy augury from that outward and visible sign of approval. It was neither genial nor infectious; it did not communicate itself to the other persons exposed to it—the caught spy who had provoked it and the armed guard who had brought him into the tent and now stood a little apart, watching his prisoner in the yellow candle-light. It was no part of that warrior's duty to smile; he had been detailed for another purpose. The conversation was resumed; it was, in fact, a trial for a capital offence.

'You admit, then, that you are a spy—that you came into my camp disguised as you are, in the uniform of a Confederate soldier, to obtain information secretly regarding the numbers and disposition of my troops?'

'Regarding, particularly, their numbers. Their disposition I already knew. It is morose.'

The General brightened again; the guard, with a severer sense of his responsibility, accentuated the austerity of his expression and stood a trifle more erect than before. Twirling his grey slouch hat round and round upon his forefinger, the spy took a leisurely survey of his surroundings. They were simple enough. The tent was a common 'wall tent', about eight feet by ten in dimensions, lighted by a single tallow-candle stuck into the haft of a bayonet, which was itself stuck into a pine-table, at which the general sat, now busily writing and apparently forgetful of his unwilling guest. An old rag-carpet covered the earthen floor; an older hair-trunk, a second chair, and a roll of blankets were about all else that the tent contained; in General Clavering's command, Confederate simplicity and penury of 'pomp and circumstance' had attained their highest development. On a large nail driven into the tent-pole at the entrance was suspended a sword-belt supporting a long sabre, a pistol in its holster and, absurdly enough, a bowie knife. Of that most unmilitary weapon it was the General's habit to explain that it was a cherished souvenir of the peaceful days when he was a civilian.

It was a stormy night. The rain cascaded upon the canvas in torrents, with the dull, drum-like sound familiar to dwellers in tents. As the whooping blasts charged upon it the frail structure shook and swayed and strained at its confining stakes and ropes.

The General finished writing, folded the half sheet of paper, and spoke to the soldier guarding Adderson: 'Here, Tassman, take that to the adjutant-general; then return.'

'And the prisoner, General?' said the soldier, saluting, with an inquiring glance in the direction of that unfortunate.

'Do as I said,' replied the officer, curtly.

The soldier took the note and ducked himself out of the tent. General Clavering turned his handsome, clean-cut face toward the Federal spy, looked him in the eyes, not unkindly, and said: 'It is a bad night, my man.'

'For me, yes.'

'Do you guess what I have written?'

'Something worth reading, I dare say. And—perhaps it is my vanity—I venture to suppose that I am mentioned in it.'

'Yes; it is a memorandum for an order to be read to the troops at reveille concerning your execution. Also some notes for the guidance of the provost-marshal in arranging the details of that event.'

'I hope, General, the spectacle will be intelligently arranged, for I shall attend it myself.'

'Have you any arrangements of your own that you wish to make? Do you wish to see a chaplain, for example?'

'I could hardly secure a longer rest for myself by depriving him of some of his.'

'Good God, man! do you mean to go to your death with nothing but jokes upon your lips? Do you not know that this is a serious matter?'

'How can I know that? I have never been dead in all my life. I have heard that death is a serious matter, but never from any of those who have experienced it.'

The general was silent for a moment; the man interested, perhaps amused, him—a type not previously encountered.

'Death,' he said, 'is at least a loss—a loss of such happiness as we have, and of opportunities for more.'

'A loss of which we will never be conscious can be borne with composure and therefore expected without apprehension. You must have observed, General, that of all the dead men with whom it is your soldierly pleasure to strew your path, none shows signs of regret.'

'If the being dead is not a regrettable condition, yet the becoming so— the act of dying—appears to be distinctly disagreeable in one who has not lost the power to feel.'

'Pain is disagreeable, no doubt. I never suffer it without more or less discomfort. But he who lives longest is most exposed to it. What you call dying is simply the last pain—there is really no such thing as dying. Suppose, for illustration, that I attempt to escape. You lift the revolver that you are courteously concealing in your lap, and——'

The general blushed like a girl, then laughed softly, disclosing his brilliant teeth, made a slight inclination of his handsome head, and said nothing. The spy continued: 'You fire, and I have in my stomach what I did not swallow. I fall, but am not dead. After a half hour of agony I *am* dead. But at any given instant of that half hour I was either alive or dead. There is no transition period.'

'When I am hanged tomorrow morning it will be quite the same; while conscious I shall be living; when dead, unconscious. Nature appears to have ordered the matter quite in my interest—the way that I should have ordered it myself. It is so simple,' he added with a smile, 'that it seems hardly worth while to be hanged at all.'

At the finish of his remarks there was a long silence. The General sat impassive, looking into the man's face, but apparently not attentive to what had been said. It was as if his eyes had mounted guard over the prisoner, while his mind concerned itself with other matters. Presently he drew a long, deep breath, shuddered, as one awakened from a dreadful dream, and exclaimed almost inaudibly: 'Death is horrible!'—this man of death.

'It was horrible to our savage ancestors,' said the spy, gravely, 'because they had not enough intelligence to dissociate the idea of consciousness from the idea of the physical forms in which it is manifested—as an even lower order of intelligence, that of the monkey, for example, may be unable to imagine a house without inhabitants, and seeing a ruined hut fancies a suffering occupant. To us it is horrible because we have inherited the tendency to think it so, accounting for the notion by wild and fanciful theories of another world—as names of places give rise to legends explaining them, and reasonless conduct to philosophies in justification. You can hang me, General, but there your power of evil ends; you cannot condemn me to heaven.'

The General appeared not to have heard; the spy's talk had merely turned his thoughts into an unfamiliar channel, but there they pursued their will independently to conclusions of their own. The storm had ceased, and something of the solemn spirit of the night had imparted itself to his reflections, giving them the sombre tinge of a supernatural dread. Perhaps there was an element of prescience in it. 'I should not like to die,' he said—'not tonight.'

He was interrupted—if, indeed, he had intended to speak further— by the entrance of an officer of his staff, Captain Hasterlick, the Provost-Marshal. This recalled him to himself; the absent look passed away from his face.

'Captain,' he said, acknowledging the officer's salute, 'this man is a Yankee spy captured inside our lines with incriminating papers on him. He has confessed. How is the weather?'

'The storm is over, sir, and the moon shining.'

'Good; take a file of men, conduct him at once to the parade-ground, and shoot him.'

A sharp cry broke from the spy's lips. He threw himself forward, thrust out his neck, expanded his eyes, clenched his hands.

'Good God!' he cried hoarsely, almost inarticulately; 'you do not mean that! You forget—I am not to die until morning.'

'I have said nothing of morning,' replied the General, coldly; 'that was an assumption of your own. You die now.'

'But, General, I beg—I implore you to remember; I am to hang! It will take some time to erect the gallows—two hours—an hour. Spies are hanged; I have rights under military law. For Heaven's sake, General, consider how short——'

'Captain, observe my directions.'

The officer drew his sword, and, fixing his eyes upon the prisoner, pointed silently to the opening of the tent. The prisoner, deathly pale, hesitated; the officer grasped him by the collar and pushed him gently forward. As he approached the tent-pole the frantic man sprang to it, and, with cat-like agility, seized the handle of the bowie knife, plucked the weapon from the scabbard, and, thrusting the Captain aside, leaped upon the General with the fury of a madman, hurling him to the ground and falling headlong upon him as he lay. The table was overturned, the candle extinguished, and they fought blindly in the darkness. The Provost-Marshal sprang to the assistance of his superior officer, and was himself prostrated upon the struggling forms. Curses and inarticulate cries of rage and pain came from the welter of limbs and bodies; the tent came down upon them, and beneath its hampering and enveloping folds the struggle went on. Private Tassman, returning from his errand and dimly conjecturing the situation, threw down his rifle, and, laying hold of the flouncing canvas at random, vainly tried to drag it off the men under it; and the sentinel who paced up and down in front, not daring to leave his beat though the skies should fall, discharged his piece. The report alarmed the camp; drums beat the long roll and bugles sounded the assembly, bringing swarms of half-clad men into the moonlight, dressing as they ran, and falling into line at the sharp commands of their officers. This was well; being in line the men were under control; they stood at arms while the General's staff and the men of his escort brought order out of confusion by lifting off the fallen tent and pulling apart the breathless and bleeding actors in that strange contention.

Breathless, indeed, was one; the Captain was dead, the handle of the bowie knife protruding from his throat and pressed back beneath his chin until the end had caught in the angle of the jaw, and the hand that delivered the blow had been unable to remove the weapon. In the dead man's hand was his sword, clenched with a grip that defied the strength of the living. Its blade was streaked with red to the hilt.

Lifted to his feet, the General sank back to the earth with a moan and fainted. Besides his bruises he had two sword-thrusts—one through the thigh, the other through the shoulder.

The spy had suffered the least damage. Apart from a broken right arm, his wounds were such only as might have been incurred in an ordinary combat with nature's weapons. But he was dazed, and seemed hardly to know what had occurred. He shrank away from those attending him, cowered upon the ground, and uttered unintelligible remonstrances. His face, swollen by blows and stained with gouts of blood, nevertheless showed white beneath his dishevelled hair—as white as that of a corpse.

'The man is not insane,' said the surgeon in reply to a question; 'he is suffering from fright. Who and what is he?'

Private Tassman began to explain. It was the opportunity of his life; he omitted nothing that could in any way accentuate the importance of his own relation to the night's events. When he had finished his story and was ready to begin it again, nobody gave him any attention.

The General had now recovered consciousness. He raised himself upon his elbow, looked about him, and, seeing the spy crouching by a camp-fire, guarded, said simply:

'Take that man to the parade-ground and shoot him.'

'The general's mind wanders,' said an officer standing near.

'His mind does *not* wander,' the Adjutant-General said. 'I have a memorandum from him about this business; he had given that same order to Hasterlick'—with a motion of the hand toward the dead Provost-Marshal—'and, by God! it shall be executed.'

Ten minutes later Sergeant Parker Adderson, of the Federal army, philosopher and wit, kneeling in the moonlight and begging incoherently for his life, was shot to death by twenty men. As the volley rang out upon the keen air of the winter midnight, General Clavering, lying white and still in the red glow of the camp-fire, opened his big blue eyes, looked pleasantly upon those about him, and said, 'How silent it all is!'

The surgeon looked at the Adjutant-General, gravely and significantly. The patient's eyes slowly closed, and thus he lay for a few moments; then, his face suffused with a smile of ineffable sweetness, he said faintly, 'I suppose this must be death,' and so passed away.

The Red Carnation

I

Madame Olga Borgensky would never, I am sure, of her own accord, have resumed her duties as political agent to the Russian Government. When, two years ago, she had married Eugen Borgensky, a Pole, she had made both to herself and to him a solemn promise to renounce once for all a *métier* which, after all, most honest-minded persons would undoubtedly call that of a spy. And when, on the occasion of His Imperial Majesty the Tsar's visit to Vienna, Count Gulohoff approached her on the subject of her returning to the service of her country, she gave him a most emphatic refusal. I have it on the surest authority that this refusal annoyed and disappointed Count Gulohoff very considerably. He was at the time head of the third section of the Russian police, and had been specially ordered to watch over his Imperial master during the latter's stay in Vienna, and there was in his mind a suspicion, almost amounting to a certainty, that some plot was being brewed by the young Poles—chiefly wealthy and of noble parentage—that lived in Vienna, and had already given the home Government one or two unpleasant nuts to crack.

Madame Olga Borgensky was just the person to help him to discover the headquarters of these young fire-eaters—she went everywhere, knew everybody—and if Count Gulohoff could have succeeded in dispatching one or two of them to cool in Siberia, he certainly would have been happier. But Madame Borgensky was obdurate—at any rate, at first.

During the early part of the evening at Princess Leminoff's ball, the indefatigable and diplomatic Count Gulohoff had made many an attack on her firmness of purpose, but she had an army of excuses and reasons at her command, and yet one little incident caused her suddenly to change her resolution.

It was after supper, during the czimbalom solo so exquisitely played by Derék Miksa, the czigány. Madame Borgensky was standing close to the band with her partner, young Prince Leminoff, and around her she noticed most of the young Poles that were such a thorn in the flesh to the Russian government. She found herself wondering, while listening to Prince Leminoff's softly whispered nothings, whether it was mere coincidence that they each wore a red carnation in their buttonhole; the next moment she distinctly caught sight of a scrap of blue paper being slipped from the hand of Count Zamoisky into that of Dimitri Golowine, and then on to young Natcheff. I suppose it must have been that slip of paper that did the mischief, for one may as well expect a spaniel not to take to the water after a wild duck, than ask Madame Olga Borgensky not to follow up a political intrigue when she had by chance caught one thread.

In an instant the old instinct was aroused, forgotten were her promises to her husband, the dangers she so often had to pass, the odiousness attached to her former calling. She saw but one thing, that was the slip of blue paper which, under cover of the pathetic Magyar love-songs, was being passed from hand to hand, and the contents of which she felt bound to know, in the interests of Russia, of the Tsar, whose life perhaps was being endangered by the plans of these fanatical plotters.

'Prince Leminoff, I feel hot and faint, please take me into the next room at once,' she sighed, half-closing her eyes, and tottering as if about to fall.

The young man started and turned a little pale. His fingers closed tightly over a scrap of blue paper that had just been thrust into his hand; but his tremor was only momentary. The next instant he was leading the now almost fainting lady into the smoking-room, where a bright blaze was burning in the hearth. Madame Borgensky sank back into an armchair close to the fire.

'Now light a cigarette, Prince,' she said when she had recovered a little; 'the smell of the smoke would do me good. Really that music had got on my nerves.' And she pushed the gold *étui* of cigarettes, that stood invitingly near, towards her young partner, who, without a moment's hesitation, and with the greatest sangfroid, folded the compromising paper he was still clutching, into a long, narrow spill, and after holding it to the fire one moment, was proceeding to light a cigarette with it when:

'Allow me, Prince, thank you,' said Madame Borgensky, gently taking it from between his fingers, and, with an apologetic smile, she lighted her own cigarette. To blow out the flame, throw the paper on the floor, and place her foot on it was the work of but a second, and the young Pole had barely realized what had actually happened, when a cheery voice spoke to him from the door.

'Prince Leminoff, the last quadrille is about to commence. Everybody is waiting for you. Are you dancing it with Madame Borgensky?' And the Abbé Rouget, smiling and rubbing his little white hands, trotted briskly into the room.

'Shall we go, Madame?' said the young Prince after a slight hesitation, and offering the lady his arm.

'Please let me stay here a little while longer and finish my cigarette in peace. I really do not feel up to dancing just at this moment. I will give you an extra valse later on if you like.'

'If Madame Borgensky will grant me the much sought for privilege,' said the Abbé, 'I should deem myself very lucky to be allowed to keep her company for half-an-hour.'

'At any other time, Monsieur l'Abbé, I should only be too happy,' said Madame Borgensky, 'but just now I really would prefer to be alone. Five minutes' quiet will set me up for the rest of the evening.'

'Your wishes are my commands, Madame; I will read my breviary till the sound of your voice calls me to your side.'

And taking Prince Leminoff's arm, the Abbé led him towards the door. As soon as they were out of earshot:

'There is something amiss,' said the Abbé. 'What is it?'

'Only this,' replied the young Pole. 'A scrap of blue paper, containing our final arrangements for tomorrow night, is at the present moment under Madame Borgensky's foot. It is partly burnt. Can your Reverence find out how much of it has remained, and if there is any danger in proceeding tomorrow?'

'Easily, my son, quite easily; and if there is, I will find means to warn you—but if all is safe, I will wear the red carnation, as usual, at Madame Borgensky's ball. Say nothing to the others till then.'

And the Abbé turned on his heel, and taking a breviary out of his pocket, sat down in a chair opposite Madame Borgensky, and proceeded to read the Latin text in a half audible voice, apparently not taking the slightest notice of the lady. Olga Borgensky, however, had not yet succeeded in picking up the paper from under her foot; she was burning with impatience to know the contents, and her excitement became such that she could only with the greatest difficulty conceal it from the Abbé.

At length she could endure the suspense no longer, and she was just stooping forward to pick up the paper at all hazards, when the voice of Count Gulohoff startled her. He drew a stool close to her, and said in a low whisper:

'*Eh bien*, Madame? You see, I come back, an unvanquished enemy, to renew the attack.'

'I may be able to serve Russia and help you, Monsieur,' Madame Borgensky said excitedly from behind her fan. 'Come to my ball tomorrow, and if I find no means of speaking to you privately before then, I will slip a letter for you inside the pink Sèvres vase that, as you know, stands in the centre of the mantelpiece in the ballroom. And now take the Abbé away if you can.' Then she said in a louder tone of voice: 'What a gay and animated dance this has been, even M. l'Abbé there has been reading his prayers with holy joy and vigorous piety, but I confess I am getting very tired, and would be so grateful if somebody will find out for me if Eugen Borgensky is in the ballroom and ready to take me home.'

'I will go and find him at once,' said Count Gulohoff rising, 'and will your Reverence,' he added, turning to the Abbé, 'give me my revenge at piquet?'

'Oh! ah! yes! Did your Excellency speak to me?' said His Reverence, as if waking from a dream. 'Forgive me, I was enjoying half-an-hour's communion with the saints, which is most refreshing during the turmoil of a mundane gathering. What did your Excellency say?'

'I merely asked if you would care now to give me my revenge at piquet; if so, we had better go at once and secure a table before there is a rush for the cardroom.'

'With all the pleasure in life,' said the cheerful little Abbé, and, putting his breviary into his pocket, he followed Count Gulohoff into the ballroom.

II

At last! She was alone! Olga Borgensky drew from under her foot the scrap of paper, and feverishly unfolded and smoothed it. It had been more than half burnt, but the contents, such as they were, fully compensated her for all the difficulties she had encountered.

This is what she read:

....ensky's ball
....his carriage
....thrown without much
....lots as to who
....alom solo, in the
....who are willing
....red· carnation in

At her ball then, in her home, which had been so hospitably opened to these young plotters, their infamous schemes were to be consummated.

No doubt existed in her mind. His Majesty the Tsar, as was well known, meant to honour her by appearing at her ball for an hour or so on the following evening.

When he re-entered 'his carriage', a bomb would be 'thrown without much' risk of detection, as the crowd would be sure to be very dense. In the meanwhile the conspirators meant to draw 'lots as to who' should be the actual assassin, and this they meant to do during the 'czimbalom solo', probably in the card or billiard-room, and those that were willing to perpetrate this dastardly deed, and thus to sacrifice themselves as well as their family, were to wear a 'red carnation', which was evidently the badge of the fraternity.

The terrible part of the whole thing in Madame Borgensky's mind was that, as the infamous plot was to be carried through in her house, she, and especially her husband, were certain to be suspected of some sort of connivance, and might thereby lose their liberty, probably their lives.

Ah! how she hated these plotters now, with a bitter, deadly hatred, the hatred of the Russian against the Pole, the hatred born of fear! How thankful she was that Count Gulohoff had induced her to spy on them; she did not regret her action now, as at one moment she feared she would do.

'Why, my darling, how pale and agitated you look,' said a loving voice, close to her elbow. 'Count Gulohoff told me you had not been well, and I have ordered the carriage to take you home.'

And Eugen Borgensky bent anxiously over his young wife, and scanned her wan-looking features and wild eyes.

'It is nothing, dear,' she said; 'a little too much excitement, I think. I will make my adieux to Princess Leminoff, and we will go home at once.'

III

The Borgensky's ball was to be one of the most brilliant functions of the season. Everybody had said so, for weeks past, ever since it had become generally known that His Imperial Majesty the Tsar meant to honour Olga Borgensky by being her guest for that evening. Everything the fair Russian did, she did well. The giving of entertainments she had studied and cultivated till she had brought it to the level of high art. She had been the Queen of Vienna society for some years now, ever since she had married Eugen Borgensky, the friend and confidant of His Eminence the Cardinal Primate of Hungary. All the doors of the most exclusive Vienna cliques had been widely thrown open for her, and *tout le monde* flocked to her soirées.

It was ten o'clock, and Madame Borgensky, exquisitely dressed and covered in diamonds, was ready to receive her guests, with the calm and grace that characterizes the 'grande dame'. A very careful observer, such as her husband probably, might, perhaps, notice that her hand shook slightly as she held it out to each fresh arrival, that her cheeks were unusually pale, and her lips quivered from time to time; also, that whenever she looked away from the door that gave access to her guests, it was to glance at the fine Italian marble mantelpiece at the furthest end of the ballroom, where a magnificent pale pink Sèvres vase of beautiful proportions and graceful lines stood in the centre among a multitude of other equally beautiful knick-knacks and silver trinkets of all kinds.

'Ah, M. l'Abbé, I am charmed to see you,' said Madame Borgensky, as the Abbé Rouget, his breviary between his fingers, his fat face beaming with promises of enjoyment, arrived at the top of the stairs and greeted his hostess. 'You will find Eugen in the cardroom, I think. I really have not seen him since I took up my post at the top of the stairs, but he was asking me whether we should have the pleasure of seeing you tonight.'

'Ah, Madame! Eugen Borgensky is too kind. The archbishop, as you know, has allowed me innocent recreation from time to time—with the exception of dancing,' he added with a half regretful little sigh.

'Besides which, M. l'Abbé, you know you can always have half-an-hour's peace in the smoking-room during which to tell your beads,' said Madame Borgensky a little sarcastically, remembering in what an agonizing plight the holy man had placed her the evening before by his persistent devotions.

'I find when I have the pleasure of coming to this house, Madame, that I can always have the billiard-room to myself for a quiet meditation some time during the evening. It is necessary for the soul not to entirely lose sight of spiritual things in the brilliancy and gaiety of a mundane function. But I must not monopolize your kind attention so long,' said the jovial Abbé, as he bowed to his hostess and began working his way through the now rapidly filling ballrooms.

Madame Borgensky looked anxiously after him, a puzzled expression on her face. Was it a mere coincidence that the Abbé had in the button-hole of his soutane a red carnation, exactly similar to the one worn by Prince Leminoff and three or four other young men she had noticed in the course of the evening, and the meaning of which was now clear to her. Surely he would not risk such a pleasant, assured position as he possessed for the sake of the destinies of a country that was not even his own.

Madame Borgensky caught herself now scanning the young men's buttonholes very curiously; there were at most only about ten or twelve of them that wore the red flower; the Abbé was certainly one, Prince Leminoff—foolish youth!—another, and . . . Ah! no! no! it is impossible, her eyes are deceiving her, her overwrought imagination is playing her own sight a cruel trick. She closed her eyes once or twice to chase away the fearful vision, but it would not go—it was true then? there, standing with his back to the pink Sèvres vase, a red carnation in his buttonhole, was Eugen Borgensky, her husband!

Ah! how could she have guessed? How could she know what a terrible deed she had done? She, Olga Borgensky, a happy, loving and loved wife, had actually spied upon and betrayed her own husband into the hands of a police that knows of no pardon. But, no; all was not lost yet, thank God! she had so far told Count Gulohoff nothing. She had devised a means of communicating with him, that she had felt would be a safe one, in case she found no chance of speaking to him privately, and now it would prove her salvation.

Feverishly she turned to go into the ballroom, heedless if anyone should notice her; what matter what people thought of her actions, as long as the terrible catastrophe is averted in time——

'His Imperial Majesty, the Tsar,' thundered the voice of the usher. All conversations ceased, and all necks were stretched forward to catch a glimpse of Alexander III, as he ascended the stairs, chatting pleasantly to Count Gulohoff.

Madame Borgensky, forced to pause, felt as if the whole room, the Tsar, her guests, were all changed into weird spectres that seemed to dance a wild, fantastic dance around her; one moment she thought her senses would leave her . . . the next instant she had bowed after the approved Court fashion, and was thanking Alexander III for the honour he was doing her, while His Majesty, with his usual affability, was conversing pleasantly with her and Eugen Borgensky. She had lost sight of Count Gulohoff, who, exchanging handshakes, nods, and smiles, worked his way through the ballroom towards the mantelpiece, where the gay little Abbé was being monopolized by a group of pious *mondaines*, and seemed to be enjoying himself thoroughly.

'Ah, your Excellency is just in time,' said his Reverence, 'to settle a most knotty point. We are having, mesdames and I, a very animated discussion on pottery and china, namely, the superiority (which I call very exaggerated) of antique over modern manufacture, and I was contending that many a connoisseur is not guided, when buying a piece of china, by the actual quality of the ware, but merely by the mark upon it.'

'Ah! M. l'Abbé is terribly sceptical of feminine knowledge,' said the Countess Zichy, 'but I am sure that in this instance he wrongs us grievously. I, myself (and I have no pretensions at being much of a connoisseur), need never look at the mark of a piece of china; I can always locate its origin, sometimes even its date. Does your Excellency doubt me?' she added, turning to Count Gulohoff, who had assumed a somewhat incredulous attitude.

'I would not do so for worlds,' said the courtly Russian, 'but I confess that I would feel very interested to test your knowledge, Comtesse; this room, for instance, is full of bibelots. Olga Borgensky has some rare and beautiful pieces; shall we experiment now, to commence with, on this exquisite pink vase?' And Count Gulohoff, inwardly thankful at the turn the conversation had taken, stretched out his hand towards the vase, from the inside of which he had already noticed protruding the corner of an envelope.

'Allow me, your Excellency,' said the Abbé, 'to lift the vase up for you.'

'No! no! I have it quite safely,' said Count Gulohoff, who hearing the faint, crisp rustle of paper inside the vase, was tilting it towards him, in the hope that he could obtain the letter unperceived.

At that moment the Abbé, who was short and somewhat rotund, apparently in trying to reach the vase must have lost his footing, for he fell forward, and, in steadying himself, jerked the arm of Count Gulohoff so violently that the latter lost the grip he had on the vase, which fell crashing to the floor.

There was general consternation among the little group of male and female connoisseurs who had gathered round to see the end of the little debate: the poor little Abbé especially seemed terribly distressed, trying to pick up the pieces, and wondering whether the valuable vase could by any possibility be repaired. Count Gulohoff was for one moment terribly disconcerted, when, in the crash, he lost sight of the letter; his mind was, however, soon set at rest, for he quickly noticed it lying on the floor, close to the priest's soutane, and he was able to pick it up unperceived.

IV

Madame Borgensky, forced in her capacity as hostess to be constantly attentive to His Imperial Majesty, doing the necessary presentations, and having to appear as gay and entertaining as possible, had not, from the end of the room where she was, noticed the little scene that was being enacted close to the mantelpiece. Had Count Gulohoff possessed himself of the letter, she wondered? The letter that denounced her husband, as well as his friends. She endured most excruciating tortures of mind, all the more unendurable as she was, for the moment, at least, perfectly powerless to do anything. She was gaily chatting the while, gradually leading Alexander III towards the further end of the ballroom, in the hope that she might yet ward off this fearful, monstrous thing.

Ah! it was too late, she had caught sight of Count Gulohoff coming towards her, and she felt, more than she actually saw, that the fatal letter was in his hand.

'Will your Majesty, and also my fair hostess, deign to allow me to take my leave,' said the Count bowing before the Tsar, while he threw a quick glance of intelligence at Madame Borgensky, who had now become deathly pale; 'serious duties call me away.'

'This dear Count!' said His Majesty laughing. 'I bet you he has discovered some conspiracy against my life, and is going to save me. I assure you, Madame, last year he discovered 365 plots, each one of which would inevitably have ended my days, were it not for the devotion and fidelity of Count Gulohoff.'

'The devotion and fidelity of all your Majesty's right-minded subjects,' said Count Gulohoff. 'Madame Borgensky, I feel sure, would do what I have done, and more, were she but given the opportunity, which, after all, may arise any day.'

'Indeed, your Majesty, and so would my husband, than whom your Majesty has no more faithful subject,' said Madame Borgensky, vainly trying to master her emotion.

'I thank you, Madame,' said the Tsar, with the charming cordiality so peculiar to him, 'and I can assure you that in coming here I quite forget that I am the guest of a Pole. Well, *au revoir, cher comte*. I shall leave soon after one o'clock, and I hope Madame Borgensky will allow me, for the moment, to monopolize her society, and let me escort her to the supper-room.'

And offering his fair hostess his arm, Alexander Nicolaïevitch led her across the room and down the stairs, followed by the respectful salutes of all, and the glances of admiration levelled at his beautiful partner, who, with eyes open wide with agonized fear, and cheeks blanched with terror, was making superhuman efforts to appear calm and self-possessed.

V

The supper was very gay. Alexander III, always a valiant trencherman, and notoriously as fond of a good glass of Tokay as of the society of a pretty woman, was graciousness itself, and deigned to enjoy himself vastly. As for the 'czigány' who were playing during supper, he declared he had never heard more entrancing music, and when, after the feast, the traditional czimbalom solo was to be played, His Majesty declared his desire to listen to it, and afterwards watch the 'csárdás' before he left.

It was while the gypsies, with that peculiarly pathetic weirdness with which they play the Magyar folksongs, played that exquisite tune, so dear to all Hungarian ears: 'There is but one beautiful girl in all the world,' that Madame Borgensky first realized that *something* after all might be done, if God would but help her, and allow her to think. Ah! how she prayed at that moment; inspiration such as she needed could but come from above.

She looked round at her guests; her husband, the Abbé Rouget, Prince Leminoff, and the dozen or so that wore the red carnation were absent. She knew where they were and oh! how terrible; knew what at that moment they were doing. Drawing lots as to who should do the assassin's deed. Oh! if it should be her husband. 'Not that! not that, oh my God, direct his hand! he does not know! he does not understand!' she pleaded. 'The Tsar is his guest! no! no! even *they* would think that deed too horrible.'

'Ah! that music was indeed divine,' said Alexander Nicolaïevitch, half dreaming, as the last chords of the czimbalom died away, 'and it will long haunt my memory after I leave Vienna tomorrow. And now, my dear Madame Borgensky, I must reluctantly bid you farewell, thanking you for your kind hospitality; believe me,' His Majesty added, looking admiringly at his beautiful hostess, 'that the remembrance of tonight will long dwell in my heart.' And the tall figure of Alexander III bent low to kiss gallantly the tips of Anna Borgensky's fingers that lay cold as ice in his hand.

'Ah! here comes our kind host,' said His Majesty, as Eugen Borgensky, very pale, approached him. 'My dear Borgensky, may I express a hope that next winter will see you and Madame at St Petersburg? I can assure you she has left many friends and admirers there.'

'Your Majesty's wishes are commands,' said Eugen Borgensky, bowing coldly.

The Tsar shot an amused glance at him. 'Jealous?' he asked Madame Borgensky *sotto voce*.

'No doubt,' she answered, trying to smile.

And Alexander III, followed by his host, and two or three gentlemen of his suite, turned his steps towards the stairway, still having on his arm Olga Borgensky, from whom he seemed loth to part, and bowing cordially to those whom he recognized among the guests, while the gypsy band struck up the Russian National Hymn: 'God Save the Tsar.'

The poor unfortunate woman walked by his side as if in a dream; her movements were those of an automaton. Now, if in the next five minutes something did not happen—something stupendous, immense—the terrible deed would be accomplished, Heaven only knew by whose hands.

Once in the hall, while two or three of the gentlemen in attendance busied themselves round their Imperial master, helping him with his furs and gloves, and the brilliant equipage drew up under the portico, Madame Borgensky shot a quick glance into the street outside. The crowd was very dense; she recognized no one. Then, as if moved by sudden inspiration, when Alexander III began at last an evidently very reluctant leave-taking, she walked up to one of the large banks of palms and cut flowers that had been erected on each side of the hall, and gathering a huge armful, she turned to the Tsar and said:

'These are for remembrance; let me place them in your carriage in memory of tonight.' And she threw him one of those glances she alone had the secret of, which quite finished turning an Imperial head, and subjugating an Imperial heart. Carrying her sweet-smelling burden, burying her head among the blossoms, she walked through the doorway to the Imperial carriage, closely followed by the Tsar; with her own hands she opened the carriage door, standing there, beautiful and defiant, daring them, the unknown assassins, to throw the bomb that would annihilate her, their hostess, the wife of their comrade, as well as him.

Then, when the Tsar had at last entered the carriage, she lingered on the steps, arranging the flowers, still chatting gaily, and when she herself had closed the carriage door, she stood, her hand in that of Alexander III; she meant to stand there, till the coachman, whipping up the horses, had borne his Imperial master out of any danger. At last the lackeys were mounted, the Tsar gave her a last military salute, the coachman gathered the reins . . . at that moment Olga Borgensky felt two vigorous arms encircling her waist, and she was thrown more than carried violently to one side, while a second later a terrific crash rent the still, night air.

There was a tremendous rush and tumult; something appeared to be smouldering some yards away in the middle of the road; while the Emperor's carriage, with its small escort of mounted *cosaques* disappeared, in a cloud of dust, along the brilliant road.

'Come in, Olga, you will catch cold,' said her husband's voice close to her, as soon as she had partially realized the situation.

There seemed to be a great commotion both outside and in. She allowed Eugen Borgensky to lead her, past her astonished and frightened guests, into a small boudoir, where she saw the Abbé Rouget sitting in a huge armchair, with eyes raised heavenwards, softly murmuring: '*Mater Dei, ora pro nobis.*' He seemed sublimely unconscious of any disturbance, and rose with alacrity to offer the half-fainting lady his seat.

At a knowing wink from the little Abbé's sparkling eyes, Eugen Borgensky, gently kissing his wife on the half-closed lids, left the two alone together.

Olga Borgensky looked pleadingly at the Abbé; she was dying for an explanation, longing to know what had happened:

'Madame,' at last said the jovial priest very earnestly, 'your brave attitude tonight has averted a terrible catastrophe. You have no sympathies with our plots and plans, you do not understand them; but you well understood that, at any cost, any risk, your life with us would be sacred.

'One of us, the one who drew the fatal number, was stationed outside your gates, to rid Russia of her autocrat. On seeing you, his heart failed him, he threw the bomb in the middle of the road, where it could not reach you, even if it hit the Tsar. Both of you, however, are safe.'

'But, Count Gulohoff,' she said, 'he knew, he and the police must have been there; did they arrest anyone? Was my husband seen?'

'No, Madame, Count Gulohoff was not present. I succeeded, by substituting a letter of my own for the one you had placed for him in the pink Sèvres vase, in inducing him to go with his minions to the other end of Vienna to seek for conspirators who will not be there. Tomorrow the Tsar and Count Gulohoff will have left Vienna. It is true our plans have utterly failed, but we are also quite safe, and not even suspected.'

'And Eugen Borgensky? my husband? M. l'Abbé.'

'I pledge you my word, Madame, that whilst I can do anything to prevent it, and I can do a great deal, he shall never again wear the red carnation.'

SIR ARTHUR QUILLER-COUCH

The Rider in the Dawn

A passage from the Memoirs of Manuel (or Manus) McNeill, agent in the Secret Service of Great Britain during the campaigns of the Peninsula (1808–13). A Spanish subject by birth, and a Spaniard in all his up-bringing, he traces in the first chapter of his Memoirs his descent from an old Highland family through one Manus McNeill, a Jacobite agent in the Court of Madrid at the time of the War of Succession, who married and settled at Aranjuez. The second chapter he devotes to his youthful adventures in the contraband trade on the Biscayan Coast and the French frontier, his capture and imprisonment at Bilbao under a two years' sentence, which was remitted on the discovery of his familiar and inherited conversance with the English tongue, and his imprisonment exchanged for a secret mission to Corsica (1794). The following extract tells of this, his first essay in the calling in which he afterwards rendered signal service to the Allies under Lord Wellington.—Q.

If I take small pleasure in remembering this youthful expedition it is not because I failed of success. It was a fool's errand from start to finish; and the Minister, Don Manuel Godoy, never meant or expected it to succeed, but furthered it only to keep his master in humour. You must know that just at this time, May, 1794, the English troops and Paoli's native patriots were between them dislodging the French from the last few towns to which they yet clung on the Corsican coast. Paoli held all the interior: the British fleet commanded the sea and from it hammered the garrisons; and, in short, the French game was up. But now came the question, What would happen when they evacuated the island? Some believed that Paoli would continue in command of his little republic, others that the crown would be offered to King George of England, or that it might go a-begging as the patriots were left to discover their weakness. I understand that, on the chance of this, two or three claimants had begun to look up their titles; and at this juncture our own Most Catholic King bethought him that once upon a time the island had actually been granted to Aragon by a certain Pope Boniface—with what right nobody could tell; but a very little right might suffice to admit Spain's hand into the lucky bag. In brief, my business was to reach the island, find Paoli (already by shabby treatment incensed against the English, as Godoy assured me), and sound him on my master's chances. Among the islanders I could pass myself off as a British agent, and some likely falsehood would have to serve me if by ill-luck I fell foul of the British soldiery. The King, who—saving his majesty—had turned the least bit childish in his old age, actually clapped his hands once or twice while his Minister gave me my instructions, which he did with a face as wooden as a grenadier's. I would give something, even at this distance of time, to know what Godoy's real thoughts were. Likely enough he and the Queen had invented this toy to amuse the husband they were both deceiving. Or Godoy may have wanted my information for his own purpose, to sell it to the French, with whom—though our armies were fighting them—he had begun to treat in private for the peace and the alliance which soon followed, and still move good Spaniards to spit at the mention of his name. But, whatever the farce was, he played it solemnly, and I took his instructions respectfully, as became me.

No: my mission was never meant to succeed: and if in my later professional pride I now think shame of it—if to this day I wince at the remembrance of Corsica—the shame comes simply from this, that I began my career as a scout by losing my way like any schoolboy. But, after all, even genius must make a beginning; and I was fated to make mine in the Corsican *macchia*.

Do you know it? If not—that is to say, if you have never visited Corsica —I despair of giving you any conception of it. But if chance has ever carried you near its coast, you will have wondered—as I did when an innocent-looking felucca from Barcelona brought me off the Gulf of Porto— at an extraordinary verdure spreading up the mountains and cut short only by the snows on their summits. You ask what this verdure may be, of which you have never seen the like. It is the *macchia*.

I declare that the scent of it—or rather, its thousand scents—came wafted down on the night air and met me on the shore as I landed at moonrise below the ruined tower, planted by the Genoese of old, at the mouth of the vale which winds up from Porto to the mountains. We had pushed in under cover of the darkness, for fear of cruisers: and as I took leave of my comrades (who were mostly Neapolitan fishermen), their skipper, a Corsican from Bastia, gave me my route. A good road would lead me up the valley to the village of Otta, where a mule might be hired to carry me on past Evvisa, through the great forest of Aïtone, and so across the pass over Monte Artica, whence below me I should see the plain of the Niolo stretching towards Corte and my goal: for at Corte, his capital, I was sure either to find Paoli or to get news of him, and if he had gone northward to rest himself (as his custom was) at his favourite Convent of Morosaglia, why the best road in Corsica would take me after him.

In the wash of the waves under the old tower I bade the skipper farewell, sprang ashore, and made my way up the valley by the light of the rising moon. Of the wonders of the island, which had shone with such promise of wonders against yesterday's sunset, it showed me little—only a white road climbing beside a deepening gorge with dark masses of foliage on either hand, and, above these, grey points and needles of granite glimmering against the night. But at every stride I drank in the odours of the *macchia*, my very skin seeming to absorb them, as my clothes undoubtedly did before my journey's end; for years later I had only to open the coffer in which they reposed, and all Corsica saluted my nostrils.

Day broke as I climbed; and soon this marvellous brushwood was holding me at gaze for minutes at a time, my eyes feasting upon it as the sun began to open its flowers and subdue the scents of night with others yet more aromatic. In Spain we know *montebaxos*, or coppice shrubs (as you might call them), and we know *tomillares*, or undergrowth; but in Corsica nature heaps these together with both hands, and the Corsican, in despair of separating them, calls them all *macchia*. Cistus, myrtle, and cactus; cytisus, lentisk, arbutus; daphne, heath, broom, juniper, and ilex—these few I recognized, but there was no end to their varieties and none to their tangle of colours. The slopes flamed with heather bells red as blood, or were snowed white with myrtle blossom: wild roses trailed everywhere, and blue vetches: on the rock ledges the cistus kept its late flowers, white, yellow, or crimson: while from shrub to shrub away to the rock pinnacles high over my left shoulder honeysuckles and clematis looped themselves in festoons as thick as a man's waist, or flung themselves over the chasm on my right, smothering the ilex saplings which clung to its sides, and hiding the water which roared three hundred feet below. I think that my month in prison must have sharpened my appetite for wild and natural beauty, for I skipped as I went, and whistled in sheer lightness of heart. 'O Corsicans!' I exclaimed, 'O favoured race of mortals, who spend your pastoral days in scenes so romantic, far from the noise of cities, the restless ambition of courts!'

At the first village of Otta, where the pass narrows to a really stupendous gorge and winds its way up between pyramidal crags soaring out of a sea of green chestnut groves, one of this favoured race (by name Giusé) attempted to sell me a mule at something like twice its value. I hired the beast instead, and also the services of its master to guide me through the two great forests which lay between me and the plain of the Niolo, one on either side of the ridge ahead. He carried a gun, and wore an air of extreme ferocity which daunted me until I perceived that all the rest of the village-men were similarly favoured. Of his politeness after striking the bargain I had no cause to complain. He accepted—and apparently with the simplest credulity—my account of myself, that I was an Englishman bound in the service of the Government to inspect and report on the forests of the interior, on the timber of which King George was prepared to lend money in support of the patriot troops. He himself had served as a stripling in Paoli's militia across the mountains on the great and terrible day of Ponte Nuovo, and by fits and starts, whenever the road allowed our two mules to travel abreast in safety, he told me the story of it, in a dialect of which I understood but one word in three, so different were its harsh aspirates and gutturals from any sounds in the Italian familiar to me.

The mules stepped out well, and in the shade of the ravine we pushed on steadily through the heat of the day. We had left the *macchia* far below us, and the road wound between and around sheer scarps of grey granite on the edge of precipices echoing the trickle of waters far below. We rode now in single file, and so continued until Evvisa was reached, and the upper hills began to open their folds. From Evvisa a rough track, yet scored with winter ruts, led us around the southern side of one of these mountain basins, and so to the skirts of the forest of Aïtone, into the glooms of which we plunged, my guide promising to bring me out long before nightfall upon the ridge of the pass, where he would either encamp with me, or (if I preferred it) would leave me to encamp alone and find his way back to Evvisa.

So, with the sun at our backs and now almost half-way below its meridian, we threaded our way up between the enormous pine-trunks, in a gloom full of pillars which set me in mind of Cordova Cathedral. From their dark roof hung myriads of cocoons white as satin and shone in every glint of sunlight. And, whether over the carpet of pine-needles or the deeper carpet of husks where the pines gave place to beech groves, our going was always easy and even luxurious. I began to think that the difficulties of my journey were over; and as we gained the *bocca* at the top of the pass and, emerging from the last outskirt of pines, looked down on the weald beyond, I felt sure of it.

The plain lay at my feet like a huge saucer filled with shadow and rimmed with snowy mountains on which the sunlight yet lingered. A good road plunged down into the gloom of Valdoniello—a forest at first glance very like that through which we had been riding, but smaller in size. Its dark green tops climbed almost to our feet, and over them Giusé pointed to the town of Niolo midway across the plain, traced with his finger the course of the Golo, and pointed to the right of it where a pass would lead me through the hill-chain to Corte.

I hesitated no longer: but thanked him, paid him his price and a trifle over, and, leaving him on the ridge, struck boldly downhill on foot towards the forest.

As with Aïtone so with Valdoniello. The road shunned its depths and, leading me down through the magnificent fringe of it, brought me out upon an open slope, if that can be called open which is densely covered to the height of a man's knees at times, and again to the height of his breast, with my old friend the *macchia*.

It was now twilight and I felt myself weary. Choosing an aromatic bed by the roadside where no prickly cactus thrust its way through the heather, I opened my wallet; pulled forth a sausage, a crust, and a skin of wine; supped; and stretched myself to sleep through the short summer night.

'The howly Mother presarve us! Whist now, Daniel Cullinan, did ye'ver hear the like of it?'

I am glad to remember now that, even as the voice fell on my ear and awoke me, I had presence enough of mind to roll quickly off my bed of heath away from the road and towards the shelter of a laurestinus bush a few paces from my elbow. But between me and the shrub lay a fern-masked hollow between two boulders, into which I fell with a shock, and so lay staring up at the heavens.

The wasted moon hung directly overhead in a sky already paling with dawn. And while I stared up at her, taking stock of my senses and wondering if here—here in Corsica—I had really heard that inappropriate sound, soon across the hillside on my left echoed an even stranger one —yet one I recognized at once as having mingled with my dreams; a woman's voice pitched at first in a long monotonous wail and then undulating in semitones above and below the keynote—a voice which seemed to call from miles away—a sound as dismal as ever fell on a man's ears.

'Arrah, let me go, Corp'ril! let me go, I tell yez! 'Tis the *banshee*— who knows it better than I?—that heard the very spit of it the day my brother Mick was drowned in Waterford harbour, and me at Ballyroan that time in Queen's County, and a long twenty-five miles away as ever the crow flies!'

'Ah, hold your whist, my son! Mebbee 'tis but some bird of the country—bad end to it!—or belike the man we're after, that has spied us, and is putting a game on us.'

'Bird!' exclaimed the man he had called Daniel Cullinan, as again the wail rang down from the hills. 'Catch the bird can talk like yondhar, and I give ye lave to eat him and me off the same dish. And if 'tis a man, and he's anywhere but on the road, here's a rare bottle of hay we'll search through for him. Rest aisy now, Corp'ril, and give it up. That man with the mules, we'll say, was a liar; and turn back before the worse befalls us!'

Through my ferny screen I saw them—two redcoats in British uniform disputing on the road not ten paces from my shelter. They moved on some fifty yards, still disputing, the first sunrays glinting on the barrels of the rifles they shouldered: and almost as soon as their backs were turned I broke cover and crept away into the *macchia*.

Now the *macchia*, as I soon discovered, is prettier to look at than to climb through. I was a fool not to content myself with keeping at a tolerably safe distance from the road. As it was, with fear at my heels and a plenty of inexperience to guide me, I crawled through thickets and blundered over sharply pointed rocks; found myself on the verge of falls from twenty to thirty feet in depth; twisted my ankles, pushed my head into cactus, tangled myself in creepers; found and followed goat-tracks which led into other goat-tracks and ended nowhere; tore my hands with briers and my shoes on jagged granite; tumbled into beds of fern, sweated, plucked at arresting thorns, and at the end of twenty minutes discovered what every Corsican knows from infancy—that to lose one's way in the *macchia* is the simplest thing in life.

I had lost mine pretty thoroughly when, happening on what seemed at least a promising track, I cast my eyes up and saw, on a ridge some two or three hundred yards ahead and sharply outlined against the blue morning sky, a horse and rider descending the slope towards me.

The horse I presently discerned to be a light roan of the island breed: and my first thought was that he seemed overweighted by his rider, who sat erect—astonishingly erect—with his head cased in a pointed hood and his body in a long dark cloak which fell from his shoulders to his knees. Although he rode with saddle and bridle, he apparently used neither stirrups nor reins, and it was a wonder to see how the man kept his seat as he did with his legs sticking out rigid as two vine-props and his arms held stiffly against his sides. I wasted no time, however, in marvelling, but ran forward as he approached and stretched out my hand to his rein, panting out, 'O, friend, be good enough to guide me out of this tangle!—for I am a stranger and indeed utterly lost.'

And with that all speech froze suddenly within me: and with good excuse—for I was looking up into the face of a corpse!

His eyes, shaded by the hood he wore, were glazed and wide, his features—the features of an old man—livid in death. As I blenched before them, I saw that a stout pole held his body upright, a pole lashed firmly at the tail of his crupper, and terminating in two forking branches like an inverted V, against which his legs had been bound with leathern thongs.

And again as I blenched from the horrible face my eyes fell on the horse, and I saw that the poor little beast was no less than distraught with fright. What I had taken for grey streaks in his roan coat were in fact lathery flakes of sweat, and he nuzzled towards me as a horse will rarely nuzzle towards a stranger and only in extremest terror. A glance told me that he had been galloping wildly and bucking to free himself of his burden, but was now worn out and thoroughly cowed. His knees quivered as I soothed and patted him; and when I pulled out a knife to cut the corpse free from its lashings, he seemed to understand at once, and rubbed his nose gratefully against my waistcoat.

A moment later the knife almost dropped from my hand at the sound of a brisk hurrah from above, and looking up I saw the stalwart form of the Irish corporal wriggling along the branch of a cork-oak which overhung the slope. He carried his rifle, and, anchoring himself in a fork of the boughs, stared down triumphantly.

'Arrah now,' he hailed, 'which of you's the man that came ashore at Porto and passed through Evvisa overnight? Spake up quick now, and surrender, for I have ye covered!'

He lifted his rifle. I cast my eye over the space of *macchia* between us, and decided that I had only his bullet to fear.

'*A poco, a poco,*' I called back. 'Be in no hurry—*piano*, my friend: this gentleman has met with an accident to his stirrup!'

'The divvle take your impudence! Step forward this moment and surrender, or it's meat I'll be making of the pair of you!'

And he meant it. I slipped behind the corpse, and hacked at its lashings as his rifle roared out; and for aught I know the corpse received the bullet. With a heave I toppled it and its ghastly frame together headlong into the fern, sprang to the saddle in its place, pointed to it, and with a shout of 'Assassino! Assassino!' shook rein and galloped down the path.

A few strides removed me out of further danger from the corporal, perched as he was in an attitude extremely inconvenient for reloading. Of his comrade I saw no signs, but judged him to be foundered somewhere in the *macchia*. The little roan had regained his wind. He took me down the precipitous track without a blunder, picked his way across the dry bed of a mountain torrent, and on the further side struck off at right angles into a path which mounted through the *macchia* towards a wedge-shaped cleft in the foothills to the north. Now and again this path returned to the very lip of the torrent, across which I looked upon cliffs descending sheer for many scores of feet from the heathery slope to the boulders below. At the pace we held it was a sight to make me shiver. But the good little horse knew his road, and I let him take it. Up and up we mounted, his pace dropping at length to a slow canter, and so at an angle of the gorge came suddenly into full view of a grassy plateau with a house perched upon it—a house so high and narrow that at first glance I took it for a tower, with the more excuse because at first glance I could discern no windows.

As we approached it, however, I saw it to be a dwelling-house, and that it had windows, though these were shuttered, and the shutters painted a light stone colour; and I had scarcely made this discovery when one of them jetted out a sudden puff of smoke and a bullet sang over my head.

The roan, which had fallen to a walk—so steep was the pitch of ground immediately beneath the house—halted at once as if puzzled; and you may guess if his dismay exceeded mine. But I reasoned from his behaviour on the road that this must be his home, and the folks behind the window shutters must recognize him. So standing high in my stirrups I waved a hand and pointed at him, at the same time shouting 'Amico! Amico!'

There was no answer. The windows still stared down upon us blankly, but to my relief the shot was not repeated. 'Amico! Amico!' I shouted again, and, alighting, led the horse towards the door.

It was opened cautiously and held a little ajar—just wide enough to give me a glimpse of a black-bearded face.

'Who are you?' a voice demanded in harsh Corsican.

'A friend,' I answered, 'and unarmed; and see, I have brought you back your horse!'

The man called to someone within the house: then addressed me again. 'Yes, it is indeed Nello. But how come you by him?'

'That is a long story,' said I. 'Be so good as either to step out or to open and admit me to your hospitality, that we may talk in comfort.'

'To the house, O stranger, I have not the slightest intention of admitting you, seeing that the windows are stuffed with mattresses, and there is no light within—no, not so much as would show your face. And even less intention have I of stepping outside, since, without calling you a liar, I greatly suspect you are here to lead me into ambush.'

'Oho!' said I, as a light broke on me. 'Is this *vendetta*?'

'It is *vendetta*, and has been *vendetta* any day since the Saturday before last, when old Stephanu Ceccaldi swindled me out of that very horse from which you have alighted: and it fills me with wonder to see him here.'

'My tale will not lessen your wonder,' said I, 'when you learn how I came by him. But as touching this Stephanu Ceccaldi?'

'As we hear, they were to have buried him last night at moonrise: for a week had not passed before my knife found him—the knife of me, Marcantonio Dezio. All night the *voceri* of the Ceccalde's women-folk have been sounding across the hills.'

'Agreeable sir, I have later news of him. The Ceccalde (let us doubt not) did their best. They mounted him upon Nello here, the innocent cause of their affliction. They waked him with dirges which—now you come to mention them—were melancholy enough to drive a cat to suicide. They tied him upright, and rode him forth to the burial. But it would seem that Nello, here, is a true son of your clan: he cannot bear a Ceccaldi on top of him. For I met him scouring the hills with the corpse on his back, having given leg-bail to all his escort.'

The Corsican has a heart, if you only know where to find it. Forgetting his dread of an ambush, or disregarding it in the violence of his emotion, Marcantonio flung wide the door, stepped forth, and casting both arms about the horse's neck and mane, caressed him passionately and even with tears.

'O Nello! O brave spirit! O true son of the Dezii!'

He called forth his family, and they came trooping through the doorway—an old man, two old women, a middle-aged matron whom I took for Marcantonio's wife, three stalwart girls, a stunted lad of about fourteen and four smaller and very dirty children. Their movements were dignified—even an infant Corsican rarely forgets his gravity—but they surrounded Nello one and all, and embraced him, and fed him on lumps of sugar. (Sugar, I may say, is a luxury in Corsica, and scarce at that.) They wept upon his mane and called him their little hero. They shook their fists towards that quarter, across the valley, in which I supposed the Ceccalde to reside. They chanted a song over the little beast while he munched his sugar with an air of conscious worth. And in short I imagined myself to be wholly forgotten in their delight at recovering him, until Marcantonio swung round suddenly and asked me to name a price for him.

'Eh?' said I. 'What—for Nello? Surely, after what has happened, you can hardly bring yourself to part with him?'

'Hardly, indeed. O stranger, it will tear my heart! But where am I to bestow him? The Ceccalde will be here presently; beyond doubt they are already climbing the pass. And for you also it will be awkward if they catch you here.'

I had not thought of this danger. 'The valley below will be barred then?' I asked.

'Undoubtedly.'

'I might perhaps stay and lend you some help.'

'This is the Dezii's private quarrel,' he assured me with dignity. 'But never fear for us, O stranger. We will give them as good as they bring.'

'I am bound for Corte,' said I.

'By following the track up to the *bocca* you will come in sight of the high-road. But you will never reach it without Nello's help, seeing that my private affairs hinder me from accompanying you. Now concerning this horse, he is one in a thousand: you might indeed say that he is worth his weight in gold.'

'At all events,' said I smiling, 'he is a ticklish horse to pay too little for.'

'A price is a price,' answered Marcantonio gravely. 'Old Stephanu Ceccaldi, catching me drunk, thought to pay but half of it, but the residue I took when I was sober. Now, between gentlefolks, what dispute could there be over eighty livres? Eighty livres!—why it is scarce the price of a good mare!'

Well, bating the question of his right to sell the horse, eighty livres was assuredly cheap: and after a moment's calculation I resolved to close with him and accept the risk rather than by higgling over a point of honesty, which after all concerned his conscience rather than mine, to incur the more unpleasant one of a Ceccaldi bullet. I searched in my wallet and paid the money, while the Dezii with many sobs, mixed a half-pint of wine in a mash and offered this last tribute to the vindicator of their family honour.

So when Nello had fed and I had drunk a cup to their very long life,

I mounted and jogged away up the pass. Once or twice I reined up on the ascent for a look back at the plateau. And always the Dezii stood there, straining their eyes after Nello and waving farewells.

On the far side of the ridge my ears were saluted by sounds of irregular musketry in the vale behind; and I knew that the second stage in the Dezio–Ceccaldi *vendetta* had opened with vigour.

Three days later I had audience with the great Paoli in his rooms in the Convent of Marosaglia. He listened to my message with patience and to the narrative of my adventures with unfeigned interest. At the end he said—

'I think you had best quit Corsica with the least possible delay. And, if I may advise you further, you will follow the road northwards to Bastia, avoiding all short cuts. In any case, avoid the Niolo. I happen to know something of the Ceccalde, and their temper; and, believe me, I am counselling you for the best.'

The Brass Butterfly

The affair of the Brass Butterfly was kept a profound secret for reasons which will be obvious.

Late on the night of 6th December 1906, I alighted at the big echoing station of Bologna, after a long and tedious journey from Charing Cross.

I was, as usual, on a secret mission, and there were strong reasons why I should not go to the Hôtel Brun or any of the other first-class houses frequented by British tourists, therefore I drove to an obscure little inn situate up a back street, called the Hôtel Tazza d'Oro. You may have seen it, a dark, frowsy, little place, dingy and so obviously unclean that, as an Englishman, you would have shuddered at the mere thought of passing a night there.

But I was not desirous of being recognized by certain persons to whom I was known in that city, therefore I registered my name as Pietro Pirelli, commercial traveller, of Naples.

I was there in order to solve a problem which had considerably puzzled us at Whitehall.

I glanced around the shabby, unclean room to which I was shown, washed my hands, and then sauntered forth along those long dark colonnaded streets that are the same today as they were back in the Middle Ages, until I had crossed the broad moonlit Piazza before the Duomo, and plunged into a maze of narrow thoroughfares which brought me eventually into a wider medieval street in front of a great, dark, almost prison-like palace of the *cinquecento* with a coat-of-arms graven in stone over the arched gateway closed by a ponderous iron-studded door.

It was the Palazzo Bardi, wherein lived the Donna Stella, the twenty-year-old daughter of the great Marquis Bardi, the millionaire landowner and Senator of the Kingdom of Italy.

The windows of the huge square stone building, almost a fortress, were closely shuttered and barred, a grim, silent place which none would believe contained such priceless works of art, or one of the most famous collections of armour in the world.

I crossed the road to the big ancient door which had withstood many a siege in those turbulent days when the Bardi so constantly fought the Ginestrelli from Pistoja, across the Appenines. Then, switching on the light of my little electric lamp, I stood on tiptoe and carefully examined the antique bronze knocker in the form of the grinning face of a satyr.

Upon one of the polished cheeks of the grotesque mask I found what I sought—a small cross, scratched by a pin.

Then, well satisfied, I turned upon my heel and retraced my steps to my obscure hotel. The Donna Stella had received my message in safety, and would meet me in secret next day.

When at noon I stood at a remote spot in the little park beyond the city, awaiting her, she came, a slim, neat-waisted figure in black, accompanied by 'Spot', her English fox-terrier. A smile of welcome lit up her handsome face as she placed her gloved hand in mine in greeting.

'You are, no doubt, surprised, signorina, at my sudden appearance in Bologna,' I said. 'But it is, in a great measure, in your interests.'

'In mine! I don't understand!' she replied in excellent English, for she had been educated at Brighton.

'In the interests of your friend Captain Devrill,' I said quietly.

Her face changed instantly.

'Have you heard anything of him? Have you just come from Vienna?'

'Unfortunately I am entirely without information,' I said. 'My friend has mysteriously disappeared.'

Jack Devrill, ex-captain of Royal Engineers, and one of the most alert and active of my colleagues, was her particular friend. They had met in England when she was still a schoolgirl, and their friendship had ripened into affection. Yet a great gulf lay between them, for it was hardly likely that she, only daughter and heiress of one of the wealthiest Roman nobles and niece of Prince von Furstenberg, the great Austrian statesman who held the office of Imperial and Royal Minister for Foreign Affairs, and who ruled at the Ballhausplatz, the Foreign Office at Vienna, would be allowed to marry the careless cosmopolitan Secret Service agent.

'I have been waiting in daily anxiety for news of him,' she sighed. 'I cannot understand it. Ah! Mr Morrice, you cannot know in what terror and dread I have existed, ever since I left Vienna twelve days ago. I—I fear that something terrible has happened to him!'

This was exactly the opinion of our Department. Jack Devrill had disappeared into space; he had fallen the victim of some enemy—betrayed, without a doubt.

The facts were briefly these. Sixteen days ago Jack and I had arrived in Vienna on a most important and secret mission. Suspicion had been aroused that something unusual was afoot at the Ballhausplatz, and we had been dispatched from Whitehall to endeavour to ascertain what was in progress.

In the gay Austrian capital we were both well-known, so we at once left cards and received many invitations. I had served as attaché there four years before, hence I knew a great many of the officials. We lived at the Hôtel Bristol, as was our habit, and the Donna Stella being on a visit to her uncle, we were both invited several times to the great official residence of the Foreign Minister in the Franzens Ring. On one of these brilliant occasions—an official ball at which the white-bearded Emperor and his suite were present—I accompanied Devrill. Donna Stella, with whom I waltzed once, looked inexpressibly dainty in turquoise chiffon, but soon afterwards I missed the pair, and concluded that they were sitting out.

That night, however, Jack mysteriously disappeared. Enquiries I made of the night-porter at the hotel next day showed that my friend had returned at about two-thirty, changed his clothes, and an hour later had gone forth—whither no one knew. I had returned an hour afterwards, but had been unaware that he was missing till near noon.

I went to his room, and there found all his belongings in perfect order, but on the table there stood a quaint antique object which he had evidently bought only a few hours before going to the ball—an old Turkish ornament in which to burn perfume—a big butterfly of polished brass.

It measured about a foot across from tip to tip of its wings, fashioned beautifully, the body perforated to allow the fragrance of the smoking pastilles to escape into the room. I examined it minutely. There was a cavity along the body, but nothing was inside. I saw at once that he had evidently bought it to add to the collection of antiques he possessed at his cosy rooms in Half Moon Street. I wondered, however, why he had not shown it to me. Whether it was on account of its unusual grotesqueness, or the delicacy of its design, I know not, yet I somehow became unusually attracted by my friend's curious purchase, and took it to an antique dealer in the Burggasse, who pronounced it to be a rare specimen of sixteenth-century work, probably from the harem of some rich pasha in the south of Turkey.

I grew alarmed at the non-return of my friend, and reported his disappearance by cipher to that cryptic telegraphic address in London

with which we are so constantly communicating. My orders were to spare
no effort to clear up the mystery. As far as could be ascertained, the political horizon was perfectly unclouded. Yet the fact of Jack's disappearance
had considerably strengthened our suspicions.

'What effort has been made to find him?' asked the girl anxiously.

'Every effort, signorina. The police of the whole Austrian Empire are
in active search for traces of him.'

'What can I do?' she asked hoarsely, pale-faced and anxious. 'This silence
of his means foul play—of that I now feel convinced.'

That was exactly my opinion, though I did not admit it. Jack Devrill
would certainly have reported himself ere that, by sending his name to
the deaths column of *The Times* 'In memoriam'.

'I'm here, signorina,' I said, 'to ask you a question. Pardon my inquis-
itiveness, but it is in Devrill's interests. On the night of the ball at His
Excellency's both you and he were absent from the room after eleven
o'clock. Were you sitting with him the whole time?'

Her face blanched, then flushed crimson. At first she became confused,
then indignant at my question.

'I really cannot see what that had to do with it,' she answered resentfully, surprising me by her antagonistic attitude. Over her handsome countenance was a cloud of undisguised displeasure that I should ask such a
question.

'I am trying to solve the cause of Jack's disappearance,' I said quietly.
'Cannot you be frank with me? Cannot you tell me what actually occurred
on that night?'

'I—I can't!' she blurted forth. Then, suddenly recovering herself, she
added: 'I don't know what you mean.'

Her attitude puzzled me.

Again I endeavoured to persuade her to relate what had occurred between
them, and there being no one in the vicinity to see or overhear, I placed
my hand tenderly upon her shapely shoulder.

'I know it is not just to him to hold back anything that took place on
that fateful night, but—but I can't tell you!' she cried, bursting into a
flood of tears. 'I—I prefer to remain here, alone and desolate, with the
memory of my dead love, than—than to reveal my shame!'

I saw that her young heart was overburdened by grief. Yet what was
the nature of the secret she would not divulge?

I argued with her for a full hour, but she refused to tell me anything.
Indeed, her attitude became more puzzling. Something had occurred on
that night, but the mystery of it was inscrutable.

I told her that I should return to Milan at four o'clock that afternoon to catch the through express from Nice to Vienna, for I intended at all hazards to solve the problem of my friend's disappearance.

'I hope you will, Mr Morrice,' was all she said as she placed her small hand in mine for a moment, then bowing, turned away and left me.

I had sent a telegram to London, and being compelled to await a reply did not leave Bologna till just before midnight. But as I stood on the platform awaiting the train I saw, to my great surprise, the Donna Stella herself. She was alone, wearing a long fur travelling-coat and toque to match, and had not seen me. She travelled by the same train to Milan as myself, and next evening I watched her descend from my train at the Südbahnhof at Vienna.

On alighting, while I still remained unseen in my wagon-lit, I saw that she was met by a short, dark-bearded man and a thin, rather angular woman in brown, with whom she held a hurried conversation. She was apparently annoyed at their presence, for as soon as possible she escaped into the fine carriage which her uncle, the Prince, had sent for her.

As I drove down the brightly lit Heugasse, to the Bristol, I could not put aside the thought that the man had used threats towards her. I had noticed the expression of fear upon her pale face, half hidden by her veil.

Yet she had deliberately concealed the truth from me, and this had aroused my suspicions.

I had kept on my sitting-room and bedroom at the hotel, and, as I entered, the first object that greeted my eyes was my missing friend's curious purchase—the Brass Butterfly. I had given up Jack's rooms, and his belongings had been transferred to mine. Taking up the curious object I gazed at it in wonder, as I had done several times. Somehow I entertained a fixed belief that its purchase was in some way connected with his disappearance. The police of Vienna had enquired of every antique dealer in the city, but the person who had sold it could not be found.

About two o'clock next day, while keeping patient watch upon the private entrance of the big house of His Excellency, the Foreign Minister in the Franzens Ring, not far from my hotel, I saw the dark-eyed girl, neat in a brown tailor-made gown, come forth, and walking as far as the corner of the Volksgarten, she entered a cab. Across the city I followed her to the Kronprinz Rudolf Strasse, where, turning down a side-street, close to the Danube, she entered a rather dingy house while her cab waited outside.

For perhaps three-quarters of an hour she remained there. When she emerged, she was accompanied by the same short, dark-bearded man who had met her at the station. He bowed to her as she drove off, but it was evident that there was a coolness between them.

The girl's sweet face was pale and haggard, and I saw that she had been greatly upset by what had transpired. Already my enquiries had revealed that the man's name was Karl von Weissenfeld, and that the woman was his sister Freda.

That evening I wrote Stella a note saying that I had seen her in Vienna, and asking her to meet me next morning in the Tirolerhof, a small, quiet café in the Weihburg, where ladies often go to drink milk. In response she rang me up on the telephone, saying that she would prefer to call at the hotel, as someone might see her at the café.

Therefore at eleven next morning she was ushered into my salon, but at sight of the Brass Butterfly she started, and drew back almost in horror. I noticed that the mere sight of the quaint object upset her.

'Why don't you put that horrible thing away, Mr Morrice—away in some place of safety? Sell it, give it away, destroy it—anything—only get rid of it!'

'Is sight of it so very painful to you, then?' I asked, greatly surprised.

'I—I don't wish to see it,' she answered, pale and agitated. 'It recalls—'

'Recalls what?' I asked, fixing my eyes upon hers as I took the old perfume-burner and placed it within a small cabinet near by.

'Ah!' she cried. 'No; do not ask me! You would not, if you knew how much I suffer, because—because I can never tell you the truth—because of my shame!'

'Then you know why Jack Devrill is missing, eh?' I said, still looking straight into her splendid eyes. 'Answer me one question, signorina. Has that Brass Butterfly any connection with his disappearance?'

She hesitated. I saw in her countenance fear and confusion. At last she nodded in the affirmative.

'Then tell me the truth, signorina—the truth of what occurred on the night of the ball?' I urged.

'I can't,' she cried. 'It shall never pass my lips!'

'And yet you are here in Vienna, because your secret is threatened with exposure,' I said very quietly, my gaze still upon her.

'*Dio!*' she gasped, starting. 'How do you know?'

'Your honour is at stake, Stella. Why not allow me to assist you against your enemies?' I asked. 'Why not tell the truth, and let me advise you? Let us combine to solve this mystery of poor Jack's disappearance. Surely you are convinced that I am your friend, as well as his?'

'If I told you, Mr Morrice, you would instantly become my enemy,' she said hoarsely, as, with a choking sob, she turned and left the room.

What did she mean? Her suggestion was that Jack's disappearance had been due to her—that she held a guilty knowledge of the truth.

That afternoon, while keeping vigilant watch upon the big house in the Franzens Ring, I saw, to my surprise, the man Von Weissenfeld call. He was admitted, and remained within for half an hour. Then he hailed a cab from the rank and drove to the Rheinisch Café, away in the Prater Strasse, where, at a table in a corner, two rather ill-dressed men awaited him. Seated where they could not observe me, I watched them holding a consultation in an undertone, and by it became convinced that some crooked business was afoot. I noticed, too, that one of the men took a pencil from his pocket, and when the waiter's back was turned he scribbled something upon the marble table-top.

At length the trio rose and, leaving the café, separated as soon as they were outside.

As soon as the waiter had gone up to the desk I left my seat, and crossing to get a newspaper which lay near, bent and discerned something very faintly written. It appeared to be 'Bristol 198–9'.

This surprised me, for the number of my room at the Bristol was 198, while 9 apparently stood for an appointment at nine o'clock.

What could it mean?

For two hours I remained there pretending to drink, until at last a tall, thin, shifty-eyed man with a reddish moustache entered, and seating himself at the table ordered a bock. Then, when the waiter had gone to obtain it, he bent and searched for the secret message. Having read it, he wetted his finger and quickly effaced it. Afterwards he drank his beer at a draught, paid, and went out.

Was it some appointment made at my rooms? I resolved to remain wary and vigilant.

Therefore, after eating my dinner that evening in the smart white-and-gold restaurant of the Bristol which you who know Vienna know so well, I ascended by the lift, and at about a quarter-past eight entered my sitting-room. Afterwards I switched off the light, and concealed myself behind the long green silk curtains which had been pulled across the windows.

Then I waited—waited so breathlessly that I could hear my own heart beat.

The clocks chimed nine. The waiter entered to make up my wood fire, and left. Then the telephone bell rang, and though I dearly wished to answer and ascertain who might wish to speak to me, I remained in my hiding-place.

Those moments of tension seemed hours. What was intended, I wondered, at nine o'clock?

About a quarter of an hour passed, as nearly as I could judge. My watch ticked with a noise like a threshing-machine.

Suddenly I heard the click of a latch, the door communicating with my bedroom slowly opened, and I saw, by the firelight, standing in the doorway the man with the red moustache. Behind him was Von Weissenfeld himself.

'It must be in here,' I heard the latter whisper in German. 'It certainly is not in the bedroom.'

'He may have sent it to London,' remarked his tall companion.

'No,' replied Von Weissenfeld. 'Stella told me today that it was here this morning. Look over there—in yonder cabinet.'

The man with the red moustache crept noiselessly across the room, opened the door of the cabinet, and with a quick exclamation of satisfaction drew forth the Brass Butterfly.

'Good!' cried Von Weissenfeld, in triumph. 'Then the secret will be ours after all!'

The fellow had transferred it to the small leather bag he carried in readiness, and was about to retire, when I sprang forth and covering him with my revolver, cried:

'I have watched you, gentlemen! You are thieves, and I shall hand you over to the police!'

And at the same moment I placed my hand behind me, locking the door leading out upon the corridor.

Von Weissenfeld remained perfectly unperturbed. Indeed, I have never seen a man take discovery so calmly.

'I do not think, Herr Morrice, that it will be exactly wise to call the police,' he replied; 'for if so, I shall explain to them that you are a secret agent of the British Government!' and he stood before me in defiance.

I was wondering why, if the Butterfly were abstracted, the secret would be theirs. What secret?

'Make what statement you like, I intend to call the police,' I said determinedly, turning to find the button of the electric bell. By this action, however, I foolishly relaxed my vigilance for a second, and when I turned again, not having found the bell-push, I discovered that both men had drawn revolvers and were covering me.

'Touch that button, and you're a dead man!' exclaimed Von Weissenfeld, determination upon his sinister face.

Instantly I saw myself in a dilemma, locked in that room with these two desperate thieves.

I demanded the return of the Brass Butterfly, but both men only laughed in my face.

'You and your friend Devrill played a clever game!' replied the dark-bearded fellow who had threatened Stella. 'But we have outwitted you. The secret is ours!'

At that moment, ere I could reply, there was a loud rapping at the door, and a woman's voice called my name.

It was Stella.

I replied that entry could be obtained through my bedroom, and next moment she burst in, accompanied by the manager of the hotel and three porters in uniform. At sight of them the intruders fell back.

'Ah, Mr Morrice!' she gasped breathlessly, 'I telephoned to you, but did not obtain a reply. I have been indiscreet. I have unwittingly told that man yonder something,' and she indicated Von Weissenfeld, 'and afterwards I felt certain he would come here tonight, in order to secure the Brass Butterfly—to kill you if necessary in order to obtain it.'

'The Butterfly is in the bag in that man's hand,' I said, pointing to it with my revolver. 'Come, give it to me!' I demanded, advancing towards him.

But the fellow thrust his weapon in my face in defiance.

'Josef!' said the hotel manager, 'just telephone for the police.' And the porter, thus addressed, crossed the room and obeyed.

Then the urbane manager induced both men to lay down their arms, an example which I followed, while ten minutes later a brigadier of police, accompanied by four agents, arrived. The bag was taken from Von Weissenfeld, the Butterfly handed back to me, and the two men, who had little to say, were arrested and afterwards conducted out.

Stella, left alone with me in the little salon, turned, and laying a trembling hand upon my arm, said in a low voice:

'Forgive me, Mr Morrice, for I ought to have revealed the whole truth to you before. I should have done so, but that man, Von Weissenfeld, forbade me, threatening to denounce me if I told you. What occurred between Jack and myself on that fateful night I can no longer conceal. We neither of us wished to dance, therefore I took him up to my uncle's smoking-room, which, you will perhaps remember, adjoins his private cabinet. Presently I left him while I went to my room to readjust my hair, which had become disarranged when waltzing with you. When I returned Jack was not there, but peeping through into my uncle's room I discovered him bending over the writing-table taking swift notes of two official-looking papers which he had taken from a drawer. At first he was unaware of my presence, but when, in horror, I charged him with espionage he admitted it, and then revealed to me his true position. I was bewildered. My first impulse was to go to my uncle and tell him, but he persuaded me to remain silent. It seems that an hour later Captain Devrill went to the central telegraph bureau, and dispatched a cipher message to London. The clerk, Von Weissenfeld, who took it over the counter, possessing some knowledge of the cipher used, made out a portion of it and, suppressing it, came to me next day to blackmail me. He was a complete stranger, but I have since ascertained that he is a secret agent of Germany, and hence, I suppose, knew something of your British cipher. He demanded that I should obtain from my uncle's writing-table the original of those two documents, and allow him to take a complete copy, otherwise he would denounce me for having given official information to my English lover. This I refused. Captain Devrill, before he left me, had entrusted me with a message for you.'

'For me!' I cried in surprise.

'Yes. He told me to tell you to unscrew the head from the Brass Butterfly and send to London what you found inside.'

With trembling hands I took up the antique brass ornament, and after some trouble found that the head really did unscrew, revealing a small cavity within.

There, concealed inside, was a piece of thin foreign notepaper covered with Jack's well-known handwriting. Glancing it through, I found, to my abject amazement, that it revealed Austria's immediate intention to defy Europe, by tearing up the Treaty of Berlin and to annex Bosnia and Herzegovina!

At first I could scarcely believe it credible. Yet previous knowledge of this amazing move which had actually received the Emperor's approval and signature, would place Downing Street in a position of defence. We would be forewarned, and consequently forearmed against being drawn into international complications!

The war-cloud had arisen, and we alone held knowledge of it! That brief telegram sent by Jack had been suppressed by Von Weissenfeld, hence our Chief was unaware of the success of our mission!

'But why did Jack disappear?' I exclaimed, speaking aloud to myself.

A postscript, addressed to me, however, explained it. 'I am going on to Sarajevo and Mostar, the capitals of Bosnia and Herzegovina,' he had scrawled. 'I shall endeavour to ascertain the feeling there, and so shall efface myself for a few weeks. There are reasons why I should leave Vienna hurriedly and disappear. Stella has discovered the truth concerning me, and others may perhaps know it. Tell the Chief I shall report myself among the deaths on 1st February. Be careful of this Brass Butterfly. I want it for my collection. Take care of yourself, old chap!'

'Ah!' I cried, 'I see quite clearly now. He feared to leave a note for me, and was compelled to catch the first train to Budapest. Therefore he hit upon the device of concealing the secret within the Brass Butterfly.'

'Why, today is the 2nd of February,' cried Stella, whose mind was greatly relieved by reading that postscript. 'Yesterday's *Times* would have arrived from London an hour ago.'

I rang and when the waiter brought the paper, we found beneath the 'In Memoriam' column:

DEVRILL.—In affectionate remembrance of Guy John Devrill, husband of Ann Devrill, who died at Belgrade, Servia, on 1st February 1901.

At midnight, while the blackmailing telegraph clerk and his companion were helpless in the police cells charged with theft at the Hotel Bristol, I rolled myself up in the wagon-lit already on my way to London via Ostend, bearing with me the precious scrap of paper which contained news of that sudden political move which, a fortnight later, took the whole world by surprise.

Three weeks afterwards Jack turned up again at Whitehall as spruce and smiling as ever, but utterly amazed at the apprehension his sudden disappearance had caused.

Later he explained that Stella had hesitated to give me his message, feeling that by revealing what the Brass Butterfly contained she would further betray her uncle's secret. She had, of course, no idea why her lover had so suddenly vanished. Further, it seemed that Von Weissenfeld had feared to denounce us, lest it should have been discovered that he was a secret agent of Germany, while the Donna Stella had, on the day following my departure, returned to Bologna.

That early knowledge of Austria's hostile actions—which no doubt surprised you when you read them in the newspapers—enabled Great Britain to unite with Russia in preventing a bloody and disastrous war in Eastern Europe. Therefore the end surely justified the means.

Jack is retiring from the service, for he is to marry Stella. Whenever I go to smoke with him in his rooms in Half Moon Street, however, I cannot help recalling how that most vital and important secret of State reposed unsuspected for so many days within the head of that quaint object which now occupies such a prominent position upon the polished table against the wall—the Brass Butterfly.

Peiffer

For a moment I was surprised to see the stout and rubicund Slingsby in Lisbon. He was drinking a vermouth and seltzer at five o'clock in the afternoon at a café close to the big hotel. But at that time Portugal was still a neutral country and a happy hunting ground for a good many thousand Germans. Slingsby was lolling in his chair with such exceeding indolence that I could not doubt his business was pressing and serious. I accordingly passed him by as if I had never seen him in my life before. But he called out to me. So I took a seat at his table.

Of what we talked about I have not the least recollection, for my eyes were quite captivated by a strange being who sat alone fairly close to Slingsby, at one side and a little behind him. This was a man of middle age, with reddish hair, a red, square, inflamed face and a bristly moustache. He was dressed in a dirty suit of grey flannel; he wore a battered Panama pressed down upon his head; he carried pince-nez on the bridge of his nose, and he sat with a big bock of German beer in front of him. But I never saw him touch the beer. He sat in a studied attitude of ferocity, his elbow on the table, his chin propped on the palm of his hand, his head pushed aggressively forward, and he glared at Slingsby through his glasses with the fixed stare of hatred and fury which a master workman in wax might give to a figure in a Chamber of Horrors. Indeed, it seemed to me that he must have rehearsed his bearing in some such quarter, for there was nothing natural or convinced in him from the brim of his Panama to the black patent leather tips of his white canvas shoes.

I touched Slingsby on the arm.

'Who is that man, and what have you done to him?'

Slingsby looked round unconcernedly.

'Oh, that's only Peiffer,' he replied. 'Peiffer making frightfulness.'

'Peiffer?'

The name was quite strange to me.

'Yes. Don't you know him? He's a product of 1914,' and Slingsby leaned towards me a little. 'Peiffer is an officer in the German Navy. You would hardly guess it, but he is. Now that their country is at war, officers in the German Navy have a marked amount of spare time which they never had before. So Peiffer went to a wonderful Government school in Hamburg, where in twenty lessons they teach the gentle art of espionage, a sort of Berlitz school. Peiffer ate his dinners and got his degrees, so to speak, and now he's at Lisbon putting obi on me.'

'It seems rather infantile, and must be annoying,' I said; but Slingsby would only accept half the statement.

'Infantile, yes. Annoying, not at all. For so long as Peiffer is near me, being frightful, I know he's not up to mischief.'

'Mischief!' I cried. 'That fellow? What mischief can he do?'

Slingsby viciously crushed the stub of his cigarette in the ashtray.

'A deuce of a lot, my friend. Don't make any mistake. Peiffer's methods are infantile and barbaric, but he has a low and fertile cunning in the matter of ideas. I know. I have had some.'

And Slingsby was to have more, very much more: in the shape of a great many sleepless nights, during which he wrestled with a dreadful uncertainty to get behind that square red face and those shining pince-nez, and reach the dark places of Peiffer's mind.

The first faint wisp of cloud began to show six weeks later, when Slingsby happened to be in Spain.

'Something's up,' he said, scratching his head. 'But I'm hanged if I can guess what it is. See what you can make of it'; and here is the story which he told.

Three Germans dressed in the black velvet corduroy, the white stockings and the rope-soled white shoes of the Spanish peasant, arrived suddenly in the town of Cartagena, and put up at an inn in a side-street near the harbour. Cartagena, for all that it is one of the chief naval ports of Spain, is a small place, and the life of it ebbs and flows in one narrow street, the Calle Mayor; so that very little can happen which is not immediately known and discussed. The arrival of the three mysterious Germans provoked, consequently, a deal of gossip and curiosity, and the curiosity was increased when the German Consul sitting in front of the Casino loudly professed complete ignorance of these very doubtful compatriots of his, and an exceeding great contempt for them. The next morning, however, brought a new development. The three Germans complained publicly to the Alcalde. They had walked through Valencia, Alicante, and Murcia in search of work, and everywhere they had been pestered and shadowed by the police.

'Our Consul will do nothing for us,' they protested indignantly. 'He will not receive us, nor will any German in Cartagena. We are poor people.' And having protested, they disappeared in the night.

But a few days later the three had emerged again at Almeria, and at a mean café in one of the narrow, blue-washed Moorish streets of the old town. Peiffer was identified as one of the three—not the Peiffer who had practised frightfulness in Lisbon, but a new and wonderful Peiffer, who inveighed against the shamelessness of German officials on the coasts of Spain. At Almeria, in fact, Peiffer made a scene at the German Vice-Consulate, and, having been handed over to the police, was fined and threatened with imprisonment. At this point the story ended.

'What do you make of it?' asked Slingsby.

'First, that Peiffer is working south; and, secondly, that he is quarrelling with his own officials.'

'Yes, but quarrelling with marked publicity,' said Slingsby. 'That, I think we shall find, is the point of real importance. Peiffer's methods are not merely infantile; they are elaborate. He is working down South. I think that I will go to Gibraltar. I have always wished to see it.'

Whether Slingsby was speaking the truth, I had not an idea. But he went to Gibraltar, and there an astonishing thing happened to him. He received a letter, and the letter came from Peiffer. Peiffer was at Algeciras, just across the bay in Spain, and he wanted an interview. He wrote for it with the most brazen impertinence.

'I cannot, owing to this with-wisdom-so-easily-to-have-been-avoided war, come myself to Gibraltar, but I will remain at your disposition here.'

'*That*,' said Slingsby, 'from the man who was making frightfulness at me a few weeks ago, is a proof of some nerve. We will go and see Peiffer. We will stay at Algeciras from Saturday to Monday, and we will hear what he has to say.'

A polite note was accordingly dispatched, and on Sunday morning Peiffer, decently clothed in a suit of serge, was shown into Slingsby's private sitting-room. He plunged at once into the story of his wanderings. We listened to it without a sign that we knew anything about it.

'So?' from time to time said Slingsby, with inflections of increasing surprise, but that was all. Then Peiffer went on to his grievances.

'Perhaps you have heard how I was treated by the Consuls?' he interrupted himself to ask suddenly.

'No,' Slingsby replied calmly. 'Continue!'

Peiffer wiped his forehead and his glasses. We were each one, in his way, all working for our respective countries. The work was honourable.

But there were limits to endurance. All his fatigue and perils went for nothing in the eyes of comfortable officials sure of their salary. He had been fined; he had been threatened with imprisonment. It was *unverschämt* the way he had been treated.

'So?' said Slingsby firmly. There are fine inflections by which that simple word may be made to express most of the emotions. Slingsby's 'So?' expressed a passionate agreement with the downtrodden Peiffer.

'Flesh and blood can stand it no longer,' cried Peiffer, 'and my heart is flesh. No, I have had enough.'

Throughout the whole violent tirade, in his eyes, in his voice, in his gestures, there ran an eager, wistful plea that we should take him at his face value and believe every word he said.

'So I came to you,' he said at last, slapping his knee and throwing out his hand afterwards like a man who has taken a mighty resolution. 'Yes. I have no money, nothing. And they will give me none. It is *unverschämt*. So,' and he screwed up his little eyes and wagged a podgy forefinger— 'so the service I had begun for my Government I will now finish for you.'

Slingsby examined the carpet curiously.

'Well, there are possibly some shillings to be had if the service is good enough. I do not know. But I cannot deal in the dark. What sort of a service is it?'

'Ah!'

Peiffer hitched his chair nearer.

'It is a question of rifles—rifles for over there,' and, looking out through the window he nodded towards Gibel Musa and the coast of Morocco.

Slingsby did not so much as flinch. I almost groaned aloud. We were to be treated to the stock legend of the ports, the new edition of the Spanish prisoner story. I, the mere tourist in search of health, could have gone on with Peiffer's story myself, even to the exact number of the rifles.

'It was a great plan,' Peiffer continued. 'Fifty thousand rifles, no less.' There always were fifty thousand rifles. 'They are buried—near the sea.' They always were buried either near the sea or on the frontier of Portugal. 'With ammunition. They are to be landed outside Melilla, where I have been about this very affair, and distributed amongst the Moors in the unsubdued country on the edge of the French zone.'

'So?' exclaimed Slingsby with the most admirable imitation of consternation.

'Yes, but you need not fear. You shall have the rifles—when I know exactly where they are buried.'

'Ah!' said Slingsby.

He had listened to the familiar rigmarole, certain that behind it there was something real and sinister which he did not know—something which he was desperately anxious to find out.

'Then you do not know where they are buried?'

'No, but I shall know if—I am allowed to go into Gibraltar. Yes, there is some one there. I must put myself into relations with him. Then I shall know, and so shall you.'

So here was some part of the truth, at all events. Peiffer wanted to get into Gibraltar. His disappearance from Lisbon, his reappearance in corduroys, his quarrelsome progress down the east coast, his letter to Slingsby, and his story, were all just the items of an elaborate piece of machinery invented to open the gates of that fortress to him. Slingsby's only movement was to take his cigarette-case lazily from his pocket.

'But why in the world,' he asked, 'can't you get your man in Gibraltar to come out here and see you?'

Peiffer shook his head.

'He would not come. He has been told to expect me, and I shall give him certain tokens from which he can guess my trustworthiness. If I write to him, "Come to me," he will say "This is a trap".'

Slingsby raised another objection:

'But I shouldn't think that you can expect the authorities to give you a safe conduct into Gibraltar upon your story.'

Peiffer swept that argument aside with a contemptuous wave of his hand.

'I have a Danish passport. See!' and he took the document from his breast pocket. It was complete, to his photograph.

'Yes, you can certainly come in on that,' said Slingsby. He reflected for a moment before he added: 'I have no power, of course. But I have some friends. I think you may reasonably reckon that you won't be molested.'

I saw Peiffer's eyes glitter behind his glasses.

'But there's a condition,' Slingsby continued sharply. 'You must not leave Gibraltar without coming personally to me and giving me twenty-four hours' notice.'

Peiffer was all smiles and agreement.

'But of course. We shall have matters to talk over—terms to arrange. I must see you.'

'Exactly. Cross by the nine-fifty steamer tomorrow morning. Is that understood?'

'Yes, sir.' And suddenly Peiffer stood up and actually saluted, as though he had now taken service under Slingsby's command.

The unexpected movement almost made me vomit. Slingsby himself moved quickly away, and his face lost for a second the mask of impassivity. He stood at the window and looked across the water to the city of Gibraltar.

Slingsby had been wounded in the early days of the war, and ever since he had been greatly troubled because he was not still in the trenches in Flanders. The casualty lists filled him with shame and discontent. So many of his friends, the men who had trained and marched with him, were laying down their gallant lives. He should have been with them. But during the last few days a new knowledge and inspiration had come to him. Gibraltar! A tedious, little, unlovely town of yellow houses and coal sheds, with an undesirable climate. Yes. But above it was the Rock, the heart of a thousand memories and traditions which made it beautiful. He looked at it now with its steep wooded slopes, scarred by roads and catchments and the emplacements of guns. How much of England was recorded there! To how many British sailing on great ships from far dominions this huge buttress towering to its needle-ridge was the first outpost of the homeland! And for the moment he seemed to be its particular guardian, the ear which must listen night and day lest harm come to it. Harm the Rock, and all the Empire, built with such proud and arduous labour, would stagger under the blow, from St Kilda to distant Lyttelton. He looked across the water and imagined Gibraltar as it looked at night, its house-lights twinkling like a crowded zone of stars, and its great search-beams turning the ships in the harbour and the stone of the moles into gleaming silver, and travelling far over the dark waters. No harm must come to Gibraltar. His honour was all bound up in that. This was his service, and as he thought upon it he was filled with a cold fury against the traitor who thought it so easy to make him fail. But every hint of his anger had passed from his face as he turned back into the room.

'If you bring me good information, why, we can do business,' he said; and Peiffer went away.

I was extremely irritated by the whole interview, and could hardly wait for the door to close.

'What knocks me over,' I cried, 'is the impertinence of the man. Does he really think that any old yarn like the fifty thousand rifles is going to deceive you?'

Slingsby lit a cigarette.

'Peiffer's true to type, that's all,' he answered imperturbably. 'They are vain, and vanity makes them think that you will at once believe what they want you to believe. So their deceits are a little crude.' Then a smile broke over his face, and to some tune with which I was unfamiliar he sang softly: 'But he's coming to Gibraltar in the morning.'

'You think he will?'

'I am sure of it.'

'And,' I added doubtfully—it was not my business to criticize—'on conditions he can walk out again?'

Slingsby's smile became a broad grin.

'His business in Gibraltar, my friend, is not with me. He will not want to meet us any more; as soon as he has done what he came for he will go—or try to go. He thinks we are fools, you see.'

And in the end it seemed almost as though Peiffer was justified of his belief. He crossed the next morning. He went to a hotel of the second class; he slept in the hotel, and next morning he vanished. Suddenly there was no more Peiffer. Peiffer was not. For six hours Peiffer was not; and then at half-past five in the afternoon the telephone bell rang in an office where Slingsby was waiting. He rushed to the instrument.

'Who is it?' he cried, and I saw a wave of relief surge into his face. Peiffer had been caught outside the gates and within a hundred yards of the neutral zone. He had strolled out in the thick of the dockyard workmen going home to Linea in Spain.

'Search him and bring him up here at once,' said Slingsby, and he dropped into his chair and wiped his forehead. 'Phew! Thirty seconds more and he might have snapped his fingers at us.' He turned to me. 'I shall want a prisoner's escort here in half an hour.'

I went about that business and returned in time to see Slingsby giving an admirable imitation of a Prussian police official.

'So, Peiffer,' he cried sternly, 'you broke your word. Do not deny it. It will be useless.'

The habit of a lifetime asserted itself in Peiffer. He quailed before authority when authority began to bully.

'I did not know I was outside the walls,' he faltered. 'I was taking a walk. No one stopped me.'

'So!' Slingsby snorted. 'And these, Peiffer—what have you to say of these?'

There were four separate passports which had been found in Peiffer's pockets. He could be a Dane of Esbjerg, a Swede of Stockholm, a Norwegian of Christiania, or a Dutchman from Amsterdam. All four nationalities were open to Peiffer to select from.

'They provide you with these, no doubt, in your school at Hamburg,' and Slingsby paused to collect his best German. 'You are a prisoner of war. *Das ist genug*,' he cried, and Peiffer climbed to the internment camp.

So far so good. Slingsby had annexed Peiffer, but more important than Peiffer was Peiffer's little plot, and that he had not got. Nor did the most careful enquiry disclose what Peiffer had done and where he had been during the time when he was not. For six hours Peiffer had been loose in Gibraltar, and Slingsby began to get troubled. He tried to assume the mentality of Peiffer, and so reach his intention, but that did not help. He got out all the reports in which Peiffer's name was mentioned and read them over again.

I saw him sit back in his chair and remain looking straight in front of him.

'Yes,' he said thoughtfully, and he turned over the report to me, pointing to a passage. It was written some months before, at Melilla, on the African side of the Mediterranean, and it ran like this:

Peiffer frequents the low houses and cafés, where he spends a good deal of money and sometimes gets drunk. When drunk he gets very arrogant, and has been known to boast that he has been three times in Bordeaux since the war began, and, thanks to his passports, can travel as easily as if the world were at peace. On such occasions he expresses the utmost contempt for neutral nations. I myself have heard him burst out: 'Wait until we have settled with our enemies. Then we will deal properly with the neutral nations. They shall explain to us on their knees. Meanwhile,' and he thumped the table, making the glasses rattle, 'let them keep quiet and hold their tongues. We shall do what we like in neutral countries.'

I read the passage.

'Do you see that last sentence? "We shall do what we like in neutral countries." No man ever spoke the mind of his nation better than Peiffer did that night in a squalid café in Melilla.'

Slingsby looked out over the harbour to where the sun was setting on the sierras. He would have given an arm to be sure of what Peiffer had set on foot behind those hills.

'I wonder,' he said uneasily, and from that day he began to sleep badly.

Then came another and a most disquieting phase of the affair. Peiffer began to write letters to Slingsby. He was not comfortable. He was not being treated as an officer should be. He had no amusements, and his food was too plain. Moreover, there were Germans and Austrians up in the camp who turned up their noses at him because their birth was better than his.

'You see what these letters mean?' said Slingsby. 'Peiffer wants to be sent away from the Rock.'

'You are reading your own ideas into them,' I replied.

But Slingsby was right. Each letter under its simple and foolish excuses was a prayer for translation to a less dangerous place. For as the days passed and no answer was vouchsafed, the prayer became a real cry of fear.

'I claim to be sent to England without any delay. I must be sent,' he wrote frankly and frantically.

Slingsby set his teeth with a grim satisfaction.

'No, my friend, you shall stay while the danger lasts. If it's a year, if you are alone in the camp, still you shall stay. The horrors you have planned you shall share with every man, woman and child in the town.'

We were in this horrible and strange predicament. The whole colony was menaced, and from the Lines to Europa Point only two men knew of the peril. Of those two, one, in an office down by the harbour, ceaselessly and vainly, with a dreadful anxiety, asked 'When?' The other, the prisoner, knew the very hour and minute of the catastrophe, and waited for it with the sinking fear of a criminal awaiting the fixed moment of his execution.

Thus another week passed.

Slingsby became a thing of broken nerves. If you shut the door noisily he cursed; if you came in noiselessly he cursed yet louder, and one evening he reached the stage when the sunset gun made him jump.

'That's enough,' I said sternly. 'Today is Saturday. Tomorrow we borrow the car'—there is only one worth talking about on the Rock—'and we drive out.'

'I can't do it,' he cried.

I continued:

'We will lunch somewhere by the road, and we will go on to the country house of the Claytons, who will give us tea. Then in the afternoon we will return.'

Slingsby hesitated. It is curious to remember on how small a matter so much depended. I believe he would have refused, but at that moment the sunset gun went off and he jumped out of his chair.

'Yes, I am fairly rocky,' he admitted. 'I will take a day off.'

I borrowed the car, and we set off and lunched according to our programme. It was perhaps half an hour afterwards when we were going slowly over a remarkably bad road. A powerful car, driven at a furious pace, rushed round a corner towards us, swayed, lurched, and swept past us with a couple of inches to spare, whilst a young man seated at the wheel shouted a greeting and waved his hand.

'Who the dickens was that?' I asked.

'I know,' replied Slingsby. 'It's Morano. He's a count, and will be a marquis and no end of a swell if he doesn't get killed motoring. Which, after all, seems likely.'

I thought no more of the man until his name cropped up whilst we were sitting at tea on the Claytons' veranda.

'We passed Morano,' said Slingsby. And Mrs Clayton said with some pride—she was a pretty, kindly woman, but she rather affected the Spanish nobility:

'He lunched with us today. You know he is staying in Gibraltar.'

'Yes, I know that,' said Slingsby. 'For I met him a little time ago. He wanted to know if there was a good Government launch for sale.'

Mrs Clayton raised her eyebrows in surprise.

'A launch? Surely you are wrong. He is devoting himself to aviation.'

'Is he?' said Slingsby, and a curious look flickered for a moment over his face.

We left the house half an hour afterwards, and as soon as we were out of sight of it Slingsby opened his hand. He was holding a visiting card.

'I stole this off the hall table,' he said. 'Mrs Clayton will never forgive me. Just look at it.'

His face had become extraordinarily grave. The card was Morano's, and it was engraved after the Spanish custom. In Spain, when a woman marries she does not lose her name. She may be in appearance more subject to her husband than the women of other countries, though you will find many good judges to tell you that women rule Spain. In any case her name is not lost in that of her husband; the children will bear it as well as their father's, and will have it printed on their cards. Thus, Mr Jones will call on you, but on the card he leaves he will be styled:

MR JONES AND ROBINSON,

if Robinson happens to be his mother's name, and if you are scrupulous in your etiquette you will so address him.

Now, on the card which Slingsby had stolen, the Count Morano was described:

MORANO Y GOLTZ.

'I see,' I replied. 'Morano had a German mother.'

I was interested. There might be nothing in it, of course. A noble of Spain might have a German mother and still not intrigue for the Germans against the owners of Gibraltar. But no sane man would take a bet about it.

'The point is,' said Slingsby, 'I am pretty sure that is not the card which he sent in to me when he came to ask about a launch. We will go straight to the office and make sure.'

By the time we got there we were both somewhat excited, and we searched feverishly in the drawers of Slingsby's writing-table.

'I shouldn't be such an ass as to throw it away,' he said, turning over his letters. 'No! Here it is!' and a sharp exclamation burst from his lips. 'Look!'

He laid the card he had stolen side by side with the card which he had just found, and between the two there was a difference—to both of us a veritable world of difference. For from the second card the 'y Goltz', the evidence that Morano was half-German, had disappeared.

'And it's not engraved,' said Slingsby, bending down over the table. 'It's just printed—printed in order to mislead us.'

Slingsby sat down in his chair. A great hope was bringing the life back to his tired face, but he would not give the reins to his hope.

'Let us go slow,' he said, warned by the experience of a hundred disappointments. 'Let us see how it works out. Morano comes to Gibraltar and makes a prolonged stay in a hotel. Not being a fool, he is aware that I know who is in Gibraltar and who is not. Therefore he visits me with a plausible excuse for being in Gibraltar. But he takes the precaution to have this card specially printed. Why, if he is playing straight? He pretends he wants a launch, but he is really devoting himself to aviation. Is it possible that the Count Morano, not forgetting Goltz, knows exactly how the good Peiffer spent the six hours we can't account for, and what his little plan is?'

I sprang up. It did seem that Slingsby was getting at last to the heart of Peiffer's secret.

'We will now take steps,' said Slingsby, and telegrams began to fly over the wires. In three days' time the answers trickled in.

An agent of Morano's had bought a German aeroplane in Lisbon. A German aviator was actually at the hotel there. Slingsby struck the table with his fist.

'What a fool I am!' he cried. 'Give me a newspaper.'

I handed him one of that morning's date. Slingsby turned it feverishly over, searching down the columns of the provincial news until he came to the heading 'Portugal'.

'Here it is!' he cried, and he read aloud. '"The great feature of the

Festival week this year will be, of course, the aviation race from Villa Real to Seville. Amongst those who have entered machines is the Count Morano y Goltz." '

He leaned back and lit a cigarette.

'We have got it! Morano's machine, driven by the German aviator, rises from the aerodrome at Villa Real in Portugal with the others, heads for Seville, drops behind, turns and makes a bee-line for the Rock, Peiffer having already arranged with Morano for signals to be made where bombs should be dropped. When is the race to be?'

I took the newspaper.

'Ten days from now.'

'Good!'

Once more the telegrams began to fly. A week later Slingsby told me the result.

'Owing to unforeseen difficulties, the Festival committee at Villa Real has reorganized its arrangements, and there will be no aviation race. Oh, they'll do what they like in neutral countries, will they? But Peiffer shan't know,' he added, with a grin. 'Peiffer shall eat of his own frightfulness.'

Mr Collingrey, MP

I have often said that there is something grossly immoral about the profession of journalism. These men who live on the woes of others, who batten on the miseries of the world, must of necessity be dead to all kindly impulse and to the gentler emotions. They must be sceptical of all that is good, and have immeasurable faith in the wickedness of human nature. They must have neither reverence for the great ones of the earth nor charity for the sins of the weak.

My experience of journalists and of English journalists particularly, had been with a Mister Haynes, who behaved with the greatest treachery toward me, insinuated himself into my office under false colours, for was he not an officer of the English Intelligence Department, and has he not, as I have reason to believe, the blood of two high-spirited German youths upon his gory hands?

In the autumn of 1916, I learnt that Berlin was sending to me a Swedish gentleman named Heigl, and I was ordered to follow his instructions and to give him all the assistance which lay in my power. I have a constitutional objection to the intrusion of outsiders and more especially to amateur intelligence officers who, in my experience, have never failed to bungle any task to which they set their hands, so I cannot say that I viewed with any enthusiasm the coming of Mr Heigl, fraught as it would be, and as I knew, with additional risks for myself and possibly the disorganization of the perfect system which I had with such labour established.

Mr Heigl proved to be a very pleasant gentleman, a merchant of Stockholm, a short man with an untidy grey beard, well dressed and having the appearance of prosperity. In fact, as I learnt, he was a gentleman of considerable wealth, and though not well born, even in a Swedish sense, he was a *persona grata* with the leaders of the Conservative Party in Sweden and was frequently consulted by his Government on all matters affecting trade.

Amongst other things he was the proprietor of a weekly newspaper published in Stockholm. All this he told me within the first hour of our meeting; in fact, on the way up from an East Coast port to whither I had gone to meet him.

'You must understand, sir,' he said with great affability, which I need hardly tell you I returned, since he was the trusted agent of my beloved country and was, moreover, a man who might be able to put a few things in my way. One never knows when one requires the help of a man of this description or, as we say in Germany, 'Don't refuse the carter the tyre, one day the wheel may be yours.'

To resume the record of our conversation.

'You understand, sir,' he said, 'that I am a citizen of a neutral state and, therefore, I can take no active part in any propaganda designed to assist Germany.'

'That is understood, excellent sir,' I replied, 'and, believe me, I will not embarrass you to the smallest extent by requesting your assistance.'

He inclined his head graciously.

'There are certain people in Berlin whom I have recently had the pleasure of meeting. They are anxious that in this great world war the German view shall not be entirely lost sight of.'

It was my turn to nod.

'The English press is not exactly friendly or inclined even to print the German point of view, save to ridicule it.'

'The English, or British press, my dear sir,' I said warmly, 'is a Government press. Every evening, as is well known, the Government send every newspaper the outlines of the leading article which they will write. So cunningly contrived are those leaders, that in some of them they criticize the Government, and nobody outside the office would realize that all those articles are written by a special band of writers who work day and night in Downing Street.'

He seemed interested at this news which was well known to me and to many of my friends.

'But I interrupted you,' I said, 'pray forgive me.'

'In Berlin,' Mr Heigl went on, 'it is thought that an excellent opportunity exists either for founding or for purchasing a newspaper. It is understood that the *Post-Herald* is for sale.'

'That is so,' I said nodding. I did not know it before, but I took his word for it. We Germans can never be caught napping.

'The price that is asked,' Mr Heigl went on, consulting a little notebook which he drew from his waistcoat pocket, 'is £100,000, that is to say, two million marks. It is a paper which has had a great deal of influence in the past but seems to have fallen away gradually until it has got into very low water indeed. We believe that if we found the right man and spent a little money the paper could be revived to its former prestige.'

'Of that I am convinced,' I said, 'and it is a view which I have often thought of advancing to Berlin. Believe me, Mr Heigl, I have not neglected the press. There is scarcely a newspaper man in Fleet Street whom I do not know. I can tell you their circulations, the family history of their editors, the names and records of their principal correspondents.'

He interrupted me with a little gesture.

'I am delighted to hear this,' he said, 'I had no idea that you had taken the matter up. In fact, they thought that you were unacquainted with the personnel of the newspapers.'

I smiled a little bitterly.

'Wilhelmstrasse is sometimes a little unjust,' I said, quietly and sadly.

'Now, what would you say the circulation of the *Post-Herald* was?' asked Mr Heigl.

It was an unfortunate and tactless question to ask at the moment, but I replied with readiness.

'I cannot tell you until I have consulted my books. There are so many newspapers in London and one cannot possibly keep their circulations in one's head.'

I could see he was a little impressed, and later he asked:

'Can you suggest a man to act as go-between? Neither you nor I can buy the paper, but if we could only get hold of a good substantial fellow, a bit of a crank preferably, we could easily hide ourselves behind a bank and a lawyer and complete the sale.'

I knitted my brows and compressed my lips, 'For the moment I cannot,' I said. 'This is much too important a matter to be settled off-hand.'

To tell the truth, gentle reader, since my making the acquaintance of Mister Haynes, I had steered clear of journalists, and the only one I knew well enough to speak to was an old gentleman in a top hat who used to stand at the corner of Salisbury Square, and borrow half-crowns from me. Even his name I did not know, but I felt with my usual good fortune and perseverance, I should not be long in finding the right kind of man.

It would not be true to say that I did not understand the British press, or that I had not given it a great deal of thought. In my humble way I have been a contributor to English journalism, and my letters, signed 'True Patriot', 'Mother of Six', and other *noms de guerre*, have appeared in newspapers of almost every colour.

The British newspaper is remarkable for its stupidity and ignorance. I do not think that even the best friends of English journalism will dispute this fact.

It is a fact which I cannot too clearly emphasize, that there is not a single London newspaper edited by a professor. Only two of the London editors have an educational degree, and none has been in the army or the navy.

I then proceeded like a good general, to examine the ground. The *Post-Herald* is an old-fashioned Whig newspaper which had fallen on evil times, due to the fact that it was owned by a family all of whom took something out of its coffers, and none of whom put any brains into its management. With true German thoroughness, I discovered that it was deeply in debt to paper manufacturers, and to a syndicate of printing-machine makers.

This poverty-stricken rag, without two penny pieces to rub against one another, had the temerity, the audacity, to attack 'unscrupulous Germany'. I confess when I opened the sheet and read the scathing and vulgar abuse of our truly great kulturland, I was filled with righteous anger. But business is business. The Fatherland has need of thee, *Post-Herald*. Thy columns shall yet scintillate with sarcasm, not directed toward the genius of Germany, but toward the vile and frivolous men who have dared the wrath of Michael! Thy readers from these dull pages shall imbibe the principles which have made Prussia feared, aye, and hated the world over. Deutschland shall be vindicated in triumphant and very clever articles written by professors of learning and translated by English hack writers.

My spirits rose and my heart glowed within me at the thought that I, Heine, should pull the strings and direct in the heart of this great and sinister city a policy which should still further enhance my beloved land.

Deutschland über alles. Also, I thought there might be some commission on the purchase, for these things can be arranged. The first thing to do was to find a go-between, a man who could be implicitly trusted, and I began to ransack my mind for a likely person. To put one of the known English pacifists in control would be to give the show away, and to upset the apple-cart, to employ two English idioms.

Collingrey was the man! It came to me in a flash of inspiration. He was a member of Parliament and hard up, having an extravagant wife and other obligations which my good German modesty prevents my describing. He had been a failure as a barrister, and a failure as a member of Parliament. He might have held a position in the Government but for certain disclosures which came to light in the matrimonial suit in which he became involved.

During the war most of his questions and speeches in Parliament had been directed against Italy—our perfidious ally! There never was a man who so hated the Italian Government as he, and with good reason, for Mr Collingrey, a year before the war started, had invested all his fortune in the purchase of two pictures by that master, Leonardo di Vinci. The Italian Government had prohibited the export of the pictures and when on top of this a lawsuit was started, which involved the ownership of these works of art, Collingrey got neither the pictures he had bought nor the money he had spent.

He had stood to make a fortune, having resold these gems to the American millionaire, Tilzer. The lawsuit dragged on, and Collingrey had declared that the Italian Government was putting every obstacle in the way of a settlement, and as the English Government refused to give him any assistance, he was doubly incensed.

He was, therefore, a bitter man, and never lost an opportunity of embarrassing the Government. His articles appeared regularly in those journals which we had subsidized—very few, alas!—in this country. He had a reputation for honesty, was a brilliant writer and a clever debater.

The thing was to secure his co-operation, and to convey to him, with as much delicacy as possible, the policy which he would be called upon to support.

I have before me the draft of instructions which I received from Berlin at a subsequent date, and I cannot do better than print these:

1. The editor will adopt a conciliatory attitude toward Germany and German War Aims. It is not necessary that the German point of view should be urged, since this would defeat the object aimed at. The Germans may even be attacked, though no uncomplimentary reference to the Great General Staff, to the Kaiser, or to any member of the German royal family must be permitted.

2. It is permissible to condemn air-raids or U-boat sinkings in a decorous and serious manner, but at the same time a note should be appended to the effect that whilst these things are unfortunate, the English have largely themselves to blame for failing at the beginning of the war to observe the distinction between open and defended towns, and also for not observing the Treaty of London.

3. At all times the editor must urge the necessity for arriving at an understanding with Germany. The cost of the war, the loss of life, must be deplored, and the possibility of avoiding further losses by meeting the Germans at a peace council must be insisted upon.

4. References to the taxation which will follow the war, and how hardly it will fall upon the working classes as well as upon the moneyed classes must be made frequently.

5. Whenever possible it should be hinted that the British have no reason for continuing the war, and that they are being bled white to support the insensate ambitions of France. French military actions should, in consequence, be criticized as far as possible.

6. Stories dealing with the humanity of the German soldier, which will be supplied from time to time, should be given prominence, and references to German strikes may be made the most of, especially at moments of industrial unrest in England.

These were only a few of the instructions. I cannot help thinking that Wilhelmstrasse made a great mistake in its moderation. If it had been left to me I would have instructed the editor to lose no opportunity of attacking every other newspaper which spoke slightingly of our great country —but then I am a patriot!

I had no difficulty in getting an introduction to Collingrey, and he invited me to dine at the British House of Commons. In a few words over a post-prandial cigar I explained the object of my visit. The good friend whose letter of introduction had procured the interview had smoothed my path by representing me to be an agent of a South American rancher (name unknown) who desired to break into London society, and in tones of gentle but amused tolerance I hinted at my client's vanity.

It was a difficult interview, because Mr Collingrey paid very little attention to what I said, but launched forth into a diatribe against the Italian Government. He was a monomaniac on the subject. He thumped the table so that all the other members in the dining-room looked round. He pounded his hand with his fist. He waved his finger in my face. He sat back, he sat forward, and all the time he spoke of the Italian Government and its iniquities. So much the better, my friend, thought I. I give you my word you shall have your fling at false Italia.

It gave me an opening to the exposition of the policy which the newspaper would support, particulars of which reached me providentially on the morning of my meeting the gentleman. Very gently and delicately I laid down the lines on which the paper would be conducted, and he agreed. Of course I did not give him all the details, for I did not desire to scare him.

'If you asked me to run a pro-Government paper I should have refused it,' he said violently, 'this is a Government of nincompoops, a Government of charlatans, a Government of Enemies of the People. I regard the war as a crowning iniquity and its continuance inexcusable but for the fact that our Ministers have sold themselves body and soul, to Italy. Take my own case, for instance. . . .'

And so I had it all over again, the story of his purchase of the di Vinci pictures from the Montimi collection, the story of the embargo, the story of the lawsuit. What bores these English members of Parliament are, how childish; what a contrast to the staid members of our own Reichstag with their serious politics and their love of the Fatherland! Mr Collingrey readily undertook to act as go-between. He entered into the spirit of the matter with great enthusiasm, and when I met him two or three days later he produced two manuscripts dealing with the Italian Government, which he read to me in the lobby of the House of Commons.

When the purchase was completed and the *Post-Herald* had passed into the possession of a certain syndicate, which it is not advisable to name, he had a manuscript on Italy in every pocket. Having done my part of the work and taken the small commission which was my right, and having seen Mr Heigl safely on his journey back to Stockholm, I had little time to bother about the newspaper, the more so since Berlin in its folly had decided that I was not to interfere in its management.

I bowed respectfully to the high authorities and to the well-born gentlemen who directed Germania's policy, but I submit in all humility that had Heine been at the helm much that subsequently happened might have been avoided.

Mr Collingrey carried out his instructions faithfully, and when they were explained with more elaborate detail he accepted his orders (to my surprise) without demur or question. His vivid leading articles on the Italian Government attracted a great deal of attention and led to a strict application of the censorship, but this only gave him a new interest in life, namely, in so couching his words that he could do the maximum amount of damage to his enemies without incurring censure. He was gentle with Germany, restrained in his reference to the U-boats, never spoke of the Kaiser except as the Emperor William, and his references to labour were invariably quoted in the extreme organs of the masses. He was indeed a most satisfactory person, and I have in my possession a letter addressed to me by the noble-born Count von Mazberg, the head of our propaganda department, congratulating me upon my most excellent choice. This I can show to any interested person who doubts my word, and especially to those evil-minded un-German journalists who have so often attacked me and my work.

I was out of London a great deal, being concerned in consultation with certain labouring men who desired to bring the war to an end by an understanding with Germany. These English patriots were organizing a strike, and, naturally, I rendered them all the assistance that lay in my power.

This meant that I had to travel with a great deal of money and could not afford to allow my attention to be distracted from the business at hand.

I arrived in London one evening and on reaching my flat discovered an urgent telegram from Mr Collingrey asking me to dine with him at the Carltonia Hotel, as he had news of the greatest importance. I immediately changed into my evening dress and drove down to the hotel where the editor was waiting impatiently. He was happier than I have ever seen him. His thin, cadaverous face was wreathed in smiles, as he heartily shook my hand, brushing aside the compliments on his conduct of the paper which I had prepared.

'Come and have dinner, my boy,' he said. 'I have got great news.'

'I am delighted to learn this,' I replied. 'Have you got one in the eye for Italy, if you will pardon the expression?'

'Oh, much better.'

Grasping my arm he led me into the dining-room.

'After all,' he said as we sat down at the table, 'perhaps I have been rather unkind about Italy—my articles have borne fruit.'

'What do you mean?' I asked in surprise.

He chuckled as he unfolded his serviette.

'They have released my pictures, my dear fellow,' he said, 'you have no idea of the weight there is off my mind. It means a tremendous lot to me—my fortune and my wife's was invested in those infernal daubs. Look here,' he took a piece of paper from his pocket and passed it across to me.

It was a cablegram which had been handed in at New York that morning:

Agree to your price, hundred and fifty thousand dollars for di Vinci pictures. Ship them by first mail-boat in charge of reliable man.—Tilzer.

'We will have a bottle of champagne on this.'

'But what induced the Government to take this step?'

'The lawsuit is ended,' said Mr Collingrey, 'and ended in my favour. I tell you it has taken ten years off my age.'

He babbled on like a boy, but presently he grew calmer and we discussed the policy of the paper, and I was glad to see that he still retained those honest convictions about Germania which had ever distinguished his writings.

It was just about this time that America was trembling on the verge of war, when the unscrupulous Wilson was making his preparations to commit the great crime against civilization of plunging his country into the horrors of strife. For me it was a time of the greatest stress and anxiety.

Cablegrams from certain neutral countries reached me every hour. Secret and confidential wireless messages from the supreme political chiefs reached me through the usual channels.

The excuse the Americans made was the initiation by our Admiralty of an unrestricted U-boat campaign against the munition ships of the Allies and it was still hoped by the superlatively clever men who guide the helm of the German state that war might be avoided.

On a night I shall never forget I received a message from Amsterdam which I decoded. It ran:

VERY URGENT.—To Chief S.S. Agents, London, Madrid, Paris, New York, Stockholm, Amsterdam.

Editors and directors of friendly and subsidized papers must be instructed to deal sympathetically with U-boat campaign. Point out iniquity blockade which is starving German women and children, and suggest a compromise between Germany and her enemies. Endeavour counteract enemy propaganda which will be unusually virulent. Prepare articles and comments in this vein. Acknowledge to chief of staff.

I wrote a brief note embodying these instructions to Mr Collingrey, telling him that the South American, the mythical proprietor of the *Post-Herald* was a big shipowner, and desired to save the shipping of the Allies. This I dispatched by special messenger and immediately dismissed the matter from my thoughts for, as I say, I had not only the organization of a great strike but also I had to condense the very heavy reports which were coming through from our agents in the various shipping centres.

I worked till three o'clock in the morning and then snatched a few hours' sleep. At seven I was at my task again with all the newspapers ready for perusal. Naturally I turned to the *Post-Herald* first. Here I knew I had material for a good report and with my code book open in front of me, I was preparing to translate the leading article into language which would pass the censor for transmission to Holland.

I opened the paper. There was the leading article, but to my amazement it was headed:

GERMAN MURDERERS AT THEIR FOUL WORK.

I gasped. From the very first word to the very last the article was the bitterest, the most vehement, the most unscrupulous attack upon Germany that had ever appeared. I grew red and white as I read it. It called the Germans assassins of the sea, barbarians, Huns, Boches, pirates, blackguards, thieves—I shudder as I recall the language which was used by Mr Collingrey.

I was in a maze, bewildered. I read on like a man in a bad dream, conscious of the awful avalanche of fury which would sweep down upon me when Berlin read this dreadful and disloyal article.

It was not till nearly the end of the leader that I began to understand Mr Collingrey's attitude. The final paragraph ran:

If any doubt existed that this nation of Hun marauders is lacking in the elements of kultur, that doubt is removed by the wanton sinking of the Italian steamship *San Salvadoro*. It was an open secret that that ill-fated vessel was carrying to England two great masterpieces of Italian art, two priceless examples of Leonardo's genius. Did that fact stay the barbarian's hand? Nay! Rather it lent zest to the lustful and bestial representative of a savage and unkultured people.

Those two masterpieces, unfortunately uninsured by their owner, lie at the bottom of the Bay of Biscay.

Let the British Government make instant reprisals. Intern the aliens in our midst! Imprison and shoot secret agents whose evil activity is seducing the allegiance of our people, whose hands are discernible even in the press itself.

I laid down the paper and wiped the perspiration from my brow. I took up a pen to indite the traitor's dismissal, but on second thoughts I put it down again.

After all, it was not my idea. Let Berlin do its own dirty work.

The Lit Chamber

He was hoisted on his horse by an ostler and two local sots from the tap-room, his valise was strapped none too securely before him, and with a farewell, which was meant to be gracious but was only foolish, he tittuped into the rain. He was as drunk as an owl, though he did not know it. All afternoon he had been mixing strong Cumberland ale with the brandy he had got from the Solway free-traders, and by five o'clock had reached that state when he saw the world all gilt and rosy and himself as an applauded actor on a splendid stage. He had talked grandly to his fellow topers, and opened to their rustic wits a glimpse of the great world. They had bowed to a master, even those slow Cumbrians who admired little but fat cattle and blood horses. He had made a sensation, had seen wonder and respect in dull eyes, and tasted for a moment that esteem which he had singularly failed to find elsewhere.

But he had been prudent. The Mr Gilbert Craster who had been travelling on secret business in Nithsdale and the Ayrshire moorlands had not been revealed in the change-house of Newbigging. There he had passed by the name, long since disused, of Gabriel Lovel, which happened to be his true one. It was a needful precaution, for the times were crooked. Even in a Border hamlet the name of Craster might be known, and since for the present it had a Whig complexion, it was well to go warily in a place where feeling ran high and at an hour when the Jacobites were on the march. But that other name of Lovel was buried deep in the forgotten scandal of London by-streets.

The gentleman late re-christened Lovel had for the moment no grudge against life. He was in the pay of a great man, no less than the lord Duke of Marlborough, and he considered that he was earning his wages. A soldier of fortune, he accepted the hire of the best paymaster; only he sold not a sword, but wits. A pedant might have called it honour, but Mr Lovel was no pedant. He had served a dozen chiefs on different sides.

For Bolingbroke he had scoured France and twice imperilled his life in Highland bogs. For Somers he had travelled to Spain, and for Wharton had passed unquiet months on the Welsh marches. After his fashion he was an honest servant and reported the truth so far as his ingenuity could discern it. But, once quit of a great man's service, he sold his knowledge readily to an opponent, and had been like to be out of employment, since unless his masters gave him an engagement for life he was certain some day to carry the goods they had paid for to their rivals. But Marlborough had seen his uses, for the great Duke sat loose to parties and earnestly desired to know the facts. So for Marlborough he went into the conclaves of both Whig and Jacobite, making his complexion suit his company.

He was new come from the Scottish south-west, for the Duke was eager to know if the malcontent moorland Whigs were about to fling their blue bonnets for King James. A mission of such discomfort Mr Lovel had never known, not even when he was a go-between for Ormonde in the Irish bogs. He had posed as an emissary from the Dutch brethren, son of an exiled Brownist, and for the first time in his life had found his regicide great-grandfather useful. The jargon of the godly fell smoothly from his tongue, and with its aid and that of certain secret letters he had found his way to the heart of the sectaries. He had sat through weary sermons in Cameronian sheilings, and been present at the childish parades of the Hebronite remnant. There was nothing to be feared in that quarter, for to them all in authority were idolaters and George no worse than James. In those moorland sojournings, too, he had got light on other matters, for he had the numbers of Kenmure's levies in his head, had visited my lord Stair at his grim Galloway castle, and had had a long midnight colloquy with Roxburghe on Tweedside. He had a pretty tale for his master, once he could get to him. But with Northumberland up and the Highlanders at Jedburgh and Kenmure coming from the west, it had been a ticklish business to cross the Border. Yet by cunning and a good horse it had been accomplished, and he found himself in Cumberland with the road open southward to the safe Lowther country. Wherefore Mr Lovel had relaxed and taken his ease in an inn.

He would not have admitted that he was drunk, but he presently confessed that he was not clear about his road. He had meant to lie at Brampton, and had been advised at the tavern of a short cut, a moorland bridle-path. Who had told him of it? The landlord, he thought, or the merry fellow in brown who had stood brandy to the company? Anyhow, it was to save him five miles, and that was something in this accursed weather. The path was clear—he could see it squelching below him, pale in the last wet daylight—but where the devil did it lead? Into the heart of a moss, it seemed, and yet Brampton lay out of the moors in the tilled valley.

At first the fumes in his head raised him above the uncertainty of his road and the eternal downpour. His mind was far away in a select world of his own imagining. He saw himself in a privy chamber, to which he had been conducted by reverent lackeys, the door closed, the lamp lit, and the Duke's masterful eyes bright with expectation. He saw the fine thin lips, like a woman's, primmed in satisfaction. He heard words of compliment—'none so swift and certain as you'—'in truth, a master-hand'—'I know not where to look for your life.' Delicious speeches seemed to soothe his ear. And gold, too, bags of it, the tale of which would never appear in any accompt-book. Nay, his fancy soared higher. He saw himself presented to Ministers as one of the country's saviours, and kissing the hand of Majesty. What Majesty and what Ministers he knew not, and did not greatly care—that was not his business. The rotundity of the Hanoverian and the lean darkness of the Stuart were one to him. Both could reward an adroit servant. . . . His vanity, terribly starved and cribbed in his normal existence, now blossomed like a flower. His muddled head was fairly ravished with delectable pictures. He seemed to be set at a great height above mundane troubles, and to look down on men like a benignant God. His soul glowed with a happy warmth.

But somewhere he was devilish cold. His wretched body was beginning to cry out with discomfort. A loop of his hat was broken and the loose flap was a conduit for the rain down his back. His old riding-coat was like a dish-clout, and he felt icy about the middle. Separate streams of water entered the tops of his riding-boots—they were a borrowed pair and too big for him—and his feet were in puddles. It was only by degrees that he realized this misery. Then in the boggy track his horse began to stumble. The fourth or fifth peck woke irritation, and he jerked savagely at the bridle, and struck the beast's dripping flanks with his whip. The result was a jib and a flounder, and the shock squeezed out the water from his garments as from a sponge. Mr Lovel descended from the heights of fancy to prosaic fact, and cursed.

The dregs of strong drink were still in him, and so soon as exhilaration ebbed they gave edge to his natural fears. He perceived that it had grown very dark and lonely. The rain, falling sheer, seemed to shut him into a queer wintry world. All around the land echoed with the steady drum of it, and the rumour of swollen runnels. A wild bird wailed out of the mist and startled Mr Lovel like a ghost. He heard the sound of men talking and drew rein; it was only a larger burn foaming by the wayside. The sky was black above him, yet a faint grey light seemed to linger, for water glimmered and he passed what seemed to be the edge of a loch. . . . At another time the London-bred citizen would have been only peevish, for Heaven knew he had faced ill weather before in ill places. But the fiery stuff he had swallowed had woke a feverish fancy. Exaltation suddenly changed to foreboding.

He halted and listened. Nothing but the noise of the weather, and the night dark around him like a shell. For a moment he fancied he caught the sound of horses, but it was not repeated. Where did this accursed track mean to lead him? Long ago he should have been in the valley and nearing Brampton. He was as wet as if he had wallowed in a pool, cold, and very weary. A sudden disgust at his condition drove away his fears and he swore lustily at fortune. He longed for the warmth and the smells of his favourite haunts—Gilpin's with oysters frizzling in a dozen pans, and noble odours stealing from the tap-room, the 'Green Man' with its tripe-suppers, Wanless's Coffee House, noted for its cuts of beef and its white puddings. He would give much to be in a chair by one of those hearths and in the thick of that blowsy fragrance. Now his nostrils were filled with rain and bog water and a sodden world. It smelt sour, like stale beer in a mouldy cellar. And cold! He crushed down his hat on his head and precipitated a new deluge.

A bird skirled again in his ear, and his fright returned. He felt small and alone in a vast inhospitable universe. And mingled with it all was self-pity, for drink had made him maudlin. He wanted so little—only a modest comfort, a little ease. He had forgotten that half an hour before he had been figuring in princes' cabinets. He would give up this business and be quit of danger and the high road. The Duke must give him a reasonable reward, and with it he and his child might dwell happily in some country place. He remembered a cottage at Guildford all hung with roses. . . . But the Duke was reputed a miserly patron, and at the thought Mr Lovel's eyes overflowed. There was that damned bird again, wailing like a lost soul. The eeriness of it struck a chill to his heart, so that if he had been able to think of any refuge he would have set spurs to his horse and galloped for it in blind terror. He was in the mood in which men compose poetry, for he felt himself a midget in the grip of immensities. He knew no poetry, save a few tavern songs; but in his youth he had had the Scriptures drubbed into him. He remembered ill-omened texts—one especially about wandering through dry places seeking rest. Would to Heaven he were in a dry place now! . . .

The horse sprang aside and nearly threw him. It had blundered against the stone pillar of a gateway.

It was now clear even to Mr Lovel's confused wits that he was lost. This might be the road to Tophet, but it was no road to Brampton. He felt with numbed hands the face of the gateposts. Here was an entrance to some dwelling, and it stood open. The path led through it, and if he left the path he would without doubt perish in a bog-hole. In his desolation he longed for a human face. He might find a good fellow who would house him; at the worst he would get direction about the road. So he passed the gateway and entered an avenue.

It ran between trees which took the force of the downpour, so that it seemed a very sanctuary after the open moor. His spirits lightened. The infernal birds had stopped crying, but again he heard the thud of hooves. That was right, and proved the place was tenanted. Presently he turned a corner and faced a light which shone through the wet, rayed like a heraldic star.

The sight gave him confidence, for it brought him back to a familiar world. He rode straight to it, crossing a patch of rough turf, where a fallen log all but brought him down. As he neared it the light grew till he saw its cause. He stood before the main door of a house and it was wide open. A great lantern, hung from a beam just inside, showed a doorway of some size and magnificence. And below it stood a servant, an old man, who at the sight of the stranger advanced to hold his stirrup.

'Welcome, my lord,' said the man. 'All is ready for you.'

The last hour had partially sobered the traveller, but, having now come safe to port, his drunkenness revived. He saw nothing odd in the open door or the servant's greeting. As he scrambled to the ground he was back in his first exhilaration. 'My lord!' Well, why not? This was an honest man who knew quality when he met it.

Humming a tune and making a chain of little pools on the stone flags of the hall, Mr Lovel followed his guide, who bore his shabby valise, another servant having led away the horse. The hall was dim with flickering shadows cast by the lamp in the doorway, and smelt raw and cold as if the house had been little dwelt in. Beyond it was a stone passage where a second lamp burned and lit up a forest of monstrous deer horns on the wall. The butler flung open a door.

'I trust your lordship will approve the preparations,' he said. 'Supper awaits you, and when you have done I will show you your chamber. There are dry shoes by the hearth.' He took from the traveller his sopping overcoat and drew from his legs the pulpy riding-boots. With a bow which might have graced a court he closed the door, leaving Mr Lovel alone to his entertainment.

It was a small square room panelled to the ceiling in dark oak, and lit by a curious magnificence of candles. They burned in sconces on the walls and in tall candlesticks on the table, while a log fire on the great stone hearth so added to the glow that the place was as bright as day. The windows were heavily shuttered and curtained, and in the far corner was a second door. On the polished table food had been laid—a noble ham, two virgin pies, a dish of fruits, and a group of shining decanters. To one coming out of the wild night it was a transformation like a dream, but Mr Lovel, half drunk, accepted it as no more than his due. His feather brain had been fired by the butler's 'my lord', and he did not puzzle his head with questions. From a slim bottle he filled himself a glass of brandy, but on second thoughts set it down untasted. He would sample the wine first, and top off with the spirit. Meantime he would get warm.

He stripped off his coat, which was dampish, and revealed a dirty shirt and the dilapidated tops of his small clothes. His stockings were torn and soaking, so he took them off, and stuck his naked feet into the furred slippers which stood waiting by the hearth. Then he sat himself in a great brocaded armchair and luxuriously stretched his legs to the blaze.

But his head was too much afire to sit still. The comfort soaked into his being through every nerve and excited rather than soothed him. He did not want to sleep now, though a little before he had been crushed by weariness. . . . There was a mirror beside the fireplace, the glass painted at the edge with slender flowers and cupids in the Caroline fashion. He saw his reflection and it pleased him. The long face with the pointed chin, the deep-set dark eyes, the skin brown with weather—he seemed to detect a resemblance to Wharton. Or was it Beaufort? Anyhow, now that the shabby coat was off, he might well be a great man in undress. 'My lord!' Why not? His father had always told him he came of an old high family. Kings, he had said—of France, or somewhere. . . . A gold ring he wore on his left hand slipped from his finger and jingled on the hearth-stone. It was too big for him, and when his fingers grew small with cold or wet it was apt to fall off. He picked it up and laid it beside the decanters on the table. That had been his father's ring, and he congratulated himself that in all his necessities he had never parted from it. It was said to have come down from ancient kings.

He turned to the table and cut himself a slice of ham. But he found he had no appetite. He filled himself a bumper of claret. It was a ripe

velvety liquor and cooled his hot mouth. That was the drink for gentlemen. Brandy in good time, but for the present this soft wine which was
in keeping with the warmth and light and sheen of silver. . . . His excitement was dying now into complacence. He felt himself in the environ-
ment for which Providence had fitted him. His whole being expanded in
the glow of it. He understood how able he was, how truly virtuous—a
master of intrigue, but one whose eye was always fixed on the star of
honour. And then his thoughts wandered to his son in the mean London
lodgings. The boy should have his chance and walk some day in silks and
laces. Curse his aliases! He should be Lovel, and carry his head as high
as any Villiers or Talbot.

The reflection sent his hand to an inner pocket of the coat now dry-
ing by the hearth. He took from it a thin packet of papers wrapped in
oil-cloth. These were the fruits of his journey, together with certain news
too secret to commit to writing which he carried in his head. He ran his
eye over them, approved them, and laid them before him on the table.
They started a train of thought which brought him to the question of his
present quarters. . . . A shadow of doubt flickered over his mind. Whose
house was this and why this entertainment? He had been expected, or
someone like him. An old campaigner took what gifts the gods sent, but
there might be questions to follow. There was a coat of arms on the plate,
but so dim that he could not read it. The one picture in the room showed
an old man in a conventional suit of armour. He did not recognize the
face or remember any like it. . . . He filled himself another bumper of
claret, and followed it with a little brandy. This latter was noble stuff,
by which he would abide. His sense of ease and security returned. He
pushed the papers farther over, sweeping the ring with them, and set his
elbows on the table, a gentleman warm, dry, and content, but much
befogged in the brain.

He raised his eyes to see the far door open and three men enter. The
sight brought him to his feet with a start, and his chair clattered on
the oak boards. He made an attempt at a bow, backing steadily towards
the fireplace and his old coat.

The faces of the newcomers exhibited the most lively surprise. All three
were young, and bore marks of travel, for though they had doffed their
riding coats, they were splashed to the knees with mud and their unpow-
dered hair lay damp on their shoulders. One was a very dark man who
might have been a Spaniard but for his blue eyes. The second was a mere
boy with a ruddy face and eyes full of dancing merriment. The third
was tall and red-haired, tanned of countenance and lean as a greyhound.

He wore trews of a tartan which Mr Lovel, trained in such matters, recognized as that of the house of Atholl.

Of the three he only recognized the leader, and the recognition sobered him. This was that Talbot, commonly known from his swarthiness as the Crow, who was Ormonde's most trusted lieutenant. He had once worked with him; he knew his fierce temper, his intractable honesty. His bemused wits turned desperately to concocting a conciliatory tale.

But he seemed to be unrecognized. The three stared at him in wild-eyed amazement.

'Who the devil are you, sir?' the Highlander stammered.

Mr Lovel this time brought off his bow. 'A storm-stayed traveller,' he said, his eyes fawning, 'who has stumbled on this princely hospitality. My name at your honour's service is Gabriel Lovel.'

There was a second of dead silence and then the boy laughed. It was merry laughter and broke in strangely on the tense air of the room.

'Lovel,' he cried, and there was an Irish burr in his speech. 'Lovel! And that fool Jobson mistook it for Lovat! I mistrusted the tale, for Simon is too discreet even in his cups to confess his name in a change-house. It seems we have been stalking the cailzie-cock and found a common thrush.'

The dark man Talbot did not smile. 'We had good reason to look for Lovat. Widrington had word from London that he was on his way to the north by the west marches. Had we found him we had found a prize, for he will play hell with Mar if he crosses the Highland line. What say you, Lord Charles?'

The Highlander nodded. 'I would give my sporran filled ten times with gold to have my hand on Simon. What devil's luck to be marching south with that old fox in our rear!'

The boy pulled up a chair to the table. 'Since we have missed the big game, let us follow the less. I'm for supper, if this gentleman will permit us to share a feast destined for another. Sit down, sir, and fill your glass. You are not to be blamed for not being a certain Scots lord. Lovel, I dare say, is an honester name than Lovat!'

But Talbot was regarding the traveller with hard eyes. 'You called him a thrush, Nick, but I have a notion he is more of a knavish jackdaw. I have seen this gentleman before. You were with Ormonde?'

'I had once the honour to serve his Grace,' said Lovel, still feverishly trying to devise a watertight tale.

'Ah, I remember now. You thought his star descending and carried your wares to the other side. And who is your new employer, Mr Lovel? His present Majesty?'

His glance caught the papers on the table and he swept them towards him.

'What have we here?' and his quick eye scanned the too legible hand-writing. Much was in cipher and contractions, but some names stood out damningly. In that month of October in that year 1715 'Ke' could only stand for 'Kenmure' and 'Nl' for 'Nithsdale'.

Mr Lovel made an attempt at dignity.

'These are my papers, sir,' he blustered. 'I know not by what author-ity you examine them.' But the protest failed because of the instability of his legs, on which his potations early and recent had suddenly a fatal effect. He was compelled to collapse heavily on the armchair by the hearth.

'I observe that the gentleman has lately been powdering his hair,' said the boy whom they called Nick.

Mr Lovel was wroth. He started upon the usual drunkard's protesta-tions, but was harshly cut short by Talbot.

'You ask me my warrant. 'Tis the commission of his Majesty King James in whose army I have the honour to hold a command.'

He read on, nodding now and then, pursing his mouth at a word, once copying something on to his own tablets. Suddenly he raised his head.

'When did his Grace dismiss you?' he asked.

Now Ormonde had been the Duke last spoken of, but Mr Lovel's pre-carious wits fell into the trap. He denied indignantly that he had fallen from his master's favour.

A grim smile played round Talbot's mouth.

'You have confessed,' he said. Then to the others: 'This fellow is one of Malbrouck's pack. He has been nosing in the Scotch westlands. Here are the numbers of Kenmure and Nithsdale to enable the great Duke to make up his halting mind. See, he has been with Roxburghe, too. . . . We have a spy before us, gentlemen, delivered to our hands by a happy incid-ent. Whig among the sectaries and with Stair and Roxburghe, and Jacobite among our poor honest folk, and wheedling the secrets out of both sides to sell to one who disposes of them at a profit in higher quarters. Faugh! I know the vermin. An honest Whig like John of Argyll I can respect and fight, but for such rats as this——What shall we do with it now that we have trapped it?'

'Let it go,' said the boy, Nick Wogan. 'The land crawls with them and we cannot go rat-hunting when we are aiming at a throne.' He picked up Lovel's ring and spun it on a fingertip. 'The gentleman has found more than news in the north. He has acquired a solid lump of gold.'

The implication roused Mr Lovel out of his embarrassment. 'I wear the ring by right. I had it from my father.' His voice was tearful with offended pride.

'The creature claims gentility,' said Talbot, as he examined the trinket. 'Lovel you call yourself. But Lovel bears barry nebuly or chevronels. This coat has three plain charges. Can you read them, Nick, for my eyes are weak! I am curious to know from whom he stole it.'

The boy scanned it closely. 'Three of something. I think they are fleur-de-lys, which would spell Montgomery. Or lions' heads, maybe, for Buchan?'

He passed it to Lord Charles, who held it to a candle's light. 'Nay, I think they are Cummin garbs. Some poor fellow dirked and spoiled.'

Mr Lovel was outraged and forgot his fears. He forgot, indeed, most things which he should have remembered. He longed only to establish his gentility in the eyes of those three proud gentlemen. The liquor was ebbing in him and with it had flown all his complacence. He felt small and mean and despised, and the talents he had been pluming himself on an hour before had now shrunk to windlestraws.

'I do assure you, sirs,' he faltered, 'the ring is mine own. I had it from my father, who had it from his. I am of an ancient house, though somewhat decayed.'

His eyes sought those of his inquisitors with the pathos of a dog. But he saw only hostile faces—Talbot's grave and grim, Lord Charles' contemptuous, the boy's smiling ironically.

'Decayed, indeed,' said the dark man, 'pitifully decayed. If you be gentle the more shame on you.'

Mr Lovel was almost whining. 'I swear I am honest. I do my master's commissions and report what I learn.'

'Aye, sir, but how do you learn it? By playing the impostor and winning your way into an unsuspecting confidence. To you friendship is a tool and honour a convenience. You cheat in every breath you draw. And what a man gives you in his innocence may bring him to the gallows. By God! I'd rather slit throats on a highway for a purse or two than cozen men to their death by such arts as yours.'

In other circumstances Mr Lovel might have put up a brazen defence, but now he seemed to have lost assurance. 'I do no ill,' was all he could stammer, 'for I have no bias. I am for no side in politics.'

'So much the worse. A man who spies for a cause in which he believes may redeem by that faith a dirty trade. But in cold blood you practise infamy.'

The night was growing wilder, and even in that sheltered room its echoes were felt. Wind shook the curtains and blew gusts of ashes from the fire. The place had become bleak and tragic and Mr Lovel felt the forlornness in his bones. Something had woke in him which shivered the fabric of a lifetime. The three faces, worn, anxious, yet of a noble hardihood, stirred in him a strange emotion. Hopes and dreams, long forgotten, flitted like spectres across his memory. He had something to say, something which demanded utterance, and his voice grew bold.

'What do you know of my straits?' he cried. 'Men of fortune like you! My race is old, but I never had the benefit of it. I was bred in a garret and have all my days been on nodding terms with starvation. . . . What should I know about your parties? What should I care for Whig and Tory or what king had his hinder-end on the throne? Tell me in God's name how should such as I learn loyalty except to the man who gives me gold to buy food and shelter? Heaven knows I have never betrayed a master while I served him.'

The shabby man with the lean face had secured an advantage. For a moment the passion in his voice dominated the room.

'Cursed if this does not sound like truth,' said the boy, and his eyes were almost friendly.

But Talbot did not relax.

'By your own confession you are outside the pale of gentility. I do not trouble to blame you, but I take leave to despise you. By your grace, sir, we will dispense with your company.'

The ice of his scorn did not chill the strange emotion which seemed to have entered the air. The scarecrow by the fire had won a kind of dignity.

'I am going,' he said. 'Will you have the goodness to send for my horse? . . . If you care to know, gentlemen, you have cut short a promising career. . . . To much of what you say I submit. You have spoken truth— not all the truth, but sufficient to unman me. I am a rogue by your reckoning, for I think only of my wages. Pray tell me what moves you to ride out on what at the best is a desperate venture?'

There was nothing but sincerity in the voice, and Talbot answered.

'I fight for the King ordained by God and for a land which cannot flourish under the usurper. My loyalty to throne, Church, and fatherland constrains me.'

Lovel's eye passed to Lord Charles. The Highlander whistled very softly a bar or two of a wild melody with longing and a poignant sorrow in it.

'That,' he said. 'I fight for the old ways and the old days that are passing.'

Nick Wogan smiled. 'And I for neither—wholly. I have a little of Talbot in me and more of Charles. But I strike my blow for romance—the little against the big, the noble few against the base many. I am for youth against all dull huckstering things.'

Mr Lovel bowed. 'I am answered. I congratulate you, gentlemen, on your good fortune. It is my grief that I do not share it. I have not Mr Talbot's politics, nor am I a great Scotch lord, nor have I the felicity to be young. . . . I would beg you not to judge me harshly.'

By this time he had struggled into his coat and boots. He stepped to the table and picked up the papers.

'By your leave,' he said, and flung them into the fire.

'You were welcome to them,' said Talbot. 'Long ere they got to Marlborough they would be useless.'

'That is scarcely the point,' said Lovel. 'I am somewhat dissatisfied with my calling and contemplate a change.'

'You may sleep here if you wish,' said Lord Charles.

'I thank you, but I am no fit company for you. I am better on the road.'

Talbot took a guinea from his purse. 'Here's to help your journey,' he was saying, when Nick Wogan, flushing darkly, intervened. 'Damn you, James, don't be a boor,' he said.

The boy picked up the ring and offered it to Mr Lovel as he passed through the door. He also gave him his hand.

The traveller spurred his horse into the driving rain, but he was oblivious of the weather. When he came to Brampton he discovered to his surprise that he had been sobbing. Except in liquor, he had not wept since he was a child.

The Reckoning with Otto Schreed

Mr Joseph P. Cray followed the usual routine observed by members of the 'Americans in London' Society on the occasion of their weekly lunches. He left his coat and hat in the cloakroom, and deposited the ticket which he received in exchange in his waistcoat pocket. Afterwards he slipped into the ante-room, where a little crowd of men were thronging around a narrow counter, exchanging hearty greetings, and indulging in various forms of pre-luncheon nourishment. Mr Cray, who had a mesmeric way of getting served over the shoulders of waiting throngs, disposed of a small cocktail in a matter of seconds, made his way to the reception-room, where the guest of the day stood by the side of his host, exchanging platitudes and handshakes with the little streams of arrivals, and a few minutes later wandered into the luncheon-room, where he discovered the round table for four at which he was placed, exchanged friendly greetings with the two men who were already in their seats, recognized the fact with a little sigh that they were not kindred spirits, and glanced with curiosity at the vacant place on his right hand, no claimant to which had as yet arrived.

It was a crowded gathering, and it takes some time for six hundred men to take their places and be seated. Mr Cray studied the menu with mild approval, glanced through the wine list, and decided to postpone for the moment his decision as to liquid refreshment, and finally, yielding to an impulse of not unnatural curiosity, he raised the card which reposed upon the tablecloth opposite the vacant chair on his right, and read it:

Mr Otto M. Schreed.

The four walls of the banqueting-room faded away. The pleasant hum of voices, the clatter of crockery and the popping of corks, fell upon deaf ears. Mr Cray's blue eyes were set in a steady stare. Gone his morning-coat, his irreproachable linen and carefully tied tie, his patent boots and well-creased trousers. He was back in the tight, ill-fitting khaki of months ago, a strange, sober figure, in the midst of the bustle of life, yet living under the shadow of death. He stood at the door of the canteen and he saw them marching by, a long, snake-like procession, some singing, some shouting cheery greetings, some pale and limping. Back to the opening in the hill he could trace them, the hill which had once been a forest and now seemed as though a cataclysm had smitten it, a nightmare of bare stumps, of shell and crater holes. The whole horizon seemed streaked with little puffs of smoke. The sound of the guns was incessant. There were times when even the ground beneath his feet shrunk. The boys were on their way to the mess tents after a stiff twelve hours. Mr Cray stepped back into the canteen, tasted the coffee in the great urn, ran through the stock of extra provisions, looked carefully round to see that all was ready for the hordes of his customers who would presently throng the place. . . . They came much sooner than they should have done, a little sullen, many of them cursing, pushed and struggled for a place at the counter, swept him clear of the whole of his stock of extra provisions. He could hear their voices.

'More of that filthy tack!'

'Say, there's some of those chaps at Washington deserve to swing!'

'What is it today, boys?' Mr Cray asked.

There was a string of lurid adjectives. Mr Cray looked as concerned as he felt.

'More of that stinking beef, eh?' he asked sympathetically.

He was met with a chorus of groans. A score or more had left the counter already, ill before they could swallow their coffee. He heard the curses of further hordes struggling to get in. Then the scene faded away. He walked down the great impromptu annexe to the hospital and spoke to one of the doctors. The doctor's adjectives made the words of his patients sound like the babbling of children.

'More cases of that bad beef,' was the plain English of what he said. 'We are just in the one corner of the line, too, where we can't rely on stores for a few days. Curse the man whoever made the stuff, and the Government inspector who passed it.'

There was a little movement by Mr Cray's side. He glanced up. A tall, well-built man of early middle-age was taking his seat. The two men exchanged greetings.

'Mr Otto Schreed?' Mr Cray observed.

The man winced a little but acknowledged his identity.

'And your name?' he asked.

'Mr Joseph P. Cray,' Mr Cray replied. 'We seem to be neighbours, Mr Schreed. Will you join me in a bottle of wine?'

'That's a great idea,' was the hearty response.

So Mr Cray did what those few months ago he would have deemed impossible—he fraternized with Mr Otto Schreed of Chicago, exporter of tinned beef. They talked together of many subjects. Their conversation was the conversation of two patriotic and high-minded Americans, with the obvious views of the well-meaning man. Mr Schreed, encouraged towards the end of the meal by his companion's friendliness, and warmed a little by the wine he had drunk, became confidential.

'Say, it's a hard question I'm going to put to you, Mr Cray,' he said, lowering his voice a little, 'but does my name suggest anything to you?'

Mr Cray took up the card and looked at it.

'Can't say that it does,' he replied, 'except that your front name reads German.'

'That ain't it,' the other observed. 'My father was a German all right, but I was born in Chicago and I am a good American citizen. It isn't that. I was one of the unlucky devils that got into some trouble with the Government contractors.'

'And I was one of those,' Mr Cray mused, 'who spent a hundred dollars cabling to the head of the YMCA in the States exactly my opinion of you.' But aloud, Mr Cray's words betrayed nothing of this fact.

'Say, that was hard luck!' he admitted. 'How did it happen?'

'Just as those things do happen,' the other explained, 'however almighty careful you may be. We were canning night and day, with Government officials standing over us, and Washington wiring all the time—"Get a move on. Get a move on. We want the stuff." I guess some of the foremen got a bit careless. I was worn out myself. The weather was moist and hot, and a load or two of stuff got in that shouldn't. Not but what I always believed,' Mr Schreed went on, 'that the complaints were exaggerated, but any way the YMCA busybodies over yonder took it up, and they got me before the Court.'

'Did it cost you much?' Mr Cray enquired.

'They fined me fifty thousand dollars,' the other replied, 'and I had to sell out. Just at the time, too,' he went on gloomily, 'when one was making money just so that you couldn't count it.'

It was precisely at this moment that Mr Cray was on the point of raising his voice and of speaking words which without doubt would have led to his neighbour's precipitate ejection from the room. And then something struck him. There was something more than the natural humiliation of a punished man in Mr Schreed's drawn face and furtive expression. There was something beyond the look of the man who has done wrong and has borne an unacceptable punishment. There was still fear, there was still terror of some unnamed possibility. Mr Cray saw this and he held his peace. He took his thoughts back a few months to the little conversation he had had with the doctor in that impromptu hospital. He recalled the latter's impassioned words and he choked down certain rebellious feelings. He decided to offer the right hand of fellowship to the unfortunate Mr Otto Schreed.

Mr Otto Schreed was alone and friendless in a strange city, with the shadow of disgrace resting upon his unattractive name. He was more than disposed, therefore, to accept the advances of this genial and companionable new acquaintance. He was not by disposition a gregarious person, but he was too uncultured to find any pleasure in books or pictures; the newspapers of London were an unknown world to him, and a certain measure of companionship became almost a necessity. It appeared that he was staying at the Milan Hotel, and it was quite natural, therefore, that he should see a great deal of his new friend during the next few days. He was not at first disposed to be communicative. He said very little about his plans, and he asked a great many personal questions, some of which Mr Cray evaded, and others of which he answered with artless candour. Mr Cray's connection with the YMCA and his work in France was not once alluded to.

'Say, what's keeping you over here?' Mr Schreed asked one day. 'You've nothing against the other side?'

'Haven't I!' Mr Cray replied. 'That's where you're making the mistake of your life. I am not a drunkard,' he went on, warming to his subject, 'but I am a man who loves his liberty, and I hate a country where the bars are crowded out with soft drinks, and where the damned waiters wink and jerk their thumbs round the corner towards the apothecary's shop when you want a drop of Scotch. I am over here, Schreed, my lad, till the United States comes to its senses on the liquor question, and over here I mean to stop until then. . . . What about yourself?'

Mr Schreed had been exceedingly close-mouthed about his own movements, but this morning he spoke with more freedom of his plans.

'I am not so strong as you on the liquor question,' he admitted, 'but I feel I have been hardly done with over there by the Government, and I'm not hurrying back yet awhile. I thought some,' he went on, after a moment's pause, glancing sideways at Mr Cray as though to watch the effect of his words, 'of taking a little tour out to the battlefields of France.'

'That's quite an idea,' Mr Cray admitted with interest.

His companion looked around to make sure that they were alone.

'I don't mind confiding to you, Cray,' he said, 'that I have another reason for wanting to get out there. When the Stores Department discovered that something was wrong with those few thousand tins of beef of mine, they burnt the lot. They sent a certificate to Washington as to its condition, upon which I was convicted and fined, although I was well able to prove that the week the defective canning must have been done, I was taking a few days' vacation. However, that's neither here nor there. I made enquiries as to whether any of it was still in existence, and I was told that before any had been opened, a matter of fifty tins or so had been doled out in some French village where the peasants hadn't got any food. Nothing was ever heard about these.'

'I see,' Mr Cray murmured, and there was nothing in his face to indicate that he had found the intelligence interesting.

'I kind of thought,' Mr Schreed continued, 'that I'd like to look around over there, and if any of these tins were still in existence I'd buy them up and destroy them, so as to avoid any further trouble. You see, they all have my name and trade-mark on the outside. The Government insisted upon that.'

'Rather like looking for a needle in a haystack,' Mr Cray remarked.

'Not so much,' the other replied. 'I know the name of the place where our men were billeted when they opened the stuff, and the name of the village to which they sent fifty tins. I thought I'd just look around there, and if there are no traces of any—well, I've done the best I could. Then I thought some of coming home by Holland.'

'Business in Holland, eh?' Mr Cray enquired.

'Not exactly business—or rather, if it is, it wouldn't take more than an hour or two,' Mr Schreed announced.

'When did you think of going?'

'Next week. They tell me they're running some tours from Paris out to the battlefields. The one that goes to Château Thierry would serve my purpose. The worst of it is I can't speak a word of the lingo.'

'It's dead easy,' Mr Cray observed. 'I've been going to Paris too many years not to have picked up a bit.'

'You wouldn't care about a trip out with me, I suppose,' Mr Schreed suggested, 'just in a friendly fashion, you understand, each paying his own dues?'

'I don't know,' Mr Cray replied cautiously. 'Next week did you say you were going?'

'I'm fixing it up to leave on Wednesday.'

'It's some trip,' Mr Cray said thoughtfully.

'A day or two in Paris wouldn't do us any harm,' Mr Schreed remarked, with a slow smile which degenerated into a leer.

'We'll take a bite together at seven o'clock tonight,' Mr Cray decided, 'and I'll let you know. I don't know as I can see anything to prevent my going, providing I can get accommodation. I might be able to help you with the language, too. Finish up in Holland, you said, eh?'

'I don't know as you'd care to go up that far with me,' Mr Schreed said, doubtfully. 'I shan't be stopping there, either. You might wait in Paris.'

Mr Cray smiled beatifically.

'Paris,' he murmured. 'Gee, I think I'll go, Schreed!'

Mr Otto Schreed was both surprised and gratified at his companion's proficiency in the French language, and his capacity for making travelling endurable. Their journey to Paris was accomplished under the most favourable circumstances, and by dint of a long argument and great tact, the very inferior accommodation which had been secured for them was cancelled, and rooms with a small *salon* and bathrooms *en suite* provided at a well-known hotel. As a guide to Paris itself, except to the American bars and the restaurants pure and simple, Mr Cray was perhaps a little disappointing, but his companion himself, during those first few days, was restless and eager to be off on their quest. On the third day, Mr Cray announced their imminent departure.

'Say, I've done better for you than these Cook's char-à-bancs,' he announced triumphantly. 'I've engaged a private car, and we can get out to Château Thierry, see the whole of that part of the line, visit the village you were speaking of, and get back before nightfall. Some hustle, what?'

'Fine!' Mr Schreed declared, showing every impatience to depart. 'Does the man speak any English?'

'I don't know as he does,' Mr Cray admitted, 'but that don't matter any, I guess, as long as I'm around all the time.'

Mr Schreed seemed a little disappointed.

'How about making the enquiries in these small grocers' shops or what you call them?'

'I shall be along,' Mr Cray reminded him. 'You can stand by my side and hear what they say.'

So the pilgrimage started. Mr Cray felt a great silence creep over him as he stood once more on well-remembered ground. It was a bright day in early October, and the familiar landmarks for many miles were visible. Behind that remnant of wood, a thousand Americans had been ambushed. On the hillside there, a great mine had been sprung. Down in the valley below, the corpses of his countrymen had lain so thick that Mr Cray found himself remembering that one awful night when every spare hand, he himself included, had been pressed into the stretcher-bearers' service. He grew more and more silent as they neared their journey's end. Mr Schreed appeared to be a trifle bored.

'Lutaples is the name of the village we want,' he announced, as they began to pass a few white-plastered cottages.

Mr Cray nodded.

'I know,' he said reminiscently. 'Our canteen was in the hollow, just at the bottom there.'

'Our canteen?' Mr Schreed repeated.

'The American canteen,' Mr Cray explained. 'I've been making enquiries for you. So far as I can gather, there was only one shop in Lutaples at the time and it's up at this end of the village. However, we'll soon find out all about it now.'

They stopped at a small *estaminet*, and here trouble nearly came, for no disguise could conceal from the warm-hearted little landlord, the kindly, absurd fat man in tight uniform, who had fed him and his wife and children and left them money to make a fresh start. Fortunately, however, Schreed had lingered behind, making a vain attempt to converse with the chauffeur, and Cray had time, in a few rapid sentences, to put a certain matter before his friend Pierre. So that when Schreed returned and took his seat by Cray's side before the marble table in the village street, Pierre was able to serve them with liqueurs and speak as though to strangers. Mr Cray conversed with him for some time.

'Well, what does he say?' Schreed asked eagerly, when he had gone in.

'There was only one grocer's shop in the village at the time we were in occupation,' Mr Cray explained, 'and the majority of the stores presented by the Americans were handed over to him for distribution. There's the place, plumb opposite—*Henri Lalarge. Epicier.*'

'That mean "grocer"?' Otto Schreed asked.

'Some of it does. Let's be getting along.'

Mr Cray led the way across the cobbled street. Monsieur Lalarge was short, fat, and black-whiskered. As they entered his shop, the landlord from the *estaminet* opposite issued from the back quarters.

'What's he been doing over here?' Schreed demanded suspiciously.

Mr Cray shrugged his shoulders.

'I suppose these fellows all live on one another's doorsteps,' he observed.

The result of the landlord's visit, however, was that although the tears of welcome glistened in the eyes of the warm-hearted Monsieur Lalarge, he greeted the two men as strangers. Mr Cray, having satisfied himself as to his companion's absolute ignorance of the language, talked fluently to the grocer in rapid French. Presently he appeared satisfied and turned to Schreed.

'He says he had fifty tins,' he explained, 'but they were distributed half an hour after he received them. The complaint was made from some of the villagers, and the unopened tins were returned and burned. There is a chemist's shop at the further end of the village where it would be as well to make enquiries. The chauffeur might take you there, and I will explain to him what you want to ask for. Meanwhile, I will see the *curé.*'

Mr Schreed saw nothing to object to in the arrangement, and drove off with the chauffeur. Monsieur Lalarge, with the tears streaming down his cheeks, threw his arms around Mr Cray and kissed him.

'Heaven has brought you back!' he exclaimed. 'Our deliverer—our Saint! But how thin—how wasted!'

'Simply a matter of clothes, Jean, my boy,' Cray assured him. 'Uncle Sam used to pinch us a bit tight about the loins. And now how goes it, eh?'

'Thanks to the benevolence of monsieur, everything prospers,' Monsieur Lalarge declared. 'His little loan—but give me time to write the cheque— it can be paid this moment.'

'Not on your life,' Mr Cray replied vigorously. 'Not a franc, Jean. We both did good work, eh, when those guns were thundering and dirty Fritz was skulking behind the hills there. Finished, Jean. I am a rich man, and what you call a loan was my little thank-offering. We did our best together for the poor people, you know.'

'But, monsieur,' the little grocer sobbed——

'About those tins,' Mr Cray interrupted. 'You have two?'

'I kept them, monsieur,' the man explained, 'because I read in the paper that some day inquiry might be held into all these matters.'

'And an inquiry is going to be held,' Mr Cray declared. 'What you have to do, Jean, is to pack those two tins securely and to send them to me by registered post to the Ritz Hotel, Paris.'

'It shall be done, monsieur.'

'Were there any who died after eating the stuff?' Mr Cray enquired.

'Two,' the grocer answered. 'They are buried in the civic cemetery. One has talked but little of these things. The Americans came as saviours, and this was an accident.'

Cray glanced down the street. His companion was still interviewing the chemist.

'One *petit verre*, Monsieur Lalarge,' he said, 'for the sake of old times.'

Monsieur Lalarge threw aside his apron.

'And to drink to the great goodness of monsieur,' he responded.

Mr Otto Schreed was in high good-humour that evening, on the way back to Paris. He insisted upon paying for a little dinner at the Ambassador's, and a box at the *Folies Bergère*. He spent money freely, for him, and drank far more wine than usual. As he drank, he expanded.

'It is like a nightmare passed away,' he confided to his companion. 'I know now that no one else in the world will ever suffer because of that terrible mistake. There is not a single tin of the condemned beef in existence.'

'A load off your mind, eh?' Mr Cray murmured.

Mr Schreed smiled a peculiar smile.

'For more reasons than you know of, my friend,' he confided. 'Now my little trip to Holland, and after that I am a free man.'

'When are you off there?' his companion enquired.

'The day after tomorrow—Thursday,' was the prompt reply. 'And, Cray——'

'Something bothering you?' the latter remarked, as Schreed hesitated.

'Just this, old fellow. My little trip to Holland is unimportant in its way, and in another sense it's a trip I want to do alone. Do you get me?'

'Sure!' Mr Cray replied. 'I am no butter in. There are some of the boys in this gay little burg I haven't had the time to look up yet. When shall you be back?'

'Monday,' was the eager reply—'Monday sure. I'll go alone, then, Cray. I guess it would be better. But look here. Get together a few of your friends, and we'll have a little dinner the night of my return. At my expense, you understand. You've been very useful to me over here and I should like to make you some slight return. Ask any one you please, and take a couple of boxes for any show you fancy. It isn't the way I live as a rule, but I've a fancy for making a celebration of it.'

'That's easy,' Mr Cray declared. 'It shall be some celebration, I can tell you. We'll dine in the hotel here, and I promise there shall be one or two people you'll be interested to meet.'

So on the following morning Mr Otto Schreed started for Holland, and Mr Joseph P. Cray, with a brown paper parcel under his arm, set out to pay a few calls in Paris.

When Mr Otto Schreed made his punctual appearance in the hotel *salon* on Monday evening at a few minutes before eight, he found Mr Cray and three other guests awaiting him. Mr Cray was busy mixing cocktails, so was unable to shake hands. He looked around and nodded.

'Glad you're punctual, Schreed,' he said. 'Pleasant trip?'

'Fine!'

'Business turn out all right?'

'Couldn't have been better. Won't you introduce me to these gentlemen, Cray?'

'Sure!' Mr Cray replied. 'Gentlemen, this is Mr Otto Schreed of Chicago—Colonel Wilmot of the American Intelligence Department, Mr Neville of the same Service, and Doctor Lemarten.'

'Delighted to meet you all, gentlemen,' Mr Schreed declared.

His outstretched hand was uselessly offered. Neville and Colonel Wilmot contented themselves with a military salute. The Frenchman bowed. Mr Schreed from the first moment was conscious of a vague feeling of uneasiness. He turned towards Cray, who was approaching with a little tray upon which were four cocktails.

'Hope you've ordered a good dinner, Cray,' he said, 'and that these gentlemen are ready to do justice to it. Why, you're a cocktail short.'

Colonel Wilmot, Mr Neville, and Doctor Lemarten had each accepted a wine-glass. Mr Cray took the other one.

'And dash it all, the table's only laid for four!' Schreed continued, as he gazed with dismay at the empty silver tray. 'Is this a practical joke?'

Mr Cray shook his head.

'One of us,' he confided, 'is not having a cocktail. One of us is not dining. That one, Otto Schreed, is you.'

Schreed was suddenly pale. He moved a little towards the door, gripping the back of a chair with his hand.

'Say, what the devil does this mean?' he demanded.

'You just stay where you are and you shall hear,' Mr Cray replied, setting down his empty glass. 'I worked out at that little village of Lutaples for the last year of the war—ran an American canteen there for the YMCA. I was there when your filthy beef was unloaded upon the boys. I saw their sufferings.'

'God!' Schreed muttered beneath his breath. 'And you never told me?'

'I never told you,' Cray assented, 'although I came pretty near telling you with an end of my fist that day at the luncheon club. Glad I didn't now. When I tumbled to it that you were scared about any more of those tins being in existence, I began to guess how things were. I came over with you to be sure you didn't get them. I got two tins from Monsieur Jean Lalarge, and a nice tale he had to tell me about the rest. Doctor Lemarten here analysed them and prepared a report. He's here to tell you about it.'

'The beef was poisoned,' the Frenchman said calmly. 'My report has been handed to Colonel Wilmot.'

'It's a lie!' Schreed declared, trembling. 'Besides, this matter has been dealt with. I have paid my fine. It is finished.'

'Not on your life,' Mr Cray replied. 'Ten thousand tins of your bully beef, Otto Schreed, contained poison. No wonder you were glad to get out of it, as you thought, with a fine. Now we'll move on a step. You've just come back from Holland.

'You may not have known it, but Mr Neville, here, of the American Intelligence Department, was your fellow-passenger. You cashed five drafts at the Amsterdam Bank, amounting in all to something like five hundred thousand dollars of American money. Half of that went to your credit in London, the other half you've got with you. Blood money, Otto Schreed—foul, stinking blood money!'

Schreed was on the point of collapse.

'You have employed spies to dog me?' he shouted.

'We don't call the officers of the American Intelligence Department spies,' Mr Cray observed coldly.

'Otto Schreed,' Colonel Wilmot said, speaking for the first time, 'I have a warrant for your arrest, and an extradition warrant from the French Government. You will leave for Cherbourg tonight and be taken back to New York!'

'On what charge?' Schreed faltered.

'Political conspiracy—perhaps murder.'

Colonel Wilmot walked to the door and called in two men who were waiting outside. Schreed collapsed.

'I've two hundred and fifty thousand dollars here,' he shrieked. 'Can't we arrange this? Cray! Colonel Wilmot!'

The two men were obliged to drag him out. Mr Cray moved to the window and threw it open.

'What we want,' he muttered, 'is fresh air.'

Colonel Wilmot smiled.

'He was a poisonous beast, Cray,' he said, 'but you've done a fine stroke of business for the United States Government, and we're anxious to drink your health.'

Two waiters, followed by a *maître d'hôtel*, were already in the room. The latter came forward and bowed.

'*Monsieur est servi*,' he announced.

Giulia Lazzari

The train started at eight. When he had disposed of his bag Ashenden walked along the platform. He found the carriage in which Giulia Lazzari was, but she sat in a corner, looking away from the light, so that he could not see her face. She was in the charge of two detectives who had taken her over from English police at Boulogne. One of them worked with Ashenden on the French side of the Lake Geneva and as Ashenden came up he nodded to him.

'I've asked the lady if she will dine in the restaurant-car, but she prefers to have dinner in the carriage, so I've ordered a basket. Is that quite correct?'

'Quite,' said Ashenden.

'My companion and I will go into the diner in turn so that she will not remain alone.'

'That is very considerate of you. I will come along when we've started and have a chat with her.'

'She's not disposed to be very talkative,' said the detective.

'One could hardly expect it,' replied Ashenden.

He walked on to get his ticket for the second service and then returned to his own carriage. Giulia Lazzari was just finishing her meal when he went back to her. From a glance at the basket he judged that she had not eaten with too poor an appetite. The detective who was guarding her opened the door when Ashenden appeared and at Ashenden's suggestion left them alone.

Giulia Lazzari gave him a sullen look.

'I hope you've had what you wanted for dinner,' he said as he sat down in front of her.

She bowed slightly, but did not speak. He took out his case.

'Will you have a cigarette?'

She gave him a glance, seemed to hesitate, and then, still without a word, took one. He struck a match and, lighting it, looked at her. He was surprised. For some reason he had expected her to be fair, perhaps from some notion that an Oriental would be more likely to fall for a blonde; but she was almost swarthy. Her hair was hidden by a close-fitting hat, but her eyes were coal-black. She was far from young, she might have been thirty-five, and her skin was lined and sallow. She had at the moment no make-up on and she looked haggard. There was nothing beautiful about her but her magnificent eyes. She was big, and Ashenden thought she must be too big to dance gracefully; it might be that in Spanish costume she was a bold and flaunting figure, but there in the train, shabbily dressed, there was nothing to explain the Indian's infatuation. She gave Ashenden a long, appraising stare. She wondered evidently what sort of man he was. She blew a cloud of smoke through her nostrils and gave it a glance, then looked back at Ashenden. He could see that her sullenness was only a mask, she was nervous and frightened. She spoke in French with an Italian accent.

'Who are you?'

'My name would mean nothing to you, *madame*. I am going to Thonon. I have taken a room for you at the Hotel de la Place. It is the only one open now. I think you will find it quite comfortable.'

'Ah, it is you the Colonel spoke to me of. You are my jailer.'

'Only as a matter of form. I shall not intrude upon you.'

'All the same you are my jailer.'

'I hope not for very long. I have in my pocket your passport with all the formalities completed to permit you to go to Spain.'

She threw herself back into the corner of the carriage. White, with those great black eyes, in the poor light, her face was suddenly a mask of despair.

'It's infamous. Oh, I think I could die happy if I could only kill that old Colonel. He has no heart. I'm so unhappy.'

'I am afraid you have got yourself into a very unfortunate situation. Did you not know that espionage was a dangerous game?'

'I never sold any of the secrets. I did no harm.'

'Surely only because you had no opportunity. I understand that you signed a full confession.'

Ashenden spoke to her as amiably as he could, a little as though he were talking to a sick person, and there was no harshness in his voice.

'Oh, yes, I made a fool of myself. I wrote the letter the Colonel said I was to write. Why isn't that enough? What is to happen to me if he does not answer? I cannot force him to come if he does not want to.'

'He has answered,' said Ashenden. 'I have the answer with me.'

She gave a gasp and her voice broke.

'Oh, show it to me, I beseech you to let me see it.'

'I have no objection to doing that. But you must return it to me.'

He took Chandra's letter from his pocket and gave it to her. She snatched it from his hand. She devoured it with her eyes, there were eight pages of it, and as she read the tears streamed down her cheeks. Between her sobs she gave little exclamations of love, calling the writer by pet names French and Italian. This was the letter that Chandra had written in reply to hers telling him, on R.'s instructions, that she would meet him in Switzerland. He was mad with joy at the prospect. He told her in passionate phrases how long the time had seemed to him since they were parted, and how he had yearned for her, and now that he was to see her again so soon he did not know how he was going to bear his impatience. She finished it and let it drop to the floor.

'You can see he loves me, can't you? There's no doubt about that. I know something about it, believe me.'

'Do you really love him?' asked Ashenden.

'He's the only man who's ever been kind to me. It's not very gay the life one leads in these music halls, all over Europe, never resting, and men—they are not much the men who haunt those places. At first I thought he was just like the rest of them.'

Ashenden picked up the letter and replaced it in his pocket-book.

'A telegram was sent in your name to the address in Holland to say that you would be at the Hotel Gibbons at Lausanne on the 14th.'

'That is tomorrow.'

'Yes.'

She threw up her head and her eyes flashed.

'Oh, it is an infamous thing that you are forcing me to do. It is shameful.'

'You are not obliged to do it,' said Ashenden.

'And if I don't?'

'I'm afraid you must take the consequences.'

'I can't go to prison,' she cried out suddenly, 'I can't, I can't; I have such a short time before me; he said ten years. Is it possible I could be sentenced to ten years?'

'If the Colonel told you so it is very possible.'

'Oh, I know him. That cruel face. He would have no mercy. And what should I be in ten years? Oh, no, no.'

At that moment the train stopped at a station and the detective waiting in the corridor tapped on the window. Ashenden opened the door and the man gave him a picture-postcard. It was a dull little view of Pontarlier, the frontier station between France and Switzerland, and showed a dusty *place* with a statue in the middle and a few plane trees. Ashenden handed her a pencil.

'Will you write this postcard to your lover. It will be posted at Pontarlier. Address it to the hotel at Lausanne.'

She gave him a glance, but without answering took it and wrote as he directed.

'Now on the other side write: "delayed at frontier but everything all right. Wait at Lausanne." Then add whatever you like, *tendresses*, if you like.'

He took the postcard from her, read it to see that she had done as he directed and then reached for his hat.

'Well, I shall leave you now, I hope you will have a sleep. I will fetch you in the morning when we arrive at Thonon.'

The second detective had now returned from his dinner and as Ashenden came out of the carriage the two men went in. Giulia Lazzari huddled back into her corner. Ashenden gave the postcard to an agent who was waiting to take it to Pontarlier and then made his way along the crowded train to his sleeping-car.

It was bright and sunny, though cold, next morning when they reached their destination. Ashenden, having given his bags to a porter, walked along the platform to where Giulia Lazzari and the two detectives were standing. Ashenden nodded to them.

'Well, good morning. You need not trouble to wait.'

They touched their hats, gave a word of farewell to the woman, and walked away.

'Where are they going?' she asked.

'Off. You will not be bothered with them any more.'

'Am I in your custody then?'

'You're in nobody's custody. I'm going to permit myself to take you to your hotel and then I shall leave you. You must try to get a good rest.'

Ashenden's porter took her hand-luggage and she gave him the ticket for her trunk. They walked out of the station. A cab was waiting for them and Ashenden begged her to get in. It was a longish drive to the hotel and now and then Ashenden felt that she gave him a sidelong glance. She was perplexed. He sat without a word. When they reached the hotel the proprietor—it was a small hotel, prettily situated at the corner of a little promenade and it had a charming view—showed them the room that had been prepared for Madame Lazzari. Ashenden turned to him.

'That'll do very nicely, I think. I shall come down in a minute.'

The proprietor bowed and withdrew.

'I shall do my best to see that you are comfortable, *Madame*,' said Ashenden. 'You are here absolutely your own mistress and you may order pretty well anything you like. To the proprietor you are just a guest of the hotel like any other. You are absolutely free.'

'Free to go out?' she asked quickly.

'Of course.'

'With a policeman on either side of me, I suppose.'

'Not at all. You are as free in the hotel as though you were in your own house and you are free to go out and come in when you choose. I should like an assurance from you that you will not write any letters without my knowledge or attempt to leave Thonon without my permission.'

She gave Ashenden a long stare. She could not make it out at all. She looked as though she thought it a dream.

'I am in a position that forces me to give you any assurance you ask. I give you my word of honour that I will not write a letter without showing it to you or attempt to leave this place.'

'Thank you. Now I will leave you. I will do myself the pleasure of coming to see you tomorrow morning.'

Ashenden nodded and went out. He stopped for five minutes at the police-station to see that everything was in order and then took the cab up the hill to a little secluded house on the outskirts of the town at which on his periodical visits to this place he stayed. It was pleasant to have a bath and a shave and get into slippers. He felt lazy and spent the rest of the morning reading a novel.

Soon after dark, for even at Thonon, though it was in France, it was thought desirable to attract attention to Ashenden as little as possible, an agent from the police-station came to see him. His name was Felix. He was a little dark Frenchman with sharp eyes and an unshaven chin, dressed in a shabby grey suit and rather down at heel, so that he looked like a lawyer's clerk out of work. Ashenden offered him a glass of wine and they sat down by the fire.

'Well, your lady lost no time,' he said. 'Within a quarter of an hour of her arrival she was out of the hotel with a bundle of clothes and trinkets that she sold in a shop near the market. When the afternoon boat came in she went down to the quay and bought a ticket to Evian.'

Evian, it should be explained, was the next place along the lake in France and from there, crossing over, the boat went to Switzerland.

'Of course she hadn't a passport, so permission to embark was denied her.'

'How did she explain that she had no passport?'

'She said she'd forgotten it. She said she had an appointment to see friends in Evian and tried to persuade the official in charge to let her go. She attempted to slip a hundred francs into his hand.'

'She must be a stupider woman than I thought,' said Ashenden.

But when next day he went about eleven in the morning to see her he made no reference to her attempt to escape. She had had time to arrange herself, and now, her hair elaborately done, her lips and cheeks painted, she looked less haggard than when he had first seen her.

'I've brought you some books,' said Ashenden. 'I'm afraid the time hangs heavy on your hands.'

'What does that matter to you?'

'I have no wish that you should suffer anything that can be avoided. Anyhow I will leave them and you can read them or not as you choose.'

'If you only knew how I hated you.'

'It would doubtless make me very uncomfortable. But I really don't know why you should. I am only doing what I have been ordered to do.'

'What do you want of me now? I do not suppose you have come only to ask after my health.'

Ashenden smiled.

'I want you to write a letter to your lover telling him that owing to some irregularity in your passport the Swiss authorities would not let you cross the frontier, so you have come here where it is very nice and quiet, so quiet that one can hardly realize there is a war, and you propose that Chandra should join you.'

'Do you think he is a fool? He will refuse.'

'Then you must do your best to persuade him.'

She looked at Ashenden a long time before she answered. He suspected that she was debating within herself whether by writing the letter and so seeming docile she could not gain time.

'Well, dictate and I will write what you say.'

'I should prefer you to put it in your own words.'

'Give me half an hour and the letter shall be ready.'

'I will wait here,' said Ashenden.

'Why?'

'Because I prefer to.'

Her eyes flashed angrily, but controlling herself she said nothing. On the chest of drawers were writing materials. She sat down at the dressing-table and began to write. When she handed Ashenden the letter he saw that even through her rouge she was very pale. It was the letter of a person not much used to expressing herself by means of pen and ink, but it was well enough, and when towards the end, starting to say how much she loved the man, she had been carried away and wrote with all her heart, it had really a certain passion.

'Now add: The man who is bringing this is Swiss, you can trust him absolutely. I didn't want the censor to see it.'

She hesitated an instant, but then wrote as he directed.

'How do you spell, absolutely?'

'As you like. Now address an envelope and I will relieve you of my unwelcome presence.'

He gave the letter to the agent who was waiting to take it across the lake. Ashenden brought her the reply the same evening. She snatched it from his hands and for a moment pressed it to her heart. When she read it she uttered a little cry of relief.

'He won't come.'

The letter, in the Indian's flowery, stilted English, expressed his bitter disappointment. He told her how intensely he had looked forward to seeing her and implored her to do everything in the world to smooth the difficulties that prevented her from crossing the frontier. He said that it was impossible for him to come, impossible, there was a price on his head, and it would be madness for him to think of risking it. He attempted to be jocular, she did not want her little fat lover to be shot, did she?

'He won't come,' she repeated, 'he won't come.'

'You must write and tell him that there is no risk. You must say that if there were you would not dream of asking him. You must say that if he loves you he will not hesitate.'

'I won't. I won't.'

'Don't be a fool. You can't help yourself.'

She burst into a sudden flood of tears. She flung herself on the floor and seizing Ashenden's knees implored him to have mercy on her.

'I will do anything in the world for you if you will let me go.'

'Don't be absurd,' said Ashenden. 'Do you think I want to become your lover? Come, come, you must be serious. You know the alternative.'

She raised herself to her feet and changing on a sudden to fury flung at Ashenden one foul name after another.

'I like you much better like that,' he said. 'Now will you write or shall I send for the police?'

'He will not come. It is useless.'

'It is very much to your interest to make him come.'

'What do you mean by that? Do you mean that if I do everything in my power and fail, that . . .'

She looked at Ashenden with wild eyes.

'Yes, it means either you or him.'

She staggered. She put her hand to her heart. Then without a word she reached for pen and paper. But the letter was not to Ashenden's liking and he made her write it again. When she had finished she flung herself on the bed and burst once more into passionate weeping. Her grief was real, but there was something theatrical in the expression of it that prevented it from being peculiarly moving to Ashenden. He felt his relation to her as impersonal as a doctor's in the presence of a pain that he cannot alleviate. He saw now why R. had given him this peculiar task; it needed a cool head and an emotion well under control.

He did not see her next day. The answer to the letter was not delivered to him till after dinner when it was brought to Ashenden's little house by Felix.

'Well, what news have you?'

'Our friend is getting desperate,' smiled the Frenchman. 'This afternoon she walked up to the station just as a train was about to start for Lyons. She was looking up and down uncertainly so I went to her and asked if there was anything I could do. I introduced myself as an agent of the Sûreté. If looks could kill I should not be standing here now.'

'Sit down, *mon ami*,' said Ashenden.

'*Merci*. She walked away, she evidently thought it was no use to try to get on the train, but I have something more interesting to tell you. She has offered a boatman on the lake a thousand francs to take her across to Lausanne.'

'What did he say to her?'

'He said he couldn't risk it.'

'Yes?'

The little agent gave his shoulders a slight shrug and smiled.

'She's asked him to meet her on the road that leads to Evian at ten o'clock tonight so that they can talk of it again, and she's given him to understand that she will not repulse too fiercely the advances of a lover. I have told him to do what he likes so long as he comes and tells me everything that is of importance.'

'Are you sure you can trust him?' asked Ashenden.

'Oh, quite. He knows nothing, of course, but that she is under surveillance. You need have no fear about him. He is a good boy, I have known him all his life.'

Ashenden read Chandra's letter. It was eager and passionate. It throbbed strangely with the painful yearning of his heart. Love? Yes, if Ashenden knew anything of it there was the real thing. He told her how he spent long long hours walking by the lakeside and looking towards the coast of France. How near they were and yet so desperately parted! He repeated again and again that he could not come, and begged her not to ask him, he would do everything in the world for her, but that he dared not do, and yet if she insisted how could he resist her? He besought her to have mercy on him. And then he broke into a long wail at the thought that he must go away without seeing her, he asked her if there were not some means by which she could slip over, he swore that if he could ever hold her in his arms again he would never let her go. Even the forced and elaborate language in which it was written could not dim the hot fire that burned the pages; it was the letter of a madman.

'When will you hear the result of her interview with the boatman?' asked Ashenden.

'I have arranged to meet him at the landing-stage between eleven and twelve.'

Ashenden looked at his watch.

'I will come with you.'

They walked down the hill and reaching the quay for shelter from the cold wind stood in the lea of the custom-house. At last they saw a man approaching and Felix stepped out of the shadow that hid them.

'Antoine.'

'*Monsieur Félix?* I have a letter for you; I promised to take it to Lausanne by the first boat tomorrow.'

Ashenden gave the man a brief glance, but did not ask what had passed between him and Giulia Lazzari. He took the letter and by the light of Felix's electric torch read it. It was in faulty German.

'*On no account come. Pay no attention to my letters. Danger. I love you. Sweetheart. Don't come.*'

He put it in his pocket, gave the boatman fifty francs, and went home to bed. But the next day when he went to see Giulia Lazzari he found her door locked. He knocked for some time, there was no answer. He called her.

'Madame Lazzari, you must open the door. I want to speak to you.'

'I am in bed. I am ill and can see no one.'

'I am sorry, but you must open the door. If you are ill I will send for a doctor.'

'No, go away. I will see no one.'

'If you do not open the door I shall send for a locksmith and have it broken open.'

There was a silence and then he heard the key turned in the lock. He went in. She was in a dressing-gown and her hair was dishevelled. She had evidently just got out of bed.

'I am at the end of my strength. I can do nothing more. You have only to look at me to see that I am ill. I have been sick all night.'

'I shall not keep you long. Would you like to see a doctor?'

'What good can a doctor do me?'

He took out of his pocket the letter she had given the boatman and handed it to her.

'What is the meaning of this?' he asked.

She gave a gasp at the sight of it and her sallow face went green.

'You gave me your word that you would neither attempt to escape nor write a letter without my knowledge.'

'Did you think I would keep my word?' she cried, her voice ringing with scorn.

'No. To tell you the truth it was not entirely for your convenience that you were placed in a comfortable hotel rather than in the local jail, but I think I should tell you that though you have your freedom to go in and out as you like you have no more chance of getting away from Thonon than if you were chained by the leg in a prison cell. It is silly to waste your time writing letters that will never be delivered.'

'*Cochon.*'

She flung the opprobrious word at him with all the violence that was in her.

'But you must sit down and write a letter that *will* be delivered.'

'Never. I will do nothing more. I will not write another word.'

'You came here on the understanding that you would do certain things.'

'I will not do them. It is finished.'

'You had better reflect a little.'

'Reflect! I have reflected. You can do what you like; I don't care.'

'Very well, I will give you five minutes to change your mind.'

Ashenden took out his watch and looked at it. He sat down on the edge of the unmade bed.

'Oh, it has got on my nerves, this hotel. Why did you not put me in the prison? Why, why? Everywhere I went I felt that spies were on my heels. It is infamous what you are making me do. Infamous! What is my crime? I ask you, what have I done? Am I not a woman? It is infamous what you are asking me to do. Infamous.'

She spoke in a high shrill voice. She went on and on. At last the five minutes were up. Ashenden had not said a word. He rose.

'Yes, go, go,' she shrieked at him.

She flung foul names at him.

'I shall come back,' said Ashenden.

He took the key out of the door as he went out of the room and locked it behind him. Going downstairs he hurriedly scribbled a note, called the boots and dispatched him with it to the police-station. Then he went up again. Giulia Lazzari had thrown herself on her bed and turned her face to the wall. Her body was shaken with hysterical sobs. She gave no sign that she heard him come in. Ashenden sat down on the chair in front of the dressing-table and looked idly at the odds and ends that littered it. The toilet things were cheap and tawdry and none too clean. There were little shabby pots of rouge and cold-cream and little bottles of black for the eyebrows and eyelashes. The hairpins were horrid and greasy. The room was untidy and the air was heavy with the smell of cheap scent. Ashenden thought of the hundreds of rooms she must have occupied in third-rate hotels in the course of her wandering life from provincial town to provincial town in one country after another. He wondered what had been her origins. She was a coarse and vulgar woman, but what had she been when young? She was not the type he would have expected to adopt that career, for she seemed to have no advantages that could help her, and he asked himself whether she came of a family of entertainers (there are all over the world families in which for generations the members have become dancers or acrobats or comic singers) or whether she had fallen into the life accidentally through some lover in the business who had for a time made her his partner. And what men must she have known in all these years, the comrades of the shows she was in, the agents and managers who looked upon it as a perquisite of their position that they should enjoy her favours, the merchants or well-to-do tradesmen, the young sparks of the various towns she played in, who were attracted for the moment by the glamour of the dancer or the blatant sensuality of the woman! To her they were the paying customers and she accepted them indifferently as the recognized and admitted supplement to her miserable salary, but to them perhaps she was romance. In her bought arms they caught sight for a moment of the brilliant world of the capitals, and ever so distantly and however shoddily of the adventure and the glamour of a more spacious life.

There was a sudden knock at the door and Ashenden immediately cried out:

'*Entrez.*'

Giulia Lazzari sprang up in bed to a sitting posture.

'Who is it?' she called.

She gave a gasp as she saw the two detectives who had brought her from Boulogne and handed her over to Ashenden at Thonon.

'You! What do you want?' she shrieked.

'*Allons, levez vous,*' said one of them, and his voice had a sharp abruptness that suggested that he would put up with no nonsense.

'I'm afraid you must get up, Madame Lazzari,' said Ashenden. 'I am delivering you once more to the care of these gentlemen.'

'How can I get up! I'm ill, I tell you. I cannot stand. Do you want to kill me?'

'If you won't dress yourself, we shall have to dress you, and I'm afraid we shouldn't do it very cleverly. Come, come, it's no good making a scene.'

'Where are you going to take me?'

'They're going to take you back to England.'

One of the detectives took hold of her arm.

'Don't touch me, don't come near me,' she screamed furiously.

'Let her be,' said Ashenden. 'I'm sure she'll see the necessity of making as little trouble as possible.'

'I'll dress myself.'

Ashenden watched her as she took off her dressing-gown and slipped a dress over her head. She forced her feet into shoes obviously too small for her. She arranged her hair. Every now and then she gave the detectives a hurried, sullen glance. Ashenden wondered if she would have the nerve to go through with it. R. would call him a damned fool, but he almost wished she would. She went up to the dressing-table and Ashenden stood up in order to let her sit down. She greased her face quickly and then rubbed off the grease with a dirty towel, she powdered herself and made up her eyes. But her hand shook. The three men watched her in silence. She rubbed the rouge on her cheeks and painted her mouth. Then she crammed a hat down on her head. Ashenden made a gesture to the first detective and he took a pair of handcuffs out of his pocket and advanced towards her.

At the sight of them she started back violently and flung her arms wide.

'*Non, non, non. Je ne veux pas.* No, not them. No. No.'

'Come, *ma fille*, don't be silly,' said the detective roughly.

As though for protection (very much to his surprise) she flung her arms round Ashenden.

'Don't let them take me, have mercy on me, I can't, I can't.'

Ashenden extricated himself as best he could.

'I can do nothing more for you.'

The detective seized her wrists and was about to affix the handcuffs when with a great cry she threw herself down on the floor.

'I will do what you wish. I will do everything.'

On a sign from Ashenden the detectives left the room. He waited for a little till she had regained a certain calm. She was lying on the floor, sobbing passionately. He raised her to her feet and made her sit down.

'What do you want me to do?' she gasped.

'I want you to write another letter to Chandra.'

'My head is in a whirl. I could not put two phrases together. You must give me time.'

But Ashenden felt that it was better to get her to write a letter while she was under the effect of her terror. He did not want to give her time to collect herself.

'I will dictate the letter to you. All you have to do is to write exactly what I tell you.'

She gave a deep sigh, but took the pen and the paper and sat down before them at the dressing-table.

'If I do this and . . . and you succeed, how do I know that I shall be allowed to go free?'

'The Colonel promised that you should. You must take my word for it that I shall carry out his instructions.'

'I *should* look a fool if I betrayed my friend and then went to prison for ten years.'

'I'll tell you your best guarantee of our good faith. Except by reason of Chandra you are not of the smallest importance to us. Why should we put ourselves to the bother and expense of keeping you in prison when you can do us no harm?'

She reflected for an instant. She was composed now. It was as though, having exhausted her emotion, she had become on a sudden a sensible and practical woman.

'Tell me what you want me to write.'

Ashenden hesitated. He thought he could put the letter more or less in the way she would naturally have put it, but he had to give it consideration. It must be neither fluent nor literary. He knew that in moments of emotion people are inclined to be melodramatic and stilted. In a book or on the stage this always rings false and the author has to make his people speak more simply and with less emphasis than in fact they do. It was a serious moment, but Ashenden felt that there were in it elements of the comic.

'I didn't know I loved a coward,' he started. 'If you loved me you couldn't hesitate when I ask you to come. . . . Underline *couldn't* twice.' He went on. 'When I promise you there is no danger. If you don't love me, you are right not to come. Don't come. Go back to Berlin where you are in safety. I am sick of it. I am alone here. I have made myself ill by waiting for you and every day I have said he is coming. If you loved me you would not hesitate so much. It is quite clear to me that you do not love me. I am sick and tired of you. I have no money. This hotel is impossible. There is nothing for me to stay for. I can get an engagement in Paris. I have a friend there who has made me serious propositions. I have wasted long enough over you and look what I have got from it. It is finished. Good-bye. You will never find a woman who will love you as I have loved you. I cannot afford to refuse the proposition of my friend, so I have telegraphed to him and as soon as I shall receive his answer I go to Paris. I do not blame you because you do not love me, that is not your fault, but you must see that I should be a stupid to go on wasting my life. One is not young for ever. Good-bye. Giulia.'

When Ashenden read over the letter he was not altogether satisfied. But it was the best he could do. It had an air of verisimilitude which the words lacked because, knowing little English, she had written phonetically, the spelling was atrocious and the handwriting like a child's; she had crossed out words and written them over again. Some of the phrases he had put in French. Once or twice tears had fallen on the pages and blurred the ink.

'I leave you now,' said Ashenden. 'It may be that when next you see me I shall be able to tell you that you are free to go where you choose. Where do you want to go?'

'Spain.'

'Very well, I will have everything prepared.'

She shrugged her shoulders. He left her.

There was nothing now for Ashenden to do but wait. He sent a messenger to Lausanne in the afternoon, and next morning went down to the quay to meet the boat. There was a waiting-room next to the ticket-office and here he told the detectives to hold themselves in readiness. When a boat arrived the passengers advanced along the pier in line and their passports were examined before they were allowed to go ashore. If Chandra came and showed his passport, and it was very likely that he was travelling with a false one, issued probably by a neutral nation, he was to be asked to wait and Ashenden was to identify him. Then he would be arrested. It was with some excitement that Ashenden watched the boat come in and the little group of people gathered at the gangway. He scanned them closely but saw no one who looked in the least like an Indian. Chandra had not come. Ashenden did not know what to do. He had played his last card. There were not more than half a dozen passengers for Thonon and when they had been examined and gone their way he strolled slowly along the pier.

'Well, it's no go,' he said to Felix who had been examining the passports. 'The gentleman I expected hasn't turned up.'

'I have a letter for you.'

He handed Ashenden an envelope addressed to Madame Lazzari on which he immediately recognized the spidery handwriting of Chandra Lal. At that moment the steamer from Geneva which was going to Lausanne and the end of the lake hove in sight. It arrived at Thonon every morning twenty minutes after the steamer going in the opposite direction had left. Ashenden had an inspiration.

'Where is the man who brought it?'

'He's in the ticket-office.'

'Give him the letter and tell him to return to the person who gave it to him. He is to say that he took it to the lady and she sent it back. If the person asks him to take another letter he is to say that it is not much good as she is packing her trunk and leaving Thonon.'

He saw the letter handed over and the instructions given and then walked back to his little house in the country.

The next boat on which Chandra could possibly come arrived about five and having at that hour an important engagement with an agent working in Germany he warned Felix that he might be a few minutes late. But if Chandra came he could easily be detained; there was no great hurry since the train in which he was to be taken to Paris did not start till shortly after eight. When Ashenden had finished his business he strolled leisurely down to the lake. It was light still and from the top of the hill he saw the steamer pulling out. It was an anxious moment and instinctively he quickened his steps. Suddenly he saw someone running towards him and recognized the man who had taken the letter.

'Quick, quick,' he cried. 'He's there.'

Ashenden's heart gave a great thud against his chest.

'At last.'

He began to run too and as they ran the man, panting, told him how he had taken back the unopened letter. When he put it in the Indian's hand he turned frightfully pale ('I should never have thought an Indian could turn that colour,' he said) and turned it over and over in his hand as though he could not understand what his own letter was doing there. Tears sprang to his eyes and rolled down his cheeks. ('It was grotesque, he's fat, you know.') He said something in a language the man did not understand and then in French asked him when the boat went to Thonon. When he got on board he looked about, but did not see him, then he caught sight of him, huddled up in an ulster with his hat drawn down over his eyes, standing alone in the bows. During the crossing he kept his eyes fixed on Thonon.

'Where is he now?' asked Ashenden.

'I got off first and Monsieur Felix told me to come for you.'

'I suppose they're holding him in the waiting-room.'

Ashenden was out of breath when they reached the pier. He burst into the waiting-room. A group of men, talking at the top of their voices and gesticulating wildly, were clustered round a man lying on the ground.

'What's happened?' he cried.

'Look,' said Monsieur Felix.

Chandra Lal lay there, his eyes wide open and a thin line of foam on his lips, dead. His body was horribly contorted.

'He's killed himself. We've sent for the doctor. He was too quick for us.'

A sudden thrill of horror passed through Ashenden.

When the Indian landed Felix recognized from the description that he was the man they wanted. There were only four passengers. He was the last. Felix took an exaggerated time to examine the passports of the first three, and then took the Indian's. It was a Spanish one and it was all in order. Felix asked the regulation questions and noted them on the official sheet. Then he looked at him pleasantly and said:

'Just come into the waiting-room for a moment. There are one or two formalities to fulfil.'

'Is my passport not in order?' the Indian asked.

'Perfectly.'

Chandra hesitated, but then followed the official to the door of the waiting-room. Felix opened it and stood aside.

'*Entrez.*'

Chandra went in and the two detectives stood up. He must have suspected at once that they were police-officers and realized that he had fallen into a trap.

'Sit down,' said Felix. 'I have one or two questions to put to you.'

'It is hot in here,' he said, and in point of fact they had a little stove there that kept the place like an oven. 'I will take off my coat if you permit.'

'Certainly,' said Felix graciously.

He took off his coat, apparently with some effort, and he turned to put it on a chair, and then before they realized what had happened they were startled to see him stagger and fall heavily to the ground. While taking off his coat Chandra had managed to swallow the contents of a bottle that was still clasped in his hand. Ashenden put his nose to it. There was a very distinct odour of almonds.

For a little while they looked at the man who lay on the floor. Felix was apologetic.

'Will they be very angry?' he asked nervously.

'I don't see that it was your fault,' said Ashenden. 'Anyhow he can do no more harm. For my part I am just as glad he killed himself. The notion of his being executed did not make me very comfortable.'

In a few minutes the doctor arrived and pronounced life extinct.

'Prussic acid,' he said to Ashenden.

Ashenden nodded.

'I will go and see Madame Lazzari,' he said. 'If she wants to stay a day or two longer I shall let her. But if she wants to go tonight of course she can. Will you give the agents at the station instructions to let her pass?'

'I shall be at the station myself,' said Felix.

Ashenden once more climbed the hill. It was night now, a cold, bright night with an unclouded sky and the sight of the new moon, a white shining thread, made him turn three times the money in his pocket. When he entered the hotel he was seized on a sudden with distaste for its cold banality. It smelt of cabbage and boiled mutton. On the walls of the hall were coloured posters of railway companies advertising Grenoble, Carcassonne and the bathing places of Normandy. He went upstairs and after a brief knock opened the door of Giulia Lazzari's room. She was sitting in front of her dressing-table, looking at herself in the glass, just idly or despairingly, apparently doing nothing, and it was in this that she saw Ashenden as he came in. Her face changed suddenly as she caught sight of his and she sprang up so vehemently that the chair fell over.

'What is it? Why are you so white?' she cried.

She turned round and stared at him and her features were gradually twisted to a look of horror.

'*Il est pris*,' she gasped.

'*Il est mort*,' said Ashenden.

'Dead! He took the poison. He had the time for that. He's escaped you after all.'

'What do you mean? How did you know about the poison?'

'He always carried it with him. He said that the English should never take him alive.'

Ashenden reflected for an instant. She had kept that secret well. He supposed the possibility of such a thing should have occurred to him. How was he to anticipate these melodramatic devices?

'Well, now you are free. You can go wherever you like and no obstacle shall be put in your way. Here are your ticket and your passport and here is the money that was in your possession when you were arrested. Do you wish to see Chandra?'

She started.

'No, no.'

'There is no need. I thought you might care to.'

She did not weep. Ashenden supposed that she had exhausted all her emotion. She seemed apathetic.

'A telegram will be sent tonight to the Spanish frontier to instruct the authorities to put no difficulties in your way. If you will take my advice you will get out of France as soon as you can.'

She said nothing, and since Ashenden had no more to say he made ready to go.

'I am sorry that I have had to show myself so hard to you. I am glad to think that now the worst of your troubles are over and I hope that time will assuage the grief that I know you must feel for the death of your friend.'

Ashenden gave her a little bow and turned to the door. But she stopped him.

'One little moment,' she said. 'There is one thing I should like to ask. I think you have some heart.'

'Whatever I can do for you, you may be sure I will.'

'What are they going to do with his things?'

'I don't know. Why?'

Then she said something that confounded Ashenden. It was the last thing he expected.

'He had a wrist-watch that I gave him last Christmas. It cost twelve pounds. Can I have it back?'

Judith

I

The average youth of twenty may expect to live for some thirty-six years. But if he was an infantry subaltern marching up into the Somme battle front in the Summer of 1916, his expectation of life was thirteen days and a bit. Some men took this contracted horizon in one way, and some in another. One virgin youth would think, 'Only a fortnight? Wouldn't do to chuck it in the straight.' Another would think, 'Only a fortnight? And life scarcely tasted! I must gather a rose while I can.'

Phil Gresson thought that he was, on the whole, for the rose. So he got a night's leave from Daours, where his Company lay for two days on its way to the mincing machine at Pozières. Then he borrowed the winking Medical Officer's horse, and trotted off into Amiens, pondering what sort of wine to have with his dinner at Gobert's famed restaurant. Burgundy, he concluded: Burgundy was the winiest wine, the central, essential and typical wine, the soul and greatest common measure of all the kindly wines of the earth, the wine that ought to be allowed to survive if it were ever decreed that, after thirteen days and a bit, only one single wine was to be left alive to do the entire work of the whole heart-gladdening lot. He thought it all out very sagely.

Gobert's was full: Gresson just bagged the last single table. Soon the rising buzz of talk drew its light screen of sound in front of the endless slow thud of the guns in the East. Soon, too, the good Burgundy did its kind office, and Phil's friendly soul was no longer alone: all the voices at the other tables had melted into one mellow voice: he recognized it as the genial voice of the whole of mankind, at its admirable best—not stiff, or cold, or forbidding, as some voices seemed at some times. It set him all a-swim in a delicious reverie about the poignant beauty of this extreme brevity that had come upon life. Thirteen days and a bit—and then all love, all liking, all delight to lie drowned for ever at the bottom of an endless night. Lovely, lovely. The individual life just a mere wisp of an eddy formed and re-formed on the face of a stream, and then smoothed away. Oh! it was good Burgundy. And Phil, a modest and a sober youth, drank more of it than he had ever drunk of any wine at a sitting.

At ten he strolled out of Gobert's, full of beautiful thoughts, and decided first to have a look at the celebrated Cathedral. He was quite an intelligent boy and had read that the great Ruskin thought it, all round, the most topping cathedral in France. So he worked northward, along the Rue St Denis, to its end and then to the left, to reach the West Front. The West Front looked all right, as far as he could see. But it was a very dark night; no moon, no lamps lit in the streets, all the shops shut. And not many people about. Far over the southern suburbs one enemy aeroplane was on duty after another, bombing the railway; and bombs addressed to a railway may be delivered anywhere else.

One ancient trade, all the same, did not slacken, bombs or no bombs. Wherever a British soldier walked, after dark, in the streets of Amiens in that year, a kind of fire-fly lamps would kindle their tiny electric lights in his path; and out of the deepened darkness that each of these made in its rear there would come a whispered assurance that some rose was there and only asked to be gathered.

In the ears of the undebauched Gresson most of these voices were more like curbs than spurs to the promptings of youth. But just as he turned from the Place Notre Dame, to go back to the Rue du Soleil, the sudden casting of one of the wee jets of electric light on his uniform and his face was followed by an English greeting that pulled him up with a jerk: 'Alone! At this late hour! What would Mother say?'

The mere words were nothing: their jaunty jocosity was the common slang of a trade. Nor was it anything out of the way that the words were spoken in English: half the sisterhood did that in France. What made him stop and say 'Hullo!' was the quality of the voice. It was everything that nobody could expect from the tongue of a street-walker hawking her person to any chance ruffian a foreign army might throw in her way. It had depths and reserves. Like some rare and gifted woman's most furtive looks, it seemed subtly to index and vouch for many old forces and causes, of slow growth and long operation—character, race, a culture carefully sheltered and long in the building. Besides, the brazen facetiousness had come out, as it were, in spite of some revolt in the speaker. And yet, as he gasped his 'Hullo!' she acted the courtesan with a will. She flashed her lamp on her own face, her hair, her bust, as if to say, 'There! See the goods, before buying.'

Gresson gasped again. The woman was a Juno; no, a Tragic Muse—tall, deep-bosomed, the regular features grave with a deep and ample expressiveness, the face of one of those most beautiful women who have achieved an intense absorption in some other thing than their own beauty. And she doing this!—she that, to see or to hear, made you feel how gloriously far a woman may be from a mere slave or a mere animal. There must be some enormous mistake somewhere, some sort of fantastic illusion. All the ardent, super-rational respect of clean-minded boys for womankind in the mass was tingling in the voice of Gresson when he made shift to answer politely, in his bad French, 'And you, Madame! Under enemy fire!'

'Enemy? German?' she asked.

He explained that the dry buzz which was then growing louder was more smoothly continuous than the hum of any British aeroplane. 'He's coming this way,' he said. 'Look!'

He pointed upwards at a white patch that had just broken out on the under-side of a cloud almost directly above them. At that place the fiery stares of two British ground searchlights had just rushed together. They had been searching the sky for the raider, each light working on its own, as two town policemen search a suspected backyard with their lanterns. Now one of them had found, and the other had instantly wheeled round to share in the find and to help keep the quarry in sight. Like a fly walking on a high ceiling, a black speck was scudding across the disk that the searchlights had painted in luminous fresco on the black dome of night. But the disk moved with the speck: wherever the speck went, its halo of brilliance was round it.

The girl gazed up eagerly. When she sighted the thing that was ranging the sky, with its glory all about it, she let out an 'Ah!' that made Gresson feel sure she was not funked at all, and yet that she was decidedly stirred.

'Like God!' she muttered. It made Gresson start. The words had an aptness, no doubt, to that enskyed engine of wrath, remote, alone, girdled with light, throbbing with power, like a Jehovah of old when he floated out on black wings over a culpable earth, with his bolt in his hand. But, Gosh! what a woman, to see it like that! French, and yet able to stand off and see a Boche bomber busy above her as anything but a foul vampire bat let out of Hell for an hour. Our Tommies might think in that detached way about enemies. But a civilian!—a woman!—a French one at that! She must be a genius.

While Gresson digested this latest course of the full meal of surprise that the evening had brought him, Jehovah let fly, to some purpose. When a bomb of some size falls anywhere near in the dark, it feels as if the big splash of flame from the burst were all round you. The sound, too, fills your whole world for a moment. Then there comes, just for a second, a quite remarkable silence, and then certain smaller noises consequent on the original smash, begin to rise clear of the silence. When Gresson's eyes and ears came to themselves, a large broken branch of a tree was settling down to the ground with a soft leafy crash of crushed boughs, some man up the street was screaming with pain, and the singular girl was a blob of black daubed anyhow on the blackish grey of the pavement. The metal of her little flash-lamp tinkled on the stone as it fell out of her slackening hand.

He grabbed the lamp and looked at her. She was alive: her eye flinched under the light. She had no obvious wound. But she had the look that Gresson, a youth now well versed in bloodshed, liked least of all the looks painted on faces and bodies by the queer artistry of scientific slaughter. It was the battered, bullied look of a mouse kicked to death in the dust. As often happened through the caprices of shell-fire, she was stripped half-naked; her hat, with its flowers, was tumbled and spoilt, the little gewgaws of her pitiful occupation were all disordered. What remained of her clothing was knocked about, dirtied and torn.

That grotesque and cruel disarraying moved the young expert in carnage more than he could have believed until he felt it. All thought of sex was gone in a moment. Now she was only a sort of poor human rag-doll that had been used as a football—that or a child caught and horribly mauled by some brute of a force while trundling her little soiled hoop through the mud. He laid her easy and straightened her dishevelled clothes as well as he could and then waited a minute, wondering whether a flake of the bomb had done her business for good, or only grazed and badly shocked her. In either case, what must he do? Get her to a hospital, he supposed. While he leant over her, thinking, she suddenly spoke, faintly but in the most earnest entreaty, as though she had detected his thought. 'Not to a hospital. No.'

'All right,' he assured her. 'Don't worry.'

She took a moment of rest and then said, in a voice that tried to be firm, 'Will you help me to rise?'

He tried, and she made a game effort. It was hopeless. One knee was clean out of action. When she attempted to use it her whole weight came upon him at once. 'Madame,' he urged, 'may I carry you to the hospital? It is two hundred yards only.'

She said, 'No, no, I beg you, for the love of God,' so piteously that he was silenced. 'You don't know,' she said in a passionate whisper, 'the way French hospital people would treat a—a woman like me.'

That brought him a new pang of compassion. He couldn't do what she dreaded so much. But, Lord! how his mess would guffaw, could they see him there now, stuck and perplexed, with the head and neck of a Midianitish tragedy queen sustained in his arms! 'But, Madame, what to do?' he said, in a voice almost as imploring as hers.

'You'll help me?—no?' she entreated, always in English. 'I live—oh; not very far off, with you helping me. I have a friend there—I'll be all right there if, with your infinite goodness——'

But no mere helping would do it. Shyly and carefully he lifted her up in his arms, said, 'You must tell me the way,' and so set off, he knew not whither, through the empty and echoing streets. She steered him up the Street of St Denis, along the Street of the Three Pebbles—the Regent Street or Broadway of Amiens—and down the smaller Street of the Three Naked Bodies without Heads to an unlighted house at its far end.

Not a soul did they meet on this picturesque progress except a corporal's party of English Military Police, out upon their everlasting quest of drunks and strays. As a matter of form, the corporal challenged the odd caravan. He was not scandalized seriously. Any natural gift for wonder with which a British soldier-policeman set out to scour the streets of Amiens in those days was much assisted to wear itself out. Even the sight of a second lieutenant bearing away a pallid Aspasia, with blood dripping from the long heels of her shoes, did not astonish. 'Pass, British officer, and all's correct' was the formula that the corporal used to disclaim further interest in the incident.

Gresson could have wished that the words described the case better. Correct! Why, not to speak of its more general lack of correctness, the girl had moved convulsively in his arms at the corporal's challenge; one of her hands had plunged somewhere into her dress and had not altogether come out again, but he could have sworn that between its half-hidden fingers he saw the shine of a silvery little pistol—the miniature kind that can give you an adequate dose, and yet have a remarkably small displacement of air in a pocket.

'I shouldn't bring that any further out if I were you,' Gresson had said at the moment—in his bad French, but in the fatherly tone that an old professional handler of arms of precision may permit himself in explaining the etiquette of their use to an inexperienced young woman. And she had taken it so—had left the firearm in its lair and had brought the hand out and shown him its palm, open and empty, and said, 'See! I am *sage*,' like a French child when it vows to be good. But why pistols at all?

And why the queer mode of their entry into the dark little house in the Street of the Three Naked Bodies? He was for ringing the bell, but she said, 'No. Please bring me near. I will knock,' and then she beat a curious little tattoo on the glass panel with a big ring that she wore. It was as if somebody had been standing just on the other side of the door, waiting in the dark for that tattoo, so immediately did a dim light appear within and the door open. Its opener was a staid woman of thirty or so, in the rig of a hospital nurse, who lost her composure at once, gave a cry of horror and flung herself on the patient with a wild outburst of sorrow and tenderness.

'She's hurt. Can't walk. A bomb, you know,' said Gresson, in his bad French. 'Permit me to carry her to her room.'

The nurse, gulping sobs and alternately charging ahead a few steps and looking anxiously back, gave him a lead up the stairs. Concerned as he still was, it was a relief to be out of the streets. Here would he see, at any rate, no British corporal. Sheltered from public derision, he could take notice of things. And what a house it was! Every lamp, every hanging, every fireplace and chair had the grim, cold, dully classical look common in French bourgeois interiors. He had been billeted in such houses. But the home of the stodgiest trader, the steeliest country attorney, had looked less drearily loyal to the conventions than this. And it an arbour for Venus, a Paphian bower! Why, it was enough to freeze a Bacchante.

These women, too! A dim lamp overhead will make almost any face appear grave, but neither of theirs needed that. They made him feel he had gained their goodwill, but also that there was something about them which he was utterly 'out of'—far outside it, and never to come any nearer, and yet unaccountably warmly regarded. Could that be common in women for whom the bedevilment of their womanhood had become a career? And how the damaged one had stuck the torments that his joggly walk must have inflicted! A Joan of Arc, begad!

He laid her reverentially down on her bed that the other showed him. Then he put on the right cheerful tone, as he thought, for the sick, and said farewell in his decentest French. 'Eh, bien, au revoir, Mesdames.'

With a most friendly earnestness the wounded woman said, 'No. Never. Never. If you should ever meet me again, by an accident, you are to think only this—that you are in danger, and go away very quickly, without looking or speaking. Please do not think me ungrateful. I was not unconscious, not for one little moment, tonight. I know all your courage and kindness and strength and your clean and delicate heart when I was abased. I only say "Never" because this is the one kind thing I can say without a disloyalty.'

She spoke with feeling, as if there were really some dreadful danger, as in the old romances, from which he was to be guarded. Well, he supposed that a 'woman of pleasure', with all that she knew, must want to warn any man, to whom she wished well—to warn him off her own world with its expense of spirit and its wastes of pain. He looked across at the older woman, as if in appeal against a judgement too drastic.

Between the two women there seemed to pass glances that questioned and answered, and then the elder one shook her head too, always with that blended expression of reticence and benevolence.

He couldn't help jibbing, at the last moment, against this decree of finality in his severance from an enigma so beautiful. 'Madame,' he said rather pleadingly, 'may I not have even a name to remember?'

She turned her dead-white face on the pillow and looked at his eager ingenuous one—the face of the English 'nice boy', at its nicest—with a sort of fierce kindness. 'Yes,' she said, 'Judith. Remember it carefully.'

She closed her eyes, and the other woman let him out of the house.

He went off straight to ring at the Hôtel du Rhin and get a bed. He felt, in a way, a little discomfited. Had he not gone forth, like others, to see life and have a good time, as they say? Had not the Medical Officer winked when he borrowed the horse? What would they say in the mess when he went back and avowed that he still had his ridiculous innocence? Wouldn't they laugh? And yet he was elated, too. He hadn't got what they thought so much of. But he had got what, somehow, was bigger. The skirts of something high and passionate had brushed him as it passed. In some indefinable way there was more in the world than before: life was a taller adventure.

II

An average, however accurately drawn, is only an average. It isn't a maximum. Not through any precaution of his, Gresson survived the next fortnight. He did well in a futile attack and under a smashing counter-attack. When the rags that were left of the Division were taken out of the line, he was the only officer left in his Company. So he was now the acting commander of all the thirty-seven NCOs and men that were left on their legs.

Through Albert and Amiens the dog-tired remnant trailed back at his heels to Ailly, on the Somme, to rest and re-fit, and one of its many long halts was made under the trees of the Boulevard du Mail at Amiens, a few minutes' walk from the Street of the Three Naked Bodies. Gresson's own legs felt like sackfuls of lead, but he plodded off to get a daylight glimpse of the casket containing the mystery. All its mystery was gone. A fly-blown 'House to Let' bill was stuck in a window: the shutters were closed.

So that was to be the absolute end of his one Arabian night's entertainment. He stumped back to the men who were lolling and chaffing under the dusty leaves, and in ten minutes more they tramped off for Picquigny and Ailly.

Gresson asked nothing more of God and the great and wise among men than that his acting command should be made substantive. But the ways of Higher Commands are not a subaltern's ways, nor are his wishes theirs. Just when the men were getting comfortably settled in and playing football rapturously in the August dust, orders came to Ailly from on high for Gresson to report at once to Colonel Mallom, of Intelligence, at GHQ.

He found this red-tabbed Colonel refreshingly unregimental. He talked to a fellow as if such things as ranks did not exist. So Gresson, he said—he seemed to know all about Gresson—had taken an engineering course at Charlottenburg, before 1914. Yes, a two-year course. Did Gresson know Germany well? Some bits of it—yes—Dusseldorf, Cologne, Bonn, Frankfort—most of the Rhineland. Did he speak German well? Even the humble-hearted Gresson couldn't deny it as flatly as he could deny any imputation of speaking good French. Hadn't he and his sister had a beloved Hanoverian governess all the days of their childhood? Anyhow, the Colonel cut out any modest shilly-shally by speaking himself, from that point onward, in German of a perfection that Gresson observed with respectful, though silent, astonishment. Gresson, in turn, seemed to make a handsome impression. 'Gad!' said the Colonel, reverting to English at last. 'Some linguist! *You* won't be a Second Loot long.'

'I'm in acting command of a Company, sir,' Gresson replied, with some pride.

'And that's a damn fine thing to be,' said Mallom cordially. 'I've tried it. I've tried only one thing that's finer. D'you guess what it is?'

'I don't, sir,' said Gresson. In fact he doubted whether the world contained such a jewel.

'It's a game,' said the Colonel, 'with much the same risk, only you take it alone, and you take it dead cold—no one within fifty miles who isn't an enemy.'

'I see it now, sir,' said Gresson.

'Of course it's a volunteer's job. I don't press you to go into Germany—don't even advise you. All I say is that, with your local knowledge and very exceptional German and—if you'll excuse me—your very ingenious mug, you might do Intelligence work of deuced high value. Feel like it?'

Gresson's heart was jumping with glee. Why, here he was, at the very heart of the rose, let into the last, inmost mystery and thrill of glorious war. 'Who wouldn't, sir?' he said.

III

In a snug country house in Artois a party of British officers seemed to be living a nice peaceful life of their own for a good part of the war. They did not dine out, but men from neighbouring messes would see two or three of them on the road and would think what an odd lot they were, and how fresh and unweathered the coveted ribbons that most of them wore, and what indoor people some of them looked, and how much time they all seemed to have on their hands for a walk or a ride. Some wag suggested that they had founded a sort of male convent, the latest wonder of the war, where all the official rewards of combatant valour were gained by an innocent life of fasting and prayer. Probably none of the neighbours noticed that now and then one of these persons of leisure would disappear for a few days, or a month, or altogether, nor knew that one of her hermits had just been listed in the *Gazette* as 'Missing': believed to have died in enemy hands.

In this shy place and in other purlieus of Intelligence the ingenious Gresson now went to school. He learnt the whole system and structure of espionage and of counter-espionage, its twin sister. He got up the 'Underground Railway'—the routes by which escaped British prisoners of war or hunted spies were guided, and passed on from guide to guide, till a 'ferry' across the enemy line had been reached and the final rush must be risked. He heard about the pigeon post and the little fire-balloons that sailed off eastward on west winds with a pigeon or two in the basket hanging below, and the little flame nicely adjusted to let the balloon down where friends would expect it, about the right distance behind the enemy's front. His mind came to see Germany and the occupied parts of Belgium and France as a map speckled thickly with infinitesimal spots of sound British red—eyes and ears of British Intelligence, noting each movement of German troops, guns, supplies, railway metal, and hospital outfit.

Those were the local agents, and now and then they had to be visited, as a merchant in New York or London visits his outlying agents in China or Africa, just to judge their efficiency and devotion, hearten them up, coach them in the latest modes of publicity, transport and salesmanship, and instil the inspiring faith that good work never passes unseen by the Olympian eyes of the firm and that shining guerdons await the virtuous. Oh! plenty to learn. And, presently, plenty to do, not obtrusively.

IV

He had become, in two years, a neat hand at the trick, and a Major with good marks to his name, when an airman still more boyish than himself put him down in the dusk of a winter evening on a great frozen field in the bend of the Rhine between Godorf and Cologne.

In the eye of reason such a descent was not possible. It was almost as if a German plane had set down passengers in Richmond Park. But some bluffs depend for success upon their very absurdity. They are too mad to be guarded against. Major Gresson's pink-faced pilot had plenty of time to bid the impudent farewell, 'So long, old son,' and then to rise cannily from the petrified mud and rough grass of the field, and to wind up his steep spiral staircase of air to the height he wanted, before every searchlight from Bonn to Cologne was groping for him all over the sky.

A German anti-aircraft gun on a fast motor lorry was on the spot in five minutes, eagerly guided for the last few hundred yards by a discharged Bavarian soldier, who had seen everything. 'A single seater, Sergeant. A small biplane,' he informed the NCO in charge of the gun. 'I think the swine had engine trouble. My God! if I'd had my old rifle! But ach! this for-ever-damned leg! I couldn't even get near him in time.'

The poor man did, indeed, walk very lame from the knee wound that had ended his soldiering days and sent him tramping the roads of the Rhineland in his old Army tunic and boots, with the interval filled by a pair of the reach-me-down trousers of peace. He also wore the Iron Cross and he made no secret of a pocketful of chits redounding enviably to his military honour. His face was young, fair and ingenious, but he took a good look at the red-worsted regimental number on the sergeant's shoulder-strap before he said much about his own regiment.

The little flutter was soon over. The sergeant presented the youthful veteran with a cigar and took himself off with his gun and its crew. Then the lame Bavarian hobbled off briskly along the high road running into the north, where a turbid red glow on the underside of a cloud marked the site of Cologne. The twilight was all but night now; a thin whistling wind stung the Bavarian's face; the black frost was hardening.

About every half mile the Bavarian stopped dead and listened carefully. Not a boot except his own was ringing on the road. After each time
that he thus made sure of being alone, he had much less of a limp, and
went much faster, till it was getting near time to listen again. When the
few bleared window-lights of the village of Roden came into sight he
limped very badly again.

That was a Tuesday evening. In the evening dusk of the following
Monday the super-boyish pilot, with nobody in the observer's seat, was
to turn off his engine, at some immense height in the sky and great distance away, and slope silently down to the very spot where he had made
his first landing. There, if still alive, a German ex-soldier was to be blowing his nose with a white hanky and whistling 'The Watch on the Rhine',
with some slight variations, but always fortissimo.

This, you perceive, was a thoroughly reasoned arrangement. Having
been caught asleep there, only six days before, the Germans were sure
to be on the watch at that point—so sure that it was also sure that no
British pilot would be such a fool as to take liberties there for a long time
to come. So sure of this were the Germans certain to be, that it was quite
a sound spec for the British Air Staff to assume that no place could be
safer for that boy to land on, next week. You see, we all grew into psy-
chologists during the war. We probed into layer below layer of our
enemy's thoughts, second thoughts, counter-thoughts, forethoughts and
afterthoughts. Sometimes we brought off grand strokes in this way. And
sometimes we didn't.

V

Gresson's long tour of calls on the agents was finished before noon on
the Sunday. He was enormously glad of it. Each call had been a separate
danger. For many spies are in the pay of both sides. It means double
money, and also protection behind either front and lots of news to be got
on each side and sold on the other. Their double game is often known
to one or both of their employers; but, even then, they may be thought
to be useful. Bits of false news may be deftly put in a double spy's way,
for him to snap up and convey to his second paymaster.

But even a double spy may have other and more intractable passions
to clash with his deep thirst for coin. He may really be backing one side:
he may secretly want it to win: and it *may* not be the right one. A spy
has been known to make a quite dramatic final break with one of his two
clients in business. The last time that one capital spy, as he had been
thought, was dropped behind the German front he took a shot with his

revolver at the English aeroplane that had just dropped him. Others 'declare to win', as we say on the turf, by denouncing a fellow-spy whom they meet in the country of their choice.

Gresson knew all this. And whatever people may say of the thrills and fine savours of peril, it was never with any flawless and whole-hearted enjoyment that he went into the house of some venal scrub who at any moment might throw up the window and yell for a policeman to lead Gresson off to the slaughter. Between each of these calls and the next he would rest from fear for a little and look into shop windows, or at the scenery, till he felt he could do with another dose of blue funk. By mid-day on Sunday he was as tired of the hard labour of holding down his apprehensions as you might be if you had been shaved thirty times in a week by a person who might or might not feel like cutting your throat—about even betting each way.

Now, Gresson, although he was getting on very well as a serpent—in a professional way and for the good of his country—was still a bit of a dove in some other ways. He was simple: he did not keep up with the more brisk-minded youth of his day; he was a poor hand at sneering; it never occurred to him that a thing must needs be wholly rubbish if other people had treasured it for a few hundred years. In fact he was unconventional, and he did and thought what he liked, without shouting about it. This careless disrespect for current fashion was privately carried so far that he went quite often to church, merely because he liked going. And, though he had no genius for prayer, as some people have, he had a private hobby of glowing, when he was in church, with intense and humble longings for things, of the more decent sort, that he specially valued or admired, and also of working up a fervent sort of gratefulness—to whom, he couldn't say—for everything that had lately gone well with him. So it occurred to him now that, having half a day free in Cologne, he would go to the afternoon service in the Cathedral.

He found an empty seat in the inner South aisle, near a pillar and slightly turned to the left, so that it gave him a view of all the huge nave. There was scarcely another man in the place. All the thousands of women who filled it were wearing dead black, and most of them the dress of widows—half a furlong of widows. Some of the faces were veiled and some not. Even of the veilless women many were soundlessly weeping: many other faces were marred with the salt scald of more secret tears.

The winter daylight was failing; the lamplight was meagre; opposite Gresson, in the North windows, the prelates and saints and heraldic blazonments were sinking into mere lustrous darkness. The dim religious light was its most sombre self: the Gothic forest gloom, the death of the short, bitter day, the shadows in the hearts of all these smitten women, the great cloud blackening over a falling nation—Gresson felt them all press in upon him together and quiet and soften him.

As the service went on, he insensibly gave himself up to it more and more wholly. He let it work upon him as it would. Soon he lost all consciousness of his disguise and his danger—indeed, of everything but the rite, the chanting, the figure implied and evoked by it all, the figure of youth and its gifts, even the gift of the clean soul's inner serenity, given up freely for love of something undeservedly beloved. Just to hold alive in his mind the idea of that was an ecstasy to be prolonged at the full height and heat of its joy by gazing intently at something, anything, the flame of a tall candle, the gleam of a lectern of brass. So he gazed level, along a row of the ranged faces, at a light burning beyond, till a trivial movement in front of him broke the precarious spell of this highly strung reverie. One of the faces had made a half-turn towards his own, as though the intensity of his gaze had emitted a jet of some sort that could brush past a cheek and be felt. A woman was gazing at him steadily with an air of utter astonishment.

He knew her at once. She wore widow's clothes: her features were thinner: some force would seem to have taken them when they were softer than now and moulded them into a fixed tragic mask: if all the lost hopes in the world had been shovelled into one grave, such a mask might have been put at its head. Yet he knew her at once. No other face, he was sure, could have had just that proud sculpturing of the brows and the chin, or the poised self-control of the lips and eyes that he had carried, in all their harlotry kit, through the streets of Amiens.

But she here! Why, of course—she, too, must be here as a spy. Not in the regular way, for she would have been on his list. Perhaps she was one of the fearful women of legend, queenly and monstrous Delilahs, the vessels of sadic vengeance that have delighted to turn an enemy's lusts into gins and knives to trap him and stab him. He fancied that France had given birth to such women before. The Medical Officer had told him so.

The service was ending, women rising wearily from their knees, shaking their skirts a little and streaming away. The chimera woman waited a little. Gresson waited too, till she gave him a look or gesture—he wasn't sure which, but he knew that he was being bidden to follow her out. As she moved towards the West door he fell in behind her.

Where a weak lamp burned under the porch she stopped, turned and said, 'So? It is you!' in the German that all must speak there.

'I trust you recovered,' he said, 'without very bad pain.'

'Pain!' she seemed to reject the idea that such pains could matter. She looked at his motley get-up as a disabled soldier, discharged, and wearing out bits of his old uniform. Her eyes softened a little. 'And so,' she said, 'all the time, you were one of us—and on duty, like me, in that horrible city—horrible!'

'Us!' His word was little more than a gasp—the escape that must come when the breath has been taken away by some smashing news or strange vision. 'May we walk on?' he said. 'There?' He pointed to the wide flagged space, east of the Domhof, where nobody used to walk then.

She nodded and walked on beside him. He used every second of silence to think the case out in his head and to plan an escape for himself. So that was what she had been—the seductress-spy of all ages—and he the British fool-officer who was to babble in her arms. She might have caught him too. Thank God for that bomb! But now she had him—caught, done for, the moment his German slipped up or he let out a fact that gave him away.

They had reached the big vacant flagged square when she asked abruptly, 'You knew what I was when you saved me? You knew I was dead if they once got me into a hospital, with the papers I had in my clothes?'

He didn't answer. He asked his own question. 'Papers, Madam? British papers? Army ones?'

'Of course. Every shred I had got on that journey in France.'

'From British officers? Whom you had——?' Imprudent but uncontrollable anger was flaming up in his mind. To think of poor devils, perhaps his own friends, under their sentence of death, trying to get their last gulp of pleasure out of this world, and then tricked by this dignified harlot into betraying the lives of their men! And yet it was part of his nature to pull in his tongue before it could say the most venomous word.

But she understood, partly. 'No,' she said. 'Yours was the first British uniform I had approached—in that way. That was the miracle. God put a German inside it, to guard me—a true German, pure-minded, brave. Yes, it was a miracle—I was like Abraham. I had risked what was most precious to me, and at the last moment my sacrifice had been spared me, and you were the last man, as well as the first, to whom I was to offer my body.'

Amazement was quenching his anger. It shouldn't have done so. It wasn't his job to be moved, or to admire. It wasn't the way to get home and bring the goods with him. And yet he was moved. There are times when you feel not to yield admiration, even to enemies, would be treason to all that is finest in life. He murmured, 'You offered that sacrifice!'

'What woman wouldn't—for Germany—if she knew all that I knew?' Her voice was not loud, but it had the brooding fervour that some women's have when they bend and doat in ecstasy over a child. They stopped short on the flags. 'Only listen!' she said, and he felt a detaining finger placed on his sleeve.

The unlighted streets had emptied. Silence was almost complete. Through it there rose to their ears the urgent whisper of a great river busy at its work, brushing a hundred piers and quays with the insistent swish of its voluminous stream. 'The Rhine!' As she breathed the word she seemed to cling to it and caress it, as if just to utter it were a key giving entrance to gardens of felicity. 'The Rhine and the vines and the forests and all the old, kind, simple life of brown, hard-working people in villages, and the songs and dear ways of our own.'

He muttered, 'How could you do it?' He had a sister who would have done much for England, but some things were almost unthinkable.

'See,' she said more quietly, as a friend reasons with a friend. 'My husband was killed in the month of our marriage. My two brothers were killed. I had no sister. My father and mother were dead. And we were losing the war, and my husband had said you could win any war if you only knew what your enemy had in his mind. And Judith had won a great war in that fearful way, and why shouldn't I? But, oh! the horror of it— yes, you're right, you understand—the thought of some foul lusting boar, half-drunk, with his slobbery tusks. And then the miracle came and you were courteous and noble and delicate in your heart and your hands. Do you know what I wished—in my mind, secretly, when I thought you were English, I wished, with all the strength of my heart—of course, it was only a wild, fantastical wish—that some day that one Englishman— only just he—might be in a danger as deadly as mine was, and I there to help him.'

'You *would* have helped him?'

'Yes.'

'Even if his were the very same danger as yours?'

'You mean, if he——?'

'Yes—if he were in Germany, doing what you did in France? If you met him here, now, skulking about in disguise, and you suddenly saw who it was?' Some thirty paces away, across the dark square, a sentry in front of a building paced up and down on his post, with a smart little stamp of a foot at each about turn. 'Would you call out to that sentry?' said Gresson.

He didn't know why he was putting it to the touch and taking her at her word. We don't know why we do many things that we do. Something other than reason, something below it, emits an imperious impulse that comes to the top like a bubble of air from the invisible bed of a pool. It must burst into action.

She saw in a moment what he was avowing. She stopped dead; she seemed to grow taller. He felt he had lost the great throw; he was done for—had tried to strike on something that might be responsible in her ferocious and generous mind, and had struck on the ferocity only. In the dark he could see her eyes burn at him like those of a beast crouching back in a cave. 'You dared!' she said, with an intense quiet fury. 'You dared to prostitute that uniform!—that Cross!'

The game was all but up. And one thing he could swear would not help him with her, and that was to whine. 'You dared worse, you brave woman,' he said. 'You were shameless.'

For a second or two she said nothing, under his taunt. She stood perfectly still. The queer clear calm which extreme danger brings to some men had come on him now. He wondered almost tranquilly—was anything within her mind struggling with anything else? Had he a single friend left in that redoubtable citadel?

When she did speak, it was low and resentfully. 'Why to God did you tell me?'

'God knows. *I* don't,' he said, quite sincerely. 'Perhaps because you had said things about yourself—frightfully intimate things. It feels better to give a bit back, in the confidence line, and not do all the taking. Sort of vanity, probably. Well, aren't you calling that sentry?' He asked almost sharply, prompted by some inarticulate guide like a wrestler's perception of when to shift his grip, or strain harder, or give for a moment.

She made some gesture—he couldn't see what it was: he guessed it to mean she put off, for a few minutes more, his sentence of death. Her voice, when it did come, was almost a wail. 'What possessed you to come? You!—a man, with clean fighting to do! A woman has nothing to use but cunning and sex. But a man! What need had *you* to turn spy? What devil possessed you?'

He did not weigh the words of his answer. A hare with the breath of a greyhound hot on her thighs does not weigh this and that. Some god gives her the tip when to double, and which way to go, and she does it. 'Listen again,' he said in his turn, and so pressingly that she too held her breath and the Rhine could again be heard whispering earnestly. 'Listen to it—you,' he said in a low voice as earnest as its. 'You think *I* have got nothing like that in my ears? I live in a house on the Thames, near a weir. When I was a boy I went off to sleep every night to the sound of the lasher—water tumbling about at the end of our garden—always the same and always changing, like somebody's voice. Well, that's *my* Rhine. That's the voice of *my* country, to *me*. It's what told me to put on this kit and come here. When I lie down in your prison tonight, I shall hear it until I'm asleep. I don't suppose all this is rational. Your Germany may be a much finer country than ours. It's love, though. Isn't that the thing to go by? Doesn't it make everything right that's done for it—even what you were going to do for it—even what I'm doing here?'

'Go quickly,' she said, 'before I remember my duty.'

He made out that she was extending a hand in farewell. He found it ungloved and kissed the back of it twice. 'You are even more splendid,' he said, before letting it go, 'than I thought you, that night in Amiens.'

'And you,' she said, 'have the great heart that I saw in you then.'

She hurried off towards the riverside quarter beyond the black bulk of the Cathedral, and Gresson hurried off, almost forgetting to limp, the opposite way, to hide in the thronged Hohe Strasse and make for the old Severin Gate in the South. Cologne was a sizeable city, but not big enough to hold that magnificent woman and him.

VI

As punctual as a constitutional King the plane glided silently down the long slant from the clouds to the field in the bend of the Rhine. 'Not nabbed, sir, yet?' the cheerful boy said airily, as Gresson scrambled in. 'Simple souls, these Germans.'

Gresson wasn't so sure. But there was no need to answer. The whirling blast from the propeller had begun to blow the hoar-frost off the turf under the plane. Nothing more could be said without effort, or easily heard, until the many-coloured lights of their home port came rushing forward and upward to bring the frozen traveller in.

The Pigeon Man

I

Flanders in '18, and March coming in like a lion. With a purr that, nearer the front, might have been confused with the thudding of distant drum-fire the icy rain beat against the panes. At the streaming window of a dingy bedroom of the Hôtel du Commerce a girl stood gazing listlessly into the street below. Outside, over the gleaming cobbles of the little Belgian town, the great grey lorries, splashed hood-high with Flanders mud, slith-ered along in an endless train, swerving from the road's greasy crown only to make way for the snorting Staff cars that, freighted with be-goggled officers in field-grey, from time to time came roaring down the street. In and out of the traffic, dispatch-riders on motorcycles whirled and rattled, staying their progress with trailing, gaitered leg to enquire the location of Operations or Intelligence offices of the Corps established there. In the hotel bedroom the crockery on the washstand jingled to the din of the street.

Without turning round from her observation post, the girl flung a ques-tion across her shoulder. She was tall, and the black frock she wore empha-sized her slimness. Her shining red hair, loosely coiled about her well-shaped head, was the only blur of positive colour among the neutral shades of the room.

'Am I to wait the convenience of the Corps Intelligence office all day?' she demanded sullenly.

At a table against the wall an officer in field-grey sat reading the *Kölnische Zeitung*. He did not lift his eyes from his newspaper at the girl's question.

'Such were Colonel von Trompeter's orders, *meine Gnädige*,' he retorted.

She stamped her foot and faced the speaker. 'This room stifles me, do you hear?' she exclaimed tensely. 'I don't mind the rain; I'm going out!'

'No!' said the officer.

'Do I understand that I'm a prisoner?'

The officer shrugged his shoulders as, stretching forth his arms, he folded back the paper. 'You're of the Service, Fräulein Sylvia,' he rejoined placidly. 'You've got to obey orders like the rest of us!'

'Agreed,' she cried. 'But they can trust me, can't they?'

The officer shrugged his shoulders again. 'Doubtless the Colonel had his reasons for not wishing civilians to roam about Corps Headquarters. . . .'

'Bah!' she broke in contemptuously. 'Do you think I'm blind? Do you really imagine, Captain Pracht, that I don't know'—she waved a slim hand towards the window and the sounding street beyond—'what all this movement means? Every railhead from the North Sea to the Vosges is pouring forth men and guns; your troops released by the Russian Revolution are gathering to deal the Allies the final——'

Pracht sprang to his feet. '*Um Gottes Willen*, mind what you're saying! You speak of things that are known to but a handful of us——'

'Quite so, my friend. But will you please remember that I am of that handful? My sources in Brussels are excellent——' She broke off and contemplated her companion's face. 'Why has Colonel von Trompeter sent for me?'

'There I can answer you quite frankly,' said the Captain. 'I don't know.'

'And if you did, you wouldn't tell me?'

The officer bowed. 'It would be hard to refuse so charming a lady anything. . . .'

She shook herself impatiently. 'Words, merely words!' she cried.

She let her eyes rest meltingly on his face. They were strange eyes, madder-brown under dark lashes. 'Have you ever been in love, Captain Pracht?'

The officer's face set doggedly, so that two small vertical lines appeared on either side of his thin lips under the clipped brown moustache. 'Never on duty, *gnädiges Fräulein*—that is'—he paused, then added—'unless commanded.'

'Why, then,' she put in merrily, 'I might have spared myself the trouble of locking my door last night.'

Captain Pracht flushed darkly, and a little pulse began to beat at his temple.

She looked at him fixedly and laughed. 'You have a charming *métier*, Herr Hauptmann!'

An ugly look crept into his face. 'The same as yours, *meine Gnädige*!'

A patch of colour crept into her pale cheeks. 'Not quite!' Her voice vibrated a little. 'Men know how to protect themselves. They go into these things with their eyes open. But almost every woman, even in the Secret Service, is blinded by love . . . once. . . .' She sighed and added: 'The first time. . . .'

'The gracious lady speaks from personal experience, no doubt,' the officer hazarded. His manner was unpleasant.

With calm disdain she looked him up and down. 'Yes,' she answered simply.

'I have always said,' the Captain announced ponderously, 'that women were too emotional for Secret Service work. Especially foreigners.'

'Romanians, for instance?' suggested the girl sweetly.

'I was not speaking personally,' retorted the officer huffily. 'If we must have women spies, then why not Germans? Our German women have an ingrained sense of discipline, a respect for orders. . . .'

The girl's gurgling laugh pealed through the room. 'But their taste in nighties is dreadful,' she broke in. 'You must remember, my dear Captain Pracht, that our battlefield is the boudoir——'

At that moment the door was flung back. An orderly, in a streaming cape stood there. 'Colonel von Trompeter's compliments,' he bawled out of a wooden face, saluting with a stamp that shook the floor, 'and will the Herr Hauptmann bring Fräulein Averescu to the office immediately.'

II

'The trouble about this job of ours, young Horst,' said Colonel von Trompeter, 'is to recognize the truth when you find it!'

A heavy man, the Herr Oberst, but handsome still with his fearless eyes of the brightest blue, straight nose, and trim white moustache. The blue and silver Hussar cap which, in defiance of all clothing regulations, he insisted on wearing with his Staff uniform, was the only evidence that he had started his army career in the light cavalry, for advancing years had endowed him with the body of a heavy dragoon. His big form, muscular yet under its swelling curves, was moulded in his well-fitting service dress of grey, frogged with the brandenburgs of the Hussars, and the broad pink stripe of the Great General Staff, together with the glossy brown field-boot into which it disappeared, set off admirably his length of leg.

A fine blade, the Herr Oberst, with a naturally intuitive mind sharpened by the intensive training of War School and Great General Staff, a gift of lightning decision and a notable aptitude for languages. But, more than this, he was a man of rugged character, of unflinching moral courage, and as such ranged head and shoulders above the swarm of silver-laced sycophants at Headquarters who assiduously lick-spittled to His Excellency Lieutenant-General Baron Hasse von dem Hasenberg, the Corps Commander. For His Excellency, a choleric old party with the brains of a louse and the self-control of a gorilla, was His Majesty's friend who with supple spine had genuflected his way up the rough road of promotion under the approving eye of the All-Highest War Lord.

His Excellency detested his Chief of Intelligence. He might have forgiven Colonel von Trompeter his outstanding ability, for brains are an asset on the staff of a Corps Commander when awkward incidents have to be covered up; and Baron Hasse had not been a lucky leader. But His Excellency was enraged by the Colonel's habit of invariably speaking his mind. It infuriated him that Colonel von Trompeter should have made his career in spite of his brutal candour. When only a Major, acting as assistant umpire at Kaiser manœuvres, had he not curtly replied to the Emperor himself, enthusiastically seeking praise for a cavalry charge led in the All-Highest Person against a nest of machine-guns: 'All dead to the last horse, your Majesty!' and been promptly exiled to an East Prussian frontier garrison for his pains?

Yet, although the victim of the All-Highest displeasure had lived the incident down, he had learned nothing by experience. To the Corps Commander's resentful fury, he flatly refused to curry favour with his immediate chief by lending himself to the great conspiracy of eyewash by means of which, in war as in peace, the War Lord was justified of his appointments to the high commands.

And so a state of open warfare existed between His Excellency—and that signified the bulk of the Headquarters Staff—and his Chief of Intelligence. Only the Intelligence Staff, who worshipped Trompeter to a man, less for his brilliant ability than for his sturdy championship of his subordinates even in the face of the epileptic ravings of His Excellency, stood by their chief. For the rest, every imaginable form of chicane and sabotage was employed in the attempt to drive Colonel von Trompeter into seeking a transfer. In almost every branch of Corps Headquarters, save only the Intelligence, it became as important to defeat Colonel von Trompeter and his assistants as to beat the English who held the line in this part of Flanders. And His Excellency proclaimed at least thrice a day to all who would hear him that Trompeter was '*ein taktloser Kerl*'.

When, therefore, on this wet March morning, 'the old man', as his staff called Trompeter, delivered himself of the apothegm set forth above, Lieutenant Horst, his youngest officer, who was examining a sheaf of aeroplane photographs at his desk in a corner of the office, glanced up with troubled eyes. It was rare, indeed, that 'the old man' allowed the daily dose of pinpricks to get under his skin. But today the Chief was restless. Ever since breakfast he had been pacing like a caged lion up and down the wet track left by the boots of visitors on the strip of matting between the door and his desk.

'Operations are making trouble about the shelling of the 176th divisional area last night,' the Colonel continued.

'With permission, Herr Oberst,' Horst put in diffidently, 'these fresh troops carry on as though they were still in Russia. Their march discipline is deplorable. They were probably spotted by aircraft——'

The Herr Oberst shook his grizzled poll. 'Won't wash, my boy. They went in after dark. *That* explanation we put up to Operations when the 58th Division had their dumps shelled last week. Operations won't swallow it again. Humph——'

He grunted and turned to stare out into the rain. A battalion was passing up the street, rank on rank of soaked and weary men. Their feet hammered out a melancholy tattoo on the cobbles. There was no brave blare of music to help them on their way. The band marched in front with instruments wrapped up against the wet. 'Fed—up', 'Fed—up', the crunching feet seemed to say.

The Colonel's voice suddenly cut across the rhythmic tramping. 'What time is Ehrhardt arriving with that prisoner from the 91st Division?' he asked.

'He was ordered for eleven, Herr Oberst!'

'It's after that now——'

'The roads are terribly congested, Herr Oberst!'

The Colonel made no reply. His fingers drummed on the window-pane. Then he said: 'Our English cousins are concentrating on the Corps area, young Horst. They've got a pigeon man out. That much was clear when that basket of pigeons was picked up in Fleury Wood last week.'

'A pigeon man, Herr Oberst?'

'I was forgetting; you're new to the game. So you don't know what a pigeon man is, young Horst?'

'No, Herr Oberst!'

'Then let me tell you something: if you ever meet a pigeon man, you can safely take your hat off to him, for you're meeting a hero. It's a job that means almost certain death. A pigeon man is a Secret Service officer who's landed by an aeroplane at some quiet spot in the enemy lines with a supply of carrier-pigeons. His job is to collect the reports which spies have already left for him at agreed hiding-places. He fastens these messages to the legs of his birds and releases them to fly back to their loft. . . .'

'Does the aeroplane wait, Herr Oberst?'

The Colonel laughed shortly. '*I wo!* The pigeon man has to make his way home the best he can. They usually head for the Dutch frontier. . . .'

'He's in plain clothes, then?'

'Of course. That's why I say the job means almost certain death. Even we Huns, as they call us, are justified in shooting an officer caught in plain clothes behind our lines.'

The young man pursed up his lips in a silent whistle. 'Brave fellows! Do we send out pigeon men, too, Herr Oberst?'

His Chief shook his head. 'They wouldn't stand an earthly. The pigeon man can operate successfully only among a friendly civilian population ——Well?'

An orderly had bounced into the office, and, stiff as a ramrod, now fronted the Colonel. 'Hauptmann Ehrhardt is here to report to the Herr Oberst.'

The clear blue eyes snapped into alertness. 'Has he brought a prisoner with him, Reinhold?'

'*Jawohl*, Herr Oberst.'

'Send him in! Prisoner and escort remain outside.' He turned to Horst as the orderly withdrew. 'Herr Leutnant, a certain lady is waiting at the Hôtel du Commerce in charge of Captain Pracht, of the Brussels command. I may ask you to send for her presently. You will not say anything to her about this prisoner, and you will be responsible to me that no one approaches him in the meantime. And see that I'm not disturbed.'

Then with bowed head the Colonel resumed his pacing up and down.

III

'As the Herr Oberst will see for himself,' said Ehrhardt, rocking slightly as he stood stiffly at attention before his chief—he was a secondary-school teacher in civil life and the military still overawed him—'the prisoner is practically a half-wit. If you speak to him, he only grins idiotically and dribbles. He looks half-starved, and as for his body—well, with respect, he's fairly crawling. God knows how long he's been wandering about the Bois des Corbeaux, where the fatigue party ran across him in the early hours of this morning. According to the Herr Oberst's orders, I had advised all units that any civilian caught in our lines was to be brought straightway to me at the Divisional Intelligence office. When this man was sent in, I rang the Herr Oberst up at once. I haven't overlooked the possibility that the fellow may be acting a part; but I'm bound to say that he seems to me to be what he looks like—a half-witted Flemish peasant. Speaking ethnologically——'

A brusque gesture cut short the imminent deadly treatise on the psychology of the Flemings. The Colonel pointed to a chair beside the desk and pushed across a box of cigars.

'Ehrhardt,' said he, 'information of the most exact description is being sent back regularly. Our troop movements are known. The 176th Division had two hundred casualties getting into their billeting area last night. These are no haphazard notes of regimental numbers jotted down at railway stations, or of movements of isolated units strung together by ignorant peasants. They are accurate reports prepared with intelligence by someone with a thorough grasp of the military situation. The English have a star man operating on this front. Who he is or what he looks like we don't know; but what we do know is that correspondence of a very secret nature which fell into the hands of one of our agents at The Hague speaks with enthusiasm of the accuracy of the reports sent by an unnamed agent concerning our present troop movements in Belgium. You are aware of my belief that an English pigeon man has been at work here'—he bent his white-tufted brows at his companion, who was gazing intently at him through gold-rimmed spectacles. 'Supposing our friend outside is the man I'm looking for. . . .'

Very positively Captain Ehrhardt shook his head. 'Of course,' he said in his pedantic fashion, 'I must bow to the Herr Oberst's experience in these matters. But for me the hypothesis is out of the question. This fellow may be a spy; but in that case he's an agent of the lowest order, a brutish Belgian peasant—not a man of the calibre you mention, an educated individual, possibly a regular officer.'

'Certainly a regular officer,' the Colonel's calm voice broke in.

'*Ausgeschlossen*, Herr Oberst! The thing's impossible, as you'll realize the moment you see him!'

'Wait, my friend! The English have an extraordinary fellow, with whom we of the Great General Staff are well acquainted, at least by repute from pre-war days. We never managed to ascertain his name or get his photograph; but we know him for a man who is a marvellous linguist, with a most amazing knowledge of the Continent and Continental peoples. Dialect is one of his specialities. What is more to the point, he is a magnificent actor, and his skill in disguises is legendary. Again and again we were within an ace of catching him, but he always contrived to slip through our fingers. We used to call him *N*, the unknown quantity. Do you see what I'm driving at?'

'*Gewiss, gewiss,* Herr Oberst!' Ehrhardt wagged his head dubiously. 'But this lout is no English officer.'

'Well,' said the Colonel, 'let's look at him, anyway.' He pressed a button on the desk, and presently, between two stolid figures in field-grey, a woebegone and miserable looking tramp shambled in.

His clothes were a mass of rags. On his head a torn and shapeless cloth cap was stuck askew, and from beneath its tattered peak a pair of hot, dark eyes stared stupidly out of a face that was clotted with grime and darkened, as to the lower part, with a stiff growth of beard. A straggling moustache trembled above a pendulous underlip that gleamed redly through bubbles that frothed at the mouth and dripped down the chin. His skin glinted yellowly through great rents in jacket and trousers, and his bare feet were thrust into clumsy, broken boots, one of which was swathed round with a piece of filthy rag. As he stood framed between the fixed bayonets of the escort, long shudders shook him continually.

Without looking up, the Colonel scribbled something on a writing-pad, tore off the slip and gave it to Horst. 'Let the escort remain outside,' he ordered. Horst and the guards clumped out. Then only did Trompeter, screwing his monocle in his eye, favour the prisoner with a long and challenging stare. The man did not budge. He continued to gaze into space, with his head rocking slightly to and fro and the saliva running down his chin.

The Colonel spoke in an aside to Ehrhardt. 'You say you found nothing on him when you searched him?'

'Only a clasp-knife, some horse-chestnuts, and a piece of string, Herr Oberst.'

'No papers?'

'No, Herr Oberst.'

The Colonel addressed the prisoner in French. 'Who are you and where do you come from?' he demanded.

Very slowly the man turned his vacuous gaze towards the speaker. He smiled feebly and dribbled, but did not speak.

'It struck me that he might be dumb,' Ehrhardt whispered across the desk, 'although he seems to hear all right.'

'Wait!' Trompeter bade him. He spoke to the prisoner again. 'Any civilian found wandering in the military zone without proper papers is liable to be shot,' he said sternly. 'Do you realize that?'

The tramp grinned feebly and made a gurgling noise like an infant. The Colonel repeated his warning in Flemish.

'Grr . . . goo . . . grr!' gibbered the prisoner.

Trompeter went round the desk and looked the man in the eye. 'See his hands, Herr Oberst,' said Ehrhardt in an undertone. The tramp's hands were coarse and horny, with blackened and broken nails. 'Are those the hands of an officer?'

The Colonel grunted, but made no other comment.

There was a smart rap at the door. Reinhold, the orderly, appeared with a tray. On it were set out a pot of coffee, a jug of milk, sugar, a plate of ham, and a hunk of greyish war bread. The Colonel signed to the man to put the tray down on a side table. Then he turned to the prisoner. 'Eat!' he bade him.

The idiot grinned broadly and broke into a cackling laugh. Then, while the two officers watched him from a distance, he fell upon the victuals. It was horrible to see him wolf the food. He tore the ham with his hands and thrust great fragments into his mouth; he literally buried his face in the bread, wrenching off great lumps with his teeth; he emptied the milk-pot at a draught, spilling a good deal of the milk down his jacket in the process. He made animal noises as he ate and drank, stuffing himself until he gasped for breath.

'Could an officer eat like that?' Ehrhardt whispered in his chief's ear. But again the Colonel proffered no remark.

When the last of the food had disappeared he said to his subordinate: 'Take the prisoner outside now, and when I ring three times send him in—alone. Alone, do you understand?'

'*Zu Befehl*, Herr Oberst!'

Left alone, Colonel von Trompeter strode across to the window and stood for an instant looking out. In the street a gang of British prisoners of war, their threadbare khaki sodden with the rain, scraped away at the mud with broom and spade. A voice at the door brought the Colonel about. Horst was there.

'Herr Oberst, the lady has arrived!'

'She's not seen the prisoner, I trust?'

'No, Herr Oberst. I put her to wait in the orderlies' room.'

Trompeter nodded approval. 'Good. I'll see her at once . . . alone.'

As Horst went away, he moved to the desk and turned the chair which Ehrhardt had vacated so that it faced the door. He himself remained standing, his hands resting on the desk at his back. With his long fingers he made sure that the bell-push in its wooden bulb was within his reach.

IV

It was commonly said of Colonel von Trompeter that he had a card-index mind. He forgot no name, no face, no date, that came into his day's work, and he had an uncanny facility at need of opening, as it were, a drawer in his brain and drawing forth a file of data.

As he helped Sylvia Averescu out of her wrap and invited her to be seated, he was mentally glancing over her record. Nineteen hundred and twelve it had been when Steuben had bought her away from the Russians at Bucharest and installed her at Brussels, that clearing-house of international espionage. For a woman, the Colonel condescendingly reflected, she had proved her worth. That affair of the signalling-book of HMS *Queen* had been her doing; and it was she who had laid the information which had led to the arrest of the English spy, Barton, at Wilhelmshaven.

'Madame,' was Trompeter's opening when he had given her a cigarette, 'I have ventured to bring you out from Brussels in this terrible weather because I need your help.'

Sylvia Averescu looked at him coldly. Her wait in a freezing cubby-hole full of damp and strongly flavoured orderlies had not improved her temper. She had entered the room resolved to give this Colonel von Trompeter a piece of her mind. Yet, somehow, his personality cowed her. Against her will she was favourably impressed by his direct gaze, good looks, and charming manners. She saw at once that he was a regular officer of the old school, a man of breeding, not a commercial traveller stuffed into uniform, like Pracht. She was flattered by the way he handed her to a chair and assisted her out of her furs as though she were a Duchess. And the Latin in her, which had always squirmed at the 'Frau' and 'Fräulein' of her German associates, was grateful for 'Madame' as a form of address.

Still, the recollection of that icy vigil yet grated on her, and she replied rather tartly: 'I don't know in what way I can be of any assistance to you, Herr Oberst.'

The Colonel's blue eyes rested for an instant on her handsome, rather discontented face. Then, brushing the ash from the end of his cigarette, he said: 'When you were in Brussels before the War, you knew the British Secret Service people pretty well, I believe?'

She shrugged her shoulders. 'It was what I was paid for.'

'You were acquainted with some of their principal agents, I take it: the star turns, I mean—men like Francise Okewood or Philip Brewster, or'—he paused—'even our friend *N*, the mysterious Unknown Quantity?'

She laughed on a hard note. 'If you'll tell me who *N* was—or is,' she returned, 'I'll tell you if I knew him. I've met the other two you mentioned.' She leaned back in her chair and blew out luxuriously a cloud of smoke. '"The Unknown Quantity," eh? What a dance he led you, Colonel! I've often wondered which of the boys he was.'

The Colonel's hand groped behind him until he found the bell. Thrice his thumb pushed the button. His eyes were on the woman as she reclined gracefully in her chair staring musingly at the ceiling. His watchful gaze did not quit her face even when the door was suddenly thrust open and a tatterdemalion figure hobbled into the room.

Trompeter, his face a mask of steel, saw how, at the sound of the door closing, the woman at his side looked up—saw, too, the little furrow of perplexity that suddenly appeared between her narrow, arching eyebrows. But the swift, suspicious glance she shot at her companion found him apparently intent on studying the end of his cigarette, yet even as her gaze switched back to the outcast, cowering in forlorn abandonment in the centre of the floor, the Colonel's bright blue eyes were quick to note the expression of horror-struck amazement which for one fleeting instant flickered across her regular features.

But the next moment she was bored and listless as before. So swift was her reaction that it was as though her face had never lost its wonted air of rather sulky indifference. She darted an amused glance at the impassive visage gazing down upon her and laughed.

'You have some queer visitors, Herr Oberst,' she said. 'Tell me'—she indicated the tramp with a comic movement of the head—'is he one of us?'

'No,' replied Trompeter, with quiet emphasis.

'Then who is he?'

'I was hoping you would be able to tell me that.'

She stared at him for a moment, then suddenly broke into a peal of merry laughter.

'Oh, my dear Colonel,' she exclaimed, 'you do their ingenuity too much honour.'

'And yet,' observed Trompeter quietly, 'he's one of their star men.' His eyes were on the prisoner as he spoke. But the tramp, leering idiotically, stared into space and dribbled feebly.

Sylvia Averescu laughed incredulously. 'Then they've changed their methods. All the British Secret Service aces I've known were serving officers, or ex-officers. You're not going to claim that this miserable creature is an English gentleman, Colonel. Why, his hands alone give you the lie!'

'Specially roughened for the job!'

'What job?'

But the Colonel left the question unanswered. 'The English are devil-ish thorough,' he added. 'I'll grant them that!'

The woman left her chair and went boldly up to the idiot. With a pointing finger she indicated a *V* of yellow skin that appeared below his uncollared neck between the lapels of his jacket.

'Look,' she vociferated in disgust, 'the man's filthy. He hasn't had a bath for years!' She turned about to face Trompeter, who had followed her. 'If this man is what you say, he would have a white skin, a properly tended body, under his rags. But this creature is disgusting!'

Trompeter stepped swiftly up to the prisoner and with brutal hands ripped the ragged jacket apart. The man wore no shirt; his coat was but-toned across his naked body. The Colonel recoiled a pace and clapped his handkerchief to his nose. '*Bfui Deibel!*' he muttered.

Something had rattled smartly on the floor. Trompeter stooped quickly with groping fingers; then, drawing himself erect, stared fixedly at the prisoner. The outside pocket of the idiot's jacket had been almost ripped away in the vigour of the Colonel's action and hung lamentably down. Trompeter's hand darted into the torn pocket and explored the lining. His fingers dredged up some tiny invisible thing which he transferred to the palm of his other hand.

With an air of triumph he swung round to the woman. 'Well,' he remarked roughly, 'he's for it, anyway. If he were a friend of yours, I should tell you to kiss him goodbye.'

At that she faltered ever so slightly. 'What do you mean?' Her voice was rather hoarse.

'What I mean,' Trompeter gave her back brutally, 'is that he's the pigeon man we've been looking for. He'll go before the court in the morning, and by noon he'll be snugly under the sod!'

So saying, he unfolded his clenched hand and thrust it close under her face. Two little shining yellow grains reposed in the open palm. 'Maize,' he announced grimly. 'Food for the birds. Pigeon men always carry it.'

With that he shut his hand and joined it to its fellow behind his back, while he dropped his square chin on his breast and sternly surveyed her.

'And do you mean to say,' she questioned unsteadily, 'that the milit-ary court would send him to his death on no other evidence than that?'

'Certainly. There was an identical case last month. Two English flying officers. They shot them in the riding school at Charleroi. Game lads they were, too!'

'But this poor devil may have picked up some maize somewhere and kept it for food. He looks half starved, anyway.'

Trompeter shrugged his shoulders. 'That's his look-out. We're not taking any chances on pigeon men. They're too dangerous, my dear. Not that I want the poor devil shot. I'd rather have him identified.'

The woman raised her head and gazed curiously at the Colonel. 'Why?' she asked, almost in a whisper.

Trompeter drew her to the window, out of earshot of the prisoner. Outside, the whole town seemed to reverberate to the passage of heavy guns, monsters, snouting under their tarpaulins, that thundered by in the wake of their tractors.

'Because,' he said in an undertone, 'I can use him to mislead the enemy. Our dear English cousins shall get their pigeon service all right, but after this the birds will carry my reports instead of our friend's. For this I must have the fellow's name.' He paused and bent his bushy eyebrows at her. 'You know this man?'

'Wait,' she bade him, rather breathless. 'Let us get this clear. If this man were identified, you would spare his life?'

The Colonel nodded curtly. His eyes never left her face.

'What guarantee have I that you will keep your word?'

'I shall hand over to you the only evidence there is against him.'

'You mean the maize?'

'Yes.'

She cast a timorous glance across the room to where the prisoner was standing, his head lolling on his shoulder. He had not changed his position. His eyes were half closed and his tongue hung out under the ragged moustache. The reek of him was pungent in the room.

Silently she held out her hand to Trompeter. Without hesitation he dropped the two grains of maize into the slender palm. She ran to the stove and dropped them in. Impassively the Colonel watched her from the window. The maps on the walls trembled in the din of gun-wheels in the street.

Slowly the woman returned to the Colonel's side. He noticed how pale her face appeared against the flame of her hair. She looked at him intently, then said, in a sort of breathless whisper: 'You're right, I know him.'

A steely light glittered in the quick blue eyes. 'Ah! Who is it?'

'Dunlop. Captain Dunlop.'

Trompeter leaned forward swiftly. 'Not "The Unknown Quantity"?'

She made a little movement of the shoulders. 'I can't tell you. He never attempted to disguise himself with me.'

'Did you meet him in Brussels?'

She nodded. 'He used to come over from London almost every week-end. . . .'

The Colonel grunted assent. 'Yes, that was the way they did it before the War.' He flashed her a scrutinizing glance. 'Did you know him well? You're sure you're not making a mistake?'

She shook her head, and there was something wistful in the gesture. 'He was my lover. . . .'

Trompeter smiled broadly. 'Ah,' he murmured, 'Steuben always managed that sort of thing so cleverly. . . .'

'Steuben had nothing to do with it,' came back her hot whisper. 'No one knew him for a secret agent—at least, not until I found him out. He told me he was an English engineer who came to Brussels on business; I was jealous of him, and one day I discovered he was visiting another woman, a Belgian. Then—then I followed things up and found out the rest. He was frank enough when I confronted him—the English are, you know. He told me he had only been carrying out his orders. And I'—she faltered—'I was part of those orders, too. . . .'

She clenched her hands tensely, and turned to stare forlornly out at the rain.

'You were fond of him, Madame?'

'My feelings have nothing to do with the business between you and me, Colonel,' she told him glacially over her shoulder.

He bowed. 'I beg your pardon. And you have told me all you know. What is his full name?'

'James, I think. I called him Jimmy.'

'How did he sign his reports? Can you tell me that?'

She nodded. ' "J. Dunlop",' she answered.

'How do you know this?'

'Because I made it my business to find out . . . afterwards!' she answered passionately, and was silent.

'And he is a regular officer?'

'Of the Royal Engineers.' She turned to the Colonel. 'And now, if you don't mind, I should like to go back to my hotel. I—I don't feel very well. I expect I must have caught a chill. This awful weather. . . .'

The Colonel rang. 'I'll send for Captain Pracht——'

Like a fury she rounded on him. 'For the love of God!' she burst forth, 'am I never to be left alone again? Can't I go back to the hotel by myself?'

Trompeter bowed. 'Certainly, if you promise to go straight there. It's in your own interest I say it. The PM is very strict about civilians just now.'

'I'll go straight back,' she retorted impatiently. 'And you'll keep to our bargain, Colonel?'

The officer inclined his head.

'What—what will you do with *him*?' she asked, rather unsteadily.

'Oh, prisoners of war camp, I suppose,' was the brisk answer.

She said no more, but moved slowly towards the door. There she paused and let her eyes rest for an instant on the scarecrow shape that mowed and gibbered between them. The Colonel saw her put forth one little hand towards the pigeon man and stand thus as though she hoped that he might turn and greet her. But the tramp with his melancholy imbecile stare paid no heed. She seemed to droop as she turned and passed out.

Then Trompeter went up to the prisoner and clapped him encouragingly on the shoulder. 'It's a wonderful disguise, Dunlop,' he said pleasantly and in flawless English, 'and I don't mind telling you that you nearly took me in. But the game's up, my friend! You're spotted. Let's have a friendly talk. I don't expect you to give anything away, but I'm anxious for news of Colonel Ross, my esteemed opposite number on the other side of no-man's-land. I heard he'd been down with this damnable *grippe*. . . .'

'Goo . . . !' mumbled the tramp, and the bubbles frothed at his mouth. The telephone on the desk rang. The Colonel left the prisoner to answer it. A well-bred voice said: 'His Excellency desires to speak with Colonel von Trompeter.' The next instant a high-pitched, furious voice came ringing over the wire.

'Is that Trompeter? So, Herr Oberst, a new division can't come into the Corps area without being shelled to ribbons! What the devil are your people doing? What's that you say? You're investigating. Investigating be damned! I want action—action, do you understand? The whole Corps knows that there's a spy in the area sending information back, and when I ask you what you propose to do about it, you tell me you're investigating! *Verdammt nochmal!* What I expect you to do is to catch the lousy fellow and shoot him, and, by God, if you don't, I'll have the collar off your back, and don't you forget it! *Himmelkreuzsakrament!* I'll show you who's in command here, you and your investigation! You'll report to me in person at six o'clock this afternoon, and I shall expect to hear then that you've laid hands on this spy. If you fail me this time, Herr Oberst, I give you fair warning that I'll get somebody I can rely upon to carry out my wishes. And you are to understand that the General is extremely dissatisfied with you. Is that clear?'

'*Zu Befehl, Exzellenz!*' replied the Colonel stiffly, and hung up the receiver. He lit a cigarette and sat at the desk for a full minute, contemplating through a swathe of blue smoke the wretched-looking outcast before him.

'Sorry, Dunlop,' he said at last. 'I'd have saved you if I could, but charity begins at home. My General demands a victim, and my head is the price. I'm a poor man, my friend, with no private means and a family to support. I've got powerful enemies, and if I lose this job my career's over. As God is my judge, Dunlop, I can't afford to keep my pledged word.' He paused and pressed his handkerchief to his lips. 'If there's anything I can do about letting your people know . . .'

He broke off expectantly, but the pigeon man made no sign. With his head cocked in the air his whole attention appeared to be directed to a fly buzzing round the wire of the electric light.

'You'll at least give me the honour,' Trompeter went on rather tremulously, 'of shaking hands with a brave man?'

But the pigeon man did not even look at him. His grimy right hand stole furtively under his tattered jacket and he writhed beneath his verminous rags. His gaze remained immutably distant, as though he were peering down some long vista. Slowly the grizzled head at the desk drooped and there was a moment's pregnant hush in the room.

Then the Colonel stood up, a stalwart figure, and moved resolutely to a press in the wall. He opened the door and disclosed, neatly hung on pegs, his steel helmet, revolver, thermos flask, map-case and saddle-bags. He unstrapped one of the saddle-bags, and, dipping in his hand, brought away in his fingers a few shining orange grains. Then he rang and told the orderly to send in Captain Ehrhardt. The officer recoiled at the grim severity of his chief's expression.

'*Also*, Herr Hauptmann,' was the Colonel's greeting, 'you searched the prisoner, did you?'

'*Jawohl*, Herr Oberst!' said Ehrhardt, in a quaking voice.

'And found nothing, I think you told me?'

'Nothing—that is, except the articles I enumerated, Herr Oberst, namely——'

The stern voice interrupted him. 'Would it surprise you to learn that I discovered maize in the prisoner's pocket when I searched him? See!' The Colonel's hand opened and spilled a few grains of maize on the blotter. 'It appears to me, Herr Hauptmann, that you have grossly neglected your duty. You've got to wake yourself up, or one of these mornings you'll find yourself back in the trenches with your regiment. Now pay attention to me! The prisoner goes before the tribunal tomorrow. You will have him washed and disinfected and issued with clean clothes immediately, and hand him over to the Provost Marshal. Horst will warn the PM. The prisoner can have anything he likes in the way of food or drink or smokes. Your evidence will be required at the trial, so you'll have to stay the night. See Horst about a bed. March the prisoner out!'

The door shut and the escort's ringing tramp died away. Grimly the Colonel shook his balled fist at the telephone.

'Break me, would you, you old sheepshead!' he muttered through his teeth. 'But my pigeon man will spike your guns, my boy! *Verdammt*, though, the price is high!'

Then, drawing himself up to his full height, he brought his heels together with a jingle of spurs and gravely saluted the door through which the pigeon man had disappeared between the fixed bayonets of his guards.

V

A week later, in an unobtrusive office off Whitehall, high above the panorama of London threaded by the silver Thames, a large, quiet man sat at his desk and frowned down at a typewritten sheet he held in his hand.

'Well,' he said, addressing an officer in khaki who stood in an expectant attitude before him, 'they've nabbed Tony, Carruthers!'

'Oh, sir!' ejaculated Carruthers in dismay. 'You were right, then?'

"Fraid so. I knew they'd pinched him when Corps forwarded those Dunlop messages that kept reachin' 'em by pigeon. Prendergast, of Rotterdam, says here he has word from a trustworthy source in Belgium that at Roulers on the 6th the Bosches shot a half-witted tramp on a charge of espionage. The trial, of course, was held in secret, but the rumour in the town is that the tramp was a British officer. That'd be Tony, all right. God bless my soul, what an actor the fellow was! I'd never have lent him for this job, only GHQ were so insistent. Well, he had a good run for his money, anyway. Our friends on the other side used to call him *N*, "The Unknown Quantity". They never managed to identify him, you see. My hat! Old Tony must be smilin' to think that he managed to take his incognito down to the grave with him.'

'But did he?'

'Obviously, otherwise the old Boches would have signed his real name to those pigeon messages of theirs which have so much amused Ross and his young men at Corps Headquarters.'

'But why "Dunlop", sir?'

The large man smiled enigmatically. 'Ah,' he remarked, 'you weren't in the Service before the war, Carruthers, or you'd have known that "Dunlop" was one of our accommodation names in the office. Most of us were Captain Dunlop at one time or another. I've been Captain Dunlop myself. We run up against some rum coves in this business, and it ain't a bad plan to have a sort of general alias. It prevents identification, and all manner of awkwardness, when the double-crossin' begins.' He broke off to chuckle audibly. 'Let's see, it's old Trompeter on that front, ain't it? I wonder where he got hold of the office alias, the foxy old devil! He's probably put up another Iron Cross over this! He'd be kickin' himself if he knew the truth. That's the catch about this job of ours, my boy—to recognize the truth when you find it!'

So saying, the large man unlocked his desk and, taking out a book, turned to a list of names. With the red pencil he scored out, slowly and methodically, a name that stood there.

Jumbo's Wife

I

When he had taken his breakfast, silently as his way was after a drunk, he lifted the latch and went out without a word. She heard his feet tramp down the flagged laneway, waking iron echoes, and, outraged, shook her fist after him; then she pulled off the old red flannel petticoat and black shawl she was wearing, and crept back into the hollow of the bed. But not to sleep. She went over in her mind the shame of last night's bout, felt at her lip where he had split it with a blow, and recalled how she had fled into the roadway screaming for help and been brought back by Pa Kenefick, the brother of the murdered boy. Somehow that had sobered Jumbo. Since Michael, the elder of the Kenefick brothers, had been taken out and killed by the police, the people looked up to Pa rather as they looked up to the priest, but more passionately, more devotedly. She remembered how even Jumbo, the great swollen insolent Jumbo had crouched back into the darkness when he saw that slip of a lad walk in before her. 'Stand away from me,' he had said, but not threateningly. 'It was a shame,' Pa had retorted, 'a confounded shame for a drunken elephant of a man to beat his poor decent wife like that,' but Jumbo had said nothing, only 'Let her be, boy, let her be! Go away from me now and I'll quieten down.' 'You'd better quieten down,' Pa had said, 'or you'll answer for it to me, you great bully you,' and he had kicked about the floor the pieces of the delf that Jumbo in his drunken frenzy had shattered one by one against the wall. 'I tell you I won't lay a finger on her,' Jumbo had said, and sure enough, when Pa Kenefick had gone, Jumbo was a quiet man.

But it was the sight of the brother of the boy that had been murdered rather than the beating she had had or the despair at seeing her little share of delf smashed on her, that brought home to Jumbo's wife her own utter humiliation. She had often thought before that she would run away from Jumbo, even, in her wild way, that she would do for him, but never before had she seen so clearly what a wreck he had made of her life. The sight of Pa had reminded her that she was no common trollop but a decent girl; he had said it, 'your decent poor wife', that was what Pa had said, and it was true; she was a decent poor woman. Didn't the world know how often she had pulled the little home together on her blackguard of a husband, the man who had 'listed in the army under a false name so as to rob her of the separation money, the man who would keep a job only as long as it pleased him, and send her out then to work in the nurseries, picking fruit for a shilling a day?

She was so caught up into her own bitter reflections that when she glanced round suddenly and saw the picture that had been the ostensible cause of Jumbo's fury awry, the glass smashed in it, and the bright colours stained with tea, her lip fell, and she began to moan softly to herself. It was a beautiful piece—that was how she described it—a beautiful, massive piece of big, big castle, all towers, on a rock, and mountains and snow behind. Four shillings and sixpence it had cost her in the Coal Quay market. Jumbo would spend three times that on a drunk; ay, three times and five times that Jumbo would spend, and for all, he had smashed every cup and plate and dish in the house on her poor little picture— because it was extravagance, he said.

She heard the postman's loud double knock, and the child beside her woke and sat up. She heard a letter being slipped under the door. Little Johnny heard it too. He climbed down the side of the bed, pattered across the floor in his nightshirt and brought it to her. A letter with the On-His-Majesty's-Service stamp; it was Jumbo's pension that he drew every quarter. She slipped it under her pillow with a fresh burst of rage. It would keep. She would hold on to it until he gave her his week's wages on Friday. Yes, she would make him hand over every penny of it even if he killed her after. She had done it before, and would do it again.

Little Johnny began to cry that he wanted his breakfast, and she rose, sighing, and dressed. Over the fire as she boiled the kettle she meditated again on her wrongs, and was startled when she found the child actually between her legs holding out the long envelope to the flames, trying to boil the kettle with it. She snatched it wildly from his hand and gave him a vicious slap across the face that set him howling. She stood turning the letter over and over in her hand curiously, and then started as she remembered that it wasn't until another month that Jumbo's pension fell due. She counted the weeks; no, that was right, but what had them sending out Jumbo's pension a month before it was due?

When the kettle boiled she made the tea, poured it out into two tin ponnies, and sat into table with the big letter propped up before her as though she was trying to read its secrets through the manilla covering. But she was no closer to solving the mystery when her breakfast of bread and tea was done, and, sudden resolution coming to her, she held the envelope over the spout of the kettle and slowly steamed its fastening away. She drew out the flimsy note inside and opened it upon the table. It was an order, a money order, but not the sort they sent to Jumbo. The writing on it meant little to her, but what did mean a great deal were the careful figures, a two and a five that filled one corner. A two and a five and a sprawling sign before them; this was not for Jumbo—or was it? All sorts of suspicions began to form in her mind, and with them a feeling of pleasurable excitement.

She thought of Pa Kenefick. Pa was a good scholar and the proper man to see about a thing like this. And Pa had been good to her. Pa would feel she was doing the right thing in showing him this mysterious paper, even if it meant nothing but a change in the way they paid Jumbo's pension; it would show how much she looked up to him.

She threw her old black shawl quickly about her shoulders and grabbed at the child's hand. She went down the low arched laneway where they lived—Melancholy Lane, it was called—and up the road to the Kenefick's. She knocked at their door, and Mrs Kenefick, whose son had been dragged to his death from that door, answered it. She looked surprised when she saw the other woman, and only then Jumbo's wife realized how early it was. She asked excitedly for Pa. He wasn't at home, his mother said, and she didn't know when he would be home, if he came at all. When she saw how crestfallen her visitor looked at this, she asked politely if she couldn't send a message, for women like Jumbo's wife frequently brought information that was of use to the volunteers. No, no, the other woman said earnestly, it was for Pa's ears, for Pa's ears alone, and it couldn't wait. Mrs Kenefick asked her into the parlour, where the picture of the murdered boy, Michael, in his Volunteer uniform hung. It was dangerous for any of the company to stay at home, she said, the police knew the ins and outs of the district too well; there was the death of Michael unaccounted for, and a dozen or more arrests, all within a month or two. But she had never before seen Jumbo's wife in such a state and wondered what was the best thing for her to do. It was her daughter who decided it by telling where Pa was to be found, and immediately the excited woman raced off up the hill towards the open country.

She knocked at the door of a little farmhouse off the main road, and when the door was opened she saw Pa himself, in shirt-sleeves, filling

out a basin of hot water to shave. His first words showed that he thought
it was Jumbo who had been at her again, but, without answering him,
intensely conscious of herself and of the impression she wished to
create, she held the envelope out at arm's length. He took it, looked at
the address for a moment, and then pulled out the flimsy slip. She saw
his brows bent above it, then his lips tightened. He raised his head and
called, 'Jim, Liam, come down! Come down a minute!' The tone in which
he said it delighted her as much as the rush of footsteps upstairs. Two
men descended a ladder to the kitchen, and Pa held out the slip. 'Look
at this!' he said. They looked at it, for a long time it seemed to her, turning it round and round and examining the postmark on the envelope.
She began to speak rapidly. 'Mr Kenefick will tell you, gentlemen, Mr
Kenefick will tell you, the life he leads me. I was never one for regulat-
ing me own, gentlemen, but I say before me God this minute, hell will
never be full till they have him roasting there. A little pitcher I bought,
gentlemen, a massive little piece—Mr Kenefick will tell you—I paid four
and sixpence for it—he said I was extravagant. Let me remark he'd spend
three times, ay, and six times, as much on filling his own gut as I'd spend
upon me home and child. Look at me, gentlemen, look at me lip where
he hit me—Mr Kenefick will tell you—I was in gores of blood.' 'Listen
now, ma'am,' one of the men interrupted suavely, 'we're very grateful to
you for showing us this letter. It's something we wanted to know this
long time, ma'am. And now like a good woman will you go back home
and not open your mouth to a soul about it, and, if himself ask you anything, say there did ne'er a letter come?' 'Of course,' she said, 'she would
do whatever they told her. She was in their hands. Didn't Mr Kenefick
come in, like the lovely young man he was, and save her from the hands
of that dancing hangman Jumbo? And wasn't she sorry for his mother,
poor little 'oman, and her fine son taken away on her? Weren't they all
crazy about her?'

The three men had to push her out the door, saying that she had squared
her account with Jumbo at last.

II

At noon with the basket of food under her arm, and the child plodding
along beside her, she made her way through the northern slums to a
factory on the outskirts of the city. There, sitting on the grass beside a
little stream—her usual station—she waited for Jumbo. He came just as
the siren blew, sat down beside her on the grass, and, without as much
as fine day, began to unpack the food in the little basket. Already she was

frightened and unhappy; she dreaded what Jumbo would do if ever he found out about the letter, and find out he must. People said he wouldn't last long on her, balloon and all as he was. Some said his heart was weak, and others that he was bloated out with dropsy and would die in great agony at any minute. But those who said that hadn't felt the weight of Jumbo's hand.

She sat in the warm sun, watching the child dabble his fingers in the little stream, and all the bitterness melted away within her. She had had a hard two days of it, and now she felt Almighty God might well have pity on her, and leave her a week or even a fortnight of quiet, until she pulled her little home together again. Jumbo ate placidly and contentedly; she knew by this his drinking bout was almost over. At last he pulled his cap well down over his eyes and lay back with his wide red face to the sun. She watched him, her hands upon her lap. He looked for all the world like a huge, fat, sulky child. He lay like that without stirring for some time; then he stretched out his legs, and rolled over and over and over downhill through the grass. He grunted with pleasure, and sat up blinking drowsily at her from the edge of the cinder path. She put her hand in her pocket. 'Jim, will I give you the price of an ounce of 'baccy?' He stared up at her for a moment. 'There did ne'er a letter come for me?' he asked, and her heart sank. 'No, Jim,' she said feebly, 'what letter was it you were expecting?' 'Never mind, you. Here, give us a couple of lob for a wet!' She counted him out six coppers and he stood up to go.

All the evening she worried herself about Pa Kenefick and his friends— though to be sure they were good-natured, friendly boys. She was glad when Jumbo came in at tea-time; the great bulk of him stretched out in the corner gave her a feeling of security. He was almost in good humour again, and talked a little, telling her to shut up when her tongue wagged too much, or sourly abusing the 'bummers' who had soaked him the evening before. She had cleared away the supper things when a motor-car drove up the road and stopped at the end of Melancholy Lane. Her heart misgave her. She ran to the door and looked out; there were two men coming up the lane, one of them wearing a mask; when they saw her they broke into a trot. 'Merciful Jesus!' she screamed, and rushed in, banging and bolting the door behind her. Jumbo stood up slowly. 'What is it?' he asked. 'That letter.' 'What letter?' 'I showed it to Pa Kenefick, that letter from the barrack.' The blue veins rose on Jumbo's forehead as though they would burst. He could barely speak but rushed to the fireplace and swept the poker above her head. 'If it's the last thing I ever do I'll have your sacred life!' he said in a hoarse whisper. 'Let me alone! Let me alone!' she shrieked. 'They're at the door!' She leaned her back against the door, and felt against her spine the lurch of a man's shoulder. Jumbo heard it; he watched her with narrowed, despairing eyes, and then beckoned her towards the back door. She went on before him on tiptoe and opened the door quietly for him. 'Quick,' he said, 'name of Jasus, lift me up this.' This was the back wall, which was fully twice his own height but had footholes by which he could clamber up. She held his feet in them, and puffing and growling, he scrambled painfully up, inch by inch, until his head was almost level with the top of the wall; then with a gigantic effort he slowly raised his huge body and laid it flat upon the spiny top. 'Keep them back, you!' he said. 'Here,' she called softly up to him, 'take this,' and he bent down and caught the poker.

It was dark in the little kitchen. She crept to the door and listened, holding her breath. There was no sound. She was consumed with anxiety and impatience. Suddenly little Johnny sat up and began to howl. She grasped the key and turned it in the lock once; there was no sound; at last she opened the door slowly. There was no one to be seen in the lane. Night was setting in—maybe he would dodge them yet. She locked the screaming child in behind her and hurried down to the archway.

The motor-car was standing where it had stopped and a man was leaning over the wheel smoking a cigarette. He looked up and smiled at her. 'Didn't they get him yet?' he asked. 'No,' she said mechanically. 'Ah, cripes!' he swore, 'with the help of God they'll give him an awful end when they ketch him.' She stood there looking up and down the road in the terrible stillness: there were lamps lighting behind every window but not a soul appeared. At last a strange young man in a trench-coat rushed down the lane towards them. 'Watch out there,' he cried. 'He's after giving us the slip. Guard this lane and the one below, don't shoot unless you can get him.' He doubled down the road and up the next laneway.

The young man in the car topped his cigarette carefully, put the butt end in his waistcoat pocket and crossed to the other side of the road. He leaned nonchalantly against the wall and drew a heavy revolver. She crossed too and stood beside him. An old lamplighter came up one of the lanes from the city and went past them to the next gas-lamp, his torch upon his shoulder. 'He's a brute of a man,' the driver said consolingly, 'sure, I couldn't but hit him in the dark itself. But it's a shame now they wouldn't have a gas-lamp at that end of the lane, huh!' The old lamplighter disappeared up the road, leaving two or three pale specks of light behind him.

They stood looking at the laneways each end of a little row of cottages, not speaking a word. Suddenly the young man drew himself up stiffly against the wall and raised his left hand towards the fading sky. 'See that?' he said gleefully. Beyond the row of cottages a figure rose slowly against a chimney-pot; they could barely see it in the twilight, but she could not doubt who it was. The man spat upon the barrel of his gun and raised it upon his crooked elbow; then the dark figure leaped out as it were upon the air and disappeared among the shadows of the houses. 'Jasus!' the young man swore softly, 'wasn't that a great pity?' She came to her senses in a flash. 'Jumbo!' she shrieked, 'me poor Jumbo! He's kilt, he's kilt!' and began to weep and clap her hands. The man looked at her in comical bewilderment. 'Well, well!' he said, 'to think of that! And are you his widda, ma'am?' 'God melt and wither you!' she screamed and rushed away towards the spot where Jumbo's figure had disappeared.

At the top of the lane a young man with a revolver drove her back. 'Is he kilt?' she cried. 'Too well you know he's not kilt,' the young man replied savagely. Another wearing a mask came out of a cottage and said 'He's dished us again. Don't stir from this. I'm going round to Samson's Lane.' 'How did he manage it?' the first man asked. 'Over the roofs. This place is a network, and the people won't stir a finger to help us.'

For hours that duel in the darkness went on, silently, without a shot being fired. What mercy the people of the lanes showed to Jumbo was a mercy they had never denied to any hunted thing. His distracted wife went back to the road. Leaving the driver standing alone by his car she tramped up and down staring up every tiny laneway. It did not enter her head to run for assistance. On the opposite side of the road another network of lanes, all steep-sloping, like the others, or stepped in cobbles, went down into the heart of the city. These were Jumbo's only hope of escape, and that was why she watched there, glancing now and then at the maze of lights beneath her.

Ten o'clock rang out from Shandon—shivering, she counted the chimes. Then down one of the lanes from the north she heard a heavy clatter of ironshod feet. Clatter, clatter, clatter; the feet drew nearer, and she heard other, lighter, feet pattering swiftly behind. A dark figure emerged through an archway, running with frantic speed. She rushed out into the middle of the road to meet it, sweeping her shawl out on either side of her head like a dancer's sash. 'Jumbo, me lovely Jumbo!' she screamed. 'Out of me way, y'ould crow!' the wild quarry panted, flying past.

She heard him take the first flight of steps in the southern laneway at a bound. A young man dashed out of the archway a moment after and gave a hasty look around him. Then he ran towards her and she stepped out into the lane to block his passage. Without swerving he rushed into her at full speed, sweeping her off her feet, but she drew the wide black shawl about his head as they fell and rolled together down the narrow sloping passage. They were at the top of the steps and he still struggled frantically to free himself from the filthy enveloping shawl. They rolled from step to step, to the bottom, he throttling her and cursing furiously at her strength; she still holding the shawl tight about his head and shoulders. Then the others came and dragged him off, leaving her choking and writhing upon the ground.

But by this time Jumbo was well beyond their reach.

III

Next morning she walked dazedly about the town, stopping every policeman she met and asking for Jumbo. At the military barrack on the hill they told her she would find him in one of the city police barracks. She explained to the young English officer who spoke to her about Pa Kenefick, and how he could be captured, and for her pains was listened to in wide-eyed disgust. But what she could not understand in the young officer's attitude to her, Jumbo, sitting over the fire in the barrack day-room, had already been made to understand, and she was shocked to see him so pale, so sullen, so broken. And this while she was panting with pride at his escape! He did not even fly at her as she had feared he would, nor indeed abuse her at all. He merely looked up and said with the bitterness of utter resignation, 'There's the one that brought me down!' An old soldier, he was cut to the heart that the military would not take him in, but had handed him over to the police for protection. 'I'm no use to them now,' he said, 'and there's me thanks for all I done. They'd as soon see me out of the way; they'd as soon see the poor old crature that served them out of the way.' 'It was all Pa Kenefick's doings,' his wife put in frantically, 'it was no one else done it. Not that my poor slob of a man ever did him or his any harm. . . .' At this the policemen round her chuckled and Jumbo angrily bade her be silent. 'But I told the officer of the swaddies where he was to be found,' she went on unheeding. 'What was that?' the policemen asked eagerly, and she told them of how she had found Pa Kenefick in the little cottage up the hill.

Every day she went to see Jumbo. When the weather was fine they sat in the little garden behind the barrack, for it was only at dusk that Jumbo could venture out and then only with military or police patrols. There were very few on the road who would speak to her now, for on the night

after Jumbo's escape the little cottage where Pa Kenefick had stayed had
been raided and smashed up by masked policemen. Of course, Pa and
his friends were gone. She hated the neighbours, and dug into her mind
with the fear of what might happen to Jumbo was the desire to be quit
of Pa Kenefick. Only then, she felt in her blind headlong way, would
Jumbo be safe. And what divil's notion took her to show him the letter?
She'd swing for Pa, she said, sizing up to the policemen.

And Jumbo grew worse and worse. His face had turned from brick-
red to grey. He complained always of pain and spent whole days in bed.
She had heard that there was a cure for his illness in red flannel, and had
made him a nightshirt of red flannel in which he looked more than ever
like a ghost, his hair grey, his face quite colourless, his fat paws growing
skinny under the wide crimson sleeves. He applied for admission to the
military hospital, which was within the area protected by the troops, and
the request was met with a curt refusal. That broke his courage. To the
military for whom he had risked his life he was only an informer, a common informer, to be left to the mercy of their enemy when his services
were no longer of value. The policemen sympathized with him, for they
too were despised by the 'swaddies' as makers of trouble, but they could
do nothing for him. And when he went out walking under cover of darkness with two policemen for an escort the people turned and laughed
at him. He heard them, and returned to the barrack consumed with a
rage that expressed itself in long fits of utter silence or sudden murder-
ous outbursts.

She came in one summer evening when the fit was on him, to find
him struggling in the day-room with three of the policemen. They were
trying to wrest a loaded carbine from his hands. He wanted blood, he
shouted, blood, and by Christ they wouldn't stop him. They wouldn't,
they wouldn't, he repeated, sending one of them flying against the hearth.
He'd finish a few of the devils that were twitting him before he was plugged
himself. He'd shoot everyone, man, woman, and child that came in his
way. His frenzy was terrifying and the three policemen were swung this
way and that, to right and left, as the struggle swept from wall to door
and back. Then suddenly he collapsed and lay unconscious upon the floor.
When they brought him round with whiskey he looked from one to the
other, and drearily, with terrible anguish, he cursed all the powers about
him, God, the King, the republicans, Ireland, and the country he had
served.

'Kimberley, Pietermaritzburg, Bethlehem, Bloemfontein,' he moaned.
'Ah, you thing, many's the hard day I put down for you! Devil's cure to

me for a crazy man! Devil's cure to me, I say! With me cane and me busby and me scarlet coat—'twas aisy you beguiled me! . . . The curse of God on you! . . . Tell them to pay me passage, d'you hear me? Tell them to pay me passage and I'll go out to Inja and fight the blacks for you!'

It was easy to see whom he was talking to.

'Go the road resigned, Jim,' his wife counselled timidly from above his head. Seeing him like this she could already believe him dying.

'I will not. . . . I will not go the road resigned.'

'. . . to His blessed and holy Will,' she babbled.

Lifting his two fists from the ground he thumped upon his chest like a drum.

''Tisn't sickness that ails me, but a broken heart,' he cried. 'Tell them to pay me passage! Ah, why didn't I stay with the lovely men we buried there, not to end me days as a public show. . . . They put the crooelty of the world from them young, the creatures, they put the crooelty of the world from them young!'

The soldiers had again refused to admit him to the military hospital. Now the police had grown tired of him, and on their faces he saw relief, relief that they would soon be shut of him, when he entered some hospital in the city, where everyone would know him, and sooner or later his enemies would reach him. He no longer left the barrack. Disease had changed that face of his already; the only hope left to him now was to change it still further. He grew a beard.

And all this time his wife lay in wait for Pa Kenefick. Long hours on end she watched for him over her half-door. Twice she saw him pass by the laneway, and each time snatched her shawl and rushed down to the barrack, but by the time a car of plain-clothes men drove up to the Kenefick's door Pa was gone. Then he ceased to come home at all, and she watched the movements of his sister and mother. She even trained little Johnny to follow them, but the child was too young and too easily outdistanced. When she came down the road in the direction of the city, all the women standing at their doors would walk in and shut them in her face.

One day the policeman on duty at the barrack door told her gruffly that Jumbo was gone. He was in hospital somewhere; she would be told where if he was in any danger. And she knew by the tone in which he said it that the soldiers had not taken Jumbo in; that somewhere he was at the mercy of his changed appearance and assumed name, unless, as was likely, he was already too far gone to make it worth the 'rebels'' while to shoot him. Now that she could no longer see him there was a great emptiness in her life, an emptiness that she filled only with brooding and hatred. Everything within her had turned to bitterness against Pa Kenefick, the boy who had been the cause of it all, to whom she had foolishly shown the letter and who had brought the 'dirty Shinners' down on her, who alone had cause to strike at Jumbo now that he was a sick and helpless man.

'God, give me strength!' she prayed. 'I'll sober him. O God, I'll put him in a quiet habitation!'

She worked mechanically about the house. A neighbour's averted face or the closing of a door in her path brought her to such a pitch of fury that she swept out into the road, her shawl stretched out behind her head, and tore up and down, screaming like a madwoman; sometimes leaping into the air with an obscene gesture; sometimes kneeling in the roadway and cursing those that had affronted her; sometimes tapping out a few dance steps, a skip to right and a skip to left, just to rouse herself. 'I'm a bird alone!' she shrieked, 'a bird alone and the hawks about me! Good man, clever man, handsome man, I'm a bird alone!' And 'That they might rot and wither, root and branch, son and daughter, born and unborn; that every plague and pestilence might end them and theirs; that they might be called in their sins'—this was what she prayed in the traditional formula, and the neighbours closed their doors softly and crossed themselves. For a week or more she was like a woman possessed.

IV

Then one day when she was standing by the archway she saw Pa Kenefick and another man come down the road. She stood back without being seen, and waited until they had gone by before she emerged and followed them. It was no easy thing to do upon the long open street that led to the quays, but she pulled her shawl well down over her eyes, and drew up her shoulders so that at a distance she might look like an old woman. She reached the foot of the hill without being observed, and after that, to follow them through the crowded, narrow side-streets of the city where every second woman wore a shawl was comparatively easy. But they walked so fast it was hard to keep up with them, and several times she had to take short-cuts that they did not know of, thus losing sight of them for the time being. Already they had crossed the bridge, and she was growing mystified; this was unfamiliar country and, besides, the pace was beginning to tell on her. They had been walking now for a good two miles and she knew that they would soon outdistance her. And all the time she had seen neither policeman nor soldier.

Gasping she stood and leaned against a wall, drawing the shawl down about her shoulders for a breath of air. 'Tell me, ma'am,' she asked of a passer-by, 'where do this road go to?' 'This is the Mallow Road, ma'am,' the other said, and since Jumbo's wife made no reply she asked was it any place she wanted. 'No, indeed,' Jumbo's wife answered without conviction. The other lowered her voice and asked sympathetically, 'Is it the hospital you're looking for, poor woman?' Jumbo's wife stood for a moment until the question sank in. 'The hospital?' she whispered. 'The hospital? Merciful God Almighty!' Then she came to her senses. 'Stop them!' she screamed, rushing out into the roadway, 'stop them!' Murder! Murder! Stop them!'

The two men who by this time were far ahead heard the shout and looked back. Then one of them stepped out into the middle of the road and signalled to a passing car. They leaped in and the car drove off. A little crowd had gathered upon the path, but when they understood what the woman's screams signified they melted silently away. Only the woman to whom she had first spoken remained. 'Come with me, ma'am,' she said. ''Tis only as you might say a step from this.'

A tram left them at the hospital gate and Jumbo's wife and the other woman rushed in. She asked for Jumbo Geany, but the porter looked at her blankly and asked what ward she was looking for. 'There were two men here a minute ago,' she said frantically, 'where are they gone to?' 'Ah,' he said, 'now I have you! They're gone over to St George's Ward. . . .'

In St George's Ward at that moment two or three nuns and a nurse surrounded the house doctor, a tall young man who was saying excitedly, 'I couldn't stop them, couldn't stop them! I told them he was at his last gasp, but they wouldn't believe me!' 'He was lying there,' said the nurse pointing to an empty bed, 'when that woman came in with the basket, a sort of dealing woman she was. When she saw him she looked hard at him and then went across and drew back the bedclothes. "Is it yourself is there, Jumbo?" says she, and, poor man, he starts up in bed and says out loud-like "You won't give me away? Promise me you won't give me away." So she laughs and says, "A pity you didn't think of that when you gave Mike Kenefick the gun, Jumbo!" After she went away he wanted to get up and go home. I seen by his looks he was dying and I sent for the priest and Doctor Connolly, and he got wake-like, and that pair came in, asking for a stretcher, and——' The nurse began to bawl.

Just then Jumbo's wife appeared, a distracted, terrified figure, the shawl drawn back from her brows, the hair falling about her face. 'Jumbo Geany?'

she asked. 'You're too late,' said the young doctor harshly, 'they've taken him away.' 'No, come back, come back!' he shouted as she rushed towards the window that opened on to the garden at the back of the hospital, 'you can't go out there!' But she wriggled from his grasp, leaving her old black shawl in his hands. Alone she ran across the little garden, to where another building jutted out and obscured the view of the walls. As she did so three shots rang out in rapid succession. She heard a gate slam; it was the little wicket gate on to another road; beside it was a stretcher with a man's body lying on it. She flung herself screaming upon the body, not heeding the little streams of blood that flowed from beneath the armpit and the head. It was Jumbo, clad only in a nightshirt and bearded beyond recognition. His long, skinny legs were naked, and his toes had not ceased to twitch. For each of the three shots there was a tiny wound, two over the heart and one in the temple, and pinned to the cheap flannelette night-shirt was a little typed slip that read

SPY.

They had squared her account with Jumbo at last.

Affaire de Cœur

Biggles hummed cheerfully as he cruised along in the new Camel which he had just fetched from the Aircraft Park. 'Another five minutes and I shall be home,' he thought, but fate willed otherwise. The engine coughed, coughed again, and with a final splutter, expired, leaving him with a 'dead' prop. He swore softly, pushed the joystick forward, and looked quickly around for the most suitable field for the now inevitable forced landing.

To the right lay the forest of Clarmes. 'Nothing doing that way,' he muttered, and looked down between his left wings. Ah! there it was. Almost on the edge of the forest was a large pasture, free from obstruction. The pilot, with a confidence born of long experience, side-slipped towards it, levelled out over the hedge and made a perfect three-point landing.

He sat in the cockpit for a minute or two contemplating his position, then he yawned, pushed up his goggles and prepared to take stock of his immediate surroundings. He raised his eyebrows appreciatively as he noted the sylvan beauty of the scene around him. Above, the sun shone from a cloudless blue sky. Straight before him a low lichen-covered stone wall enclosed an orchard through which he could just perceive a dull red pan-tiled roof. To the right lay the forest, cool and inviting. To the left a stream meandered smoothly between a double row of willows.

'Who said there was a war on,' he murmured, lighting a cigarette, and climbing up on to the 'hump' of his Camel, the better to survey the enchanting scene. 'Well, well, let's see if anyone is at home.' He sprang lightly to the ground, threw his leather coat across the fuselage and strolled towards the house. An old iron gate opened into the orchard; entering, he paused for a moment, uncertain of the path.

'Are you looking for me, monsieur?' said a voice, which sounded to Biggles as musical as ice tinkling in a cocktail glass.

Turning, he beheld a vision of blonde loveliness wrapped up in blue silk, smiling at him. For a moment he stared as if he had been raised in a monastery and had never seen a woman before. He closed his eyes, shook his head, and opened them again—the vision was still there, dimpling.

'You were looking for me, perhaps?' said the girl again.

Biggles saluted like a man sleep-walking.

'Mademoiselle,' he said earnestly, 'I've been looking for you all my life. I didn't think I'd ever find you.'

'Then why did you land here?' asked the girl.

'I landed here because my mag. shorted,' explained Biggles.

'What would have happened if you had not landed when your bag shorted?' enquired the vision, curiously.

'Not bag—mag. Short for magneto, you know,' replied Biggles, grinning. 'Do you know, I've never even thought of doing anything but land when a mag. shorts; if I didn't, I expect that I should fall from a great altitude and collide with something substantial.'

'What are you going to do now?'

'I don't know—it takes thinking about. It may be necessary for me to stay here for some time. Anyway, the War will still be on when I get back. But, pardon me, mademoiselle, if I appear impertinent; are you English? I ask because you speak English so well.'

'Not quite, monsieur. My mother was English and I have been to school in England,' replied the girl.

'Thank you, Miss—er——'

'Marie Janis is my name.'

'A charming name, more charming even than this spot of heaven,' said Biggles warmly. 'Have you a telephone, Miss Janis? You see, although the matter is not urgent, if I do not ring up my Squadron to say where I am, someone may fly around to look for me,' he explained.

The thought of Mahoney spotting his Camel from the air and landing, did not, in the circumstances, fill him with the enthusiasm one might normally expect.

'Come and use the telephone, m'sieur le Capitaine,' said the girl, leading the way. 'May I offer you *un petit verre?*'

'May you?' responded Biggles, warmly. 'I should say you may!'

Five hours later Biggles again took his place in the cockpit of the Camel which a party of ackemmas had now repaired. He took off and swung low over the orchard, waving gaily to a slim blue-clad figure that looked upwards and waved back.

Rosy clouds drifted across the horizon as he made the short flight back to the aerodrome. 'That girl's what I've been reading about,' he told himself. 'She's the "Spirit of the Air", and she's going to like me an awful lot if I know anything about it. Anyway, I'd be the sort of skunk who'd give rat poison to orphans if I didn't go back and thank her for her hospitality.'

Biggles, a week later, seated on an old stone bench in the orchard, sighed contentedly. The distant flickering beam of a searchlight on the war-stricken sky meant nothing to him; the rumble of guns along the line seemed very far away. His arm rested along the back of the seat; a little head, shining whitely in the moonlight, nestled lightly on his sleeve. In the short time that had elapsed since his forced landing, he had made considerable progress.

'Tell me, Marie,' he said, 'do you ever hear from your father?'

'No, m'sieur,' replied the girl, sadly. 'I told you he was on a visit to the north when war was declared. In the wild panic of the Boche advance he was left behind in what is now the occupied territory. Communication with that part of France is forbidden, but I have had two letters from him which were sent by way of England by friends. I have not even been able to tell him that maman is—dead!'

Tears shone for a moment in her eyes, and Biggles stirred uncomfortably.

'It is a hell of a war,' he said compassionately.

'If only I could get a letter to him to say that maman—*est morte*, and that I am looking after things until he returns, I should be happy. Poor Papa!'

'I suppose you don't even know where he is?' said Biggles sympathetically.

'But yes,' answered the girl quickly, 'I know where he is. He is still at our friend's château, where he was staying when the Boche came.'

'Where's that?' asked Biggles in surprise.

'At Vinard, near Lille; le Château Boreau,' she replied, 'but he might as well be in Berlin,' she concluded sadly, shrugging her shoulders.

'Good Lord!' ejaculated Biggles suddenly.

'Why did you say that, monsieur?'

'Nothing—only an idea struck me, that's all,' said Biggles.

'Tell me.'

'No. I'm crazy. Better forget it.'

'Tell me—please.'

Biggles wavered. 'All right,' he said, 'say "please, Biggles," and I'll tell you.'

'Please, Beegles.'

Biggles smiled at the pronunciation. 'Well, if you must know,' he said, 'it struck me that I might act as a messenger for you.'

'Beegles! How?'

'I had some crazy notion that I might be able to drop a letter from my machine,' explained Biggles.

'Mon dieu!' The girl sprang to her feet in excitement, but Biggles held her arm and pulled her towards him. For a moment she resisted, and then slipped into his arms.

'Beegles—please.'

'Marie,' whispered Biggles, as their lips met. Then, his heart beating faster than archie or enemy aircraft had ever caused it to beat, he suddenly pushed her aside, rose to his feet and looked at the luminous dial of his watch. 'Time I was getting back to quarters,' he said unsteadily.

'But Beegles, it is not yet so late.'

Biggles sat down, passed his hand over his face and then laughed. 'My own mag. was nearly shorting then,' he said.

They both laughed, and the spell was broken.

'Tell me, Beegles, is it possible to drop such a letter to papa?' said the girl presently.

'I don't know,' said Biggles, a trifle anxiously. 'I don't know what orders are about that sort of thing, and that's a fact. There wouldn't be any harm in it, and they wouldn't know about it, anyway. You give me the letter and I'll see what I can do.'

'Beegles—you——'

'Well?'

'Never mind. Come to the house and we will write the letter together.'

Hand in hand they walked slowly towards the house. The girl took a writing-pad from a desk and began to write; the door opened noiselessly and Antoine, Marie's elderly man-servant appeared.

'Did you ring, mademoiselle?' he asked.

'Merci, Antoine.'

'Do you know,' said Biggles, after the man had withdrawn, 'I don't like the look of that bloke. I never saw a nastier looking piece of work in my life.'

'But what should I do without Antoine and Lucille, his wife. They are the only two that stayed with me all the time. Antoine is a dear, he only thinks of me,' said the girl reproachfully.

'I see,' said Biggles. 'Well, go ahead with the letter.'

The girl wrote rapidly.

'Look,' she smiled when it was finished. 'Read it and tell me if you do not think it is a lovely letter to a long-lost father.'

Biggles read the first few lines and skipped the rest, blushing. 'I don't want to read your letter, kid,' he said.

Marie sealed the letter, addressed it, and tied it firmly to a small paperweight. 'Now,' she said, 'what can we use for a banner?'

'You mean a streamer,' laughed Biggles.

'Yes, a streamer. Why! here is the very thing.' She took a black and white silk scarf from the back of a chair and tied the paperweight to it. 'There you are, *mon aviateur*,' she laughed. 'Take care, do not hit papa on the head or he will wish I had not written.'

Biggles slipped the packet into the pocket of his British 'warm' and took her in his arms impatiently.

Arriving at the aerodrome he went to his quarters and flung the coat on his bed, and then made his way across to the mess for a drink. As the door of his quarter closed behind him, two men—an officer in uniform and a civilian—entered his room. Without a moment's hesitation the civilian picked up the coat and removed the letter from the pocket.

'You know what to do,' he said grimly.

'How long will you be?'

'An hour. Not more. Keep him until 11.30, to be on the safe side,' said the civilian.

'I will,' replied the officer, and followed Biggles into the mess.

Biggles, humming gaily, headed for home. His trip had proved uneventful and the dropping of Marie's letter ridiculously simple. He had found the château easily, and swooping low had seen the black and white scarf flutter on to the lawn. Safely back across the line he was now congratulating himself upon the success of his mission. 287, the neighbouring SE5 Squadron, lay below, and it occurred to him to land and pass the time of day with them.

Conscious that many eyes would be watching him, he side-slipped in and flattened out for his most artistic landing. There was a sudden crash, the Camel swung violently and tipped up on to its nose. Swearing savagely he climbed out and surveyed the damage.

'Why the devil don't you fellows put a flag or something on this sunken road?' he said bitterly to Wilkinson and other pilots who had hurried to the scene; and pointing to the cause of his misadventure, 'look at that mess.'

'Well, most people know about that road,' said Wilkinson. 'If I'd have known you were coming I'd have had it filled in altogether. Never mind; its only a tyre and the prop. gone. Our fellows will have it right by tomorrow. Come and have a drink; I'll find you transport to take you home. The CO's on leave, so you can use his car.'

'Righto, but I'm not staying to dinner,' said Biggles, emphatically, 'I'm on duty tonight,' he added, thinking of a moonlit orchard and an old stone seat.

It was nearly eight o'clock when he left the aerodrome, seated at the wheel of the borrowed car. He had rung up Major Mullen and told him that he would be late, and now, thrilling with anticipation, he headed for the home of the girl who was making life worth living and the war worth fighting for.

The night was dark, for low clouds were drifting across the face of the moon; a row of distant archie-bursts made him look up, frowning. A bomb raid, interrupting the story of his successful trip, was the last thing he wanted. His frown deepened as the enemy aircraft and the accompanying archie drew nearer. 'They're coming right over the house, blast 'em,' he said, and switching off his lights raced for the orchard. 'God! they're low,' he muttered, as he tore down the road, the roar of the engines of the heavy bombers in his ears. 'They're following this road, too.' He wondered where they were making for, trying to recall any possible objective on their line of flight. That he himself might be in danger did not even occur to him. He was less than five miles from the house now, and taking desperate chances to race the machines. 'The poor kid'll be scared stiff if they pass over her as low as this.'

With every nerve taut he tore down the road. He caught his breath suddenly. What was that! A whistling screech filled his ears and an icy hand clutched his heart. Too well he knew the sound. Boom! Boom! Boom! Three vivid flashes of orange fire leapt towards the sky. Boom! Boom! Boom!—and then three more.

'My God! what are they fanning, the fools? There is only the forest there,' thought Biggles, as, numb with shock, he raced round the last bend. Six more thundering detonations, seemingly a hundred yards ahead, nearly split his eardrums, but still he did not pause. He tried to think, but could not; he had lost all sense of time and reason. He seemed to have been driving for ever, and he cursed as he drove. Searchlights probed the sky on all sides and subconsciously he noticed that the noise of the engines was fading into the distance.

'They've gone,' he said, trying hard to think clearly. God! if they've hit the house! He jammed on his brakes with a grinding screech as two men sprang out in front of the car as he turned in the gates, but he was not looking at them. One glance showed him that the house was a blazing pile of ruins. He sprang out of the car and darted towards the conflagration, but a hand closed on his arm like a vice. Biggles, white-faced, turned and struck out viciously. 'My girl's in there, blast you,' he muttered.

A sharp military voice penetrated his stunned brain.

'Stand fast, Captain Bigglesworth,' it said.

'Let me go, damn you,' snarled Biggles, struggling like a madman.

'One more word from you Captain Bigglesworth and I'll put you under close arrest,' said the voice, harshly.

'You'll what?' Biggles turned, his brain fighting for consciousness. 'You'll what?' he cried again incredulously. He saw the firelight gleam on the fixed bayonets of a squad of Tommies; Colonel Raymond of Wing Head-quarters and another man stood near them. Biggles passed his hand over his eyes, swaying.

'I'm dreaming,' he said, 'that's it, dreaming. God! what a hell of a nightmare. I wish I could wake up.'

'Take a drink, Bigglesworth, and pull yourself together,' said Colonel Raymond passing him a flask. Biggles emptied the flask and handed it back.

'I'm going now,' said the Colonel, 'I'll see you in the morning. This officer will tell you all you need to know,' he concluded, indicating a dark-clad civilian standing near. 'Good-night, Bigglesworth.'

'Good-night, sir.'

'Tell me,' said Biggles, with an effort, 'is she—in there?'

The man nodded.

'Then, that's all I need to know,' said Biggles, slowly turning away.

'I'm sorry, but there are other things you will have to know,' returned the man.

'Who are you?' said Biggles curiously.

'Major Charles, of the British Intelligence Service.'

'Intelligence!' repeated Biggles, the first ray of light bursting upon him.

'Come here a moment.' Major Charles switched on the lights of his car. 'Yesterday, a lady asked you to deliver a message for her, did she not?' he asked.

'Why—yes.'

'Did you see it?'

'Yes!'

'Was this it?' said Major Charles, handing him a letter.

Biggles read the first few lines, dazed. 'Yes,' he said, 'that was it.'

'Turn it over.'

Unconsciously Biggles obeyed. He started as his eyes fell on a tangle of fine lines that showed up clearly. In the centre was a circle.

'Do you recognize that?'

'Yes.'

'What is it?'

'It is a map of 266 Squadron aerodrome,' replied Biggles, like a child reciting a catechism.

'You see the circle?'

'Yes.'

'The Officers' mess. Perhaps you understand now. The letter you were asked to carry had been previously prepared with a solution of invisible ink and contained such information that, had you delivered it, your entire squadron would have been wiped out tonight, and you as well. The girl sent you to your death, Captain Bigglesworth.'

'I'll not believe it,' said Biggles distinctly. 'But I did deliver the letter, anyway,' he cried suddenly.

'Not this one,' said Major Charles smiling queerly. 'You delivered the one we substituted.'

'Substituted!'

'We have watched this lady for a long time. You have been under surveillance since the day you force-landed, although your record put you above suspicion.'

'And on the substituted plan you marked her home to be bombed instead of the aerodrome?' sneered Biggles. 'Why?'

Major Charles shrugged his shoulders. 'The lady was well connected. There may have been unexpected difficulties connected with an arrest, yet her activities had to be checked. She had powerful friends in high places. Well, I must be going; no doubt you will hear from Wing in the morning.'

Biggles walked a little way up the garden path. The old stone seat glowed dully crimson. 'Bah!' he muttered, turning, 'what a fool I am. What a hell of a war this is.'

He drove slowly back to the aerodrome. On his table lay a letter. Ripping it open eagerly he read:

CHERE,

I have something important to ask you—something you must do for me. Tonight at seven o'clock I will come for you. It is important. Meet me in the road by the aerodrome. I will be very kind to you, my Biggles.

MARIE.

Biggles, with trembling hands, sat on the bed and re-read the letter, trying to reason out its purport. 'She timed the raid for eight,' he said to himself, 'when all officers would be dining in mess. She knew I should be there and wrote this to bring me out. She knew I'd never leave her waiting on the road—that was the way of it. She must have cared, or she wouldn't have done that. When I didn't come she went back home. She didn't even know I hadn't seen her letter—how could she? Now she's dead. If I hadn't landed at 287 I should be with her now. Well, she'll never know.' He rose wearily. Voices were singing in the distance, and he smiled bitterly as he heard the well-remembered words:

> Who minds to the dust returning,
>   Who shrinks from the sable shore,
> Where the high and haughty yearning
>   Of the soul shall be no more?

> So stand by your glasses steady,
>   This world is a world of lies;
> A cup to the dead already,
>   Hurrah! for the next man that dies.

A knock on the door aroused him from his reverie. An orderly of the guard entered.

'A lady left this for you,' he said, holding out a letter.

'A lady?—when?' said Biggles, holding himself in hand with a mighty effort.

'About ten minutes ago, sir. Just before you came in. She came about eight and said she must see you, sir, but I told her you weren't here.'

'Where is she now?'

'She's gone, sir, she was in a car. She told me to bring the letter straight to you when you returned, sir.'

'All right—you may go.'

Biggles took the letter, fighting back a wild desire to shout, opened it, and read:

Good-bye, my Biggles,

You know now. What can I say? Only this. Our destinies are not always in our own hands—always try and remember that, my Biggles. That is all I may say. I came tonight to take you away or die with you, but you were not here. And remember that one thing in this world of war and lies is true: my love for you. It may help you, as it helps me. Take care of yourself. Always I shall pray for you. If anything happens to you I shall know, but if to me, you will never know. My last thought will be of you. We shall meet again, if not in this world then in the next, so I will not say good-bye,

Au revoir,
MARIE.

'And they think she's dead,' said Biggles softly. She risked her life to tell me this. He kissed the letter tenderly, then held it to the candle and watched it burn away.

He was crumbling the ashes between his fingers when the door opened, and Mahoney entered. 'Hullo! laddie, what's wrong; had a fire?' he enquired.

'Yes,' replied Biggles, slowly, 'foolish of me; got my fingers burnt a bit, too.'

Flood on the Goodwins

Dundas looked out into the fog and blew reflectively on his finger-tips. The night was cold, raw with the steady drift of the westerly wind, and the fog poured over the dark bulk of the harbour wall as flood water pours over a breach in the dykes—as evenly, as endlessly, as ominously.

The last greyness was fading out of it now, and within twenty minutes at the outside the night would be down, and the sea as lost as the black earth in a snowdrift. Dundas blew again; not a night for fishing, he decided. Not even for war-time fishing, when food was scarce and prices high.

The complete darkness of the harbour was daunting. No lights showed even on a clear night now—save when the immediate necessities of shipping demanded it. Even to find one's way through the narrow entrance was a matter for caution and skill. Dundas knew that he could do it despite the fog—but whether he could find his way home again was another matter—and this fog might easily be a two-day affair.

It was not as if he were a regular local fisherman—though, heaven knew, even the 'locals' had not gone out this night. Dundas was a 'deep sea' man, third mate he had been when the war began, third mate of the *Rosvean*, five thousand tons, flush decked, running regularly like a ferry in the Rio Plata maize trade.

In the May of 1917 he had watched the *Rosvean* sink off the Casquets. The incident had made a considerable impression on him, but had in no way affected his nerves. His principal reaction had been largely one of scorn at the poorness of the shooting of the submarine which had put them down.

In the July he went down with his next ship, the *Moresby*, because the torpedo gave them rather less warning than the gun of the previous sinking.

He was picked up after two hours by a destroyer, and her commander commended him on his swimming ability.

That left him with nothing worse than a cold in the head, and at the end of July he signed on again. By this time he had won promotion. He signed on as second mate.

His new office lasted precisely seven hours, allowing for three hours in dock before the ship sailed. Off Selsey Bill, he being then on the poop supervising the readjustment of a hatch tarpaulin, the ship was struck just for'ard of the engine-room by a mine.

The explosion cracked five ribs, dislocated his shoulder, and three parts drowned him.

After he was brought ashore the doctors told him to take it easy for at least a month. By way of taking it easy he went down to Ramsgate, where his uncle had one of the new motor fishing boats. After five days of his aunt's cooking he began to get restless for the sea again. After seven days he was skipper of his uncle's fishing boat, and his uncle was taking a holiday.

It was a small boat, eighteen feet long, open, with the engine under a little dog-kennel cover, and no particular virtues. Tonight the engine had been sulky, diffident over starting, and secretive about its disabilities.

Dundas was inclined to thank it. If the engine had started easily, he would now be out in the very thick of the fog. When he came down to the dock there had been little sign that it would close down on them suddenly an hour later.

He bent down after a moment's rest, and began tinkering with it again. He had found the trouble—dirt in the magneto—and nothing remained now but to put the pieces together again.

The lantern he was working by made a pleasant pool of reddish light in the wide blackness about him. There was little more to do now. He felt curiously alone. Save for the steady lap and splash of the water against the sides of the boat and the stone of the wall, the night was empty of sound. Even the long low chorus of bellows and wails and grunts that normally accompanies a Channel fog was absent.

He finished piecing the engine together, replaced the cover, rolled the strap round the groove, and, giving a mighty heave, jerked it into sudden life.

After a moment he throttled down and listened contentedly to the steady purring.

Above him a voice spoke suddenly. It was an educated voice, pleasant, with a faint burr to it. 'May I come aboard?' said the unknown.

'Who are you?' said Dundas, startled suddenly out of the calm emptiness that had enclosed him.

'Cutmore's my name,' said the unknown. 'I'm from the minesweeper down the wall. Taking a breather before turning in.'

'Mind the weed on the ladder as you come down,' said Dundas.

The unknown came slowly down, a pair of long legs coming first into the glow of the lamp, followed gradually by a long body. The unknown wore a heavy overcoat, which appeared to impede somewhat his freedom of action.

'Been having trouble with that?' he said, indicating the engine. 'I heard you cursing when I passed a few minutes ago.'

'Yes,' said Dundas; 'she's a bitch, she is, but I think I've fixed her.'

'Going sweetly now?' said the unknown.

'Yes,' said Dundas.

'What can you get out of her?'

'Seven knots or thereabouts,' said Dundas.

'And what's her range with full tanks?'

'Eighty miles or so, I suppose,' said Dundas. 'I've never tried her out, really.'

'Tanks full now?' said the stranger.

'Yes—er——' Dundas's tone suddenly changed. 'May I ask why you are cross-examining me like this?'

'Forgive me,' said the stranger, 'but can you keep your mouth shut?'

'I—well, I suppose so; what is it?'

'As a matter of fact,' said the stranger, 'I'm a member of the Naval Intelligence service, and it is urgently necessary that I should be landed on the Belgian coast tonight. Almost anywhere along the coast will do, as long as it's clear of the German lines. I've an extraordinarily important job on hand, and it's got to be done in complete secrecy.'

Dundas lifted his face away from the glow of the lamp.

'Question of getting close enough in. You know the Belgian coast, I suppose. You know how it shoals? Difficult to get a destroyer close enough in to land me with comfort. The size is against it, too, she might easily be seen by the shore posts. It's essential that I should go by a small boat. As a matter of fact, the sweeper up the wall was to have taken me along, but she's developed engine-room defects. . . . That's why I came along to see if there was any possibility up here. They told me there was a motor-boat here. I came along, missed you the first time, and then found you by the noise of your engine.'

'You said you heard me the first time,' said Dundas. 'Heard me swearing.'

'Oh, yes,' said the stranger. 'I heard somebody swearing, but I didn't know it was you. As a matter of fact I went along to another boat up there, and they told me you were further back.'

'And that,' said Dundas, feeling in the dark for a screw wrench, 'proves you to be a liar, for there was only Terris up the wall, and he called good-night to me an hour ago. Your story's a lot of bull. You're coming along with me to the sweeper now.'

'I was wondering how long you'd take to see through it,' said the stranger coolly. 'No, don't move, I've got my foot on the monkey wrench, and I've got you covered with a fairly large calibre revolver. Now listen to me. . . .'

'You swine . . .' said Dundas provocatively.

'No you don't,' said the stranger. 'Keep absolutely still, because I shall shoot if you make the slightest movement, and I can hardly miss. I use soft-nosed bullets, too. Listen, I'm going to make you a fair offer. I want to charter this boat; it's absolutely necessary that I should charter it, and if you want it back you'll have to come with me. I've got to get to Bruges before ten o'clock tomorrow, and that means I've got to be on the Belgian coast by dawn. This boat can do it, and this fog makes it possible. If you'll take me there I'll give you sixty pounds, in one-pound notes. It's all I've got. If you won't do it, I'm going to shoot you now, and make a run for it myself. I can find my way out of this tin-pot basin, and I guess I can find the Belgian coast by myself. It's a fine night for yachting.'

The stranger used the same tone as he had used in the early stages of his conversation, but a faint overtone of menace had crept into it. Dundas, thinking as swiftly as the other talked, decided that he meant what he said.

'You wouldn't dare,' said he after a moment. 'The shot would rouse the whole harbour, and the sentries on the wall would get you long before you could clear the entrance.'

'In this fog?' said the stranger scornfully. 'I'll take the chance.'

'There's a boom across the mouth,' said Dundas.

'That's an afterthought,' said the stranger equably. 'I don't blame you. I'd lie myself if I were in your position, but it isn't any use, you know. Are you going to accept my offer?'

'No,' said Dundas. He thought rapidly for a moment. If he could edge back slowly he could perhaps slip the tiller out of its socket and, hitting blindly in the dark, knock the other out of the boat.

The stranger seemed to be able to read his mind. 'No you don't,' he said. 'If you edge back another inch I'll shoot, and I don't mind telling you that I am a prize-winner at revolver shooting.'

'Give me a minute to think it over,' said Dundas.

'I will if you turn round with your back to me. Do it slowly now. If you move too quickly I'll shoot.'

Dundas moved slowly round, shuffling cautiously on the floor boards. Immediately he felt something prod him in the back.

'This bullet will rip your spine clear out,' said the stranger softly. 'I warn you to make up your mind quickly. If this fog clears I'm done for, you see, and I'm not taking any risks.'

Dundas trod his mind as a squirrel treads its mill, but no help came. It was clear that this man was desperate. Whatever he had done, whatever he wanted to do, it was sufficiently obvious that he was prepared to risk his own life. It was equally obvious that he would not allow the life of any other to obstruct his purpose.

'Come on,' said the stranger again; 'sixty pounds is sixty pounds to a fisherman—and the season's bad, I know. Heroics won't help you if you're a corpse. Better take my offer and keep your mouth shut about it. Nobody will know, you can say you got lost in the fog, and couldn't get home again—engine broke down or something. Any tale. . . . Come on!'

'Can you give me any help when we get near the Belgian coast?' said Dundas suddenly. 'I don't know the marks.'

'Good man,' said the stranger; 'then you'll do it. No, I shan't be able to help you much. I don't know much about it.'

'Oh, well,' said Dundas slowly. 'Doesn't seem as if I've any choice, and I don't suppose it'll do much harm.'

'That's right,' said the stranger. 'That's splendid. Shall we unloosen the ropes.'

'Er—cast off—er, yes. Just a minute. Let me light the binnacle lamp. It'll be no joke working through in the fog, you know.'

'I know,' said the other, 'but I've been waiting for a fog for a whole week now.'

Dundas knelt down and, striking a match, lit the tiny lamp of the boat compass that he carried. The green card shone wanly in its glow. He could feel the muzzle of the stranger's revolver still pressed against his back.

'Sorry,' said the other, 'but I must safeguard myself till we're out of the harbour anyway.'

Fumbling, Dundas cleared the mooring lines, and the boat drifted away from the wall. Immediately she was lost to the world.

Dundas jerked at the starting strap, and the engine came throatily to life. Foam swirled under the stern of the boat, and she surged forward through the unseen water. The fog dragged past them, faintly gold in the light of the lamp.

'We'll have that out,' said Dundas after a moment; 'the visibility's impossible as it is.'

The stranger had squatted himself down next to the engine casing on the starboard side. He stretched out and grasped the lamp, found the wick lever, and turned it out.

They went on into the blackness with only the faint green eye of the binnacle making sign of life in it all.

After a minute or two Dundas put down the helm gently. 'We ought to make the entrance now,' he said.

The boat lifted to a little swell in immediate answer, and there was a momentary glance of a high black wall. From its top some one challenged, and Dundas answered, giving his name and the name of the boat.

The next instant they were outside in the live water, pitching a little to the lop that came up from the Downs.

'A-ah,' said the stranger relaxing. 'And that's that. Now you play me straight, young fellow, and you'll be sixty pounds the richer. How soon can we get across. It's about fifty-five miles, I should say—that's seven hours by this boat?'

Dundas shrugged in the darkness. 'It's sixty-five miles as the crow flies. We'll have to reckon with the tides though.'

'When's high tide?' said the stranger.

'High tide—oh, you mean the flood? Well, I'm not exactly sure,' said Dundas slowly. 'I'll tell you what I'm going to do. I'll go south and a little east now, and round the heel of the Goodwins, and then stand out with the flood, and get right across. With luck we'll make it by two o'clock.'

'That'll suit me,' said the stranger, 'but why not go straight?'

'Well, you see, this is an underpowered boat . . .' said Dundas slowly. 'Don't you know anything about the sea?'

'Nothing,' said the other airily. 'I was in the cavalry.'

'The Uhlans?' said Dundas swiftly.

'Don't ask questions, my little friend. You look after your steering.' He settled himself more comfortably. 'Remember,' he added after a moment, 'I still have my revolver in my hand. If you betray me, take me up to one of your patrol ships or anything, we will both die.'

Dundas grunted and peered into the binnacle.

For a long hour there was silence. Only the steady mutter of the engine, and the occasional lift and rattle of the screw in the stern glands, broke across the silence of the night. Water noises from the bow, and the lap-lap along the sides were somehow merged in the immense silence of the sea.

Only once, far away, they heard a bell buoy, and once the clatter of a ship's bell at anchor. At the end of the hour Dundas spoke again. 'We will have cleared the Goodwins now,' he said. 'I'm going to stand out across the heel of them. Like to see the course we're making?'

'How?' said the other.

'Look at the compass,' said Dundas.

'And bring my head in front of you with my back to you?' said the other. 'No, no, my little friend. Remember only that I have my revolver and the soft-nosed bullets—and that if I die, you die too. The steering is your business—so long as you remember that.'

Dundas grunted again, and shifted his helm very slightly.

For another hour they held on in silence, then Dundas heard a slight noise from for'ard. A faint, rasping noise. A moment later it came again, an unmistakable snore.

He nodded grimly to himself.

The snoring went on, grew louder, became more steady, more settled. It was plain that the stranger was fast asleep. For three hours it went on, varied occasionally by little grunts and slight pauses following a change of position.

Dundas occupied himself steadily with his helm, making tiny alterations of course from time to time, checking them carefully with a great silver watch that he held in the light of the binnacle lamp.

Quarter of an hour before midnight the stranger awoke. Dundas felt the jerk as he straightened up, hurriedly.

'You've been asleep', he said quietly, 'for a long time.'

The other muttered incoherently for a moment, and then said yes. Presently the implication seemed to strike him. 'And you tried nothing, no, no funny business.' He paused. 'That was good,' he said. 'You are being sensible, my young friend. Sixty pounds is sixty pounds. Ach—I was tired. Three days and three nights without sleep, most of them spent in the fields of the wretched country behind Ramsgate. *Lieber Gott*, I was tired.'

'Three days and three nights. That's since Monday, then?'

'Yes,' said the other.

'Monday was the day of the big explosion?'

'What of it?' said the other.

'You. . . .'

'Partly,' said the other cynically. 'Since you are being sensible it does not matter if you know.'

'But you are English, aren't you? Your voice. . . .'

'Come, come,' said the stranger. 'I was at an English school, but you knew from the start. . . .'

'I suppose so,' said Dundas grudgingly.

'And how near are we?'

'Not far now,' said Dundas. 'We should get there a little earlier than I thought, half-past one perhaps.'

'Good,' said the German.

With long spells of silence and occasional brief conversations they pressed on through the night. Once or twice the fog thinned slightly, so that they could see a boat's length from them over the darkling water. Twice Dundas tried to get the German to tell him why he had to be at Bruges in so painful a hurry, but the other avoided his questions adroitly.

Every now and then he seemed to be listening.

'Strange,' he said once. 'Strange, we should have heard the sound of the guns by now.'

'Nothing strange in fog,' said Dundas; 'you can hear something that's miles away sometimes, and another time miss a fog gun when you're right on top of it.'

The night was getting on now. When Dundas next looked at his watch it was a quarter past one. 'We should be very nearly there,' he said. 'Can you take a sounding?'

'What do I do?' said the other.

'Feel in the locker to your right and see if you can find a fishing line with a lead,' said Dundas. 'I'll slow down, and you throw it ahead of you, feel when it touches the bottom, and then measure it with your arms outstretched.'

The other fumbled for a bit, experimented once, and then after a second cast said, 'Nine times.'

'Call it eight fathoms,' said Dundas. 'We're closing in on the coast.'

Five minutes later he slowed for another cast.

'Six times,' said the German.

'Getting there; we're inside the five fathom line.'

Five minutes later they heard the sound of little seas on sand, a soft rustle that was yet loud enough to come over the noise of the engine, and the rustle and rush of their progress. Somewhere in the darkness a sleepy gull called.

'We're there,' said Dundas whispering; 'get ready.'

The other stood up, wrapping his coat about him. Even as he did so Dundas switched off the engine, and in absolute silence they glided in.

Suddenly the boat grated, dragged forward, and grated again. The German lurched, steadied himself with a hand on the thwart and said: 'Lieber Gott.'

'The money,' said Dundas.

'But yes,' said the German, fumbling in his pocket. 'You are sure this is Belgium?'

'By the distance we've run,' said Dundas, 'and the time, it must be.'

'Ha,' said the other, 'take it!'

Dundas met the other's hand and took a rolled bundle of notes. 'Thank you,' he said. 'Get out over the bows; there'll be a little more than a foot of water, and give me a shove off before you go. I must get afloat again.'

The other lumbered over the side, splashed for a moment, and then, bending down, heaved. The boat slid astern, Dundas pushing on the other side with the loom of an oar.

In a moment it floated free, surging back into deepish water. Dundas straightened himself, the starting strap in his hand.

'High tide's at three,' he called out loudly.

He heard the other splash through the shallows, and then a scrunch as he reached the dry sand beyond. A voice came clear out of the fog to him: 'What's that?'

He heard the feet run on, scrunching over the sand and then stop suddenly. The voice came out to him again. 'There's water here. A strip of sand and then. . . .'

'High tide's at three,' shouted Dundas again, 'but the Goodwins are covered before the flood.' He bent down and jerked at the starting strap and the engine woke to life. Sitting down he headed the boat round until her bows pointed a little west of north.

Swiftly he crossed the four-mile circle of water inside the Goodwin sands that he had thrashed round and round so many times during the long night. There was six miles between home and the neck of the South Goodwins, upon which a lone man stood watching the slow, relentless, upward movement of the tide.

'Thirty dead in the big explosion,' said Dundas softly to himself. 'Women, too. Well . . .' he fingered the roll of notes. 'Dirty money's as good as clean to the Red Cross fund. And the Goodwins pays for all.'

How Ryan Got Out of Russia

'Once again,' said Jorkens suddenly, either in answer to some remark that I had not heard or to some fierce memory that awoke in his mind, 'once again I must protest that anyone who finds anything unusual in any story that I may ever have happened to tell knows little of the stories that men do tell, daily, hourly, in fact all the time. All the twenty-four hours of every day there is someone telling some tale here in London, not to mention everywhere else, that is far less credible than anything I ever told. Then why do they single me out for what I can only call incredulity? Can you answer me that? No. And can you tell me any tale I have ever told you that has been definitely disproved in a properly scientific manner? No,' he added before giving anyone very much time, not that anyone seemed ready with any case in point. 'And I'll tell you what,' Jorkens went on: 'I'm ready to prove what I say. I'm ready to take anyone now and show him someone within a mile from here who is telling stranger tales than I've ever told, at this very minute. And if he isn't, he'll begin as soon as we ask him. As many of you as you like. Now, who'll come?'

'Very well, very well,' Jorkens went on. 'You'll none of you come. Then please never say, or allow anyone else to say, that I tell any more unusual tales than other people. Because I've given you an opportunity of putting it to the proof; and you won't take it. Very well. Waiter.'

In another moment Jorkens would have settled down to a large whiskey; he would have soothed himself with it; he would then have slept a little; when he awoke he would have forgotten his anger, for he is never angry for long, and with his anger he would have forgotten the whole episode, including the man to whom he offered to take us. I don't say that Jorkens's tales are unusual, or that they are usual; I leave the reader to judge that; but I do say that anyone whose tales were more unusual would certainly have something to tell that was distinctly out of the way. So before Jorkens had caught the waiter's eye, before any whiskey had had time to be brought to him, I said: 'That is unsporting of them, Jorkens. You have offered to prove that your stories are not unusual, as stories go. They should give you a chance to prove it. I'll come.'

Jorkens looked for a moment a little regretfully in the direction of the screen at the far end of the room, behind which were the waiters, and then said: 'Very well.' So away we went from the Billiards Club, and soon we were in a taxi, going towards Soho, with Tutton, another member, who at the last moment came too.

I thought that even in the taxi Jorkens was regretting his whiskey, for he sat silent; but when we got to the dingy café to which he had directed the driver, a dark little place called 'The Universe', and we went in and he saw at once the man he was looking for, he brightened up a good deal. The man was seated alone at one of the tables, eating some odd foreign dish. 'Look at his forehead,' said Jorkens.

'Yes,' I said. 'He hasn't got one.'

'Well, a pair of bulging eyebrows,' said Jorkens. 'But no forehead. As you say. Not a man to imagine anything.'

'Not in the least,' I said.

'No, no,' said Tutton.

'Very well,' said Jorkens.

He took hold of a couple of chairs then, and dragged them up to the man's table, while I brought one for myself.

'A couple of friends,' said Jorkens, 'who would like to hear your tale.' And all at the same moment he made a sign with one finger to a waiter whose home I would have placed as the East of Europe, though I could get no nearer than that; and the sign meant evidently absinthe, for one came. The man had not spoken yet; then he tasted the absinthe; tasted it again, to be sure it was all right; then started at once. 'I was in a Russian prison,' he said. 'The walls were ten feet thick. And I was sentenced to death.'

'Begin at the beginning,' said Jorkens.

'Sentenced to die next morning, as a matter of fact,' the man went on; 'so there wasn't much time. And I was working on the mortar round one of the big stones with the edge of a button off my trousers.'

'At the beginning,' said Jorkens.

'Oh,' said the man; and he looked up from his absinthe, his clipped black moustache wet with it, his eyes groping with memory. Then he started again.

'I never knew who I was spying for,' he said.

'Tell them how you came to be spying,' said Jorkens.

'I got into a chess-club in Paris,' said the man. And he took another drink from his glass of absinthe and it all seemed to come back to him. 'It was a dark low sty of a place. I only went there twice. It was only the second time I ever went there that I looked up from the game I was play-ing, at one of the other tables. I was having a good enough game and getting a bit the best of it, and I turned to look at one of the other tables while my man was making his move, a table level with mine on the other side of the gangway, and got the shock of my life. I saw all of a sudden that one of the two players didn't know the move of the knight. He was moving it anyhow, and his opponent was taking no notice. Well, it wasn't a chess club.

'I'd been introduced to the place by a man of whom I knew nothing. No help there. The man I was playing with was a chess-player all right, but one swallow doesn't make a summer. I glanced at a few other boards, and saw pretty much the same thing going on as I had seen at the table beside me. Chess was a blind. What did go on there? I was a long way from the door, and I felt most damnably alone.'

'You've never told me, you know,' said Jorkens, 'what you were doing in Paris.'

'Just looking round to see what would turn up,' said the man.

'Oh well, go on,' replied Jorkens.

He took another sip at the absinthe, and went on.

'I began looking round at the door then, and seeing how many men there were sitting between me and it. I couldn't have done anything worse. I couldn't have made myself more conspicuous if I'd made a dash for it. They followed the turn of my eyes, and all seemed to read my thoughts. And a man got up from another table presently, and loafed my way as though he were not coming up to me. But I knew he was. He passed my table, but turned round at once, and spoke to me. 'Are you one of us?' he said.

'It was no use saying Yes. You can't invent passwords. They'd have plenty of them all right. I knew the kind of people they were, the moment I discovered what they were not.

'So I said, "No, but I wish to be."

'It was the only thing to do. But it let me in for a lot of oaths, of which I can tell you nothing; with penalties attached, you know. And I became a member of the lowest degree, of an association of which I still know practically nothing at all. All I really knew of its aims was that they seemed to be to give orders to members of the degree to which I belonged. And you had to obey those orders. Otherwise, several unpleasant things, behind the screen at the end of that dingy room, the far end from the door of course, and the Seine afterwards.

'Well, I got away from that room, and I went back to Mimi. I haven't told you about Mimi. And I said to her: "Mimi, that chess-club isn't a chess-club; it's something else, and I've got to leave Paris."

'And she said at once: "Don't you go. People like that would be sure to watch you. Don't let them see you trying to get away. It's not safe."

'And, do you know, she was right. But all I said to her was: "People like that, Mimi? But I've not told you what they are like."

'And all she would say was: "I know that type," and went on urging me not to try to go.

'She was right, sure enough. They were watching me. I saw Mimi gazing out of the window next morning, and saying nothing, just gazing, till I went up and gazed too. And there was a man outside looking too unconcerned, looking a shade too thoughtfully up at the sky; and I knew Mimi was right.

'So I merely stayed with Mimi. And one day the order came. I was to go round to the chess-club that evening to receive instructions from the Grand Master. Well, I went. I had a pretty shrewd idea as to what those instructions would be. But I went.

'Well, there he was all dressed up, at the dark end of the room, dingy and curtained off, and a couple of candles.

'"You will go to Russia," he said; and before he had time to get in another word I slipped in with what I had to say. "Not to assassinate anybody," I said. I slipped in with in then because once he had given me my orders there was an end of it. If I disobeyed after that it was the Seine, with certain accessories: if I let him see now that I wouldn't do it for certain, there seemed the ghost of a chance. Why put themselves to the trouble of carrying a sack all the way to the Seine at night, I thought, if they knew they had nothing to gain by it? It was a slender chance. He seemed surprised, and was silent a moment. "And if he has already signed the death-warrants of two hundred thousand innocent men and women?" he said.

'"That's his affair," I said. "I attend to mine."

'"You wouldn't kill even such a man?" he said.

'"No," I answered.

'He was silent again; so were the others; the sort of silence that seemed like earthquake, or any awful natural disaster; and the sort of robes they were wearing rustled against the silence. It was only two seconds, probably, before he spoke again.

'"I have not commanded you to assassinate anyone," he said.

'So it worked, my slender chance.

'"You are to destroy something deadlier than a man," he said, "But perhaps your scruples won't let you hurt a machine?"

'The words sound simple, but he said them nastily enough.

'"I obey," I said.

'"You will go to Russia," he repeated. "There is a machine in Novarsinsk that makes certain munitions. There are only three of them in Russia. They are the three deadliest machines in the world. You will wreck one of them."

'He ceased speaking. Others gave me my passport, money, railway tickets, and a varnished walking-stick half of which was a steel bar. I was to break off the bar later on and secrete it in my clothing, and drop it one day into the machine. And they gave me a testimonial that seemed to make me out one of the world's best experts in the handling of that particular machine, signed by some fellow that seemed to cut a good deal of ice in Russia; forged of course. I knew something of engineering, but not that much.

'"What will I do with the machine?" I asked.

'But they were busy closing down their meeting. "You won't be there long," said one of them, "before you drop the bar in. Then you get back here as quickly as possible." And he rather hustled me out. He was the man that saw me off next day, by the train across Europe. I tried to tell Mimi something about it without giving anything away. There's a lot I haven't told you: I told Mimi still less. And yet she seemed to guess a good deal of it. And the odd thing was she said I'd come back all right. Lord knows how she knew. And I remembered what she said, through the oddest experiences, and when a thousand to one against her being right looked like a safe bet to lay. And what odds wouldn't it be safe to lay against the life of a man in prison in Russia, sentenced to death, with walls round him ten feet thick; and guilty too?

'Well I went all through Europe, past the German rye-fields, silvery green, and a great many other things, but I wasn't thinking so much of scenery as of my chances of ever seeing it again, coming the other way. You see, I fancied I should come out of Russia by train, if I ever came out at all. You can waste your time guessing how I did come out, if you like. Certainly I never guessed it.

'Well, I arrived and showed my testimonial. It looked a good one to me when first I saw it, but nothing to what it looked to them: I was evidently just the one man in the world they were waiting for; they seemed a bit short of engineers. They brought me along to their machine; and, except that it was a machine and needed oiling, I knew very little about it. It was a huge affair, as big as the engines of a small ship; and there it was roaring away underneath me, and they looking at it as though—well, there simply weren't any standards of comparison; they hadn't any religion, and no king, and didn't care overmuch about human life, so it's no use saying it was like one of their children to them, or a god or anything else; but I saw, from the way they looked at it, roughly what they would do to anybody that hurt it. Well, I went round oiling it, but as that was about all I was able to do for it, for a wage of £2,000 a year, I thought the sooner I wrecked it and cleared out the better. And so I did. Not the clearing out; they saw to that; but the wrecking of it. I pushed the steel bar, a foot and a half of it, in through a grating with my fore-finger at the end of it, with which I gave it a good send off, and it went down like an arrow in amongst the great cogs of the wheels, till a heaving piston hid it out of my sight, and it didn't heave any more, and the roar of the engine that had been like a huge purr changed its note suddenly. I didn't like that change of note coming as quick as it did. I don't know what else I expected. I see now that I might as well have tried to kill a tiger in the Zoo with a spike, and expect that none of the keepers would notice, as expect to smash a machine like that quietly. Of course I was alone when I did it, but the thing began roaring like a wounded gorilla that has been trapped in a china shop, and the Bolshies rushed in on me. Of course I said I knew nothing about it, and they didn't try to mob me. They said there would have to be a trial and they took me to prison, but they were rather polite than otherwise. I got the idea that they would never be able to prove anything, and that my chances were quite good. What I was worrying mostly about was that they might keep me a long time in prison before they had any trial, several months perhaps; but they were in more of a hurry to deal with me than I knew. As for my chances, the first shadow came over them when one of the Russians came to the prison to question me. "You can prove nothing whatever," I had remarked to him.

'"Prove things," he answered. "We don't waste time proving things when we know perfectly well what has happened."

'"You have to in a court of law," I said.

'"Have to? Why?" he asked.

'"Because you might punish an innocent man otherwise," I told him.

'He laughed rather a nasty laugh at that. "And if we stopped the course of the law for that," he said, "we'd stop ploughing the steppes with our motor-tractors for fear of killing a worm."

'I was on the point of telling him things were different in England, and stopped myself in time and did a good deal of thinking.

'And then the trial came on, very soon, as I said. I'd worked out a good enough defence. Who had ever seen me with a steel bar? How could I have concealed it? Why should I wreck a machine that was to pay me £2,000 a year? And a lot more points besides. But somehow when I looked at them in their law-court I got the idea that they were up to all that. And at the very last moment I felt I must do something better.

'The charge was read out and the judge looked straight at me. "Did you do it?" he said.

'"Yes," I replied, on the spur of the moment.

'"Why?" he asked.

'"I was compelled to, by capitalists," I answered.

'They were interested at once. "Of what country?" he asked me.

'"England," I said; and watched how the answer went down.

'"Who gave you your orders?" asked the judge.

'"The Archbishop of Canterbury," I said, and saw that I had said the right thing. I didn't expect to get off scot-free, but if I could get the blame on to English capitalists I felt sure they would spare my life.

'"Where did he give you your orders?" said the judge.

'"At the back of his cathedral," I answered.

'It was just right. They'd never have heard of Lambeth, and they'd have known that a secular conversation of that sort would not have gone on within the cathedral; but the shadow of its huge walls, at the back, out of the way, would have been the perfect scene for it. And they believed me too. I could see that.

'"What were his exact words?" said the judge.

'And that was where I crashed. I had nothing prepared, and with the judge's eyes on my face I had no time to prepare it now.

'"Those accursed Russians have a machine," I began; but I saw from a change in their faces that it was no good. And one watches men's faces pretty closely when one's life hangs on what they are thinking about. You see, I hadn't liked to blackguard them too much to their faces, but my silly politeness ruined me; I should have given them the talk that they would have expected from a prominent personage of a capitalist country, instead of mincing my words as I did. Look what they had done to religion. They would have expected the archbishop to talk pretty stiffly about them, and I was altogether too mild. So all I got for trying to spare their feelings was a death sentence. I saw they had stopped believing me, and somehow after that my answers were merely silly. And in a minute or two the judge took a pull at his cigarette and leaned back and looked at me, then shot the smoke out of his lungs and said two words in Russian.

'"Tell him it's death," I heard one of them say. And the sentry standing beside me, with a very nasty-looking bayonet fixed, took out his cigarette and said: "It's death," and went on with his smoking.

'They hadn't got my real name yet, and now they asked for it, just when it seemed not to matter any longer. I gave them the name of Bourk.'

'And what name do you give us?' asked Jorkens.

The man thought for a moment, and then said: 'Ryan.'

'This is where the tale gets a little unusual,' said Jorkens to us. And the man went on.

'When they took me back to the prison I knew I hadn't got very long. The English idea on these occasions is to give a man a little time to look after his soul; but in Russia, where you don't have one, they weren't likely to keep me waiting.

'I'd looked at the stones in my prison wall pretty thoughtfully; square grey blocks that had once had plaster over them; and now I decided to work the mortar away and get one out, after which some of the others should come more easily, and see where the hole led to. I had ten buttons on my trousers; metal ones; and by bending one of them double I got some sort of a point, and I started to scrape away the mortar at once, so as not to waste time, which was precious. The mortar came easily, being old and full of damp, and presently I began to hope. I had a chair in the cell, and I kept it handy: whenever I heard the lock in my door beginning to move I slewed the chair round and sat on it with my back to the stone I was working on. The lock didn't move often; a man came twice a day with my food, and sometimes loafed in at an odd hour, making three times in all; but on this day he came in once oftener, attracted, I suppose, by the interesting news that they had condemned me to death. I always had my chair in place by the time the key had turned, and was sitting on it before the door began to open. By nightfall I had the stone loose, and had only used two buttons, and even they were by no means finished. That night I got it out, and worked till dawn on one of the stones behind it; then I tidied up the dust, eating some of it, and put the stone back, and had some sleep for an hour or two. But I didn't want to waste much time on sleep, as I didn't know how long I'd got; and early that morning I was at work again, this time on the next stone. And I was getting along splendidly.

'They are devils. They know how to make you despair. I had never despaired in all my life before. I had held back from despair as you keep from the brink of a precipice. But those Russians brought me to it. They must have been watching me through some spy-hole they had; for the lock turned and one of them came in, and there was I sitting comfortably in my chair with my back to the loose stones, and the bent bit of button in my pocket. And he never said a word. Just threw a hammer and a good sharp chisel down on the floor in front of me, and walked out of the cell. Then I knew that those walls must be about ten feet thick, and that nothing was any good, and I left the hammer and chisel where they had fallen and gave myself up to despair. If he had put me into a lower dungeon, or manacled me, or flogged me, I could have held out against it, but that hammer and chisel somehow or other seemed the very last notes of doom.

'The man that came in with my food just looked at the chisel, as you might take a look at a snake, just to see that I wasn't near enough to use it on him; then he left it and the hammer lying there.

'Next day I was sitting there hopeless, when in walked another fellow, a good deal neater than the rest. I looked up.

'"Do you want a reprieve?" he said.

'But I had seen the look on his face. I don't know what I thought he was going to ask for; to betray all those people in Paris, I suppose. But the look on his face was enough, and I said: "No, thank you."

'"Not want a reprieve?" he asked.

'"No, not today, thank you," I answered.

'"If it's not today, you'll not want it at all," he said. "You're for the cellar tomorrow morning."

'And he hung about near the door, to see if I'd changed my mind. But I wouldn't. I felt sure that there must be some crab in it, from the look I had seen on his face.

'Well, a little while later another man came in, as though the first hadn't come in at all.

'"I've got a reprieve for you," he said.

'"What have I got to do for it?" I asked him.

'"We want to explore a distant place; perhaps to colonize it," he said. "We want you to go there first, and light a fire as a sign when you get there."

'"What else?" I asked.

'"Nothing else," he said.

'"How do I get there?" said I.

'"We send you," he said.

'"Where is it?" I asked.

"'The moon,' he replied.

"'Nonsense,' I said.

"'Yes, to capitalists,' he answered. "They're all two hundred years behind Russia; and imperialism is as far as they can think. But the moon is well within the scope of our scientists."

"'How would you get me there?' I asked.

"'Shoot you out of a gun,' he said.

"'Well, there's two reasons why you couldn't do that,' I told him.

"'Well?' he said with a superior smile.

"'Firstly,' I said, "the thing would smash to fragments on landing; or more likely melt."

"'There's a parachute that you can release from a spring inside,' he said, "as soon as you see you're close. The head of the shell is crystal."

"'Well, there's another reason,' I said. "Starting off at a thousand feet per second would merely finish one. Why, even a railway train . . .'"

"'You don't,' he said. "You're moving at nearly three hundred miles an hour when you enter the gun."

"'How do you manage that?' I asked.

'Always the slow superior smile, as though their scientists were all grown up and the people in other countries only children.

"'We've rails,' he said, "and the shell is on very low wheels. It runs on those rails over what is almost a precipice, four or five hundred feet of it, and that's how it gets its pace. The moment it enters the tunnel a steel door falls behind it. The tunnel's the gun. As in any gun, the near end, the chamber, is larger, and the powder is stacked there all round you; but when you get to the barrel it exactly fits the shell, even to a groove for the wheels. The powder is ignited behind you the moment you pass, slow-burning big blocks of black powder, slow-burning I mean when compared with modern explosives, and by the time you leave the muzzle you have your maximum speed. Is that simple enough for you?"

"'Is the gun rifled?' I asked.

'Again the smile, as though he spoke to a child. "Of course," he said. "The grooves for the wheels are twisted round the barrel."

"'Then the spin will addle my brains,' I said, "and I shan't unloose any parachute."

"'There's a gyroscope in your cabin,' he answered.

"'What? The outside spins, while the gyroscope holds the cabin?'

"'Of course,' he said.

"'And what will I breathe?' I asked.

"'Oxygen,' he replied.

'"And eat and drink?"

'"We give you supplies," said he.

'"And how long will they last on the moon?" I asked.

'"We'll send over more shells," he said.

'"Supposing one of them hits me," I said.

'"Very unlikely," he answered. "Whereas our man in the cellar was working hard all through the busy time, perhaps fifty thousand cases, and he's never missed yet."

'I could see they were pretty keen for me to go, from that tactful reference to the swine in the cellar. Well, I wasn't keen on the cellar, and I accepted. A bit longer to live, and that was to the good, and anyway I would get out of Russia.

'They released me from the prison and housed me decently; as a matter of fact there was tapestry all over the walls; but it wasn't any easier to escape; they saw to that all right. There was a courtyard all round the palace in which they kept me, and a thirty-foot wall beyond, and plenty of soldiers walking about between.

'What they were keenest on was my lighting a fire when I got there: they gave me a packet of powder to spread over a hundred yards square, and they were going to watch with their telescopes. They were keen on Russia being the first to do it, and keen on proving they had. Any Russians that they could spare they had probably killed already, so they had to send people like me. If I lit the fire they would send other men after me; if I didn't they would send over no more provisions. They fed me well, very well indeed, in fact they seemed as fond of me as a farmer is of a good fat turkey when it is getting near Christmas. They took me out and showed me their apparatus; a huge high iron scaffold on a hill, with a lift running up it, and the rails running airily down over a flimsy viaduct, and their long steel tunnel lying along the fields, slanting very slightly upwards, just enough for the shell to clear the low hills in the West on its way to the new moon. New, you see, so that it would most of it be in darkness and they would be able to see my fire. And there was the shell all ready, waiting at the end of its rail. And they opened it and showed me my bunk inside, like the smallest berth on a boat you ever saw; barely room to turn round; a nasty place to spend ten days or a fortnight. And the gadgets they showed me too, the oxygen gas-mask for use on the moon and the switch for releasing the parachute that was to steady the shell before landing. When it came to the switch for the parachute I pointed out that there wasn't much air on the moon. "Not much," said one of them, the same man that first offered me the reprieve; "but we have evidence that there is some. Four or five hundred feet would be all you'd want for the parachute," brushing aside lightly enough what was probably the principal drawback. I bet he'd have worried more about that air if he'd been the one that was going.

'Then we went down and had a look at the tunnel, with its steel door up in the air like a guillotine, the door that was to fall behind me the moment the shell ran in, and would close the breech of the gun. We walked in and saw the big blocks of black powder lying beside the rails and stacked round the walls, and then the sudden narrowing of the tunnel.

'"The bigger the blocks of powder the slower they burn," said my friend, if one can use such a word of the man who had sneeringly offered reprieve. "The explosion gradually increases in force all the time you are in the gun."

'I may say that that moon-shooting tunnel was nearly three hundred yards long.

'There seemed sense in what they told me about the gun, but I couldn't get over my fear that the lunar atmosphere would be too thin for the parachute, and that I should crash through it and melt on landing. I watched them talking among themselves in the tunnel and knew what they were saying, though I didn't know Russian: they were boasting that the USSR would do it.

'"It's a thousand to one against getting there," I blurted out to the man who talked English.

'"Russia will do it," he answered. "Our scientists don't leave things to prayer or chance, like the people in capitalist countries. If it's a thousand to one we'll send a thousand men, and get one there, and then a thousand more, and as many thousands as we need to get enough there to colonize it."

'So that was the sort of men they were.

'Well, there seemed nothing for it but to try to live as long as I could. "Will you give me a fortnight's holiday before I start?" I said.

'And to my surprise they said Yes. Well, next day Eisen called for me rather early; that's what the sneering man called himself, the man whose reprieve I'd refused; and he said that he wanted to show me all over the shell again so that I should know all about it, and that after that we'd go to a theatre, and to a dance with some girls he knew. He talked of the girls all the way to the high, gaunt tower, and they really seemed very nice. One in particular, he said, would be very glad to meet me: he knew her tastes. He said this just as I got inside the shell; he had been describing her all the way up in the lift. The moon, a little past full, was high in the sky behind us as I got in, the long gun pointing away from it. Eisen put his hand in and began showing me things; then he questioned me about everything in the shell, because he said that I had to know all about it before I went on my holiday, and he kept on explaining about spreading the powder on a hundred yards square on the moon. "She's a very pretty one, that girl," he said all of a sudden. Then he showed me how the door shut.

'There was a grinding of wheels at once. Lord! we were off! I thought at first that it was an accident, but I've found that, however easily people fool you, you find it out when you think it over, sometimes long afterwards. Having the moon behind me was one thing that helped to fool me. It never occurred to me that the gun might be aiming at just where the moon would be ten days to a fortnight later, when the shell would be due to arrive. Well, it was a sickening feeling, dropping down the rails from that tower. I lay there on the sort of bed, wondering when we'd come to the tunnel. As a matter of fact I remember nothing of that. It was all very well for them to talk of the increase of speed being gradual, but somewhere or other in that tunnel I must have had a jolt that was a bit too much for my brains; for I opened my eyes feeling very sleepy indeed, and when I remembered what had been happening and looked out through the crystal window, there was nothing but sky in sight.

'That damned Russian had turned on the oxygen, or I wouldn't have been alive. How many hours or days had passed since leaving earth I had no idea, nor any idea how far we were away from it. Nor could I see the moon. All I knew was that I was rushing through space at the pace of a bullet, and all I felt was the most absolute stillness, the most absolute stillness that I have ever known; and no sound but the purr of my gyroscope that was keeping my cabin steady while the shell rotated. No sound of any wind or the passage of air; so I knew I was outside Earth's atmosphere. An intolerable glitter oppressed me, a glare still and unflickering, sunlight rushing through space unhindered by clouds or air. I shut my eyes to escape it, but could not sleep; and so hours went by. And then a shadow came over us that I felt through my closed eyes, and I looked through the crystal again, and at once the stars came out. This blessed shadow wrapped us for half an hour, and passed away again and the glare returned.'

'What made the shadow?' I asked.

And Ryan looked up wearily from his absinthe, weary still, it seemed, from the memory of that long journey, unsheltered in sunlight: 'Sunset,' he said, 'and then in half an hour it came up on the other side. We were as far as that from Earth.'

'How awful,' I couldn't help saying.

'But I was out of Russia,' he said. 'Still I couldn't see the moon. I didn't know where I was or how long we'd been going. I ate some food: I didn't know how many hours or days I had been without it; and I drank some water, and it tasted good. And then a curious thing happened. I'd been lying back in my bunk, facing the way we were going, with my feet a lot higher than my head.'

'You should never sleep like that,' said Jorkens.

'No,' replied Ryan, 'and it probably helped to keep me unconscious much longer than I should have been otherwise. But I don't know. But now I was sliding down more and more to the other end, and pressing against my feet. The head of the shell had been higher than its base, and was now evidently lower. I drank a lot more water during the next few hours, which I seemed to want more than food; and nothing else changed. And then my bed seemed to be a little steeper, and I was pressing a little harder against my feet. And suddenly through the crystal head of the shell the weary steely glitter disappeared, and a soft grey took its place. The relief to the eye, and the brain itself, was immense. But I had no idea where I was, or what was happening. And then sound came again, the sound of what could only be air. And the soft grey darkened. It came to me with extraordinary suddenness, and nearly too late, that it was time to use the parachute. It worked, and there was a bump that broke the end of my bed. We had landed. The first thing I did was to slip on the oxygen gas-mask, that they had given me to wear when walking about on the Moon. I could see nothing at all, for most of the crystal nose of the shell was buried, and the rest of it was all blurred, with some atmospheric disturbance that looked like rain. Then I opened the door that Eisen had shut in Russia, and walked out wearing my gas-mask; and sure enough it was rain, and it splashed on my eye-pieces and dimmed them at once, and it seemed to be evening. From a soft patch of soil in which we had luckily landed I stepped at once on an expanse that I could feel rather than see to be utterly devoid of all vegetation. In fact it was exactly the sandy or gravelly waste that I had expected to find by the shore of some dried-up lunar sea. But our anticipations do not always guide us aright; for suddenly just behind me I heard the words: "Are you aware you are trespassing?"

'Yes, it was England. England all over. And a man who couldn't have been either a Russian or an inhabitant of the moon came towards me, looking at me out of his eye-glass, along his gravel drive. My shell had landed in one of his flower-beds, and the parachute draped all over it looked like a fallen tent. Well, I'm not a lunatic. So I didn't say to him: "I have come out of a gun in Russia, but I was looking for the moon." No, I said: "I'm very sorry, sir, but I'm down from London, camping; and I didn't know it was private. I'll go away at once." He gave one disgusted look at his flower-bed, and went away with his nose in the air. You see, I'd told him exactly what he'd expected, as when I told the Russians about the Archbishop of Canterbury, and there was no more for him to say. Well, I didn't like to leave that shell for the Press of the world to write about. I was none too sure I mightn't get extradited over that business of the steel bar. So I got hold of the powder that was to light up the moon, and mixed it with everything inflammable in the shell and put the oxygen canisters on top of it; and, protecting it all from the rain with the parachute, I set the whole thing alight. It made a fine glow in the sky; but they wouldn't have seen that in Russia: they were looking for it in the wrong place. And I doubt if what was left of the shell after that got into even the local papers. And by the evening of the next day I saw Mimi again, as she had told me I would.'

'Now, you know, that's unusual,' said Jorkens to Tutton and me. 'I should say distinctly unusual.'

A Patriot

The other day I was told a true story, which I remember vaguely
hearing or reading about during the war, but which is worth retelling for
those who missed it, for it has certain valuable ironic implications and a
sort of grandeur. It concerns one of those beings who, when they spy
upon us, are known by that word of three letters, as offensive as any in
the language, and when they spy for us are dignified by the expression
'Secret Service', and looked on as heroes of at least second water.

You will recollect that when the war broke out, the fifteen hundred
persons engaged in supplying Germany with information, mainly trivial
and mostly erroneous, concerning our condition and arrangements, were
all known by the authorities and were put out of action at a single swoop.
From that moment there was not one discovered case of espionage by
spies already resident in England when war was declared. There were,
however, a few and, I am told, unimportant discovered cases of espionage
by persons who developed the practice or went into England for the purpose, during the war. This story concerns one of the latter.

In August 1914 there was living in America a business man of German
birth and American citizenship, called—let us say, for it was not his name—
Lichtfelder, who had once been an officer in the German Army; a man
of about fifty, of square and still military appearance, with rather short
stiff hair, a straight back to his head, and a patriotic conscience too strong
for his American citizenship. It was not long then before an American
called Lightfield landed in Genoa and emerged as Lichtfelder at the German
headquarters of his old regiment, offering his services.

'No,' they said to him, 'you are no longer a young and active man, and
you are an American citizen. We are very disappointed with our Secret
Service in England; something seems to have gone wrong. You can be
of much greater service to the Fatherland if, having learned our codes,

you will go to England as an American citizen and send us all the information you can acquire.'

Lichtfelder's soul was with his old regiment; but, being a patriot, he consented. During the next two months he made himself acquainted with all the tricks of his new trade, took ship again at Genoa, and reappeared as Lightfield in the United States. Soon after this he sailed for Liverpool, well stocked with business addresses and samples, and supplied with his legitimate American passport in his own American name.

He spent the first day of his 'Secret Service' wandering about the docks of a town which, in his view—if not in that of other people—was a naval station of importance; he also noted carefully the half-militarized appearance of the khaki figures in the streets; and in the evening he penned a business letter to a gentleman in Rotterdam, between the lines of which, devoted to the more enlightened forms of—shall we say?—plumbing, he wrote down in invisible ink all he had seen—such and such ships arrived or about to sail; such and such 'khaki' drilling or wandering about the streets; all of which had importance in his view, if not in fact. He ended with the words: 'Morgens Dublin Lichtfelder', and posted the letter.

Now, unfortunately for this poor but simple patriot, there was a young lady in the General Post Office who was spending her days in opening all letters with suspected foreign addresses, and submitting them to the test for invisible ink. To her joy—for she was weary at the dearth of that useful commodity—between the lines of this commercial screed, which purported to be concerned with the refinements of plumbing, out sprang the guilty ink. To a certain Department were telephoned the incautious 'Morgens Dublin Lichtfelder'. Now, no alien in those days was suffered to leave for Ireland save through a bottle-neck at Holyhead. To the bottle-neck then went the message: 'Did man called Lichtfelder travel yesterday to Dublin?' The answer came quickly: 'American called Lightfield went Dublin yesterday returned last night, is now on train for Euston.' At Euston our patriot, after precisely three days of secret service, was arrested, and lodged wherever they were then lodged.

'I am,' he said, 'an American citizen called Lightfield.'

'That,' said the British Cabinet, not without disagreement, 'makes a difference. You shall be tried by ordinary process of law, and defended by counsel chosen by the American Embassy at our expense, instead of by court martial.'

Speedily—for in those days the law's delays were short—the American citizen called Lightfield, alias Lichtfelder, was put on his trial for supplying information to the enemy; and for three days, at the Government's expense, a certain eminent counsel gave the utmost of his wits to preparing his defence. But a certain great advocate, whose business it was to prosecute, had given the utmost of his wits to considering with what question he should open his cross-examination, since it is well known how important is the first question; and there had come to him an inspiration.

'Mr Lichtfelder,' he said, fixedly regarding that upright figure in the dock, 'tell me: have you not been an officer in the German Army?'

The hands of the American citizen went to his sides, and his figure stiffened. For hours he had been telling the Court how entirely concerned he was with business, giving his references, showing his samples, explaining that—as for the lines in invisible ink in this letter, which he admitted sending—well, it was simply that he had met a Dutch journalist on board the ship coming out, who had said to him: 'You know, we can get no news at all, we neutrals—do send us *something*—not, of course, harmful to England, but *something* we can say.' And he had sent it. Was it harmful? It was nothing but trifles he had sent. And now, at that first question, he was standing suddenly a little more erect, and—silent.

And the great advocate said:

'I won't press you now, Mr Lichtfelder: we will go on to other matters. But I should like you to think that question over, because it is not only the first question that I ask you—it will also be the last.'

And the Court adjourned, the cross-examination not yet over, with that question not yet asked again.

In the early morning of the following day, when the warder went to the cell of Lichtfelder, there, by his muffler, dangled his body from the grating. Beneath the dead feet the cell Bible had been kicked away; but since, with the stretching of the muffler, those feet had still been able to rest on the ground, the patriot had drawn them up, until he was choked to death. He had waited till the dawn, for on the cell slate was written this:

I am a soldier with rank I do not desire to mention . . . I have had a fair trial of the United Kingdom. I am not dying as a spy, but as a soldier. My fate I stood as a man, but I can't be a liar and perjure myself. . . . What I have done I have done for my country. I shall express my thanks, and may the Lord bless you all.

And from the ten lawyers—eight English and two American—who, with me, heard the story told, there came, as it were, one murmur: 'Jolly fine!'

And so it was!

A Double Double-Cross

I

In an attractive villa between Nîmes and Avignon lives Roanne—to be precise, Roanne Lucrezia Loranoff. It was believed by the assortment of individuals who still meet, occasionally, in the little room upstairs at Père Benoit's, in Ostend, that Loranoff was not her actual surname but that it was a much more important name. John Varnak of the yellow beard and loud laugh—that same Varnak who was stabbed last August in a mean alley in Leningrad—said that she was a princess. It was, however, agreed that the point was immaterial. She was Roanne—which was sufficient.

In the years which followed the ending of the first war, when open diplomacy was so fashionable that the secret service and intelligence departments of every country were worked to death, Roanne functioned very adequately. She was one of the few aristocratic young women who had escaped from the Soviets with no harm, except a twisted little finger—caused by some ruffian tearing off a too-well-fitting ring—and a desire to annoy anybody who was a man.

She did none of the things which *émigrées* did. She left the stage, the Parisian cabarets and New York society severely alone. She called herself Loranoff, and spied—most excellently. In a year she had made a reputation on counter-espionage work which made old hands jealous. Half a dozen countries employed Roanne at different times. But she served only one master at once. She was dependable. Male secret service people, carefully warned against her wiles, went down like ninepins. In 1920 she rifled John Varnak's dispatch-case while he, driven desperate by the pain of her supposed toothache, wandered about Milan at three o'clock in the morning in search of a dentist. He said afterwards that he knew it would happen, but that he 'couldn't *not* believe her', when she said she was hurt.

From her feet upwards she was the woman that most men dream of. She was supple and slim, but not too slim; her taste in clothes and her method of wearing them were exquisite. Her skin was like milk, and when she pulled off her hat, you expected, for some reason, to see black hair. You did not. She was an ash blonde. Even women gazed after her when she walked. This was Roanne, who, at this moment, lives at the Villa Lucretia between Nîmes and Avignon.

II

When Duplessis stepped off the boat at Dieppe, Roanne, standing on the railway side of the *octroi*, spotted him immediately.

Maltazzi (she was working for Italy at this time) was with her, and she spoke quickly to him.

'Listen, Maltazzi,' she said. 'That must be Duplessis. Somehow I shall get into conversation with him on the train. But do not let him see you.'

Maltazzi nodded, and went off to the train. Roanne watched Duplessis get into a first-class carriage which was unoccupied. Then she pulled up the big chinchilla collar of her cloak round her face, gave a little tug at her cloche hat, darted one quick look at her stockings (like all well-groomed women, she hated the wrinkle which sometimes appears under the knee, even in the best silk stocking) and ordered her porter to put her suitcase in the carriage where Duplessis sat. The porter, somewhat clumsily, knocked the suitcase against the doorway, slightly tearing the leather cover and attracting for a moment the attention of Duplessis, who was reading. He looked up and saw both the tear in the suitcase cover and Roanne, who was just about to enter the carriage. Duplessis looked at Roanne's face and forgot all about everything else.

That look was sufficient for Roanne. The momentary gleam which had appeared in the grey eyes of Duplessis, and her quick glance at his humorous and sensitive mouth, convinced her that he would be easy prey; providing always that he had not been warned and had not recognized her from one of the innumerable dossiers which every Intelligence record possessed.

As a matter of fact, Duplessis had not the remotest notion, at that moment, that she was Roanne. He realized simply that she was a remarkably beautiful woman with a wicked little gleam in her eyes; that she had a twisted little finger—he was observant, was Duplessis—and that the idiot porter had torn the patent leather corner of her suitcase. The first realization nearly ruined Duplessis; the last saved him.

Probably every man who has done Secret Service work has a complex about beautiful women. His mind, so continuously occupied with the fact that 'the other side' may be employing some international beauty to trap him, becomes more than cautious about them and, paradoxically, that makes them more attractive.

The train moved off on its way towards Paris. Duplessis sat in his corner, reading a magazine and stealing covert glances over the top at Roanne. She, in the diagonally opposite corner—her plan of campaign definitely settled—composed her features into an expression of heart-broken sadness, and twiddled nervously with her lace handkerchief. Beneath the long lashes her eyes watched Duplessis, who was obviously interested.

For half an hour Roanne did nothing. She sat and looked sad. Then, after some decided twitching of her long fingers and with a spasmodic movement which betokened intense effort of self-control, a sob broke from her. She put her hands to her face, her body relaxed, and she sobbed, bitterly and openly. Roanne was an excellent actress.

It worked. Within three minutes Duplessis was sitting by her side, offering condolence, sympathy, asking if he could do something—would she like some tea? Tea was so refreshing; such a stimulant to the nerves. Roanne, still sobbing, admitted that she would like tea, and Duplessis, rather pleased with himself, went off to get it. While he was gone Roanne arranged her face against his return, and Maltazzi, observing from his distant part of the train the peregrinations of Duplessis in search of tea, grinned a little cynically. He knew Roanne.

It was very natural that, after Duplessis had procured the tea and after Roanne had drunk it, Duplessis should endeavour to find out what the trouble was, and if he could be of any assistance.

You have heard already that Duplessis was not an amazingly clever man. His business in the Secret Service was mainly confined to opening reluctant safes for the more clever people, who afterwards dealt with the contents. Being entirely innocent at the moment as to what his mission to Paris might be, he did not suspect Roanne in the remotest degree.

Punctuated by the most charming sobs and with an occasional side-long glance at Duplessis, which was not without its effect, Roanne halt-ingly told her story. Her name was Marie d'Enverde. Her mother had died, leaving her certain bonds, payable at sight, in the charge of her young brother Etienne. Etienne, it appeared, was a bad young man; he drank, he doped; in fact, he did everything that he should not do. Also, he refused to hand over Roanne's legacy.

'Why not take proceedings against him?' Duplessis asked, naturally enough.

To this Roanne replied that she could not bear the publicity. In any event, too much had been heard in Paris of the doings of the aforesaid Etienne. After another little outburst of tears, during which Duplessis sat by Roanne's side and patted her hand in a manner which grew less fatherly at every moment, Roanne went on to say that in a fit of desperation she had even hired a burglar to break into Etienne's flat, open the safe and steal the bonds. But alas! the cracksman could not open the safe. It was a marvellous safe, an entirely new invention, a Duplex safe. Duplessis smiled to himself at hearing this, for in all probability he was the only man in Europe who could open a Duplex safe.

So that, continued Roanne, life was entirely impossible. She was almost penniless. Yet, in this safe of her brother's reposed a small fortune of a million francs, which was rightfully hers, though she could not obtain it. She indulged in another spasm of tears, this time on her comforter's shoulder.

Then the idea came to Duplessis. A wonderful idea! Of course, it was the idea that the clever and beautiful Roanne had intended should come to him—the idea that *he* should open the safe! He pointed out to Roanne that he was an engineer occupied in the manufacture of safes, that he knew all about them and that the whole thing would be easy. Roanne was very diffident. She took a great deal of persuading, but eventually she allowed herself to be persuaded.

'It will be quite, quite simple, my dear, my very dear friend,' she murmured eventually, 'because, you see, my brother will not be at his flat tonight. It is the first-floor flat, thirty-seven, rue Clichy. The concierge is a friend of mine. I will telephone him that you will be there at nine o'clock tonight. I can give you a key of the flat. Luckily, I have one in my handbag.'

She opened her handbag and gave Duplessis the key.

'Oh!' She gave a little exclamation. 'Here is something else too. Here is an exact replica of the leather case in which the bonds are. I had it made for my unsuccessful burglar to leave in place of the other one, so that my brother should not miss it too quickly. Will you take this and leave it in the place of the one which you take out of the safe? And then if you do open the safe, do you think you can bring my bonds to me at the Hotel Continental? I shall be there at ten o'clock. And perhaps,' continued Roanne, with a positively devastating glance, 'you might care to have supper with me.'

Duplessis agreed to everything. By this time, like many much cleverer men, he was head-over-heels in love with the exquisite Roanne. And when the train arrived at the Gare du Nord he was congratulating himself on being lucky enough to be able to do her a service.

On the station she bade him an affectionate farewell and got into a large car which awaited her. Duplessis watched the car until it disappeared in the dusk.

Two hundred yards from the station Roanne's car pulled up. Maltazzi jumped from a following taxicab. He hurried to Roanne's car, opened the door and smiled at her. She sat back in the corner, wrapped in her cloak. Her eyes were shining.

'Well?' asked Maltazzi.

'My friend,' said Roanne, 'it worked. This Duplessis was easy. At nine o'clock he will go to the flat and open the safe. Therefore the occupant of the flat, Bayarde, who would guard those papers with his life, must somehow be removed. You must find a way to do that.'

'Easy,' said Maltazzi. 'It has been arranged that I call on Bayarde tonight with reference to some business in which he is interested in Paris. I am supposed to be one Gauteuil, a commercial traveller.'

Roanne laughed. 'Maltazzi,' she said, 'you don't look very much like a commercial traveller, but if you put on your hat a little straight, and get your shoes dusty, and—yes!—take my suitcase, you will probably look the part much more; but please return my suitcase carefully—my evening gowns are in it.'

Maltazzi nodded and picked up the case from the floor of the car. 'Easy,' he said again. 'When I get into the flat I shall ask Bayarde to examine some papers. As he does so I shall press a wad, soaked in chloroform, over his nose. There is no one else in the flat and I shall drag him into the next flat, which belongs to one of my men. He will see that Bayarde remains there sleeping quietly until our friend Duplessis has done his work.'

'Excellent,' said Roanne.

Maltazzi nodded and lit a cigarette.

'It is all very well, mademoiselle,' he continued. 'I can arrange all that easily enough, but supposing this innocent Duplessis takes it into his head, after he has opened the safe, to examine the papers. He will quickly discover that, far from being bonds, they are copies of two important secret treaties. What will he do then? Why obviously, he will take them to his own chief in Paris and all our troubles will have been for nothing. What a curse it is that I could not get that safe open myself!'

'I've thought of all that,' replied Roanne. 'It's quite possible our charming Duplessis will examine the papers, in which event he would, as you say, take them straight off to his chief. It is even possible that he will report to his chief this evening. If so, he would be told that he has been sent for by his own service to open the identical safe in the rue Clichy in order that Britain may have these papers, and then the affair will become a little difficult; but I'm hoping he will be so inspired by my distress over my wicked brother'—here Roanne laughed softly—'that he will put off reporting to his chief until tomorrow. With regard to the second point, that he examines the papers when he *has* opened the safe, that, my friend, must be dealt with by you.'

'How?' asked Maltazzi.

'Easily enough,' said Roanne. 'When Duplessis leaves the flat in the rue Clichy tonight it will be quite dark. He must be set on by three or four *apaches*. They will take everything on him, papers, watch, chain, money, everything. It will look like an ordinary robbery. We shall in any event get the papers, and all that remains for my poor Duplessis to do is to come to me at ten o'clock, with tears in his nice eyes, and to inform me that, after actually getting my bonds from my wicked brother's safe, they have been stolen from him in the street. Quite simple, isn't it?'

Maltazzi laughed. 'You're a clever woman, Roanne,' he said, looking at her with sincere admiration. 'I can arrange that. It will be dark when he comes out, and as there have been one or two robberies in the neighbourhood of the rue Clichy during the last week, no one will think anything of it.'

'Excellent!' said Roanne. 'But one thing, Maltazzi. My nice Duplessis must not be hurt. I shouldn't like that. He was so kind to me. He got tea for me, and patted my hand, and was so sympathetic.'

Maltazzi smiled again. 'Rest assured, mademoiselle,' he said, 'we shall not hurt him. I will promise you that.'

He raised his hat and, quite pleased with himself, disappeared into the crowd. He would not have been so pleased had he realized that in the business of chloroforming the unfortunate Bayarde he, Maltazzi, would forget Roanne's suitcase and leave it on the floor in the corner of Bayarde's sitting-room. All of which goes to prove that the cleverest international agent, like the most foolish criminal, can make a mistake.

III

Duplessis, having watched Roanne's car out of sight, took a cab and went straight to the rooms where he stayed when in Paris, near the Grand Boulevard Montmartre.

Roanne had made one mistake in assessing Duplessis's character. He was not the type of man to disregard his duty, and his first business, after dumping his attaché-case in the corner, was to ring up Slavin—who was at that time Chief of the British Service in Paris—and to ask him whether he was wanted immediately.

'Oh no, Duplessis,' said Slavin cheerily on the telephone. 'I want you to do a job for me, but it can easily wait until tomorrow. Still, I'd like to talk it over with you, so perhaps you will come round to my place about ten tonight.'

Duplessis said he would. He thought that he could have the little business in the rue Clichy finished at nine-thirty, dash round to Slavin, hear what he had to say, and then make straight for the Hotel Continental and Roanne.

The very thought of Roanne stirred Duplessis. Dimly, in some remote place at the back of his mind, a vague idea of marrying Roanne was germinating. How he was going to do this he had not the remotest notion, but the idea was there. He realized also that the first step towards making this vague idea a little more practical was to carry through successfully the business of returning to Roanne her bonds.

He bathed, put on a dinner-suit, ate an excellent dinner, and at ten minutes to nine, having put his little kitbag of tools, most of which were his own inventions, into the pocket of his overcoat, he took a taxi to the rue Clichy.

He paid off the cab on this side of Zelie's and walked slowly towards his destination, examining the houses carefully. Soon he realized that a postcard-seller, whom he had noticed when he got out of his cab, was sidling behind him. The man whispered hoarsely in his ear: 'M'sieu, everything is arranged. Mademoiselle's brother is out and the concierge has been amenable to reason. It is the first-floor flat; your way is clear before you. *Bonne chance*, M'sieu!'

Duplessis nodded, and walked on. He turned casually into the entrance to Number Thirty-seven, acknowledged the greeting of the concierge and ran quickly up the stairs. The front door of the flat yielded easily to his key. He looked quickly through the rooms until he found the safe. Then he switched on the light and set to work.

Opening that safe was one of the toughest jobs which Duplessis had ever experienced. It took twenty-five minutes' hard work and it was nearly half-past nine as he swung the ponderous door open. Before him, on the steel shelf of the safe, lay the leathern wallet, the exact duplicate of the dummy in his pocket. He had put out his hand for it when his observant eye fell on something in the corner—something which made him start. In the corner of the room was a very ordinary suitcase; *but* the corner of this suitcase was torn. Duplessis immediately recognized it as Roanne's case, which the clumsy porter had torn when putting it into the railway carriage at Dieppe.

I have said that Duplessis was not an extraordinarily clever man, but, very naturally, he asked himself why this case should be in the flat. Why, for some unknown reason, should this case, part of Roanne's luggage— which should have gone with her straight to her hotel—be in this flat in the rue Clichy? Either Roanne had been there herself or someone else had brought it there. Was it likely that Roanne, who was such bad friends with her brother, would come round to the flat, and, if she did, leave her attaché-case there?

Duplessis's eye fell on the clock on the mantelpiece. It was twenty to ten. He remembered his appointment with Slavin. The very thought of Slavin suggested something to Duplessis. The idea came to him, for the first time, that Roanne was not all that she seemed and that, possibly, he had walked into a trap.

He tiptoed out of the flat and looked down the stairs. The concierge was deep in conversation with two rough-looking individuals, one of whom was the man who had told Duplessis that the way was clear in the rue Clichy. Then Duplessis realized that when he got outside he would probably be set upon and the wallet stolen.

There was a telephone in the corner of the room, but he knew that it was no use telephoning the police. It isn't usual for employees of the Secret Service to get mixed up in foreign police courts. Suddenly the whole thing became clear to Duplessis. Slavin wanted those documents in the safe! And Duplessis had been sent over to Paris because he was the only man who could open it. These other people, whoever they were, wanted them too. And he, like a fool, had walked straight into the trap that had been laid for him.

For some minutes Duplessis stood in the middle of the room, thinking deeply. Then he walked over to the attaché-case and opened it. In it were three evening gowns. Their filminess and the suggestion of perfume which greeted Duplessis's nostrils reminded him vividly of Roanne.

An idea come to him and he laughed quietly to himself. Then he went to the telephone, found the number of the Hotel Continental, rang up the hotel and asked for Mademoiselle d'Enverde. A few minutes later the sound of Roanne's soft voice came to him over the telephone.

'Mademoiselle,' said Duplessis, 'I am delighted to tell you that I have just opened the safe and that the leather wallet containing your bonds, which, of course, I have not opened, is in my hands.'

'Excellent!' said Roanne softly. 'I am so indebted to you, Monsieur Duplessis—my dear Monsieur Duplessis—how can I ever repay you?'

'Quite easily, mademoiselle,' replied Duplessis. 'I have been thinking. You remember you said that I might come to you for supper. Would it be asking too great a reward for my services if I asked you to have supper with me at ten-thirty at the Café de la Paix? If that is agreeable I will call for you at ten-fifteen.'

'But how I should love that, my friend,' said Roanne. 'But, alas! I have no evening gowns . . .' Duplessis's heart leapt when he heard this. 'Do you mind if I come in a day gown?'

'Mademoiselle,' said Duplessis, 'I am terribly disappointed. You see, I think that I am very fond of you, and all the while I was working on this safe I had a little picture in my mind, a picture of us supping together, with you wearing the most wonderful evening gown. I thought,' said Duplessis, 'that it would probably be a black one. I am certain you would look so nice in black. . . .' He remembered the black gown in the attaché-case.

Roanne laughed. 'Very well, my friend,' she said, 'you have deserved well. I will wear a black evening gown. It is a little inconvenient because my evening gowns are not here, but I will send for them. Nothing is too much trouble for you, my good friend.'

Duplessis murmured suitable thanks, said '*Au revoir*', and hung up the receiver. Five minutes later, having shut the safe door, he noisily descended the stairs, said 'Good night' to the concierge, and turned into the rue Clichy. Seven minutes later a very burly individual, coming suddenly out of a side street, neatly tripped Mr Duplessis. With great promptitude four other individuals who appeared out of the shadows which abound in the rue Clichy held him down and very systematically relieved him of everything in his possession, including his tiepin. They then disappeared as quickly as they came.

Duplessis got up, brushed himself, and, with a beatific smile, got the first cab which appeared. In it he drove straight round to Slavin who, when he had heard Duplessis's story, laughed long and loudly; and that, if you know anything about Mr Slavin, was a very strange thing.

IV

At ten minutes past ten Duplessis called at the Hotel Continental.

Roanne received him smilingly, but, as he shook hands with her, Duplessis's face was a picture of abject misery.

'Mademoiselle,' he said, 'I do not know how to tell you the terrible

news. I hope you will understand. When I left the apartment in the rue
Clichy tonight I was set upon by *apaches*. They took everything that I
had, including the wallet with your bonds in it. I would have rung you
up sooner, but I could not bear the thought of your disappointment.'

Roanne smiled. She was looking utterly delicious in a black evening
gown—the top one in the attaché-case, Duplessis noted with satisfaction.

'My poor friend,' she said, 'do not be concerned on my account.
Naturally, I am sorry that the bonds are lost, but since I last saw you
certain business has taken place which will mean that I am to receive a
large sum of money. Therefore do not let us think any more about these
bonds which have been the cause of so much trouble. Let us go and sup
and talk about more pleasant things. For you must know,' said Roanne
admiringly, 'I am beginning to feel quite an affection for you.'

And this was true. In spite of her varied acquaintance amongst some
of the cleverest men in Europe, Roanne really felt herself attracted to this
rather quiet and straightforward Englishman, this specialist in opening
reluctant safes of whom she had made such good use.

At this moment the telephone rang loudly. Roanne, with a murmured
excuse, went to it. After a moment's conversation she called through the
door leading from the sitting-room, in which they were, to her bedroom.
'Marie, there is somebody downstairs, a Monsieur Leblanc who insists
on speaking to me personally on an urgent matter. I don't know him,
and I don't want him up here. Go down and see what he wants.'

The maid went off, and Duplessis smiled to himself.

Two minutes afterwards the maid returned and informed Roanne that
Monsieur Leblanc was sorry, but that he must see her personally. It was
a matter of the utmost urgency, and Roanne, with apologies to Duplessis,
went downstairs.

Immediately she had gone Duplessis turned to the maid. 'How silly of
me,' he said, 'I have just remembered. The Monsieur Leblanc downstairs
wishes to see me, and, knowing that I should be with mademoiselle, he
has probably asked for her by mistake. Run after her and explain. And
tell him he must come and see me tomorrow morning.'

The maid, looking rather surprised, went off. As the door closed
behind her, Duplessis dashed across the room and into Roanne's bedroom, from which he emerged in time to seat himself in his original chair
as Roanne and her maid returned.

As they sat over their coffee, Roanne watched Duplessis covertly. She
felt that he would make a nervous confession of love at any moment, a

process to which she was quite accustomed, for most men proposed to Roanne at some time or other.

But she found herself rather interested in the forthcoming avowal from Duplessis. She felt that it would be different. He looked troubled and his hand, holding the coffee-spoon, trembled a little.

Eventually he spoke, and she, with a little inward and gratified sigh—in which women indulge on these occasions—braced herself to listen with much pleasure. Her surprise grew as Duplessis continued speaking.

'Mademoiselle Loranoff,' said Duplessis—she sat back a little at that. So he knew her name!—'I am very unhappy because I am very fond of you and I feel that the news I have to break to you will make you hate me. However, I will tell you at once that the wallet, which your friends took from me on the rue Clichy this evening, is the dummy one which you yourself gave me. . . .'

Roanne smiled a little. She was a good loser.

'So . . .' she murmured, 'and the real one?'

'By this time safe at the British Embassy,' said Duplessis. 'You see, mademoiselle, I am not at all a clever man. When I received instructions to report here, I could not guess that it was to open that safe of Bayarde's in order that my own people might get hold of those plans. I believed your story and was keen to help you, because I had already become interested in you . . .'

Roanne's eyes were glistening.

'How did you get the papers away from the flat in the rue Clichy?' she asked.

Duplessis grinned. 'That was quite easy,' he said. 'You see, the first thing that aroused my suspicions was your suitcase in Bayarde's flat. When you left me at the Gare du Nord it was put into your car. I noticed this. Directly I saw it at the flat I recognized it because I had seen the porter tear the corner slightly getting it into the carriage at Dieppe. Then I began to suspect you and when I saw the concierge whispering with the man who had spoken to me in the rue Clichy I thought that I should probably be set on directly I got out of the flat.

'Therefore, having discovered that your evening gowns were in the suitcase and that the top one was black, I telephoned you, and asked you to wear an evening gown, knowing that you would probably send round for the case. I then hid the real wallet in the empty pocket in the lid of the suitcase, and put the dummy in my pocket. As I thought, you sent round for the suitcase. You remember the mysterious Monsieur Leblanc who called to see you while I was with you at the Continental? Well, this was a young gentleman in the employ of our service here, and I used him to get both you and your maid out of your suite while I went into your room and took the wallet from the suitcase which lay open on your bed.

'The Embassy messenger was awaiting me here in the cloakroom when I arrived with you, and I handed him the wallet.'

Duplessis looked at her. He looked thoroughly miserable. Roanne, looking into his eyes, came to the conclusion that Duplessis was a thoroughly sound Englishman and that he was not half such a fool as he liked to pretend.

'I am sorry, mademoiselle,' said Duplessis, 'that you have lost this little game. I am a loser too.'

Roanne smiled and her eyes were very soft. Remember that she was very much of a woman and that Duplessis was the first man to outwit her.

'M'sieu Duplessis,' she said, 'you are the only man who has ever beaten me at my own game. I think that I like being outwitted—the experience is new. But you must be punished. I shall, therefore, marry you! Well——?'

It took Duplessis five minutes to recover his breath and another twenty to be persuaded that Roanne was speaking the truth. When he told Slavin the next morning that worthy refused, point blank, to believe him.

But the fact remained that 'Roanne Lucrezia Loranoff', sometime Princess Roanne Lucrezi Demiroff, and now Mrs John Duplessis, lives in an attractive villa between Nîmes and Avignon, and awaits the periodic return of her spouse who, in the intervals of feeding chickens, occasionally points out how clever she is, and what an awful fool she must think him.

When they ask Duplessis—in the little room upstairs at Père Benoit's, in Ostend—how he got Roanne to marry him, he says he doesn't know.

And, strangely enough, although no one believes him, he doesn't.

The Army of the Shadows

It is three years since Llewellyn removed my appendix; but we still meet occasionally. I am dimly related to his wife: that, at least, is the pretext for the acquaintanceship. The truth is that, during my convalescence, we happened to discover that we both like the same musicians. Before the war we usually met when there was some Sibelius being played and went to hear it together. I was a little puzzled when, about three weeks ago, he telephoned with the suggestion that I should dine at his house that night. There was not, I knew, a concert of any sort in London. I agreed, however, to grope my way round to Upper Wimpole Street shortly before eight o'clock.

It was not until he had presented me with a brandy that I found out why I had been invited to dinner.

'Do you remember,' he said suddenly, 'that I spent a week or so in Belgrade last year? I missed Beecham doing the Second through it. There was one of those international medical bun fights being held there, and I went to represent the Association. My German is fairly good, you know. I motored. Can't stick trains. Anyway, on the way back a very funny thing happened to me. Did I ever tell you about it?'

'I don't think so.'

'I thought not. Well'—he laughed self-consciously—'it was so funny now there's a war on that I've been amusing myself by writing the whole thing down. I wondered whether you'd be good enough to cast a professional eye over it for me. I've tried'—he laughed again—'to make a really literary job of it. Like a story, you know.'

His hand had been out of sight behind the arm of his chair, but now it emerged from hiding holding a wad of typewritten sheets.

'It's typed,' he said, planking it down on my knees. And then, with a theatrical glance at his watch, 'Good Lord, it's ten. There's a telephone call I must make. Excuse me for a minute or two, will you?'

He was out of the room before I could open my mouth to reply. I was left alone with the manuscript.

I picked it up. It was entitled 'A Strange Encounter'. With a sigh, I turned over the title-page and began, rather irritably, to read:

The Stelvio Pass is snowed up in winter, and towards the end of November most sensible men driving to Paris from Belgrade or beyond take the long way round via Milan rather than risk being stopped by an early fall of snow. But I was in a hurry and took a chance. By the time I reached Bolzano I was sorry I had done so. It was bitterly cold, and the sky ahead was leaden. At Merano I seriously considered turning back. Instead, I pushed on as hard as I could go. If I had had any sense I should have stopped for petrol before I started the really serious part of the climb. I had six gallons by the gauge then. I knew that it wasn't accurate, but I had filled up early that morning and calculated that I had enough to get me to Sargans. In my anxiety to beat the snow I overlooked the fact that I had miles of low-gear driving to do. On the Swiss side and on the Sargans road where it runs within a mile or two of the Rhätikon part of the German frontier, the car spluttered to a standstill.

For a minute or two I sat there swearing at and to myself and wondering what on earth I was going to do. I was, I knew, the only thing on the road that night for miles.

It was about eight o'clock, very dark and very cold. Except for the faint creaking of the cooling engine and the rustle of the breeze in some nearby trees, there wasn't a sound to be heard. Ahead, the road in the headlights curved away to the right. I got out the map and tried to find out where I was.

I had passed through one village since I left Klosters, and I knew that it was about ten kilometres back. I must, therefore, either walk back ten kilometres to that village, or forward to the next village, whichever was the nearer. I looked at the map. It was of that useless kind that they sell to motorists. There was nothing marked between Klosters and Sargans. For all I knew, the next village might be fifteen or twenty kilometres away.

An Alpine road on a late November night is not the place to choose if you want to sleep in your car. I decided to walk back the way I had come.

I had a box of those small Italian waxed matches with me when I started out. There were, I thought, about a hundred in the box, and I calculated that, if I struck one every hundred metres, they would last until I reached the village.

That was when I was near the lights of the car. When I got out of sight of them, things were different. The darkness seemed to press against the backs of my eyes. It was almost painful. I could not even see the shape of the road along which I was walking. It was only by the rustling and the smell of resin that I knew that I was walking between fir trees. By the time I had covered a mile I had six matches left. Then it began to snow.

I say 'snow'. It had been snow; but the Sargans road was still below the snow-line, and the stuff came down as a sort of half-frozen mush that slid down my face into the gap between my coat collar and my neck.

I must have done about another mile and a half when the real trouble began. I still had the six matches, but my hands were too numb to get them out of the box without wetting them, and I had been going forward blindly, sometimes on the road and sometimes off it. I was wondering whether I would get along better if I sang, when I walked into a telegraph post.

It was of pre-cast concrete and the edge was as sharp as a razor. My face was as numb as my hands and I didn't feel much except a sickening jar; but I could taste blood trickling between my teeth and found that my nose was bleeding. It was as I held my head back to stop it that I saw the light, looking for all the world as if it were suspended in mid-air above me.

It wasn't suspended in mid-air, and it wasn't above me. Darkness does strange things to perspective. After a few seconds I saw that it was showing through the trees on the hillside, up to the right of the road.

Anyone who has been in the sort of mess that I was in will know exactly how my mind worked at that moment. I did not speculate as to the origin of that God-forsaken light or as to whether or not the owner of it would be pleased to see me. I was cold and wet, my nose was bleeding, and I would not have cared if someone had told me that behind the light was a maniac with a machine-gun. I knew only that the light meant there was some sort of human habitation near me and that I was going to spend the night in it.

I moved over to the other side of the road and began to feel my way along the wire fence I found there. Twenty yards or so further on, my hands touched a wooden gate. The light was no longer visible, but I pushed the gate open and walked on into the blackness.

The ground rose steeply under my feet. It was a path of sorts, and soon I stumbled over the beginnings of a flight of log steps. There must have been well over a hundred of them. Then there was another stretch of path, not quite so steep. When I again saw the light, I was only about twenty yards from it.

It came from an oil reading-lamp standing near a window. From the shape of the window and the reflected light of the lamp, I could see that the place was a small chalet of the kind usually let to families for the summer season or for the winter sports. That it should be occupied at the end of November was curious. But I didn't ponder over the curiosity: I had seen something else through the window besides the lamp. The light from a fire was flickering in the room.

I went forward up the path to the door. There was no knocker. I hammered on the wet, varnished wood with my fist and waited. There was no sound from inside. After a moment or two I knocked again. Still there was no sign of life within. I knocked and waited for several minutes. Then I began to shiver. In desperation I grabbed the latch of the door and rattled it violently. The next moment I felt it give and the door creaked open a few inches.

I think that I have a normal, healthy respect for the property and privacy of my fellow-creatures; but at that moment I was feeling neither normal nor healthy. Obviously, the owner of the chalet could not be far away. I stood there for a moment or two, hesitating. I could smell the wood smoke from the fire, and mingled with it a bitter, oily smell which seemed faintly familiar. But all I cared about was the fire. I hesitated no longer and walked in.

As soon as I was inside I saw that there was something more than curious about the place, and that I should have waited.

The room itself was ordinary enough. It was rather larger than I had expected, but there were the usual pinewood walls, the usual pinewood floor, the usual pinewood staircase up to the bedrooms, and the usual tiled fireplace. There were the usual tables and chairs, too: turned and painted nonsense of the kind that sometimes finds its way into English tea shops. There were red gingham curtains over the windows. You felt that the owner probably had lots of other places just like it, and that he made a good thing out of letting them.

No, it was what had been added to the room that was curious. All the furniture had been crowded into one half of the space. In the other half, standing on linoleum and looking as if it were used a good deal, was a printing press.

The machine was a small treadle platten of the kind used by jobbing printers for running off tradesmen's circulars. It looked very old and decrepit. Alongside it on a trestle table were a case of type and a small

proofing press with a locked-up forme in it. On a second table stood a
pile of interleaved sheets, beside which was a stack of what appeared to
be some of the same sheets folded. The folding was obviously being done
by hand. I picked up one of the folded sheets.

It looked like one of those long, narrow business-promotion folders
issued by travel agencies. The front page was devoted to the reproduc-
tion, in watery blue ink, of a lino-cut of a clump of pines on the shore
of a lake, and the display of the name 'TITISEE'. Page two and the page
folded in to face it carried a rhapsodical account in German of the beauties of Baden in general and Lake Titisee in particular.

I put the folder down. An inaccessible Swiss chalet was an odd place
to choose for printing German travel advertisements; but I was not disposed to dwell on its oddity. I was cold.

I was moving towards the fire when my eye was caught by five words
printed in bold capitals on one of the unfolded sheets on the table:
'DEUTSCHE MÄNNER UND FRAUEN, KAMERADEN!'

I stood still. I remember that my heart thudded against my ribs as suddenly and violently as it had earlier that day on the Stelvio when some
crazy fool in a Hispano had nearly crowded me off the road.

I leaned forward, picked the folder up again, and opened it right out.
The Message began on the second of the three inside pages.

GERMAN MEN AND WOMEN, COMRADES! We speak to you with the voice of
German Democracy, bringing you news. Neither Nazi propaganda nor the
Gestapo can silence us, for we have an ally which is proof against floggings, an
ally which no man in the history of the world has been able to defeat. That
ally is Truth. Hear then, people of Germany, the Truth which is concealed
from you. Hear it, remember it, and repeat it. The sooner the Truth is known,
the sooner will Germany again hold up its head among the free nations of the
world.

Then followed a sort of news bulletin consisting of facts and figures
(especially figures) about the economic condition of Germany. There was
also news of a strike in the Krupp works at Essen and a short description of a riot outside a shipyard in Hamburg.

I put it down again. Now I knew why these 'travel advertisements' were
being printed in an inaccessible Swiss chalet instead of in Germany itself.
No German railway official would distribute these folders. That business
would be left to more desperate men. These folders would not collect
dust on the counters of travel agencies. They would be found in trains

and in trams, in buses and in parked cars, in waiting rooms and in bars, under restaurant plates and inside table napkins. Some of the men that put them there would be caught and tortured to betray their fellows; but the distribution would go on. The folders would be read, perhaps furtively discussed. A little more truth would seep through Goebbels' dam of lies to rot still further the creaking foundation of Nazidom.

Then, as I stood there with the smell of wood smoke and printing ink in my nostrils, as I stood staring at that decrepit little machine as if it were the very voice of freedom, I heard footsteps outside.

I suppose that I should have stood my ground. I had, after all, a perfectly good explanation of my presence there. My car and the blood from my nose would confirm my story. But I didn't reason that way. I had stumbled on a secret, and my first impulse was to try to hide the fact from the owner of the secret. I obeyed that impulse.

I looked around quickly and saw the stairs. Before I had even begun to wonder if I might not be doing something excessively stupid, I was up the stairs and opening the first door I came to on the landing. In the half-light I caught a glimpse of a bed; then I was inside the room with the door slightly ajar. I could see across the landing and through the wooden palings along it to the top of the window at the far side of the room below.

I knew that someone had come in: I could hear him moving about. He lit another lamp. There was a sound from the door and a second person entered.

A woman's voice said in German, 'Thank God, Johann has left a good fire.'

There was an answering grunt. It came from the man. I could almost feel them warming their hands.

'Get the coffee, Freda,' said the man suddenly. 'I must go back soon.'

'But Bruno is there. You should take a little rest first.'

'Bruno is a Berliner. He is not as used to the cold as I am. If Kurt should come now he would be tired. Bruno could only look after himself.'

There was silence for a moment. Then the woman spoke again.

'Do you really think he will come now, Stephan? It is so late.' She paused. Her voice had sounded casual, elaborately casual; but now, as she went on, there was an edge to it that touched the nerves. 'I can keep quite calm about it, you see, Stephan. I wish to believe, but it is so late, isn't it? You don't think he will come now, do you? Admit it.'

He laughed, but too heartily. 'You are too nervous, Freda. Kurt can take care of himself. He knows all the tricks now. He may have been waiting for the first snow. The frontier guards would not be so alert on a night like this.'

'He should have been back a week ago. You know that as well as I do, Stephan. He has never been delayed so long before. They have got him. That is all. You see, I can be calm about it even though he is my dear husband.' And then her voice broke. 'I knew it would happen sooner or later. I knew it. First Hans, then Karl, and now Kurt. Those swine, those—' She sobbed and broke suddenly into passionate weeping. He tried helplessly to comfort her.

I had heard enough. I was shaking from head to foot; but whether it was the cold or not, I don't know. I stood back from the door. Then, as I did so, I heard a sound from behind me.

I had noticed the bed as I had slipped into the room, but the idea that there might be someone in it had not entered my head. Now, as I whipped around, I saw that I had made a serious mistake.

Sitting on the edge of the bed in which he had been lying was a very thin, middle-aged man in a nightshirt. By the faint light from the landing I could see his eyes, bleary from sleep, and his grizzled hair standing ludicrously on end. But for one thing I should have laughed. That one thing was the large automatic pistol which he held pointed at me. His hand was as steady as a rock.

'Don't move,' he said. He raised his voice. 'Stephan! Come quickly!'

'I must apologize . . .' I began in German.

'You will be allowed to speak later.'

I heard Stephan dash up the stairs.

'What is it, Johann?'

'Come here.'

The door was pushed open behind me. I heard him draw in his breath sharply.

'Who is it?'

'I do not know. I was awakened by a noise. I was about to get up when this man came into the room. He did not see me. He has been listening to your conversation. He must have been examining the plant when he heard you returning.'

'If you will allow me to explain . . .' I began.

'You may explain downstairs,' said the man called Stephan. 'Give me the pistol, Johann.'

The pistol changed hands and I could see Stephan, a lean, raw-boned fellow with broad, sharp shoulders and dangerous eyes. He wore black oilskins and gum boots. I saw the muscles in his cheeks tighten.

'Raise your hands and walk downstairs. Slowly. If you run, I shall shoot immediately. March.'

I went downstairs.

The woman, Freda, was standing by the door, staring blankly up at me as I descended. She must have been about thirty and had that soft rather matronly look about her that is characteristic of so many young German women. She was short and plump, and as if to accentuate the fact, her straw-coloured hair was plaited across her head. Wisps of the hair had become detached and clung wetly to the sides of her neck. She too wore a black oilskin coat and gum boots.

The grey eyes, red and swollen with crying, looked beyond me.

'Who is it, Stephan?'

'He was hiding upstairs.'

We had reached the foot of the stairs. He motioned me away from the door and towards the fire. 'Now, we will hear your explanation.'

I gave it with profuse apologies. I admitted that I had examined the folders and read one. 'It seemed to me,' I concluded, 'that my presence might be embarrassing to you. I was about to leave when you returned. Then, I am afraid, I lost my head and attempted to hide.'

Not one of them was believing a word that I was saying: I could see that from their faces. 'I assure you,' I went on in exasperation, 'that what I am telling . . .'

'What nationality are you?'

'British. I . . .'

'Then speak English. What were you doing on this road?'

'I am on my way home from Belgrade. I crossed the Yugoslav frontier yesterday and the Italian frontier at Stelvio this afternoon. My passport was stamped at both places if you wish to . . .'

'Why were you in Belgrade?'

'I am a surgeon. I have been attending an international medical convention there.'

'Let me see your passport, please.'

'Certainly. I have . . .' And then with my hand in my inside pocket, I stopped. My heart felt as if it had come right into my throat. In my haste to be away after the Italian Customs had finished with me, I had thrust my passport with the Customs carnet for the car into the pocket beside me on the door of the car.

They were watching me with expressionless faces. Now, as my hand reappeared empty, I saw Stephan raise his pistol.

'Well?'

'I am sorry.' Like a fool I had begun to speak in German again. 'I find that I have left my passport in my car. It is several kilometres along the road. If . . .'

And then the woman burst out as if she couldn't stand listening to me any longer.

'Don't you see? Don't you see?' she cried. 'It is quite clear. They have found out that we are here. Perhaps after all these months Hans or Karl has been tortured by them into speaking. And so they have taken Kurt and sent this man to spy upon us. It is clear. Don't you see?'

She turned suddenly, and I thought she was going to attack me. Then Stephan put his hand on her arm.

'Gently, Freda.' He turned to me again, and his expression hardened. 'You see my friend, what is in our minds? We know our danger, you see. The fact that we are in Swiss territory will not protect us if the Gestapo should trace us. The Nazis, we know, have little respect for frontiers. The Gestapo have none. They would murder us here as confidently as they would if we were in the Third Reich. We do not underrate their cunning. The fact that you are not a German is not conclusive. You may be what you say you are: you may not. If you are, so much the better. If not, then, I give you fair warning, you will be shot. You say your passport is in your car several kilometres along the road. Unfortunately, it is not possible for us to spare time tonight to see if that is true. Nor is it possible for one of us to stand guard over you all night. You have already disturbed the first sleep Johann has had in twenty-four hours. There is only one thing for it, I'm afraid. It is undignified and barbaric; but I see no other way. We shall be forced to tie you up so that you cannot leave.'

'But this is absurd,' I cried angrily. 'Good heavens, man, I realize that I've only myself to blame for being here; but surely you could have the common decency to . . .'

'The question,' he said sternly, 'is not of decency, but of necessity. We have no time tonight for six-kilometre walks. One of our comrades has been delivering a consignment of these folders to our friends in Germany. We hope and believe that he will return to us across the frontier tonight. He may need our help. Mountaineering in such weather is exhausting. Freda, get me some of the cord we use for tying the packages.'

I wanted to say something, but the words would not come. I was too angry. I don't think that I've ever been so angry in my life before.

She brought the cord. It was thick grey stuff. He took it and gave the pistol to Johann. Then he came towards me.

I don't think they liked the business any more than I did. He had gone a bit white and he wouldn't look me in the eyes. I think that I must have been white myself; but it was anger with me. He put the cord under one of my elbows. I snatched it away.

'You had better submit,' he said harshly.

'To spare your feelings? Certainly not. You'll have to use force, my friend. But don't worry. You'll get used to it. You'll be a good Nazi yet. You should knock me down. That'll make it easier.'

What colour there was left in his face went. A good deal of my anger evaporated at that moment. I felt sorry for the poor devil. I really believe that I should have let him tie me up. But I never knew for certain; for at that moment there was an interruption.

It was the woman who heard it first—the sound of someone running up the path outside. The next moment a man burst wildly into the room.

Stephan had turned. 'Bruno! What is it? Why aren't you at the hut?'

The man was striving to get his breath, and for a moment he could hardly speak. His face above the streaming oilskins was blue with cold. Then he gasped out.

'Kurt! He is at the hut! He is wounded—badly!'

The woman gave a little whimpering cry and her hands went to her face. Stephan gripped the newcomer's shoulder.

'What has happened? Quickly!'

'It was dark. The Swiss did not see him. It was one of our patrols. They shot him when he was actually on the Swiss side. He was wounded in the thigh. He crawled on to the hut, but he can go no further. He . . .'

But Stephan had ceased to listen. He turned sharply. 'Johann, you must dress yourself at once. Bruno, take the pistol and guard this man. He broke in here. He may be dangerous. Freda, get the cognac and the iodine. We shall need them for Kurt.'

He himself went to a cupboard and got out some handkerchiefs, which he began tearing feverishly into strips, which he knotted together. Still gasping for breath, the man had taken the pistol and was staring at me with a puzzled frown. Then the woman reappeared from the kitchen carrying a bottle of cognac and a small tube of iodine of the sort that is sold for dabbing at cut fingers. Stephan stuffed them in his pockets with the knotted handkerchiefs. Then he called up the stairs, 'Hurry, Johann. We are ready to leave.'

It was more than I could bear. Professional fussiness, I suppose.

'Has any one of you,' I asked loudly, 'ever dealt with a bullet wound before?'

They stared at me. Then Stephan glanced at Bruno.

'If he moves,' he said, 'shoot.' He raised his voice again. 'Johann!'

There was an answering cry of reassurance.

'Has it occurred to you,' I persisted, 'that even if you get him here alive, which I doubt, as you obviously don't know what you're doing, he will need immediate medical attention? Don't you think that one of you had better go for a doctor? Ah, but of course; the doctor would ask questions about a bullet wound, wouldn't he? The matter would be reported to the police.'

'We can look after him,' Stephan grunted. 'Johann! Hurry!'

'It seems a pity,' I said reflectively, 'that one brave man should have to die because of his friends' stupidity.' And then my calm deserted me. 'You fool,' I shouted. 'Listen to me. Do you want to kill this man? You're going about it the right way. I'm a surgeon, and this is a surgeon's business. Take that cognac out of your pocket. We shan't need it. The iodine too. And those pieces of rag. Have you got two or three clean towels?'

The woman nodded stupidly.

'Then get them, please, and be quick. And you said something about some coffee. Have you a flask for it? Good. Then we shall take that. Put plenty of sugar in it. I want blankets, too. Three will be enough, but they must be kept dry. We shall need a stretcher. Get two poles or broomsticks and two old coats. We can make a stretcher of sorts by putting the pole through the sleeves of them. Take this cord of yours too. It will be useful to make slings for the stretcher, and hurry! The man may be bleeding to death. Is he far away?'

The man was glowering at me. 'Four kilometres. In a climbing hut in the hills this side of the frontier.' He stepped forward and gripped my arm. 'If you are tricking us . . .' he began.

'I'm not thinking about you,' I snapped. 'I'm thinking about a man who's been crawling along with a bullet in his thigh and a touching faith in his friends. Now get those poles, and hurry.'

They hurried. In three minutes they had the things collected. The exhausted Bruno's oilskins and gum boots had, at my suggestion, been transferred to me. Then I tied one of the blankets round my waist under my coat, and told Stephan and Johann to do the same.

'I,' said the woman, 'will take the other things.'

'You,' I said, 'will stay here, please.'

She straightened up at that. 'No,' she said firmly, 'I will come with you. I shall be quite calm. You will see.'

'Nevertheless,' I said rather brutally, 'you will be more useful here. A bed must be ready by the fire here. There must also be hot bricks and plenty of blankets. I shall need, besides, both boiled and boiling water. You have plenty of ordinary salt, I suppose?'

'Yes, *Herr Doktor*. But . . .'

'We are wasting time.'

Two minutes later we left.

I shall never forget that climb. It began about half a mile along the road below the chalet. The first part was mostly up narrow paths between trees. They were covered with pine needles and, in the rain, as slippery as the devil. We had been climbing steadily for about half an hour when Stephan, who had been leading the way with a storm lantern, paused.

'I must put out the light here,' he said. 'The frontier is only three kilometres from here, and the guards patrol to a depth of two kilometres. They must not see us.' He blew out the lamp. 'Turn round,' he said then. 'You will see another light.'

I saw it, far away below us, a pinpoint.

'That is our light. When we are returning from Germany, we can see it from across the frontier and know that we are nearly home and that our friends are waiting. Hold on to my coat now. You need not worry about Johann behind you. He knows the path well. This way, *Herr Doktor*.'

It was the only sign he gave that he had decided to accept me for what I said I was.

I cannot conceive of how anyone could know that path well. The surface soon changed from pine needles to a sort of rocky rubble, and it twisted and turned like a wounded snake. The wind had dropped, but it was colder than ever, and I found myself crunching through sugary patches of half-frozen slush. I wondered how on earth we were going to bring down a wounded man on an improvised stretcher.

We had been creeping along without the light for about twenty minutes when Stephan stopped and, shielding the lamp with his coat, relit it. I saw that we had arrived.

The climbing hut was built against the side of an overhanging rock face. It was about six feet square inside, and the man was lying diagonally across it on his face. There was a large blood-stain on the floor beneath him. He was semi-conscious. His eyes were closed, but he mumbled something as I felt for his pulse.

'Will he live?' whispered Stephan.

I didn't know. The pulse was there, but it was feeble and rapid. His breathing was shallow. I looked at the wound. The bullet had entered on the inner side of the left thigh just below the groin. There was a little bleeding, but it obviously hadn't touched the femoral artery and, as far as I could see, the bone was all right. I made a dressing with one of the towels and tied it in place with another. The bullet could wait. The immediate danger was from shock aggravated by exposure. I got to work with the blankets and the flask of coffee. Soon the pulse strengthened a little, and after about half an hour I told them how to prepare the stretcher.

I don't know how they got him down that path in the darkness. It was all I could do to get down by myself. It was snowing hard now in great fleecy chunks that blinded you when you moved forward. I was prepared for them to slip and drop the stretcher; but they didn't. It was slow work, however, and it was a good forty minutes before we got to the point where it was safe to light the lamp.

After that I was able to help with the stretcher. At the foot of the path up to the chalet, I went ahead with the lantern. The woman heard my footsteps and came to the door. I realized that we must have been gone for the best part of three hours.

'They're bringing him up,' I said. 'He'll be all right. I shall need your help now.'

She said, 'The bed is ready.' And then, 'Is it serious, Herr Doktor?'

'No.' I didn't tell her then that there was a bullet to be taken out.

It was a nasty job. The wound itself wasn't so bad. The bullet must have been pretty well spent, for it had lodged up against the bone without doing any real damage. It was the instruments that made it difficult. They came from the kitchen. He didn't stand up to it very well, and I wasn't surprised. I didn't feel so good myself when I'd finished. The cognac came in useful after all.

We finally got him to sleep about five.

'He'll be all right now,' I said.

The woman looked at me and I saw the tears begin to trickle down her cheeks. It was only then that I remembered that she wasn't a nurse, but his wife.

It was Johann who comforted her. Stephan came over to me.

'We owe you a great debt, Herr Doktor,' he said. 'I must apologize for our behaviour earlier this evening. We have not always been savages, you know. Kurt was a professor of zoology. Johann was a master printer. I was an architect. Now we are those who crawl across frontiers at night and plot like criminals. We have been treated like savages, and so we live like them. We forget sometimes that we were civilized. We ask your pardon. I do not know how we can repay you for what you have done. We . . .'

But I was too tired for speeches. I smiled quickly at him.

'All that I need by way of a fee is another glass of cognac and a bed to sleep in for a few hours. I suggest, by the way, that you get a doctor in to look at the patient later today. There will be a little fever to treat. Tell the doctor he fell on his climbing axe. He won't believe you, but there'll be no bullet for him to be inquisitive about. Oh, and if you could find me a little petrol for my car . . .'

It was five in the afternoon and almost dark again when Stephan woke me. The local doctor, he reported, as he set an enormous tray of food down beside the bed, had been, dressed the wound, prescribed, and gone. My car was filled up with petrol and awaited me below if I wished to drive to Zurich that night. Kurt was awake and could not be prevailed upon to sleep until he had thanked me.

They were all there, grouped about the bed, when I went downstairs. Bruno was the only one who looked as if he had had any sleep.

He sprang to his feet. 'Here, Kurt,' he said facetiously, 'is the *Herr Doktor*. He is going to cut your leg off.'

Only the woman did not laugh at the jest. Kurt himself was smiling when I bent over to look at him.

He was a youngish-looking man of about forty with intelligent brown eyes and a high, wide forehead. The smile faded from his face as he looked at me.

'You know what I wish to say, *Herr Doktor*?'

I took refuge in professional brusqueness. 'The less you say, the better,' I said, and felt for his pulse. But as I did so his fingers moved and gripped my hand.

'One day soon,' he said, 'England and the Third Reich will be at war. But you will not be at war with Germany. Remember that, please, *Herr Doktor*. Not with Germany. It is people like us who are Germany, and in our way we shall fight with England. You will see.'

I left soon after.

At nine that night I was in Zurich.

Llewellyn was back in the room. I put the manuscript down. He looked across at me.

'Very interesting,' I said.

'I'd considered sending it up to one of these magazines that publish short stories,' he said apologetically. 'I thought I'd like your opinion first, though. What do you think?'

I cleared my throat. 'Well, of course, it's difficult to say. Very interesting, as I said. But there's no real point to it, is there? It needs something to tie it all together.'

'Yes, I see what you mean. It sort of leaves off, doesn't it? But that's how it actually happened.' He looked disappointed. 'I don't think I could invent an ending. It would be rather a pity, wouldn't it? You see, it's all true.'

'Yes, it would be a pity.'

'Well, anyway, thanks for reading it. Funny thing to happen. I really only put it down on paper for fun.' He got up. 'Oh, by the way. I was forgetting. I heard from those people about a week after war broke out. A letter. Let's see now, where did I put it? Ah, yes.'

He rummaged in a drawer for a bit, and then tossed a letter over to me.

The envelope bore a Swiss stamp and the postmark was Klosters, 4 September 1939. The contents felt bulky. I drew them out.

The cause of the bulkiness was what looked like a travel agent's folder doubled up to fit the envelope. I straightened it. On the front page was a lino-cut of a clump of pines on the shore of a lake and the name 'TITISEE'. I opened out the folder.

'GERMAN MEN AND WOMEN, COMRADES!' The type was worn and battered. 'Hitler has led you into war. He fed you with lies about the friendly Polish people. In your name he has now committed a wanton act of aggression against them. As a consequence, the free democracies of England and France have declared war against Germany. Comrades, right and justice are on their side. It is Hitler and National Socialism who are the enemies of peace in Europe. Our place as true Germans is at the side of the democracies against Hitler, against National Socialism. Hitler cannot win this war. But the people of Germany must act. All Germans, Catholics, Protestants, and Jews, must act now. Our Czech and Slovak friends are already refusing to make guns for Hitler. Let us stand by their sides. Remember . . .'

I was about to read on when I saw that the letter which accompanied the folder had fluttered to the carpet. I picked it up. It consisted of a few typewritten lines on an otherwise blank sheet of paper.

Greetings, *Herr Doktor*. We secured your address from the Customs carnet in your car and write now to wish you good luck. Kurt, Stephan, and Bruno have made many journeys since we saw you and returned safely each time. Today, Kurt leaves again. We pray for him as always. With this letter we send you Johann's newest work so that you shall see that Kurt spoke the truth to you.

We are the army of the shadows. We do not fight for you against our country-men; but we fight with you against National Socialism, our common enemy.

Auf Wiedersehen.

Freda, Kurt, Stephan, Johann, and Bruno.

Llewellyn put my glass down on the table beside me. 'Help yourself to a cigarette. What do you think of that? Nice of them, wasn't it?' he added. 'Sentimental lot, these Germans.'

ROBERT SHECKLEY

Citizen in Space

I'm really in trouble now, more trouble than I ever thought possible. It's a little difficult to explain how I got into this mess, so maybe I'd better start at the beginning.

Ever since I graduated from trade school in 1991 I'd had a good job as sphinx valve assembler on the Starling Spaceship production line. I really loved those big ships, roaring to Cygnus and Alpha Centaurus and all the other places in the news. I was a young man with a future, I had friends, I even knew some girls.

But it was no good.

The job was fine, but I couldn't do my best work with those hidden cameras focused on my hands. Not that I minded the cameras themselves; it was the whirring noise they made. I couldn't concentrate.

I complained to Internal Security. I told them, look, why can't I have new, quiet cameras, like everybody else? But they were too busy to do anything about it.

Then lots of little things started to bother me. Like the tape recorder in my TV set. The FBI never adjusted it right, and it hummed all night long. I complained a hundred times. I told them, look, nobody else's recorder hums that way. Why mine? But they always gave me that speech about winning the cold war, and how they couldn't please everybody.

Things like that make a person feel inferior. I suspected my government wasn't interested in me.

Take my Spy, for example. I was an 18-D Suspect—the same classification as the Vice-President—and this entitled me to part-time surveillance. But my particular Spy must have thought he was a movie actor, because he always wore a stained trench coat and a slouch hat jammed over his eyes. He was a thin, nervous type, and he followed practically on my heels for fear of losing me.

Well, he was trying his best. Spying is a competitive business, and I couldn't help but feel sorry, he was so bad at it. But it was embarrassing, just to be associated with him. My friends laughed themselves sick whenever I showed up with him breathing down the back of my neck. 'Bill,' they said, 'is *that* the best you can do?' And my girl friends thought he was creepy.

Naturally, I went to the Senate Investigations Committee, and said, look, why can't you give me a *trained* Spy, like my friends have?

They said they'd see, but I knew I wasn't important enough to swing it.

All these little things put me on edge, and any psychologist will tell you it doesn't take something big to drive you bats. I was sick of being ignored, sick of being neglected.

That's when I started to think about Deep Space. There were billions of square miles of nothingness out there, dotted with too many stars to count. There were enough Earth-type planets for every man, woman and child. There had to be a spot for me.

I bought a Universe Light List, and a tattered Galactic Pilot. I read through the Gravity Tide Book, and the Interstellar Pilot Charts. Finally I figured I knew as much as I'd ever know.

All my savings went into an old Chrysler Star Clipper. This antique leaked oxygen along its seams. It had a touchy atomic pile, and space-warp drives that might throw you practically anywhere. It was dangerous, but the only life I was risking was my own. At least, that's what I thought.

So I got my passport, blue clearance, red clearance, numbers certificate, space-sickness shots and deratification papers. At the job I collected my last day's pay and waved to the cameras. In the apartment, I packed my clothes and said goodbye to the recorders. On the street, I shook hands with my poor Spy and wished him luck.

I had burned my bridges behind me.

All that was left was final clearance, so I hurried down to the Final Clearance Office. A clerk with white hands and a sun-lamp tan looked at me dubiously.

'Where did you wish to go?' he asked me.

'Space,' I said.

'Of course. But where in space?'

'I don't know yet,' I said. 'Just space. Deep Space. Free Space.'

The clerk sighed wearily. 'You'll have to be more explicit than that, if you want a clearance. Are you going to settle on a planet in American Space? Or did you wish to emigrate to British Space? Or Dutch Space? Or French Space?'

'I didn't know *space* could be owned,' I said.

'Then you don't keep up with the times,' he told me, with a superior smirk. 'The United States has claimed all space between coordinates 2XA and D2B, except for a small and relatively unimportant segment which is claimed by Mexico. The Soviet Union has coordinates 3DB to LO2— a very bleak region, I can assure you. And then there is the Belgian Grant, the Chinese Grant, the Ceylonese Grant, the Nigerian Grant—'

I stopped him. 'Where is Free Space?' I asked.

'There is none.'

'None at all? How far do the boundary lines extend?'

'To infinity,' he told me proudly.

For a moment it fetched me up short. Somehow I had never considered the possibility of every bit of infinite space being owned. But it was natural enough. After all, *somebody* had to own it.

'I want to go into American Space,' I said. It didn't seem to matter at the time, although it turned out otherwise.

The clerk nodded sullenly. He checked my records back to the age of five—there was no sense in going back any further—and gave me the Final Clearance.

The spaceport had my ship all serviced, and I managed to get away without blowing a tube. It wasn't until Earth dwindled to a pinpoint and disappeared behind me that I realized I was alone.

Fifty hours out I was making a routine inspection of my stores, when I observed that one of my vegetable sacks had a shape unlike the other sacks. Upon opening it I found a girl, where a hundred pounds of potatoes should have been.

'Well,' she said, 'are you going to help me out? Or would you prefer to close the sack and forget the whole thing?'

I helped her out. She said, 'Your potatoes are lumpy.'

I could have said the same of her, with considerable approval. She was a slender girl, for the most part, with hair the reddish blonde colour of a flaring jet, a pert, dirt-smudged face and brooding blue eyes. On Earth, I would gladly have walked ten miles to meet her. In space, I wasn't so sure.

'Could you give me something to eat?' she asked. 'All I've had since we left is raw carrots.'

I made her a sandwich. While she ate, I asked, 'What are you doing here?'

'You wouldn't understand,' she said, between mouthfuls.

'Sure I would.'

She walked to a porthole and looked out at the spectacle of stars— American stars, most of them—burning in the void of American space.

'I wanted to be free,' she said.

'Huh?'

She sank wearily on my cot. 'I suppose you'd call me a romantic,' she said quietly. 'I'm the sort of fool who recites poetry to herself in the black night, and cries in front of some absurd little statuette. Yellow autumn leaves make me tremble, and dew on a green lawn seems like the tears of all Earth. My psychiatrist tells me I'm a misfit.'

She closed her eyes with a weariness I could appreciate. Standing in a potato sack for fifty hours can be pretty exhausting.

'Earth was getting me down,' she said. 'I couldn't stand it—the regimentation, the discipline, the privation, the cold war, the hot war, everything. I wanted to laugh in free air, run through green fields, walk unmolested through gloomy forests, sing—'

'But why did you pick on me?'

'You were bound for freedom,' she said. 'I'll leave if you insist.'

That was a pretty silly idea, out in the depths of space. And I couldn't afford the fuel to turn back.

'You can stay,' I said.

'Thank you,' she said very softly. 'You *do* understand.'

'Sure, sure,' I said. 'But we'll have to get a few things straight. First of all—' But she had fallen asleep on my cot, with a trusting smile on her lips.

Immediately I searched her handbag. I found five lipsticks, a compact, a phial of Venus V perfume, a paper-bound book of poetry, and a badge that read: *Special Investigator, FBI*.

I had suspected it, of course. Girls don't talk that way, but Spies always do.

It was nice to know my government was still looking out for me. It made space seem less lonely.

The ship moved into the depths of American Space. By working fifteen hours out of twenty-four, I managed to keep my spacewarp drive in one piece, my atomic piles reasonably cool, and my hull seams tight. Mavis O'Day (as my Spy was named) made all meals, took care of the light housekeeping, and hid a number of small cameras round the ship. They buzzed abominably, but I pretended not to notice.

Under the circumstances, however, my relations with Miss O'Day were quite proper.

The trip was proceeding normally—even happily—until something happened.

I was dozing at the controls. Suddenly an intense light flared on my starboard bow. I leaped backwards, knocking over Mavis as she was inserting a new reel of film into her number three camera.

'Excuse me,' I said.

'Oh, trample me any time,' she said.

I helped her to her feet. Her supple nearness was dangerously pleasant, and the tantalizing scent of Venus V tickled my nostrils.

'You can let me go now,' she said.

'I know,' I said, and continued to hold her. My mind inflamed by her nearness, I heard myself saying, 'Mavis—I haven't known you very long, but—'

'Yes, Bill?' she asked.

In the madness of the moment I had forgotten our relationship of Suspect and Spy. I don't know what I might have said. But just then a second light blazed outside the ship.

I released Mavis and hurried to the controls. With difficulty I throttled the old Star Clipper to an idle, and looked around.

Outside, in the vast vacuum of space, was a single fragment of rock. Perched upon it was a child in a space suit, holding a box of flares in one hand and a tiny space-suited dog in the other.

Quickly we got him inside and unbuttoned his space suit.

'My dog—' he said.

'He's all right, son,' I told him.

'Terribly sorry to break in on you this way,' the lad said.

'Forget it,' I said. 'What were you doing out there?'

'Sir,' he began, in treble tones, 'I will have to start at the start. My father was a spaceship test pilot, and he died valiantly, trying to break the light barrier. Mother recently remarried. Her present husband is a large, black-haired man with narrow, shifty eyes and tightly compressed lips. Until recently he was employed as a ribbon clerk in a large department store.

'He resented my presence from the beginning. I suppose I reminded him of my dead father, with my blond curls, large oval eyes and merry outgoing ways. Our relationship smouldered fitfully. Then an uncle of his died (under suspicious circumstances) and he inherited holdings in British Space.

'Accordingly, we set out in our spaceship. As soon as we reached this deserted area, he said to Mother, "Rachel, he's old enough to fend for himself." My mother said, "Dirk, he's so young!" But soft-hearted, laughing Mother was no match for the inflexible will of the man I would never call Father. He thrust me into my space suit, handed me a box of flares, put Flicker into his own little suit, and said, "A lad can do all right for himself in space these days." "Sir," I said, "there is no planet within two hundred light years." "You'll make out," he grinned, and thrust me upon this spur of rock.'

The boy paused for breath, and his dog Flicker looked up at me with moist oval eyes. I gave the dog a bowl of milk and bread, and watched the lad eat a peanut butter and jelly sandwich. Mavis carried the little chap into the bunk room and tenderly tucked him into bed.

I returned to the controls, started the ship again, and turned on the intercom.

'Wake up, you little idiot!' I heard Mavis say.

'Lemme sleep,' the boy answered.

'Wake up! What did Congressional Investigation *mean* by sending you here? Don't they realize this is an FBI case?'

'He's been reclassified as a 10-F Suspect,' the boy said. 'That calls for full surveillance.'

'Yes, but *I'm* here,' Mavis cried.

'You didn't do so well on your last case,' the boy said. 'I'm sorry, ma'am, but Security comes first.'

'So they send you,' Mavis said, sobbing now. 'A twelve-year-old child—'

'I'll be thirteen in seven months.'

'A twelve-year-old child! And I've tried so hard! I've studied, read books, taken evening courses, listened to lectures—'

'It's a tough break,' the boy said sympathetically. 'Personally, I want to be a spaceship test pilot. At my age, this is the only way I can get in flying hours. Do you think he'll let me fly the ship?'

I snapped off the intercom. I should have felt wonderful. Two full-time Spies were watching me. It meant I was really someone, someone to be watched.

But the truth was, my Spies were only a girl and a twelve-year-old boy. They must have been scraping bottom when they sent those two.

My government was still ignoring me, in its own fashion.

We managed well on the rest of the flight. Young Roy, as the lad was called, took over the piloting of the ship, and his dog sat alertly in the co-pilot's seat. Mavis continued to cook and keep house. I spent my time patching seams. We were as happy a group of Spies and Suspects as you could find.

We found an uninhabited Earth-type planet. Mavis liked it because it was small and rather cute, with the green fields and gloomy forests she had read about in her poetry books. Young Roy liked the clear lakes, and the mountains, which were just the right height for a boy to climb.

We landed, and began to settle.

Young Roy found an immediate interest in the animals I animated from the freezer. He appointed himself guardian of cows and horses, protector of ducks and geese, defender of pigs and chickens. This kept him so busy that his reports to the Senate became fewer and fewer, and finally stopped altogether.

You really couldn't expect any more from a Spy of his age.

And after I had set up the domes and force-seeded a few acres, Mavis and I took long walks in the gloomy forest, and in the bright green and yellow fields that bordered it.

One day we packed a picnic lunch and ate on the edge of a little waterfall. Mavis's unbound hair spread lightly over her shoulders, and there was a distant enchanted look in her blue eyes. All in all, she seemed extremely un-Spylike, and I had to remind myself over and over of our respective roles.

'Bill,' she said after a while.

'Yes?' I said.

'Nothing.' She tugged at a blade of grass.

I couldn't figure that one out. But her hand strayed somewhere near mine. Our fingertips touched, and clung.

We were silent for a long time. Never had I been so happy.

'Bill?'

'Yes?'

'Bill dear, could you ever—'

What she was going to say, and what I might have answered, I will never know. At that moment our silence was shattered by the roar of jets. Down from the sky dropped a spaceship.

Ed Wallace, the pilot, was a white-haired old man in a slouch hat and a stained trench coat. He was a salesman for Clear-Flo, an outfit that cleansed water on a planetary basis. Since I had no need for his services, he thanked me, and left.

But he didn't get very far. His engines turned over once, and stopped with a frightening finality.

I looked over his drive mechanism, and found that a sphinx valve had blown. It would take me a month to make him a new one with hand tools.

'This is terribly awkward,' he murmured. 'I suppose I'll have to stay here.'

'I suppose so,' I said.

He looked at his ship regretfully. 'Can't understand how it happened,' he said.

'Maybe you weakened the valve when you cut it with a hacksaw,' I said, and walked off. I had seen the tell-tale marks.

Mr Wallace pretended not to hear me. That evening I overheard his report on the interstellar radio, which functioned perfectly. His home office, interestingly enough, was not Clear-Flo, but Central Intelligence.

Mr Wallace made a good vegetable farmer, even though he spent most of his time sneaking around with camera and notebook. His presence spurred young Roy to greater efforts. Mavis and I stopped walking in the gloomy forest, and there didn't seem time to return to the yellow and green fields, to finish some unfinished sentences.

But our little settlement prospered. We had other visitors. A man and his wife from Regional Intelligence dropped by, posing as itinerant fruit pickers. They were followed by two girl photographers, secret representatives of the Executive Information Bureau, and then there was a young newspaper man, who was actually from the Idaho Council of Spatial Morals.

Every single one of them blew a sphinx valve when it came time to leave.

I didn't know whether to feel proud or ashamed. A half-dozen agents were watching *me*—but every one of them was a second-rater. And invariably, after a few weeks on my planet, they became involved in farmwork and their Spying efforts dwindled to nothing.

I had bitter moments. I pictured myself as a testing ground for novices, something to cut their teeth on. I was the Suspect they gave to Spies who were too old or too young, inefficient, scatter-brained, or just plain incompetent. I saw myself as a sort of half-pay retirement plan Suspect, a substitute for a pension.

But it didn't bother me too much. I did have a position, although it was a little difficult to define. I was happier than I had ever been on Earth, and my Spies were pleasant and co-operative people.

Our little colony was happy and secure.

I thought it could go on for ever.

Then, one fateful night, there was unusual activity. Some important message seemed to be coming in, and all radios were on. I had to ask a few Spies to share sets, to keep from burning out my generator.

Finally all radios were turned off, and the Spies held conferences. I heard them whispering into the small hours. The next morning, they were all assembled in the living room, and their faces were long and sombre. Mavis stepped forward as spokeswoman.

'Something terrible has happened,' she said to me. 'But first, we have something to reveal to you. Bill, none of us are what we seemed. We are all Spies for the government.'

'Huh?' I said, not wanting to hurt any feelings.

'It's true,' she said. 'We've been spying on you, Bill.'

'Huh?' I said again. 'Even you?'

'Even me,' Mavis said unhappily.

'And now it's all over,' young Roy blurted out.

That shook me. '*Why?*' I asked.

They looked at each other. Finally Mr Wallace, bending the rim of his hat back and forth in his calloused hands, said, 'Bill, a re-survey has just shown that this sector of space is not owned by the United States.'

'What country does own it?' I asked.

'Be calm,' Mavis said. 'Try to understand. This entire sector was overlooked in the international survey, and now it can't be claimed by any country. As the first to settle here, this planet, and several million miles of space surrounding it, belong to you, Bill.'

I was too stunned to speak.

'Under the circumstances,' Mavis continued, 'we have no authorization to be here. So we're leaving immediately.'

'But you can't!' I cried. 'I haven't repaired your sphinx valves!'

'All Spies carry spare sphinx valves and hacksaw blades,' she said gently.

Watching them troop out to their ships, I pictured the solitude ahead of me. I would have no government to watch over me. No longer would I hear footsteps in the night, turn, and see the dedicated face of a Spy behind me. No longer would the whirr of an old camera soothe me at work, nor the buzz of a defective recorder lull me to sleep.

And yet, I felt even sorrier for them. Those poor, earnest, clumsy, bungling Spies were returning to a fast, efficient, competitive world. Where would they find another Suspect like me, or another place like my planet?

'Good-bye, Bill,' Mavis said, offering me her hand.

I watched her walk to Mr Wallace's ship. It was only then that I realized that she was no longer *my* Spy.

'Mavis!' I cried, running after her. She hurried towards the ship. I caught her by the arm. 'Wait. There was something I started to say in the ship. I wanted to say it again on the picnic.'

She tried to pull away from me. In most unromantic tones I croaked, 'Mavis, I love you.'

She was in my arms. We kissed, and I told her that her home was here, on this planet with its gloomy forests and yellow and green fields. Here with me.

She was too happy to speak.

With Mavis staying, young Roy reconsidered. Mr Wallace's vegetables were just ripening, and he wanted to tend them. And everyone else had some chore or other that he couldn't drop.

So here I am—ruler, king, dictator, president, whatever I want to call myself. Spies are beginning to pour in now from *every* country—not only America.

To feed all my subjects, I'll soon have to import food. But the other rulers are beginning to refuse me aid. They think I've bribed their Spies to desert.

I haven't, I swear it. They just come.

I can't resign, because I own this place. And I haven't the heart to send them away. I'm at the end of my rope.

With my entire population consisting of former government Spies, you'd think I'd have an easy time forming a government of my own. But no. They're completely uncooperative. I'm the absolute ruler of a planet of farmers, dairymen, shepherds, and cattle raisers, so I guess we won't starve after all. But that's not the point. The point is: how am I supposed to rule?

Not a single one of these people will Spy for me.

Risico

'In this pizniss is much risico.'

The words came softly through the thick brown moustache. The hard black eyes moved slowly over Bond's face and down to Bond's hands which were carefully shredding a paper match on which was printed *Albergo Colomba d'Oro*.

James Bond felt the inspection. The same surreptitious examination had been going on since he had met the man two hours before at the rendezvous in the Excelsior bar. Bond had been told to look for a man with a heavy moustache who would be sitting by himself drinking an Alexandra. Bond had been amused by this secret recognition signal. The creamy, feminine drink was so much cleverer than the folded news-paper, the flower in the buttonhole, the yellow gloves that were the hoary, slipshod call-signs between agents. It had also the great merit of being able to operate alone, without its owner. And Kristatos had started off with a little test. When Bond had come into the bar and looked round there had been perhaps twenty people in the room. None of them had a moustache. But on a corner table at the far side of the tall, discreet room, flanked by a saucer of olives and another of cashew nuts, stood the tall-stemmed glass of cream and vodka. Bond went straight over to the table, pulled out a chair and sat down.

The waiter came. 'Good evening, sir. Signor Kristatos is at the telephone.'

Bond nodded. 'A Negroni. With Gordon's, please.'

The waiter walked back to the bar. 'Negroni. Uno. Gordon's.'

'I am so sorry.' The big hairy hand picked up the small chair as if it had been as light as a matchbox and swept it under the heavy hips. 'I had to have a word with Alfredo.'

There had been no handshake. These were old acquaintances. In the same line of business, probably. Something like import and export. The younger one looked American. No. Not with those clothes. English.

Bond returned the fast serve. 'How's his little boy?'

The black eyes of Signor Kristatos narrowed. Yes, they had said this man was a professional. He spread his hands. 'Much the same. What can you expect?'

'Polio is a terrible thing.'

The Negroni came. The two men sat back comfortably, each one satisfied that he had to do with a man in the same league. This was rare in 'The Game'. So many times, before one had even started on a tandem assignment like this, one had lost confidence in the outcome. There was so often, at least in Bond's imagination, a faint smell of burning in the air at such a rendezvous. He knew it for the sign that the fringe of his cover had already started to smoulder. In due course the smouldering fabric would burst into flames and he would be *brûlé*. Then the game would be up and he would have to decide whether to pull out or wait and get shot at by someone. But at this meeting there had been no fumbling.

Later that evening, at the little restaurant off the Piazza di Spagna called the Colomba d'Oro, Bond was amused to find that he was still on probation. Kristatos was still watching and weighing him, wondering if he could be trusted. This remark about the risky business was as near as Kristatos had so far got to admitting that there existed any business between the two of them. Bond was encouraged. He had not really believed in Kristatos. But surely all these precautions could only mean that M's intuition had paid off—that Kristatos knew something big.

Bond dropped the last shred of match into the ashtray. He said mildly: 'I was once taught that any business that pays more than ten per cent or is conducted after nine o'clock at night is a dangerous business. The business which brings us together pays up to one thousand per cent and is conducted almost exclusively at night. On both counts it is obviously a risky business.' Bond lowered his voice. 'Funds are available. Dollars, Swiss francs, Venezuelan bolivars—anything convenient.'

'That makes me glad. I have already too much lire.' Signor Kristatos picked up the folio menu. 'But let us feed on something. One should not decide important pizniss on a hollow stomach.'

A week earlier M had sent for Bond. M was in a bad temper. 'Got anything on, 007?'

'Only paperwork, sir.'

'What do you mean, only paperwork?' M jerked his pipe towards his loaded in-tray. 'Who hasn't got paperwork?'

'I meant nothing active, sir.'

'Well, say so.' M picked up a bundle of dark red files tied together with tape and slid them so sharply across the desk that Bond had to catch them. 'And here's some more paperwork. Scotland Yard stuff mostly—their narcotics people. Wads from the Home Office and the Ministry of Health, and some nice thick reports from the International Opium Control people in Geneva. Take it away and read it. You'll need today and most of tonight. Tomorrow you fly to Rome and get after the big men. Is that clear?'

Bond said that it was. The state of M's temper was also explained. There was nothing that made him more angry than having to divert his staff from their primary duty. This duty was espionage, and when necessary sabotage and subversion. Anything else was a misuse of the Service and of Secret Funds which, God knows, were meagre enough.

'Any questions?' M's jaw stuck out like the prow of a ship. The jaw seemed to tell Bond to pick up the files and get the hell out of the office and let M move on to something important.

Bond knew that a part of all this—if only a small part—was an act. M had certain bees in his bonnet. They were famous in the Service, and M knew they were. But that did not mean that he would allow them to stop buzzing. There were queen bees, like the misuse of the Service, and the search for true as distinct from wishful intelligence, and there were worker bees. These included such idiosyncrasies as not employing men with beards, or those who were completely bilingual, instantly dismissing men who tried to bring pressure to bear on him through family relationships with members of the Cabinet, mistrusting men or women who were too 'dressy', and those who called him 'sir' off-duty; and having an exaggerated faith in Scotsmen. But M was ironically conscious of his obsessions, as, thought Bond, a Churchill or a Montgomery were about theirs. He never minded his bluff, as it partly was, being called on any of them. Moreover, he would never have dreamed of sending Bond out on an assignment without proper briefing.

Bond knew all this. He said mildly: 'Two things, sir. Why are we taking this thing on, and what lead, if any, have Station I got towards the people involved in it?'

M gave Bond a hard, sour look. He swivelled his chair sideways so that he could watch the high, scudding October clouds through the broad window. He reached out for his pipe, blew through it sharply, and then, as if this action had let off the small head of steam, replaced it gently on the desk. When he spoke, his voice was patient, reasonable. 'As you can imagine, 007, I do not wish the Service to become involved in this drug business. Earlier this year I had to take you off other duties for a fortnight so that you could go to Mexico and chase off that Mexican grower. You nearly got yourself killed. I sent you as a favour to the Special Branch. When they asked for you again to tackle this Italian gang I refused. Ronnie Vallance went behind my back to the Home Office and the Ministry of Health. The Ministers pressed me. I said that you were needed here and that I had no one else to spare. Then the two Ministers went to the PM.' M paused. 'And that was that. I must say the PM was very persuasive. Took the line that heroin, in the quantities that have been coming in, is an instrument of psychological warfare—that it saps a country's strength. He said he wouldn't be surprised to find that this wasn't just a gang of Italians out to make big money—that subversion and not money was at the back of it.' M smiled sourly. 'I expect Ronnie Vallance thought up that line of argument. Apparently his narcotics people have been having the devil of a time with the traffic—trying to stop it getting a hold on the teenagers as it has in America. Seems the dance halls and the amusement arcades are full of pedlars. Vallance's Ghost Squad have managed to penetrate back up the line to one of the middle-men, and there's no doubt it's all coming from Italy, hidden in Italian tourists' cars. Vallance has done what he can through the Italian police and Interpol, and got nowhere. They get so far back up the pipeline, arrest a few little people, and then, when they seem to be getting near the centre, there's a blank wall. The inner ring of distributors are too frightened or too well paid.'

Bond interrupted. 'Perhaps there's protection somewhere, sir. That Montesi business didn't look so good.'

M shrugged impatiently. 'Maybe, maybe. And you'll have to watch out for that too, but my impression is that the Montesi case resulted in a pretty extensive clean-up. Anyway, when the PM gave me the order to get on with it, it occurred to me to have a talk with Washington. CIA were very helpful. You know the Narcotics Bureau have a team in Italy. Have had ever since the War. They're nothing to do with CIA—run by the American Treasury Department, of all people. The American Treasury control a so-called Secret Service that looks after drug smuggling and counterfeiting. Pretty crazy arrangement. Often wonder what the FBI must think of it. However,' M slowly swivelled his chair away from the window. He linked his hands behind his head and leaned back, looking across the desk at Bond. 'The point is that the CIA Rome Station works pretty closely with this little narcotics team. Has to, to prevent crossed lines and so on. And CIA—Alan Dulles himself, as a matter of fact—gave me the name of the top narcotics agent used by the Bureau.

Apparently he's a double. Does a little smuggling as cover. Chap called Kristatos. Dulles said that of course he couldn't involve his people in any way and he was pretty certain the Treasury Department wouldn't welcome their Rome Bureau playing too closely with us. But he said that, if I wished, he would get word to this Kristatos that one of our, er, best men would like to make contact with a view to doing business. I said I would much appreciate that, and yesterday I got word that the rendezvous is fixed for the day after tomorrow.' M gestured towards the files in front of Bond. 'You'll find all the details in there.'

There was a brief silence in the room. Bond was thinking that the whole affair sounded unpleasant, probably dangerous and certainly dirty. With the last quality in mind, Bond got to his feet and picked up the files. 'All right, sir. It looks like money. How much will we pay for the traffic to stop?'

M let his chair tip forward. He put his hands flat down on the desk, side by side. He said roughly: 'A hundred thousand pounds. In any currency. That's the PM's figure. But I don't want you to get hurt. Certainly not picking other people's coals out of the fire. So you can go up to another hundred thousand if there's bad trouble. Drugs are the biggest and tightest ring in crime.' M reached for his in-basket and took out a file of signals. Without looking up he said: 'Look after yourself.'

Signor Kristatos picked up the menu. He said: 'I do not beat about bushes, Mr Bond. How much?'

'Fifty thousand pounds for one hundred per cent results.'

Kristatos said indifferently: 'Yes. Those are important funds. I shall have melon with prosciutto ham and a chocolate ice-cream. I do not eat greatly at night. These people have their own Chianti. I commend it.'

The waiter came and there was a brisk rattle of Italian. Bond ordered Tagliatelli Verdi with a Genoese sauce which Kristatos said was improbably concocted of basil, garlic, and fir cones.

When the waiter had gone, Kristatos sat and chewed silently on a wooden toothpick. His face gradually became dark and glum as if bad weather had come to his mind. The black, hard eyes that glanced restlessly at everything in the restaurant except Bond, glittered. Bond guessed that Kristatos was wondering whether or not to betray somebody. Bond said encouragingly: 'In certain circumstances, there might be more.'

Kristatos seemed to make up his mind. He said: 'So?' He pushed back his chair and got up. 'Forgive me. I must visit the toiletta.' He turned and walked swiftly towards the back of the restaurant.

Bond was suddenly hungry and thirsty. He poured out a large glass of Chianti and swallowed half of it. He broke a roll and began eating, smothering each mouthful with deep yellow butter. He wondered why rolls and butter are delicious only in France and Italy. There was nothing else on his mind. It was just a question of waiting. He had confidence in Kristatos. He was a big, solid man who was trusted by the Americans. He was probably making some telephone call that would be decisive. Bond felt in good spirits. He watched the passers-by through the plate-glass window. A man selling one of the Party papers went by on a bicycle. Flying from the basket in front of the handlebars was a pennant. In red on white it said: PROGRESSO?—SI!—AVVENTURI?—NO! Bond smiled. That was how it was. Let it so remain for the rest of the assignment.

On the far side of the square, rather plain room, at the corner table by the *caisse*, the plump fair-haired girl with the dramatic mouth said to the jovial good-living man with the thick rope of spaghetti joining his face to the plate: 'He has a rather cruel smile. But he is very handsome. Spies aren't usually so good-looking. Are you sure you are right, mein Täubchen?'

The man's teeth cut through the rope. He wiped his mouth on a napkin already streaked with tomato sauce, belched sonorously and said: 'Santos is never wrong about these things. He has a nose for spies. That is why I chose him as the permanent tail for that bastard Kristatos. And who else but a spy would think of spending an evening with the pig? But we will make sure.' The man took out of his pocket one of those cheap tin snappers that are sometimes given out, with paper hats and whistles, on carnival nights. It gave one sharp click. The maître d'hôtel on the far side of the room stopped whatever he was doing and hurried over.

'Si, padrone.'

The man beckoned. The maître d'hôtel went over and received the whispered instructions. He nodded briefly, walked over to a door near the kitchens marked UFFICIO, and went in and closed the door behind him.

Phase by phase, in a series of minute moves, an exercise that had long been perfected was then smoothly put into effect. The man near the *caisse* munched his spaghetti and critically observed each step in the operation as if it had been a fast game of chess.

The maître d'hôtel came out of the door marked UFFICIO, hurried across the restaurant and said loudly to his No. 2: 'An extra table for four. Immediately.' The No. 2 gave him a direct look and nodded. He followed the maître d'hôtel over to a space adjoining Bond's table, clicked his fingers for help, borrowed a chair from one table, a chair from another table and, with a bow and an apology, the spare chair from Bond's table. The fourth chair was being carried over from the direction of the door marked UFFICIO by the maître d'hôtel. He placed it square with the others, a table was lowered into the middle and glass and cutlery were deftly laid. The maître d'hôtel frowned. 'But you have laid a table for four. I said three—for three people.' He casually took the chair he had himself brought to the table and switched it to Bond's table. He gave a wave of the hand to dismiss his helpers and everyone dispersed about their business.

The innocent little flurry of restaurant movement had taken about a minute. An innocuous trio of Italians came into the restaurant. The maître d'hôtel greeted them personally and bowed them to the new table, and the gambit was completed.

Bond had hardly been conscious of it. Kristatos returned from whatever business he had been about, their food came and they got on with the meal.

While they ate they talked about nothing—the election chances in Italy, the latest Alfa Romeo, Italian shoes compared with English. Kristatos talked well. He seemed to know the inside story of everything. He gave information so casually that it did not sound like bluff. He spoke his own kind of English with an occasional phrase borrowed from other languages. It made a lively mixture. Bond was interested and amused. Kristatos was a tough insider—a useful man. Bond was not surprised that the American Intelligence people found him good value.

Coffee came, Kristatos lit a thin black cigar and talked through it, the cigar jumping up and down between the thin straight lips. He put both hands flat on the table in front of him. He looked at the tablecloth between them and said softly: 'This pizniss. I will play with you. To now I have only played with the Americans. I have not told them what I am about to tell you. There was no requirement. This machina does not operate with America. These things are closely regulated. This machina operates only with England. Yes? Capito?'

'I understand. Everyone has his own territory. It's the usual way in these things.'

'Exact. Now, before I give you the informations, like good commercials we make the terms. Yes?'

'Of course.'

Signor Kristatos examined the tablecloth more closely. 'I wish for ten thousand dollars American, in paper of small sizes, by tomorrow lunchtime.

When you have destroyed the machina I wish for a further twenty thousand.' Signor Kristatos briefly raised his eyes and surveyed Bond's face. 'I am not greedy. I do not take all your funds, isn't it?'

'The price is satisfactory.'

'Bueno. Second term. There is no telling where you get these informations from. Even if you are beaten.'

'Fair enough.'

'Third term. The head of this machina is a bad man.' Signor Kristatos paused and looked up. The black eyes held a red glint. The clenched dry lips pulled away from the cigar to let the words out. 'He is to be destrutto—killed.'

Bond sat back. He gazed quizzically at the other man who now leaned slightly forward over the table, waiting. So the wheels had now shown within the wheels! This was a private vendetta of some sort. Kristatos wanted to get himself a gunman. And he was not paying the gunman, the gunman was paying him for the privilege of disposing of an enemy. Not bad! The fixer was certainly working on a big fix this time—using the Secret Service to pay off his private scores. Bond said softly: 'Why?'

Signor Kristatos said indifferently: 'No questions catch no lies.'

Bond drank down his coffee. It was the usual story of big syndicate crime. You never saw more than the tip of the iceberg. But what did that matter to him? He had been sent to do one specific job. If his success benefited others, nobody, least of all M, could care less. Bond had been told to destroy the machine. If this unnamed man was the machine, it would be merely carrying out orders to destroy the man. Bond said: 'I cannot promise that. You must see that. All I can say is that if the man tries to destroy me, I will destroy him.'

Signor Kristatos took a toothpick out of the holder, stripped off the paper and set about cleaning his fingernails. When he had finished one hand he looked up. He said: 'I do not often gamble on incertitudes. This time I will do so because it is you who are paying me, and not me you. Is all right? So now I will give you the informations. Then you are alone—solo. Tomorrow night I fly to Karachi. I have important pizniss there. I can only give you the informations. After that you run with the ball and—' he threw the dirty toothpick down on the table—'Che sera, sera.'

'All right.'

Signor Kristatos edged his chair nearer to Bond. He spoke softly and quickly. He gave specimen dates and names to document his narrative. He never hesitated for a fact and he did not waste time on irrelevant detail. It was a short story and a pithy one. There were two thousand

American gangsters in the country—Italian-Americans who had been convicted and expelled from the United States. These men were in a bad way. They were on the blackest of all police lists and, because of their records, their own people were wary of employing them. A hundred of the toughest among them had pooled their funds and small groups from this élite had moved to Beirut, Istanbul, Tangier, and Macao—the great smuggling centres of the world. A further large section acted as couriers, and the bosses had acquired, through nominees, a small and respectable pharmaceutical business in Milan. To this centre the outlying groups smuggled opium and its derivatives. They used small craft across the Mediterranean, a group of stewards in an Italian charter airline and, as a regular weekly source of supply, the through carriage of the Orient Express in which whole sections of bogus upholstery were fitted by bribed members of the train cleaners in Istanbul. The Milan firm— Pharmacia Colomba SA—acted as a clearing-house and as a convenient centre for breaking down the raw opium into heroin. Thence the couriers, using innocent motor cars of various makes, ran a delivery service to the middlemen in England.

Bond interrupted. 'Our Customs are pretty good at spotting that sort of traffic. There aren't many hiding-places in a car they don't know about. Where do these men carry the stuff?'

'Always in the spare wheel. You can carry twenty thousand pounds worth of heroin in one spare wheel.'

'Don't they ever get caught—either bringing the stuff in to Milan or taking it on?'

'Certainly. Many times. But these are well-trained men. And they are tough. They never talk. If they are convicted, they receive ten thousand dollars for each year spent in prison. If they have families, they are cared for. And when all goes well they make good money. It is a co-operative. Each man receives his *tranche* of the *brutto*. Only the chief gets a special *tranche*.'

'All right. Well, who is this man?'

Signor Kristatos put his hand up to the cheroot in his mouth. He kept the hand there and spoke softly from behind it. 'Is a man they call "The Dove", Enrico Colombo. Is the padrone of this restaurant. That is why I bring you here, so that you may see him. Is the fat man who sits with a blonde woman. At the table by the cassa. She is from Vienna. Her name is Lisl Baum. A luxus whore.'

Bond said reflectively: 'She is, is she?' He did not need to look. He had noticed the girl, as soon as he had sat down at the table. Every man in the restaurant would have noticed her. She had the gay, bold, forth-coming looks the Viennese are supposed to have and seldom do. There was a vivacity and a charm about her that lit up her corner of the room. She had the wildest possible urchin cut in ash blonde, a pert nose, a wide laughing mouth and a black ribbon round her throat. James Bond knew that her eyes had been on him at intervals throughout the evening. Her companion had seemed just the type of rich, cheerful, good-living man she would be glad to have as her lover for a while. He would give her a good time. He would be generous. There would be no regrets on either side. On the whole, Bond had vaguely approved of him. He liked cheer-ful, expansive people with a zest for life. Since he, Bond, could not have the girl, it was at least something that she was in good hands. But now? Bond glanced across the room. The couple were laughing about some-thing. The man patted her cheek and got up and went to the door marked UFFICIO and went through and shut the door. So this was the man who ran the great pipeline into England. The man with M's price of a hun-dred thousand pounds on his head. The man Kristatos wanted Bond to kill. Well, he had better get on with the job. Bond stared rudely across the room at the girl. When she lifted her head and looked at him, he smiled at her. Her eyes swept past him, but there was a half smile, as if for herself, on her lips, and when she took a cigarette out of her case and lit it and blew the smoke straight up towards the ceiling there was an offering of the throat and the profile that Bond knew were for him.

It was nearing the time for the after-cinema trade. The maître d'hôtel was supervising the clearing of the unoccupied tables and the setting up of new ones. There was the usual bustle and slapping of napkins across chair-seats and tinkle of glass and cutlery being laid. Vaguely Bond noticed the spare chair at his table being whisked away to help build up a nearby table for six. He began asking Kristatos specific questions—the personal habits of Enrico Colombo, where he lived, the address of his firm in Milan, what other business interests he had. He did not notice the casual progress of the spare chair from its fresh table to another, and then to another, and finally through the door marked UFFICIO. There was no reason why he should.

When the chair was brought into his office, Enrico Colombo waved the maître d'hôtel away and locked the door behind him. Then he went to the chair and lifted off the squab cushion and put it on his desk. He unzipped one side of the cushion and withdrew a Grundig tape-recorder, stopped the machine, ran the tape back, took it off the recorder and put it on a play-back and adjusted the speed and volume. Then he sat down at his desk and lit a cigarette and listened, occasionally making further adjustments and occasionally repeating passages. At the end, when Bond's tinny voice said 'She is, is she?' and there was a long silence interspersed with background noises from the restaurant, Enrico Colombo switched off the machine and sat looking at it. He looked at it for a full minute. His face showed nothing but acute concentration on his thoughts. Then he looked away from the machine and into nothing and said softly, out loud: 'Son-a-beech.' He got slowly to his feet and went to the door and unlocked it. He looked back once more at the Grundig, said 'Son-a-beech' again with more emphasis and went out and back to his table.

Enrico Colombo spoke swiftly and urgently to the girl. She nodded and glanced across the room at Bond. He and Kristatos were getting up from the table. She said to Colombo in a low, angry voice: 'You are a disgusting man. Everybody said so and warned me against you. They were right. Just because you give me dinner in your lousy restaurant you think you have the right to insult me with your filthy propositions'—the girl's voice had got louder. Now she had snatched up her handbag and had got to her feet. She stood beside the table directly in the line of Bond's approach on his way to the exit.

Enrico Colombo's face was black with rage. Now he, too, was on his feet. 'You goddam Austrian beech——'

'Don't dare insult my country, you Italian toad.' She reached for a half-full glass of wine and hurled it accurately in the man's face. When he came at her it was easy for her to back the few steps into Bond who was standing with Kristatos politely waiting to get by.

Enrico Colombo stood panting, wiping the wine off his face with a napkin. He said furiously to the girl: 'Don't ever show your face inside my restaurant again.' He made the gesture of spitting on the floor between them, turned and strode off through the door marked UFFICIO.

The maître d'hôtel had hurried up. Everyone in the restaurant had stopped eating. Bond took the girl by the elbow. 'May I help you find a taxi?'

She jerked herself free. She said, still angry: 'All men are pigs.' She remembered her manners. She said stiffly: 'You are very kind.' She moved haughtily towards the door with the men in her wake.

There was a buzz in the restaurant and a renewed clatter of knives and forks. Everyone was delighted with the scene. The maître d'hôtel, looking solemn, held open the door. He said to Bond: 'I apologize, Monsieur. And you are very kind to be of assistance.' A cruising taxi slowed. He beckoned it to the pavement and held open the door.

The girl got in. Bond firmly followed and closed the door. He said to Kristatos through the window: 'I'll telephone you in the morning. All right?' Without waiting for the man's reply he sat back in the seat. The girl had drawn herself away into the furthest corner. Bond said: 'Where shall I tell him?'

'Hotel Ambassadori.'

They drove a short way in silence. Bond said: 'Would you like to go somewhere first for a drink?'

'No thank you.' She hesitated. 'You are very kind, but tonight I am tired.'

'Perhaps another night.'

'Perhaps, but I go to Venice tomorrow.'

'I shall also be there. Will you have dinner with me tomorrow night?'

The girl smiled. She said: 'I thought Englishmen were supposed to be shy. You are English, aren't you? What is your name? What do you do?'

'Yes, I'm English—My name's Bond—James Bond. I write books—adventure stories. I'm writing one now about drug smuggling. It's set in Rome and Venice. The trouble is that I don't know enough about the trade. I am going round picking up stories about it. Do you know any?'

'So that is why you were having dinner with that Kristatos. I know of him. He has a bad reputation. No. I don't know any stories. I only know what everybody knows.'

Bond said enthusiastically: 'But that's exactly what I want. When I said "stories" I didn't mean fiction. I meant the sort of high-level gossip that's probably pretty near the truth. That sort of thing's worth diamonds to a writer.'

She laughed. 'You mean that . . . diamonds?'

Bond said: 'Well, I don't earn all that as a writer, but I've already sold an option on this story for a film, and if I can make it authentic enough I dare say they'll actually buy the film.' He reached out and put his hand over hers in her lap. She did not take her hand away. 'Yes, diamonds. A diamond clip from Van Cleef. Is it a deal?'

Now she took her hand away. They were arriving at the Ambassadori. She picked up her bag from the seat beside her. She turned on the seat so that she faced him. The commissionaire opened the door and the light from the street turned her eyes into stars. She examined his face with a certain seriousness. She said: 'All men are pigs, but some are lesser pigs than others. All right. I will meet you. But not for dinner. What I may tell you is not for public places. I bathe every afternoon at the Lido. But not at the fashionable plage. I bathe at the Bagni Alberoni, where the

English poet Byron used to ride his horse. It is at the tip of the peninsula. The Vaporetto will take you there. You will find me there the day after tomorrow—at three in the afternoon. I shall be getting my last sunburn before the winter. Among the sand-dunes. You will see a pale yellow umbrella. Underneath it will be me.' She smiled. 'Knock on the umbrella and ask for Fräulein Lisl Baum.'

She got out of the taxi. Bond followed. She held out her hand. 'Thank you for coming to my rescue. Goodnight.'

Bond said: 'Three o'clock then. I shall be there. Goodnight.'

She turned and walked up the curved steps of the hotel. Bond looked after her thoughtfully, and then turned and got back into the taxi and told the man to take him to the Nazionale. He sat back and watched the neon signs ribbon past the window. Things, including the taxi, were going almost too fast for comfort. The only one over which he had any control was the taxi. He leant forward and told the man to drive more slowly.

The best train from Rome to Venice is the Laguna express that leaves every day at midday. Bond, after a morning that was chiefly occupied with difficult talks with his London Headquarters on Station I's scrambler, caught it by the skin of his teeth. The Laguna is a smart, streamlined affair that looks and sounds more luxurious than it is. The seats are made for small Italians and the restaurant car staff suffer from the disease that afflicts their brethren in the great trains all over the world—a genuine loathing for the modern traveller and particularly for the foreigner. Bond had a gangway seat over the axle in the rear aluminium coach. If the seven heavens had been flowing by outside the window he would not have cared. He kept his eyes inside the train, read a jerking book, spilled Chianti over the tablecloth and shifted his long, aching legs and cursed the Ferrovie Italiane dello Stato.

But at last there was Mestre and the dead straight finger of rail across the eighteenth-century aquatint into Venice. Then came the unfailing shock of the beauty that never betrays and the soft swaying progress down the Grand Canal into a blood-red sunset, and the extreme pleasure—so it seemed—of the Gritti Palace that Bond should have ordered the best double room on the first floor.

That evening, scattering thousand-lira notes like leaves in Vallombrosa, James Bond sought, at Harry's Bar, at Florian's, and finally upstairs in the admirable Quadri, to establish to anyone who might be interested that he was what he had wished to appear to the girl—a prosperous writer who lived high and well. Then, in the temporary state of euphoria that a first night in Venice engenders, however high and serious the purpose of the visitor, James Bond walked back to the Gritti and had eight hours dreamless sleep.

May and October are the best months in Venice. The sun is soft and the nights are cool. The glittering scene is kinder to the eyes and there is a freshness in the air that helps one to hammer out those long miles of stone and terrazza and marble that are intolerable to the feet in summer. And there are fewer people. Although Venice is the one town in the world that can swallow up a hundred thousand tourists as easily as it can a thousand—hiding them down its side-streets, using them for crowd scenes on the piazzas, stuffing them into the vaporetti—it is still better to share Venice with the minimum number of packaged tours and Lederhosen.

Bond spent the next morning strolling the back-streets in the hope that he would be able to uncover a tail. He visited a couple of churches—not to admire their interiors but to discover if anyone came in after him through the main entrance before he left by the side door. No one was following him. Bond went to Florian's and had an Americano and listened to a couple of French culture-snobs discussing the imbalance of the containing façade of St Mark's Square. On an impulse, he bought a postcard and sent it off to his secretary who had once been with the Georgian Group to Italy and had never allowed Bond to forget it. He wrote: 'Venice is wonderful. Have so far inspected the railway station and the Stock Exchange. Very aesthetically satisfying. To the Municipal Waterworks this afternoon and then an old Brigitte Bardot at the Scala Cinema. Do you know a wonderful tune called "O Sole Mio?" It's v. romantic like everything here. JB.'

Pleased with his inspiration, Bond had an early luncheon and went back to his hotel. He locked the door of his room and took off his coat and ran over the Walther PPK. He put up the safe and practised one or two quick draws and put the gun back in the holster. It was time to go. He went along to the landing-stage and boarded the twelve-forty vaporetto to Alberoni, out of sight across the mirrored lagoons. Then he settled down in a seat in the bows and wondered what was going to happen to him.

From the jetty at Alberoni, on the Venice side of the Lido peninsula, there is a half mile dusty walk across the neck of land to the Bagni Alberoni facing the Adriatic. It is a curiously deserted world, this tip of the famous

peninsula. A mile down the thin neck of land the luxury real estate development has petered out in a scattering of cracked stucco villas and
bankrupt housing projects, and here there is nothing but the tiny fishing
village of Alberoni, a sanatorium for students, a derelict experimental station belonging to the Italian Navy and some massive weed-choked gun
emplacements from the last war. In the no man's land in the centre of
this thin tongue of land is the Golf du Lido, whose brownish undulating fairways meander around the ruins of ancient fortifications. Not many
people come to Venice to play golf, and the project is kept alive for its
snob appeal by the grand hotels of the Lido. The golf course is surrounded by a high wire fence hung at intervals, as if it protected something of great value or secrecy, with threatening Vietatos and Prohibitos.
Around this wired enclave, the scrub and sandhills have not even been
cleared of mines, and amongst the rusting barbed wire are signs saying
MINAS. PERICOLO DI MORTE beneath a roughly stencilled skull and crossbones. The whole area is strange and melancholy and in extraordinary
contrast to the gay carnival world of Venice less than an hour away across
the lagoons.

Bond was sweating slightly by the time he had walked the half mile
across the peninsula to the plage, and he stood for a moment under the
last of the acacia trees that had bordered the dusty road to cool off while
he got his bearings. In front of him was a rickety wooden archway whose
central span said BAGNI ALBERONI in faded blue paint. Beyond were the
lines of equally dilapidated wooden cabins, and then a hundred yards of
sand and then the quiet blue glass of the sea. There were no bathers and
the place seemed to be closed, but when he walked through the archway
he heard the tinny sound of a radio playing Neapolitan music. It came
from a ramshackle hut that advertised Coca-Cola and various Italian soft
drinks. Deck-chairs were stacked against its walls and there were two
pedalos and a child's half inflated seahorse. The whole establishment looked
so derelict that Bond could not imagine it doing business even at the
height of the summer season. He stepped off the narrow duckboards into
the soft, burned sand and moved round behind the huts to the beach.
He walked down to the edge of the sea. To the left, until it disappeared
in the autumn heat haze, the wide empty sand swept away in a slight
curve towards the Lido proper. To the right was half a mile of beach
terminating in the seawall at the tip of the peninsula. The seawall stretched
like a finger out into the silent mirrored sea, and at intervals along its top
were the flimsy derricks of the octopus fishermen. Behind the beach were
the sandhills and a section of the wire fence surrounding the golf course.

On the edge of the sandhills, perhaps five hundred yards away, there was a speck of bright yellow.

Bond set off towards it along the tide-line.

'Ahem.'

The hands flew to the top scrap of bikini and pulled it up. Bond walked into her line of vision and stood looking down. The bright shadow of the umbrella covered only her face. The rest of her—a burned cream body in a black bikini on a black and white striped bath-towel—lay offered to the sun.

She looked up at him through half closed eyelashes. 'You are five minutes early and I told you to knock.'

Bond sat down close to her in the shade of the big umbrella. He took out a handkerchief and wiped his face. 'You happen to own the only palm tree in the whole of this desert. I had to get underneath it as soon as I could. This is the hell of a place for a rendezvous.'

She laughed. 'I am like Greta Garbo. I like to be alone.'

'Are we alone?'

She opened her eyes wide. 'Why not? You think I have brought a chaperone?'

'Since you think all men are pigs . . .'

'Ah, but you are a gentleman pig,' she giggled. 'A milord pig. And anyway, it is too hot for that kind of thing. And there is too much sand. And besides this is a business meeting, no? I tell you stories about drugs and you give me a diamond clip. From Van Cleef. Or have you changed your mind?'

'No. That's how it is. Where shall we begin?'

'You ask the questions. What is it you want to know?' She sat up and pulled her knees to her between her arms. Flirtation had gone out of her eyes and they had become attentive, and perhaps a little careful.

Bond noticed the change. He said casually, watching her: 'They say your friend Colombo is a big man in the game. Tell me about him. He would make a good character for my book—disguised, of course. But it's the detail I need. How does he operate, and so on? That's not the sort of thing a writer can invent.'

She veiled her eyes. She said: 'Enrico would be very angry if he knew that I had told any of his secrets. I don't know what he would do to me.'

'He will never know.'

She looked at him seriously. 'Lieber Mr Bond, there is very little that he does not know. And he is also quite capable of acting on a guess. I would not be surprised'—Bond caught her quick glance at his watch—

'if it had crossed his mind to have me followed here. He is a very suspicious man.' She put her hand out and touched his sleeve. Now she looked nervous. She said urgently: 'I think you had better go now. This has been a great mistake.'

Bond openly looked at his watch. It was three-thirty. He moved his head so that he could look behind the umbrella and back down the beach. Far down by the bathing huts, their outlines dancing slightly in the heat haze, were three men in dark clothes. They were walking purposefully up the beach, their feet keeping step as if they were a squad.

Bond got to his feet. He looked down at the bent head. He said drily: 'I see what you mean. Just tell Colombo that from now on I'm writing his life-story. And I'm a very persistent writer. So long.' Bond started running up the sand towards the tip of the peninsula. From there he could double back down the other shore to the village and the safety of people.

Down the beach the three men broke into a fast jogtrot, elbows and legs pounding in time with each other as if they were long-distance runners out for a training spin. As they jogged past the girl, one of the men raised a hand. She raised hers in answer and then lay down on the sand and turned over—perhaps so that her back could now get its toasting, or perhaps because she did not want to watch the man-hunt.

Bond took off his tie as he ran and put it in his pocket. It was very hot and he was already sweating profusely. But so would the three men be. It was a question who was in better training. At the tip of the peninsula, Bond clambered up on to the seawall and looked back. The men had hardly gained, but now two of them were fanning out to cut round the edge of the golf course boundary. They did not seem to mind the danger notices with the skull and crossbones. Bond, running fast down the wide seawall, measured angles and distances. The two men were cutting across the base of the triangle. It was going to be a close call.

Bond's shirt was already soaked and his feet were beginning to hurt. He had run perhaps a mile. How much further to safety? At intervals along the seawall the breeches of antique cannon had been sunk in the concrete. They would be mooring posts for the fishing fleets sheltering in the protection of the lagoons before taking to the Adriatic. Bond counted his steps between two of them. Fifty yards. How many black knobs to the end of the wall—to the first houses of the village? Bond counted up to thirty before the line vanished into the heat haze. Probably another mile to go. Could he do it, and fast enough to beat the two flankers? Bond's breath was already rasping in his throat. Now even his suit was soaked with sweat and the cloth of his trousers was chafing his legs. Behind him, three hundred yards back, was one pursuer. To his right, dodging among the sand-dunes and converging fast, were the other two. To his left was a twenty-foot slope of masonry to the green tide ripping out into the Adriatic.

Bond was planning to slow down to a walk and keep enough breath to try and shoot it out with the three men, when two things happened in quick succession. First he saw through the haze ahead a group of spear-fishermen. There were about half a dozen of them, some in the water and some sunning themselves on the seawall. Then, from the sand-dunes came the deep roar of an explosion. Earth and scrub and what might have been bits of a man fountained briefly into the air, and a small shock-wave hit him. Bond slowed. The other man in the dunes had stopped. He was standing stock-still. His mouth was open and a frightened jabber came from it. Suddenly he collapsed on the ground with his arms wrapped round his head. Bond knew the signs. He would not move again until some-one came and carried him away from there. Bond's heart lifted. Now he had only about two hundred yards to go to the fishermen. They were already gathering into a group, looking towards him. Bond summoned a few words of Italian and rehearsed them. 'Mi Ingles. Prego, dove il carabinieri.' Bond glanced over his shoulder. Odd, but despite the witnessing spear-fishers, the man was still coming on. He had gained and was only about a hun-dred yards behind. There was a gun in his hand. Now, ahead, the fisher-men had fanned out across Bond's path. They had harpoon guns held at the ready. In the centre was a big man with a tiny red bathing-slip hang-ing beneath his stomach. A green mask was slipped back on to the crown of his head. He stood with his blue swim-fins pointing out and his arms akimbo. He looked like Mr Toad of Toad Hall in Technicolor. Bond's amused thought died in him stillborn. Panting, he slowed to a walk. Automatically his sweaty hand felt under his coat for the gun and drew it out. The man in the centre of the arc of pointing harpoons was Enrico Colombo.

Colombo watched him approach. When he was twenty yards away, Colombo said quietly: 'Put away your toy, Mr Bond of the Secret Service. These are CO_2 harpoon guns. And stay where you are. Unless you wish to make a copy of Mantegna's St Sebastian.' He turned to the man on his right. He spoke in English. 'At what range was that Albanian last week?'

'Twenty yards, padrone. And the harpoon went right through. But he was a fat man—perhaps twice as thick as this one.'

Bond stopped. One of the iron bollards was beside him. He sat down and rested the gun on his knee. It pointed at the centre of Colombo's big stomach. He said: 'Five harpoons in me won't stop one bullet in you, Colombo.'

Colombo smiled and nodded, and the man who had been coming softly up behind Bond hit him once hard in the base of the skull with the butt of his Luger.

When you come to from being hit on the head the first reaction is a fit of vomiting. Even in his wretchedness Bond was aware of two sensations—he was in a ship at sea, and someone, a man, was wiping his forehead with a cool wet towel and murmuring encouragement in bad English. 'Is okay, amigo. Take him easy. Take him easy.'

Bond fell back on his bunk, exhausted. It was a comfortable small cabin with a feminine smell and dainty curtains and colours. A sailor in a tattered vest and trousers—Bond thought he recognized him as one of the spear-fishermen—was bending over him. He smiled when Bond opened his eyes. 'Is better, yes? Subito okay.' He rubbed the back of his neck in sympathy. 'It hurts for a little. Soon it will only be a black. Beneath the hair. The girls will see nothing.'

Bond smiled feebly and nodded. The pain of the nod made him screw up his eyes. When he opened them the sailor shook his head in admonition. He brought his wrist-watch close up to Bond's eyes. It said seven o'clock. He pointed with his little finger at the figure nine. 'Mangiare con Padrone, Si?'

Bond said: 'Si.'

The man put his hand to his cheek and laid his head on one side. 'Dormire.'

Bond said 'Si' again and the sailor went out of the cabin and closed the door without locking it.

Bond got gingerly off the bunk and went over to the wash basin and set about cleaning himself. On top of the chest of drawers was a neat pile of his personal belongings. Everything was there except his gun. Bond stowed the things away in his pockets, and sat down again on the bunk and smoked and thought. His thoughts were totally inconclusive. He was being taken for a ride, or rather a sail, but from the behaviour of the sailor it did not seem that he was regarded as an enemy. Yet a great deal of trouble had been taken to make him prisoner and one of Colombo's men had even, though inadvertently, died in the process. It did not seem to be just a question of killing him. Perhaps this soft treatment was the preliminary to trying to make a deal with him. What was the deal—and what was the alternative?

At nine o'clock the same sailor came for Bond and led him down a short passage to a small, blowzy saloon, and left him. There was a table and two chairs in the middle of the room, and beside the table a nickel-plated trolley laden with food and drinks. Bond tried the hatchway at the end of the saloon. It was bolted. He unlatched one of the portholes and looked out. There was just enough light to see that the ship was about two hundred tons and might once have been a large fishing-vessel. The engine sounded like a single diesel and they were carrying sail. Bond estimated the ship's speed at six or seven knots. On the dark horizon there was a tiny cluster of yellow lights. It seemed probable that they were sailing down the Adriatic coast.

The hatchway bolt rattled back. Bond pulled in his head. Colombo came down the steps. He was dressed in a sweat-shirt, dungarees and scuffed sandals. There was a wicked, amused gleam in his eyes. He sat down in one chair and waved to the other. 'Come, my friend. Food and drink and plenty of talk. We will now stop behaving like little boys and be grown-up. Yes? What will you have—gin, whisky, champagne? And this is the finest sausage in the whole of Bologna. Olives from my own estate. Bread, butter, Provelone—that is smoked cheese—and fresh figs. Peasant food, but good. Come. All that running must have given you an appetite.'

His laugh was infectious. Bond poured himself a stiff whisky and soda, and sat down. He said: 'Why did you have to go to so much trouble? We could have met without all these dramatics. As it is you have prepared a lot of grief for yourself. I warned my chief that something like this might happen—the way the girl picked me up in your restaurant was too childish for words. I said that I would walk into the trap to see what it was all about. If I am not out of it again by tomorrow midday, you'll have Interpol as well as Italian police on top of you like a load of bricks.'

Colombo looked puzzled. He said: 'If you were ready to walk into the trap, why did you try and escape from my men this afternoon? I had sent them to fetch you and bring you to my ship, and it would all have been much more friendly. Now I have lost a good man and you might easily have had your skull broken. I do not understand.'

'I didn't like the look of those three men. I know killers when I see them. I thought you might be thinking of doing something stupid. You should have used the girl. The men were unnecessary.'

Colombo shook his head. 'Lisl was willing to find out more about you, but nothing else. She will now be just as angry with me as you are. Life is very difficult. I like to be friends with everyone, and now I have made two enemies in one afternoon. It is too bad.' Colombo looked genuinely sorry for himself. He cut a thick slice of sausage, impatiently tore the rind off it with his teeth and began to eat. While his mouth was still full he took a glass of champagne and washed the sausage down with it. He said, shaking his head reproachfully at Bond: 'It is always the same, when I am worried I have to eat. But the food that I eat when I am worried I cannot digest. And now you have worried me. You say that we could have met and talked things over—that I need not have taken all this trouble.' He spread his hands helplessly. 'How was I to know that? By saying that, you put the blood of Mario on my hands. I did not tell him to take a short cut through that place.' Colombo pounded the table. Now he shouted angrily at Bond. 'I do not agree that this was all my fault. It was your fault. Yours only. You had agreed to kill me. How does one arrange a friendly meeting with one's murderer? Eh? Just tell me that.' Colombo snatched up a long roll of bread and stuffed it into his mouth, his eyes furious.

'What the hell are you talking about?'

Colombo threw the remains of the roll on the table and got to his feet, holding Bond's eyes locked in his. He walked sideways, still gazing fixedly at Bond, to a chest of drawers, felt for the knob of the top drawer, opened it, groped and lifted out what Bond recognized as a tape-recorder playback machine. Still looking accusingly at Bond, he brought the machine over to the table. He sat down and pressed a switch.

When Bond heard the voice he picked up his glass of whisky and looked into it. The tinny voice said: 'Exact. Now, before I give you the informations, like good commercials we make the terms. Yes?' The voice went on: 'Ten thousand dollars American ... There is no telling where you get these informations from. Even if you are beaten ... The head of this machina is a bad man. He is to be destrutto—killed.' Bond waited for his own voice to break through the restaurant noises. There had been a long pause while he thought about the last condition. What was it he had said? His voice came out of the machine, answering him. 'I cannot promise that. You must see that. All I can say is that if the man tries to destroy me, I will destroy him.'

Colombo switched off the machine. Bond swallowed down his whisky. Now he could look up at Colombo. He said defensively: 'That doesn't make me a murderer.'

Colombo looked at him sorrowfully. 'To me it does. Coming from an

Englishman. I worked for the English during the War. In the Resistance. I have the King's Medal.' He put his hand in his pocket and threw the silver Freedom medal with the red, white and blue striped ribbon on to the table. 'You see?'

Bond obstinately held Colombo's eyes. He said: 'And the rest of the stuff on that tape? You long ago stopped working for the English. Now you work against them, for money.'

Colombo grunted. He tapped the machine with his forefinger. He said impassively: 'I have heard it all. It is lies.' He banged his fist on the table so that the glasses jumped. He bellowed furiously: 'It is lies, lies. Every word of it.' He jumped to his feet. His chair crashed down behind him. He slowly bent and picked it up. He reached for the whisky bottle and walked round and poured four fingers into Bond's glass. He went back to his chair and sat down and put the champagne bottle on the table in front of him. Now his face was composed, serious. He said quietly: 'It is not all lies. There is a grain of truth in what that bastard told you. That is why I decided not to argue with you. You might not have believed me. You would have dragged in the police. There would have been much trouble for me and my comrades. Even if you or someone else had not found reason to kill me, there would have been scandal, ruin. Instead I decided to show you the truth—the truth you were sent to Italy to find out. Within a matter of hours, tomorrow at dawn, your mission will have been completed.' Colombo clicked his fingers. 'Presto—like that.'

Bond said: 'What part of Kristatos's story is not lies?'

Colombo's eyes looked into Bond's calculating. Finally he said: 'My friend, I am a smuggler. That part is true. I am probably the most successful smuggler in the Mediterranean. Half the American cigarettes in Italy are brought in by me from Tangier. Gold? I am the sole supplier of the black valuta market. Diamonds? I have my own purveyor in Beirut with direct lines to Sierra Leone and South Africa. In the old days, when these things were scarce, I also handled aureomycin and penicillin and such medicines. Bribery at the American base hospitals. And there have been many other things—even beautiful girls from Syria and Persia for the houses of Naples. I have also smuggled out escaped convicts. But,' Colombo's fist crashed on the table, 'drugs, heroin, opium, hemp—no! Never! I will have nothing to do with these things. These things are evil. There is no sin in the others.' Colombo held up his right hand. 'My friend, this I swear to you on the head of my mother.'

Bond was beginning to see daylight. He was prepared to believe Colombo. He even felt a curious liking for this greedy, boisterous pirate who had so nearly been put on the spot by Kristatos. Bond said: 'But why did Kristatos put the finger on you? What's he got to gain?'

Colombo slowly shook a finger to and fro in front of his nose. He said: 'My friend, Kristatos is Kristatos. He is playing the biggest double game it is possible to conceive. To keep it up—to keep the protection of American Intelligence and their Narcotics people—he must now and then throw them a victim—some small man on the fringe of the big game. But with this English problem it is different. That is a huge traffic. To protect it, a big victim was required. I was chosen—by Kristatos, or by his employers. And it is true that if you had been vigorous in your investigations and had spent enough hard currency on buying information, you might have discovered the story of my operations. But each trail towards *me* would have led you further away from the truth. In the end, for I do not underestimate your Service, I would have gone to prison. But the big fox you are after would only be laughing at the sound of the hunt dying away in the distance.'

'Why did Kristatos want you killed?'

Colombo looked cunning. 'My friend, I know too much. In the fraternity of smugglers, we occasionally stumble on a corner of the next man's business. Not long ago, in this ship, I had a running fight with a small gunboat from Albania. A lucky shot set fire to their fuel. There was only one survivor. He was persuaded to talk. I learnt much, but like a fool I took a chance with the minefields and set him ashore on the coast north of Tirana. It was a mistake. Ever since then I have had this bastard Kristatos after me. Fortunately,' Colombo grinned wolfishly, 'I have one piece of information he does not know of. And we have a rendezvous with this piece of information at first light tomorrow—at a small fishing-port just north of Ancona, Santa Maria. And there,' Colombo gave a harsh, cruel laugh, 'we shall see what we shall see.'

Bond said mildly. 'What's your price for all this? You say my mission will have been completed tomorrow morning. How much?'

Colombo shook his head. He said indifferently: 'Nothing. It just happens that our interests coincide. But I shall need your promise that what I have told you this evening is between you and me and, if necessary, your Chief in London. It must never come back to Italy. Is that agreed?'

'Yes. I agree to that.'

Colombo got to his feet. He went to the chest of drawers and took out Bond's gun. He handed it to Bond. 'In that case, my friend, you had better have this, because you are going to need it. And you had better get some sleep. There will be rum and coffee for everyone at five in the morning.' He held out his hand. Bond took it. Suddenly the two men were friends. Bond felt the fact. He said awkwardly 'All right, Colombo,' and went out of the saloon and along to his cabin.

The *Colombina* had a crew of twelve. They were youngish, tough-looking men. They talked softly among themselves as the mugs of hot coffee and rum were dished out by Colombo in the saloon. A storm lantern was the only light—the ship had been darkened—and Bond smiled to himself at the Treasure Island atmosphere of excitement and conspiracy. Colombo went from man to man on a weapon inspection. They all had Lugers, carried under the jersey inside the trouser-band, and flick-knives in the pocket. Colombo had a word of approval or criticism for each weapon. It struck Bond that Colombo had made a good life for himself—a life of adventure and thrill and risk. It was a criminal life— a running fight with the currency laws, the State tobacco monopoly, the Customs, the police—but there was a whiff of adolescent rascality in the air which somehow changed the colour of the crime from black to white— or at least to grey.

Colombo looked at his watch. He dismissed the men to their posts. He dowsed the lantern and, in the oyster light of dawn, Bond followed him up to the bridge. He found the ship was close to a black, rocky shore which they were following at reduced speed. Colombo pointed ahead. 'Round that headland is the harbour. Our approach will not have been observed. In the harbour, against the jetty, I expect to find a ship of about this size unloading innocent rolls of newsprint down a ramp into a ware-house. Round the headland, we will put on full speed and come along-side this ship and board her. There will be resistance. Heads will be broken. I hope it is not shooting. We shall not shoot unless they do. But it will be an Albanian ship manned by a crew of Albanian toughs. If there is shooting, you must shoot well with the rest of us. These people are ene-mies of your country as well as mine. If you get killed, you get killed. Okay?'

'That's all right.'

As Bond said the words, there came a ting on the engine-room tele-graph and the deck began to tremble under his feet. Making ten knots, the small ship rounded the headland into the harbour.

It was as Colombo had said. Alongside a stone jetty lay the ship, its sails flapping idly. From her stern a ramp of wood planks sloped down towards the dark mouth of a ramshackle corrugated iron warehouse, inside which burned feeble electric lights. The ship carried a deck cargo of what appeared to be rolls of newsprint, and these were being hoisted one by one on to the ramp whence they rolled down under their own momentum through the mouth of the warehouse. There were about twenty men in sight. Only surprise would straighten out these odds. Now Colombo's craft was fifty yards away from the other ship, and one or two of the men had stopped working and were looking in their direction. One man ran off into the warehouse. Simultaneously Colombo issued a sharp order. The engines stopped and went into reverse. A big searchlight on the bridge came on and lit the whole scene brightly as the ship drifted up alongside the Albanian trawler. At the first hard contact, grappling-irons were tossed over the Albanian's rail fore and aft, and Colombo's men swarmed over the side with Colombo in the lead.

Bond had made his own plans. As soon as his feet landed on the enemy deck, he ran straight across the ship, climbed the far rail and jumped. It was about twelve feet to the jetty and he landed like a cat, on his hands and toes, and stayed for a moment, crouching, planning his next move. Shooting had already started on deck. An early shot killed the searchlight and now there was only the grey, luminous light of dawn. A body, one of the enemy, crunched to the stone in front of him and lay spread-eagled, motionless. At the same time, from the mouth of the warehouse, a light machine gun started up, firing short bursts with a highly professional touch. Bond ran towards it in the dark shadow of the ship. The machine-gunner saw him and gave him a burst. The bullets zipped round Bond, clanged against the iron hull of the ship and whined off into the night. Bond got to the cover of the sloping ramp of boards and dived forward on his stomach. The bullets crashed into the wood above his head. Bond crept forward into the narrowing space. When he had got as close as he could, he would have a choice of breaking cover either to right or left of the boards. There came a series of heavy thuds and a swift rumble above his head. One of Colombo's men must have cut the ropes and sent the whole pile of newsprint rolls down the ramp. Now was Bond's chance. He leapt out from under cover—to the left. If the machine-gunner was waiting for him, he would expect Bond to come out firing on the right. The machine-gunner was there, crouching up against the wall of the warehouse. Bond fired twice in the split second before the bright muzzle of the enemy weapon had swung through its small arc. The dead man's finger clenched on the trigger and, as he slumped, his gun made a brief Catherine-wheel of flashes before it shook itself free from his hand and clattered to the ground.

Bond was running forward towards the warehouse door when he

slipped and fell headlong. He lay for a moment, stunned, his face in a pool of black treacle. He cursed and got to his hands and knees and made a dash for cover behind a jumble of the big newsprint rolls that had crashed into the wall of the warehouse. One of them, sliced by a burst from the machine gun, was leaking black treacle. Bond wiped as much of the stuff off his hands and face as he could. It had the musty sweet smell that Bond had once smelled in Mexico. It was raw opium.

A bullet whanged into the wall of the warehouse not far from his head. Bond gave his gun-hand a last wipe on the seat of his trousers and leapt for the warehouse door. He was surprised not to be shot at from the interior as soon as he was silhouetted against the entrance. It was quiet and cool inside the place. The lights had been turned out, but it was now getting brighter outside. The pale newsprint rolls were stacked in orderly ranks with a space to make a passageway down the centre. At the far end of the passageway was a door. The whole arrangement leered at him, daring him. Bond smelled death. He edged back to the entrance and out into the open. The shooting had become spasmodic. Colombo came running swiftly towards him, his feet close to the ground as fat men run. Bond said peremptorily: 'Stay at this door. Don't go in or let any of your men in. I'm going round to the back.' Without waiting for an answer he sprinted round the corner of the building and down along its side.

The warehouse was about fifty feet long. Bond slowed and walked softly to the far corner. He flattened himself against the corrugated iron wall and took a swift look round. He immediately drew back. A man was standing up against the back entrance. His eyes were at some kind of spyhole. In his hand was a plunger from which wires ran under the bottom of the door. A car, a black Lancia Granturismo convertible with the hood down, stood beside him, its engine ticking over softly. It pointed inland along a deeply tracked dust road.

The man was Kristatos.

Bond knelt. He held his gun in both hands for steadiness, inched swiftly round the corner of the building and fired one shot at the man's feet. He missed. Almost as he saw the dust kick up inches off the target, there was the rumbling crack of an explosion and the tin wall hit him and sent him flying.

Bond scrambled to his feet. The warehouse had buckled crazily out of shape. Now it started to collapse noisily like a pack of tin cards. Kristatos was in the car. It was already twenty yards away, dust fountaining up from the traction on the rear wheels. Bond stood in the classic pistol-shooting pose and took careful aim. The Walther roared and kicked three times. At the last shot, at fifty yards, the figure crouched over the wheel jerked backwards. The hands flew sideways off the wheel. The head craned briefly into the air and slumped forward. The right hand remained sticking out as if the dead man was signalling a right-hand turn. Bond started to run up the road, expecting the car to stop, but the wheels were held in the ruts and, with the weight of the dead right foot still on the accelerator, the Lancia tore onwards in its screaming third gear. Bond stopped and watched it. It hurried on along the flat road across the burned-up plain and the cloud of white dust blew gaily up behind. At any moment Bond expected it to veer off the road, but it did not, and Bond stood and saw it out of sight into the early morning mist that promised a beautiful day.

Bond put his gun on safe and tucked it away in the belt of his trousers. He turned to find Colombo approaching him. The fat man was grinning delightedly. He came up with Bond and, to Bond's horror, threw open his arms, clutched Bond to him and kissed him on both cheeks.

Bond said: 'For God's sake, Colombo.'

Colombo roared with laughter. 'Ah, the quiet Englishman! He fears nothing save the emotions. But me,' he hit himself in the chest, 'me, Enrico Colombo, loves this man and he is not ashamed to say so. If you had not got the machine-gunner, not one of us would have survived. As it is, I lost two of my men and others have wounds. But only half a dozen Albanians remain on their feet and they have escaped into the village. No doubt the police will round them up. And now you have sent that bastard Kristatos motoring down to hell. What a splendid finish to him! What will happen when the little racing-hearse meets the main road? He is already signalling for the right-hand turn on to the autostrada, I hope he will remember to drive on the right.' Colombo clapped Bond boisterously on the shoulder. 'But come, my friend. It is time we got out of here. The cocks are open in the Albanian ship and she will soon be on the bottom. There are no telephones in this little place. We will have a good start on the police. It will take them some time to get sense out of the fishermen. I have spoken to the head man. No one here has any love for Albanians. But we must be on our way. We have a stiff sail into the wind and there is no doctor I can trust this side of Venice.'

Flames were beginning to lick out of the shattered warehouse, and there was billowing smoke that smelled of sweet vegetables. Bond and Colombo walked round to windward. The Albanian ship had settled on the bottom and her decks were awash. They waded across her and climbed on board the *Colombina*, where Bond had to go through some more handshaking and backslapping. They cast off at once and made for the headland guarding the harbour. There was a small group of fishermen standing by their boats that lay drawn up on the beach below a huddle of stone cottages. They made a surly impression, but when Colombo waved and shouted something in Italian most of them raised a hand in farewell, and one of them called back something that made the crew of the *Colombina* laugh. Colombo explained: 'They say we were better than the cinema at Ancona and we must come again soon.'

Bond suddenly felt the excitement drain out of him. He felt dirty and unshaven, and he could smell his own sweat. He went below and borrowed a razor and a clean shirt from one of the crew, and stripped in his cabin and cleansed himself. When he took out his gun and threw it on the bunk he caught a whiff of cordite from the barrel. It brought back the fear and violence and death of the grey dawn. He opened the porthole. Outside, the sea was dancing and gay, and the receding coastline, that had been black and mysterious, was now green and beautiful. A sudden delicious scent of frying bacon came downwind from the galley. Abruptly Bond pulled the porthole to and dressed and went along to the saloon.

Over a mound of fried eggs and bacon washed down with hot sweet coffee laced with rum, Colombo dotted the i's and crossed the t's.

'This we have done, my friend,' he said through crunching toast. 'That was a year's supply of raw opium on its way to Kristatos's chemical works in Naples. It is true that I have such a business in Milan and that it is a convenient depot for some of my wares. But it fabricates nothing more deadly than cascara and aspirin. For all that part of Kristatos's story, read Kristatos instead of Colombo. It is he who breaks the stuff down into heroin and it is he who employs the couriers to take it to London. That huge shipment was worth perhaps a million pounds to Kristatos and his men. But do you know something, my dear James? It cost him not one solitary cent. Why? Because it is a gift from Russia. The gift of a massive and deadly projectile to be fired into the bowels of England. The Russians can supply unlimited quantities of the charge for the projectile. It comes from their poppy fields in the Caucasus, and Albania is a convenient entrepôt. But they have not the apparatus to fire this projectile. The man Kristatos created the necessary apparatus, and it is he, on behalf of his masters in Russia, who pulls the trigger. Today, between us, we have destroyed, in half an hour, the entire conspiracy. You can now go back and tell your people in England that the traffic will cease. You can also tell them the truth—that Italy was not the origin of this terrible underground weapon of war. That it is our old friends the Russians. No doubt it is some psychological warfare section of their Intelligence apparatus. That I cannot tell you. Perhaps, my dear James,' Colombo smiled encouragingly, 'they will send you to Moscow to find out. If that should happen, let us hope you will find some girl as charming as your friend Fräulein Lisl Baum to put you on the right road to the truth.'

'What do you mean "my friend"? She's yours.'

Colombo shook his head. 'My dear James, I have many friends. You will be spending a few more days in Italy writing your report, and no doubt,' he chuckled, 'checking on some of the things I have told you. Perhaps you will also have an enjoyable half an hour explaining the facts of life to your colleagues in American Intelligence. In between these duties you will need companionship—someone to show you the beauties of my beloved homeland. In uncivilized countries, it is the polite custom to offer one of your wives to a man whom you love and wish to honour. I also am uncivilized. I have no wives, but I have many such friends as Lisl Baum. She will not need to receive any instructions in this matter. I have good reason to believe that she is awaiting your return this evening.' Colombo fished in his trousers pocket and tossed something down with a clang on the table in front of Bond. 'Here is the good reason.' Colombo put his hand to his heart and looked seriously into Bond's eyes. 'I give it to you from my heart. Perhaps also from hers.'

Bond picked the thing up. It was a key with a heavy metal tag attached. The metal tag was inscribed *Albergo Danielli. Room 68.*

Keep Walking

He strolled quietly away from the mailbox, knowing that the game was up. This was the end, and he was not prepared for it. He had always expected it to come—if it had to come—at home or in the course of some police check. But evidently they had not found out his name. They only knew about the mailbox and the timing. He would learn how they knew after his second or third interrogation, if he had any curiosity left. Now there was nothing for it but to keep walking until those two security agents came alongside and gripped his arms.

The trick had worked for nearly a year. He dropped his reports in the mailbox just before the time for collection. The envelope would then be at the top or conspicuous among the top four or five. Thus it was easy for the postman to pocket and pass on the letter. One had only to be sure that the right man was on duty. It had even been possible, in an emergency, to bypass the censorship of foreign mail.

Today he had not given himself away by any change of expression or sudden movement. He could count on that. After dropping the letter in the box he had continued on his way at an even pace. Behind his eyes remained a photograph of the scene. He had time to run it through memory and develop it as he walked.

On the opposite pavement, where usually only a handful of women could be seen scurrying home to prepare lunch, two men had been talking together. They were in no way remarkable. They might have been two door-to-door salesmen comparing notes. It was the greatest luck that he knew one of them by sight, the most abominable luck that he had not spotted him before the letter was mailed.

The photograph in his mind also showed two more men on his side of the street, looking in a shop window. They might be innocent passersby but, if they were not, they fell neatly into the composition. One pair would wait until the collection was made from the box; the others would make the arrest.

He did not look round. He tried to believe himself a plain respectable citizen so that neither his walk, his back, nor his hands could possibly suggest guilt. Now, what would experienced police agents do? Their case could not be quite complete. True, it would be unshakable as soon as that envelope at the top of the box was opened. But for the moment? Well, since their suspect appeared unworried and walking fairly purposefully, they would tail him; it might be profitable to find out where he was going and to whom he talked.

But they could take no risks. None at all. If he hailed a taxi or jumped on a bus, that would be the end. He could not be allowed to break contact. They would instantly obstruct any move which gave him the slightest chance of escaping.

So keep walking. A harmless human activity.

He knew very well what a lot of evidence could be extracted from it. Tail a man who was walking, tail him for an hour, and one could almost tell his fortune, let alone his character, his income, the state of his digestion and his fears.

His fears. God, it was difficult not to show any! Death was the least. Death was a companion just as present in his personal war as in any public one. What appalled him was the certainty that when at last he died he wouldn't be recognizable to himself in body or mind. Well, he had always accepted that. Why? The answer was something neutral for half his brain to think about while he kept walking. Patriotism? Democracy? Or hatred? Hatred of a system, a government that hung more oppressively over his country every day?

Hardest of all was not to look round. If he did they might arrest him at once. His only chance of delaying the end was to show himself clearly and absolutely unconscious that he was followed.

Having been a security man himself, he could imagine the messages going back to headquarters by walkie-talkie—or by telephone perhaps, if there were a third person who could leave the hunt to use it.

'We have got him,' they would say, 'but it's worth seeing where he is going . . . No, sir, no danger of losing him. He doesn't know. Couldn't know.'

Better make quite certain that he was not merely returning to an office or on any daily routine such as shopping or visiting a café. He very slightly quickened his pace, settling down, so far as pavement and people allowed, to a steady five and a half kilometers an hour. He might be going home, but, if he was, why not take his usual bus? So long as they were kept guessing, so long as they could not jump to any conclusion, they would follow.

Direction had been decided for him on leaving the mailbox. He could not change it too abruptly. He had to appear intent on something. Well, his present course would do. It led straight to the inner suburbs on the east of the city. After twenty minutes he thought it wise to offer them a little diversion. A taxi was approaching. He hesitated as if about to stop it. When the driver began to pull in, he shook his head and walked on. That would give them something to think about if they were still behind him. Were they? He dared not find out. One single suggestion that he was suspicious and they would no longer take the risk of losing him.

He wondered if they could tell that he was armed. That was not an urgent matter yet, nor likely to be. Still, it was worth a thought. Certainly they would know, after such long detailed observation, if the gun had been in a shoulder holster or pocket. He doubted, however, if an automatic nestling across the navel could be spotted from behind. They might reasonably assume that a man who might be searched would not be such a fool as to carry one. They would be on their guard, of course, but not keeping the question continually in the forefront of consciousness. That might be important . . .

They had been following for six kilometers now, tiring and inclined to forego the contact to whom he might be leading them. Their keen sense of duty, their strong instinct against running him in at once, ought to be revived. He decided to display more caution, as if he were nearing his destination. It would be the first quick glance over his shoulder that they had seen, and therefore important.

He looked behind him. He could not spot any followers at all. Had the walk and the discipline been all for nothing? Careful! That could not be assumed yet. It was all very well to force himself to ignore terror, but don't overdo it! He reminded his body of what was going to happen to it.

He chose a long residential street. There were very few pedestrians. If the hunters were still determined to take no action and stick to the trail, they would have to be very careful. However casual they appeared, they were bound to be out of place and conspicuous. His experience had taught him how they—if they still followed—would arrange that one. It would show how relentless the pursuit really was. If they knew their job (and no one knew it better) there ought to be a car moving more or less on parallel lines. As soon as his two shadows were forced to fall too far behind, they would signal the car to take over.

He spotted the car. It drove past in the same direction and parked on the other side of the road. He could not really have said why he was certain it was the car. Perhaps because it did exactly what it should, covering the road he was in and two side streets into which he might turn. Perhaps because nobody opened the door in answer to the bell which the driver was ringing or pretending to ring. Perhaps it was the instinct of the hunted.

It was oddly comforting to get his fear back. Now he knew that he had not imagined they were after him. Also he had proof that so far he had decoyed them into believing his movements significant. That report collected from the mailbox must already have been read. His guilt was beyond question. Yet they still thought it worthwhile to see where he was going before they struck.

He continued eastward. He was now passing through a local shopping center, and the two could safely close up. He longed to confirm that they were still on his trail, but every trick he knew for seeing who was behind him was equally well known to them. Show absolute unconcern, and they would wait. Keep walking, and they had to know the reason why. The view of his steadily moving back must be beginning to hypnotize them.

All the same it was tempting to make a dash for it. Through a house or shop? Into a back garden? The bushes of a park? But he hadn't a hope and knew it. There would always be a car or two on that parallel course and uniformed police somewhere in the background . . .

Nearly two hours now. Ten kilometers more or less. To do more in a straight line might not be convincing. They would accept it as normal that he should not take a taxi all the way to his rendezvous, but why not take one part of the way? He could imagine the debate behind him, one of them in favor of picking him up without delay, the other protesting against such a waste of the long grind.

So it was time for another sweetener. He looked at his watch and began to stroll more gently. He walked around two blocks and came back to his starting-point. He saw the car again. That was careless of them. It confirmed that they had never detected any hint that he was on his guard.

Again he looked at his watch and made a gesture of impatience— hardly perceptible but they wouldn't miss it. He started to stride out at a good pace toward the outskirts of the city, and allowed that hypnotizing back view of his to show some anxiety.

He knew where he was going and when he meant to arrive. There might be a hope for him, just a slight hope, if the same two obstinate men continued on the job. Probably they would. After all their trouble they would ask permission to carry on. Headquarters would be very impressed indeed if they could follow their man across the whole city and out of it and discover his contact in the end. There was little point in substituting fresh agents for the two who by now were familiar with the suspect.

The real difficulty was not these two, but their unknown colleagues. The field. The rest of the hunt. Some occupation must be found to delay them. There was a newspaper seller ahead on the other side of the road. That would do. A shop would not. If he entered any sort of shop it would break the spell.

He crossed the road, bought two papers almost without slowing his stride, and walked straight on, feeling sorry for the newsdealer who was sure to be investigated in case more than a coin had passed between them.

He rolled up the papers as he walked, but had trouble in keeping them rolled. He needed two rubber bands or strips of gummed paper. He didn't have either. A couple of stamps were the only available means. And who the devil would take something from an inner pocket and stick it on rolled newspapers without stopping? Well, he must not stop, not on any account. They would have to work it out for themselves.

He kept walking, holding a rolled paper in each hand until the stamps held, the gum was safely dry. He knew what he wanted—a high fence or wall. In that district of builders' yards and small workshops it should not be hard to find. He saw the proper setting at last, up a turning to the right. There was a big printing works on one side, small houses on the other.

He turned sharply into the street, threw one of his newspapers over the printer's wall, and walked on. As soon as the two turned the corner and took up the trail, they wouldn't miss the obvious inference that one paper had gone over the wall and the other was still to be delivered.

He wouldn't be arrested now! He was really worth following. Especially since the printer happened to be a government printer. The newspaper would—presumably—be easily found, but what had been rolled up in it and who had picked it up? That unfortunate printing works was going to be turned inside out. He reckoned that the whole of the team would be instantly and urgently occupied except for his two followers. They had to stay with him as long as their feet held out.

He was clear of the inner suburbs and among the factories. The main avenue was landscaped, bordered by lawns and imposing offices. Behind it were the service roads, the waste lots, the dumps, the uninviting cafés. He looked at his watch, on this occasion because he really wanted to know the time. It was going to be a close thing, but he must not hurry.

Keeping his even, persuasive pace he turned off the avenue into the worst stretch of all, empty and far too long. Surely they must realize what was going to happen and arrest him now? He imagined he heard their footsteps closing up, but he dared not look back or run.

The third corner was a possibility. Far from perfect, but all the chance he was ever going to get. He shot round it and crouched behind a lump of concrete, once part of a wall and now standing shapeless among thistles. There were a few workers further along the road, all busily occupied with brooms or vehicles or last-minute loading.

The two followed almost at once without any precautions at all, startled out of their trance by his sudden evasion just as he hoped they would be. They were still the same pair, seen once near the mailbox two and a half hours earlier. Hurrying to restore the broken contact, they passed within two yards of his silenced gun with their eyes fixed ahead on the parked vehicles and the factory gate. He let them pass. It had not been his intention, but why take an unnecessary risk? Lucky for them that they had panicked and tried to catch up instead of searching the corner itself.

The factory clock struck six. Cars, bicycles, and pedestrians surged out of the gate and surrounded them. He saw them trying, he thought, to give orders. He took off his coat and tie, and unobtrusively mingled with the crowd when it reached him. At last he allowed himself to appear as tired as he felt, putting twenty years on his age. That would fix them, if they were in any position at all to pick out the back view of individuals from the mass.

He kept walking, now no longer alone, until he saw a bus ready to start. Where it went was unimportant; for him the destination was freedom. His identity was still unknown and his papers were in perfect order. After a few professional, very simple alterations in his appearance he could cross the frontier. He had earned freedom.

Paper Casualty

It was a still day. The grey stone house was lifeless, like a prehistoric shrine in some long-forgotten jungle. The lower windows were shuttered, but the upper ones reflected the bleached sky, their grimy panes glinting dully like fake diamonds in a pawned tiara. The hard tennis court was covered in nettles. On the terrace forget-me-nots hovered like mist, and dead daffodils, now only shrunken vellum relics of their blooms, were infiltrated by bluebells. The wood was dark. There, fern stalks curled liked poised vipers and disguised as soft green lace prepared to strangle the nettles in a fight for the patches of sunlight that stabbed through the trees.

Beyond the drive, this anarchy ceased. Flag plants grew out of the mud like bright green sabres, each bloom a polished brass hilt. Uniform in size, shape, and colour, and spaced like guardsmen, they marked the place where in winter the river broke its banks. Today the water raced noisily over drowned trees and the collapsed embankment's stones. A young man, dressed in an old jacket and corduroy trousers tied at the knees, picked his way carefully along the overgrown path beside the water. A sow grunted loudly enough to alarm him, but he smiled as she turned and forced a noisy way through the undergrowth. He disturbed other creatures: pigeons that chortled loudly, and game birds that broke cover almost under his feet with a mighty rattle of anxious wings.

He went through the wrought-iron gate that marked the end of a short avenue of cedars. Beyond it, amid a chaos of roses, a collapsed portico, dock, nettles, and daisies, there was a small heap of kindling. As he walked towards it his boots hit the pearly globes of dandelion so that he left a trail of seeds suspended in the air behind his feet. He picked up an armful of twigs, selecting the driest ones and including a few thick pieces. From here there was a fine view of the house and the landscape behind it. The scene was timeless, until an aeroplane passed over at thirty thousand feet, leaving a condensation trail that soon went blobby in the high-altitude winds and then smudged twenty miles across Kent before it disappeared. The man kept a watch upon the curve of the front drive; that was the way they would come. He went to a derelict outhouse and lit the stove there. From time to time he consulted a gold wrist-watch which he kept in his trousers pocket.

There were several false alarms. The sow wandered back that way and made as much noise coming through the bushes as a recruit infantry pla-toon. When the soldiers finally arrived they were two Corporals, each on a BSA motor-cycle. The senior wore a scarf across his face. He unwound it as he walked over to the civilian.

'Empty, eh?'

'That's right.'

'How long?'

'A long time; five years, perhaps.'

'Bloody fool! How long since they retreated through here, I mean.'

'Very late last night. I heard tanks and motor-cycles about midnight.' The Corporal nodded; that fitted with what his officer had told him. These two Corporals were 'point': the men at the very tip of an advancing army. Point discovered mines, traps, pill boxes, and eventually the fortified posi-tions at which a retreating army turned to fight again. Sometimes they didn't. Sometimes the defenders let the point pass by and saved their energies for the infantry and tanks, or even for the soft transport that came after. This dangerous duty left a mark upon the faces of men. One of them lit a cigarette and the other looked at his watch. They were early. They brought their motor-cycles up to the front terrace and rubbed the dirty glass of the porch, trying to see inside. The furniture was covered with white sheets and the carpets had been taken up. After ten minutes the two Corporals went away. They returned along the front drive as far as the road but they didn't follow the retreating enemy; they turned back north.

When the sound of tanks could be heard in the gardens of the house the civilian climbed the embankment behind the stables. From there he could see them; eight infantry tanks—Valentines, perhaps—were mov-ing along the main road on the far side of Ten-Acre Field. It was difficult to identify them because of the leafy branches and netting that they wore. The commander of the lead tank was standing up in his turret talking into his microphone and looking ahead to where the two men on motor-cycles had by now disappeared. The other tanks were closed down for action.

The civilian descended from his vantage-point and went back to his stove. He searched for a cigarette and lit it carefully. This was the easiest way to infiltrate an army; let it advance right over you. It was an hour before any other soldiers came near the house. At 10.30 hours a 30-cwt lorry bumped up on to the little lawn adjacent to the gate house. Three soldiers climbed out, swearing. One of them lit a pressure stove to brew tea while the others changed the wheel. The civilian watched them from the end of the drive but they did not see him. Within twenty-five minutes they had finished, and accelerated away to catch up with their convoy.

At lunchtime a small Austin car came up the drive. It was painted khaki and had a Divisional sign, but was clearly one of those vehicles that the army had commandeered. Two subalterns got out and hammered on the door. The civilian shouted from the kitchen garden to tell them that the house was empty. The two officers were suspicious of him. They were all togged up in webbing, steel helmets and pistols, and seemed uncertain whether to hold the civilian at pistol-point. The man shrugged and offered to show them through the house if they wanted to see it.

He unlocked the oak door, and they kicked aside a broken dog-basket and ancient advertisements that had been put through the letter-box. The two officers kicked the staircase, too, and jumped up and down upon the wooden floor of the library to decide if it was sound. They tried the taps in the kitchen and the scullery, and got dirty searching the wine cellar.

It was the pink drawing-room that pleased the officers most. When they drew back the heavy curtains the sunlight came in like gold bars and made the mirrors flash. The french windows came unstuck with a creak. The dusty panes went white as they swung open and revealed childish rude words scrawled on the glass. Those walls would hold the maps, and the room was big enough to hold the sort of briefing that the Divisional commander wanted.

The Div HQ must already have been on the road, for they began to arrive by three o'clock. There were lorries and Jeeps and staff cars in such profusion that they had to put a redcap on the terrace to arrange the parking. The first-floor study became the map room, refreshments were to be served in the dining-room, and the drawing-room was filled with ten rows of stacking chairs ready for the briefing.

The telephones were installed in the vinery because, by breaking a glass pane, the signallers were able to pay out cables to rear windows at all levels and put a field telephone on each sill. The soldiers did other damage; heavy lorries demolished part of the wall near the gate house by turning too sharply into the drive. Sappers cleared young trees and bushes from the near side of the pond so that the sentries could see all the meadow as far as the stream. The stables became a strong-point with a Bren in the loft, and they removed a few bricks to give it a traverse. A carrier left track marks right through the flowerbeds to the azaleas.

The interior of the house suffered, too. When they were fixing the maps a ladder cracked one of the ornamental mirrors, and two fine gilt chairs were broken by soldiers who stacked them carelessly in the base-ment kitchen. General Parkstone assigned an officer to record each dam-aged item and decide whether the culprit should be punished. Parkstone was not the sort of man who tolerated vandalism, even in a war.

When he arrived at the house, General Parkstone was asleep for the first time in forty hours. He was hunched across the back seat of his Humber with his cap tipped over his face and a book of poetry on the floor. His pale-blue eyes blinked awake as his driver opened the door. He recognized the cornices and the superb front door. He'd seen this house before. He'd seen almost every Georgian house in southern England. Prospect, this one was called, and Parkstone saw in that name the promise of a happy life as well as a fine vista. He felt a moment of envy for the man who'd designed and sited this mansion. He hurried inside where his batman had prepared a hot bath, clean clothes, and a bowl of tinned soup.

This wasn't Parkstone's first war, as one glance at his greying hair and the ribbons on his chest confirmed. Before going to the Staff College in 1918 he'd won a DSO and Bar and an MC. Some said that the action at Polygon Wood, when Parkstone brought in four casualties under fire and got a mention, would have got a VC for a lower rank. Not that Parkstone's past valour did him much good in his present job. Decorations from the First World War dated him. Beaten in France by a dynamic Panzer Army, the British had suddenly decided that youthful commanders were the secret of victory. 'Suspect,' a very senior officer had told Parkstone, tap-ping his medal ribbons, 'suspect, General!' Outraged by the injustice of such treatment, Parkstone had nodded. Even to remember it made him flush with shame.

For Major-General A. G. Parkstone was no blimp. A close friend of Swinton and Fuller, he'd been a tank man when such heresies were a great impediment to his career. Now that armoured warfare had become the epitome of fashion, Parkstone was accused of being the same sort of fogey that he'd spent his career opposing.

Lieutenant Fane came into the dining-room and checked the number of cups on the sideboard before opening a tin of biscuits that he had been jealously guarding for a week. He put them out on the plates, roughly calculating at three biscuits per officer. He was a tall elderly man with a bony nose and thin lips that he sometimes bit bloodless rather than lose his temper. Lieutenant Fane was Camp Commandant. He had spent most of his life as a senior NCO. In order to take charge of the domestic side of this Divisional HQ he'd got a commission, but he had no illusions about it. To the men around him he was still an NCO despite the salutes that he now got from his clerks and waiters, and Fane was satisfied that it should be so.

He looked around the room approvingly; his clerks had done a good job. It was almost impossible to believe that it had only been inhabited for a couple of hours. He'd found the carpets in the attic, and they were bright and clean as ever they'd been. He had chivvied the Catering Sergeant into lighting one of the kitchen stoves, and they'd found a collection of odd teacups and saucers in a tea-chest in the pantry. There was an army blanket over the dining-room table to protect it from careless cigarettes or hot teapots.

'A good effort, Camp,' said Parkstone.

'Sir!' Fane went to the door and placed a notice there: COMMANDING OFFICER'S CONFERENCE. NO ADMISSION. He nodded to the sentry. 'No one else.'

'Sir.'

The past inhabitants of the house would have rejoiced to see the dining-room that Tuesday afternoon in 1941. It had been as lively as this when young Victoria was crowned, and as sunny when Uncle Arthur celebrated his knighthood. There had been fireworks on the lawn at Mafeking, and an orchestra in the summerhouse for Emily's twenty-first. But never had the dining-room vibrated with the sound of so many polished masculine voices as when the senior officers of Parkstone's Division greeted their comrades, ragged their school chums, and artfully probed the credentials of newcomers. They had all arrived by ten minutes to four, none of them wishing to face the cold greeting that Parkstone reserved for people who were merely punctual.

Major-General Parkstone, a slight, pale figure, circulated among his officers. Colonel Lee—who commanded one of the armoured regiments from inside his tank—was wearing clean, pressed overalls. Mitchell, Lee's Brigadier, was in shirtsleeve order, his khaki shirt bleached almost white. Chaps back from the desert liked to advertise the fact, thought Parkstone. He'd never got along well with Brigadier Mitchell, a blond thirty-seven-year-old with a tanned skin and a nose full of broken capillaries. Mitchell and his protégé Lee had both got mentions the previous winter, when the 7th Armoured Division chased Berganzoli and his Italians across Cyrenaica. Those two had smelled the scent of victory, and breathed it proudly among colleagues who had tasted the sand of Dunkirk. Parkstone nodded to the two men and moved past them to where his GSO1, Colonel Joyce, was standing near the sideboard, examining a bowl of wax fruit inside its dusty glass dome.

Joyce offered his commander a plate of biscuits. The plump little Irishman, dark skinned from a quarter-century of Indian sun, had still not got used to rooms and streets full of white faces. He also had known victory, in Africa, with his Punjabis. But defending the mountain stronghold of Keren, the Italians had fought like tigers. Joyce had watched his Indians die on every crag. He had no illusions about blitzkriegs.

'Those oatmeal ones are grand.' Even after all the time away, there were still traces of Kerry. The voice was known to everyone in the room. Like every chief-of-staff, he was able to manage on little or no sleep and spent almost all his waking hours giving wireless orders. He'd had only brief moments out of his command vehicle since the battle had started.

Parkstone smiled and took a biscuit. Joyce was an old friend. He, more than anyone, knew the difficulties he faced. Armoured Divisions were the newest toys of the General Staff. They only awarded them to their brightest boys, that's why everyone wanted one. Some said it was more difficult to get than a Corps.

'I'll take two, Joycey, while I've got the chance.' They both smiled.

Lieutenant Fane appeared at the Irishman's elbow with a glass of ice-cold beer. 'You're a darling man, Camp,' said Joyce in a stage-Irish accent.

The old boy was a great organizer, thought Parkstone, the best Camp Commandant he'd known. He did most of the Quartermaster's work, too. Parks nodded to Fane to tell him that they should soon be moving into the drawing-room. He wondered who the portraits could be: the girl in the pink dress, the two young country squires on horseback and the old man so proud of his knighthood that he'd had a scroll painted around his head like the halo on a martyr.

There was a noise that rattled the cut-glass chandelier as a formation of fighters came over the house at one thousand feet. Some of the officers moved to the french windows to catch sight of them before they disappeared over the tree tops.

'Spitfires,' said Mitchell.

'Off to the real war.' Colonel Lee brushed a biscuit crumb off his immaculate tankman's overalls.

'It won't be long now.' Mitchell smiled at his protégé. Unlike the others, they knew all about the real war. 'The Two Hussars', the others called them derisively but they liked this label; they relished its connotations of vigour and *élan*.

In the kitchen garden the young man also looked up at the Spitfires before glancing back at the senior officers moving past the hall window as they filed into the drawing-room. He'd tried to get around the terrace to glimpse the map on the wall, but there was an armed sentry on duty each side of the shrubbery, and even from here he could see that the drawing-room curtains were closed. He cursed his own stupidity in not hiding those curtains before the soldiers had arrived.

Major-General Parkstone lit a cigarette himself to avoid giving formal permission to smoke. It was dark in the curtained drawing-room, apart from the battery of lights that had been arranged to shine upon the blackboard and the map that were mounted on the platform.

'Two squadrons of armoured cars will be ahead as far as Maidstone. The infantry attached to the armoured brigade—that is to say, Sammy's battalion—will maintain contact with Brigadier Mitchell by means of the command tank. It is imperative that tank crews realize that the speed of advance will be dictated by the pace of the infantry. Infantry are the eyes of the advance; without them, closed-down tanks will get into trouble. I'll deal personally with any breach of this order.' Parkstone could see that the commander of one of the armoured regiments was fidgeting. 'Colonel Lee, you have a question?'

'Affirmative,' said Lee. He spoke in strange staccato bursts, like economical machine-gun fire. 'Maidstone: south of the river. Could give us a chance to break out. The recce squadrons give me the green light. I'd punch one of my sabre squadrons southwards and keep going.'

'The Guderian approach,' nodded Parkstone. It was strange that he had spent most of his life advocating breakthrough armour tactics without response. Then came Dunkirk, and now it had become necessary to curb everyone's desire to stage a blitzkrieg. 'This is not Sedan,' said Parkstone, 'we are not fighting the French . . .' he paused before adding, 'and you are not Guderian.' He gave the room a moment or two to absorb the reprimand he'd given Lee. 'If we put an armoured column down the Ashford road the enemy will tear open the flank of the whole Corps. Look.' Patiently Parkstone ran his hands across the map to explain the strategy of the battle from Portsmouth to Margate. Parkstone's Division was protecting London. Now that the Corps was advancing, Parkstone's task was to maintain contact with his flanks. Only that morning the Corps

Commander had pointed out that Parkstone's front would be stretched by advancing. Strategically, the less he advanced the safer London would remain.

Outside, by the flowerbeds that skirted the croquet lawn, the man in civilian clothes made a decision. He had gathered a large bunch of mixed flowers and walked slowly towards the servants' entrance. Outhouses surrounded a cobbled yard on the east side of the house, and on a clothes-line stretched across the yard hung khaki shirts and underclothes. Three batmen were sitting in the derelict dairy. They had got a fire going in an old stove near by and were drinking tea and chatting. The last of the row of outhouses had once been the head gardener's house, and an old sofa and some chairs were still there. The Military Police Sergeant had claimed it as his office. The man in civilian clothes pushed open the double gates to enter the courtyard and found himself half strangled by the Police Sergeant before he knew what was happening.

'And where are you off to, my pretty maid?'

'Flowers for the Officers' Mess dining-room,' grunted the man. The Police Sergeant did not relax his hold. 'Just drop them on the floor, chummy.' The flowers dropped to the cobbles and, still holding the man, the sergeant kicked them gently with his toe to be sure there was nothing concealed there. He released the man, who rubbed his neck and said, 'A nice mess you've made of the flowers now.'

'And a nice mess my General would have made of me if you'd gone waltzing into the house,' said the Police Sergeant. 'Who are you, anyway?'

'Pepper. I'm the gardener for Mr Matthews who owns Prospect. I'm the one that will get into trouble for all the damage your lot are doing.' He finished picking up the flowers. 'Am I allowed to take them inside now, or will you do it?'

The Police Sergeant patted Pepper's pockets and under his arms. Before the war he had been a prison warder, and he searched him with a swift professional flourish. 'OK Mr Pepper. Just as far as the kitchen door. Hand them to one of the cooks. I'll be watching you.' He glanced towards the house. The drawing-room was over the kitchen, but the curtains were still tightly closed.

'Just as you like,' said the man. When he got to the kitchen door he didn't knock, but took from his pocket four tin-tacks and a piece of red paper and fixed a notice to the door. The Police Sergeant ran to him, but the man in civilian clothes just stood and grinned. On the piece of paper was crudely printed the word 'Bomb'. In the bottom right-hand corner it was signed by a Captain Ridley on behalf of Lieutenant-General Post, the senior referee of the whole Southern Command Exercise.

'But good God Almighty,' said Parkstone, 'you can't kill a man with a sheet of paper.' He had the red paper in his hand and he kept examining it as though some new information might appear there.

'It's ridiculous,' agreed Colonel Joyce. 'I've been on to Command, but it seems our move this morning has rather outstripped the referees.'

'He was searched?' Parkstone asked for the fifth time.

'He was, sir, very thoroughly, by Sergeant Albany.'

'If he'd really had a bomb he would have found it.'

'Exactly, sir.'

'After all,' said Parkstone, forcing a smile, 'I could have sent the whole staff a postcard with "bullet" written on it. What then?'

Joyce nodded.

'You can't kill a roomful of chaps with a sheet of paper, Joycey, or the War Office would have obliterated the Jerries in the first week of war, eh?'

Joyce smiled.

'It's buggered the briefing.'

'Yes, sir, and I think you had them ready to go.'

'I think I did, Joycey.'

The General looked at his watch again. How long would this bloody referee be? Inevitably, his senior officers would be talking about this business. He wondered what they would be saying about it.

'Everyone thinks it's quite idiotic, sir.'

'Do you think we could find them all a real drink, Joycey?'

'If we used up your personal bar, sir. Then we could squeeze them out a small one.'

'Do that.'

The General sat down on his desk and sorted through his piles of paperwork: fire support, boundaries, water, fuel, daily objectives. But he couldn't take his mind off the paper bomb.

When the referee arrived it was Brigadier Frederick. Until Dunkirk, 'Bunny' Frederick had been noted for his immaculate appearance: Sam Browne, riding-boots, starched collars, the finest of gold-wire badges and a riding-crop in his formally gloved hands. Now, Parkstone noted sardonically, it was the age of the private soldier. Frederick was wearing an old battledress with a webbing belt and gaiters and a steel helmet with netting. His cloth badges had been carefully dirtied—to avoid snipers—

and he'd exchanged his gold spectacles for a steel pattern frame that the army issued to recruits. He saluted.

'Hello, Bunny,' said General Parkstone.

'A fine how-do-you-do this is, Parks, old boy.'

'How do you want to do this, Bunny? Set up an office here and see this so-called spy and my Police Sergeant?'

'No needs, Parks. I know all the details, there's nothing to settle. The fellow has blown up your whole Div HQ. There's not one senior commander between Green Force and London. If they exploit the gap they'll be in London by tonight. Sorry old fellow.' The brigadier spoke rapidly and tonelessly, like a child reciting a poem that it didn't understand.

'But Bunny, for Lord's sake listen. This chap was searched. All he had was a piece of paper—'

'Piece of paper to you, bomb to me.' He smiled. 'We're up against a tough opponent, Parks. The Hun is going to use every damned trick in the book and a few not in the book. Look at Holland: parachute troops dressed as nuns.' He slapped his thigh with an imaginary riding-crop.

'Must have been damned draughty up their skirts,' said Parks. 'I've never believed that stuff about paratroop nuns, a bit too much like some of those atrocity stories that came out of Belgium in the first lot.'

'Yes, well, you remember the first lot, of course. But this is a different sort of war we're fighting, Parks. You don't believe in nuns and you don't believe in spies—'

'I didn't say I don't believe in spies,' said General Parkstone. 'I don't believe in things that are not evidenced. I don't believe in paper bombs.'

'You underrate the enemy, sir,' said Bunny Frederick, 'if you don't mind me saying so.'

'I don't think I agree,' said Parkstone.

'Well, luckily it wasn't up to me. I went over to Army before coming here. That's what made me a bit late. The fact is, Parks, that the exercise will stop at 18.00 hours. It was agreed that there is no point in continuing with so many senior officers pulled out of the battle.' Frederick tugged at the brassard that had a large R on it. 'Five referees gave evidence and that was the decision. Sorry, Parks.'

'Did they say anything about me?'

Frederick shuffled, and pulled the strap of his respirator case so that it fitted more comfortably on his shoulder. 'The chief was in a black mood, Parks. They all were except Simms—you know, the G2 Major—it was his idea, the bomb. He was almost jubilant—expounding his theories about infiltration, you know.'

'I know.' Parks nodded. 'Think I'll lose the Division, Bunny?'

'Of course not, Parks.'

'You'd better tell me, Bunny. I'd sooner know from you.'

'It's only talk.'

'Say on.'

'It might go to Mitchell. The Chief wants young commanders. You can't blame him, Parks . . . the press, the PM, the politicians, all keep talking about Britain's new young army . . . recruiting jaw-jaw, don't you know.'

'A triumph for the Hussars.' He couldn't keep the bitterness out of his voice.

'Yes, Mitchell's lad Lee will probably get Mitchell's Brigade.'

Frederick walked across the room to look out of the window. He didn't want to look at Parkstone. He asked himself if he'd handled it terribly badly. He wished desperately that he had the deft touch of a diplomat, so that he could have lessened the blow. But Bunny Frederick wasn't a diplomat, or even a very good soldier. At Sandhurst where Under-Officer Parkstone was still something of a legend, Gentleman Cadet Bunny Frederick had been a dud, swotting like mad and sometimes cheating, just to end up with a pass into the army. His sympathy could be no comfort to a man like Parks. It would make him feel even worse; but at least Bunny Frederick knew this. 'Must have been a magnificent place once,' he said. 'You've always liked these Georgian country houses.'

'Detailing is a bit heavy,' said Parkstone mechanically, 'but the cornice is good and the front-door is pure Queen Anne.'

'Well, everyone knows you're an expert, Parks.'

Including Major Simms, thought Parkstone; he guessed I couldn't resist Prospect as a Div HQ. Parkstone had been in shirtsleeves, but now that the sun was behind the trees he felt cold. He put on his jacket and fastened the buttons carefully. It gave him a chance to think. Only half an hour ago he'd been sure that you can't kill a man with a sheet of paper; now he wasn't so sure.

Signal Tresham

'You are my Member,' said Colonel Mounteagle.

'Indeed, yes,' said Mr Pocock, sipping nervously at the glass of sherry which the colonel had thrust on to him when he arrived.

'You represent my interests in Parliament.'

'Yours, and other people's.'

'Never mind about other people. It isn't other people's land this feeder road is going to ruin. It's my land.'

'That's one way of looking at it,' agreed Mr Pocock. 'But you have to bear in mind that by taking the pressure off the road between your lodge gates and the roundabout, a number of people with houses on that stretch will be relieved of the heavy flow of traffic just outside their front gates. Danger to children—'

'Irrelevant,' said the colonel. 'People who buy houses on the main road must expect to see a bit of traffic. That's not the point. When a road is going to invade the privacy of a landowner—is going to trespass across *his* fields—he *must* be allowed some say in the matter. That's right, isn't it?'

'Up to a point.'

'Right. Have some more sherry.' Without allowing Mr Pocock to say yes or no he refilled his glass. 'Now, you've got a chance to do what's needed. You've drawn a place—third place, I believe—in the ballot for private members' bills. I've told you what's wanted. A simple three- or four-clause bill saying that where a new road is planned the landowners affected by it will have a right to veto it. If there are several of them, the verdict to be by a straight majority. That's democratic, isn't it?'

'In a way,' said Mr Pocock. He wished he could dispose of the sherry, but if he drank it too quickly he was going to choke. 'But one has to look at the other side of the coin. The new road will be a great benefit to a number of householders.'

'Including you.'

'Yes. It's true that my present house happens to be on that stretch of road. But I hope you don't impute—'

'I don't impute anything,' said the colonel. 'I state facts. Mine is the only property which is going to be invaded, and that means that I am the only person directly concerned.'

He gazed out of the window. From where he stood he could see, across two fields, the line of hedge which marked the main road—a thick hedge of well matured beech. What he now had to face was the thought of a road, a loathsome snake of tar macadam, giving right of access to every Tom, Dick, and Harry with a stinking motor car or a roaring motor cycle, violating lands which had been in the Mounteagle family for two and a half centuries. Was it for this that they had fought Napoleon, Kaiser William, and Hitler, that one Mounteagle had fallen in the breach at Badajoz, and another in the sodden wastes of Passchendaele, that he himself—?

He looked down at his left hand from which three of the middle fingers were gone. Mr Pocock, not fancying the expression on his face, managed to swallow most of the sherry in his glass.

'It may not be easy to push such a bill through,' said the colonel. 'But it's a chance. And maybe your last chance to settle this matter without bloodshed.'

'Metaphorically, I hope you mean,' said Mr Pocock with a nervous smile.

'I'm not in the habit of talking in metaphors,' said the colonel. 'If you put me with my back to the wall, I shall fight.'

'And, oh dear,' said Mr Pocock to his wife that evening, 'I've got a feeling he meant it.'

'You can't possibly promote an anti-social bill of that sort.'

'If I did, it would be the end of me, politically. And it wouldn't get a second reading. It would be laughed out of Parliament, and me with it.'

'Then,' said his wife, 'what's the difficulty? You just say no.'

'You didn't see his face,' said Mr Pocock.

'When I was in India,' said Mr Fortescue, 'there was a saying that all sappers were mad, married, or Methodist. Colonel Mounteagle is a bachelor, and a staunch upholder of the established Church.'

'So he must be mad,' said Mr Calder.

When Mr Fortescue, Manager of the Westminster Branch of the London and Home Counties Bank, wished to make contact with Mr Calder or Mr Behrens, both of whom lived in Kent, he would convey a message to them that their accounts were causing him concern. The precise form of the message indicated the gravity of the situation. On this occasion it had been of very moderate urgency, and directed to Mr Calder only.

'Madness is an imprecise term,' said Mr Fortescue. He steepled the tips of his fingers and looked severely at Mr Calder over his glasses.

'If you mean, is he certifiably insane, the answer must be in the negative. But his conduct in recent months has been causing concern in certain quarters. A number of my people have, as you know, succeeded in establishing themselves in positions of some confidence in IRA cells in this country. One of my people has managed to become friendly with Michael Scullin.'

Mr Calder knew that the people referred to were very brave men who took their lives into their hands every day of the year. He also knew that the systematic penetration of IRA groups was one of the ways in which bomb outrages were kept within manageable limits.

He said, 'Scullin? He's their electronics expert, isn't he?'

'One of them. He specializes in detonation by remote control, and devices of that sort. He learned his trade in Russia.'

'I'm surprised that we don't take steps to abate him.'

'On the whole it is more useful to keep him under observation. It can produce surprising results—as it has on this occasion. It seems that recently he has been paid substantial sums of money by a certain Colonel Mounteagle for what I can only describe as a refresher course in the use of high explosive.'

'A refresher course?'

'Certainly. As a young officer, in 1945, Mounteagle had a considerable reputation. He was a member of the task force charged with clearing the mouth of the Scheldt, and blowing up the submarine pens. They were jobs which had to be done against time, and this involved the acceptance of risks. There was a procedure by which unmanned barges filled with explosive could be directed into the underground pens and exploded. The danger lay in the variety of underwater devices which had first to be brought to the surface and dismantled. It was while he was engaged in this work that the colonel lost three fingers of his left hand—and gained an immediate DSO.'

'He sounds quite a lad,' said Mr Calder. 'Do we know what is leading him to a renewed interest in the forces of destruction?'

'He is annoyed with the authorities for wishing to build a road across his park and with his local MP for failing to introduce a private bill to stop them.'

Mr Calder thought for a moment that Mr Fortescue was joking, then realized that he was serious. He said, 'What sort of reprisals do you think he might be intending?'

'He could be laying a number of booby traps in his park. Alternatively, or in addition, he may be planning to blow up the MP concerned, a Mr Pocock. Two nights ago Mr Pocock was awakened by mysterious noises. He telephoned the police. When they arrived they found that the door of his garage had been forced. From the garage an unlocked door leads into the house.'

'I see,' said Mr Calder. 'The colonel sounds like a determined character. Perhaps Mr Pocock would be wise to press on with his bill.'

Mr Fortescue said, 'I think we must take a hand. The loss of an occasional Member of Parliament may not be a matter of concern, but we don't want some innocent bulldozer driver destroyed. I suggest you make yourself known to the colonel. His address is Mounteagle Hall, Higham. He is managing director of his own family firm, The Clipstone Sand and Gravel Company. It is on the river, north of Cooling. I will alert Behrens as to the position, but I imagine you will be able to handle this yourself.'

Mr Calder's methods were usually simple and straightforward. On this occasion he put on his oldest clothes, armed himself with a fishing rod, and sat down to fish at a point just outside the boundary fence of the Clipstone Sand and Gravel Company. Soon after he had started, a man came out of a gate in the fence and stood watching him. From his appearance and walk he was an ex-naval type, Mr Calder guessed. At this moment he succeeded in hooking a sizeable fish.

This served as a convenient introduction, and Mr Calder was soon deep in conversation with Chief Petty Officer Seward. He mentioned that he was putting up for a few days at the local pub. Seward agreed that the beer there was drinkable, and that he might be down there himself after work.

By ten o'clock that evening, in the friendly atmosphere of the saloon bar, Mr Calder had learned a good deal about the Clipstone Sand and Gravel Company and its owner.

'He's all right,' said Seward. 'I mean, you don't find many like him nowadays. He knows what he wants, and he likes to get his own way, no messing about. But if he likes you, he'll do anything for you.'

'And if he doesn't like you?'

'If he doesn't like you,' said Seward with a grin, 'you clear out quick. We had a chap once who set himself up as a sort of shop steward. Wanted to get us unionized. The colonel soon put a stop to it.'

'How did he manage to do that?'

'Threw him in the river.'

'I see,' said Calder thoughtfully.

'I don't say he would have got away with it in the usual outfit, but we're more a sort of family business. All ex-service. We've even got our own fleet.'

Mr Calder had seen the neat row of grey metal barges anchored to the jetty.

'Lovely jobs,' said Seward. 'Self-powered. One man can handle them easily. Built to ferry stuff ashore on the beaches at D-day. Picked them up from the Crown Agents after the war. Most of our stuff—sand and aggregate, that is—goes up by river. And they bring back timber piling and iron sheeting. When we're opening a new section of quarry we have to blanket off each section as we go—'

He expounded the intricacies of the quarryman's job, and Mr Calder, who always liked to learn about other people's work, listened with interest.

He said to Mr Behrens when he met him three days later—'Mounteagle's a real buccaneer. The sort of man who used to go out to India in the seventeenth century and come back with a fortune and a hobnailed liver. But he's running a very useful outfit, and his men swear by him.'

'Would he be capable of blowing up a Member of Parliament?' said Mr Behrens.

'Think nothing of it. He chucked a shop steward into the river.'

On the following Sunday Mr Calder paid a visit, by appointment, to the modest villa residence of Alfred Pocock, MP. It stood, with five similar residences, on the far side of the road which skirted Colonel Mounteagle's park. He found Mr Pocock at home, alone and depressed. He said, 'I've sent my wife away to stay with her mother. She didn't want to go but I thought it would be safer.'

'Much safer,' said Mr Calder. 'I take it the explosives experts have given your house a clean bill of health.'

'They poked around with some sort of machine which reacts to explosives. They didn't find anything.'

'I expect it was just a reconnaissance. The colonel's a methodical man.'

'He's a public menace,' said Mr Pocock indignantly. 'I'm told that the

workmen who should have started on the new road a week ago have refused
to proceed without police protection.'

'I'm not sure that policemen would be much use. What they need is
a military reconnaissance screen, armed with mine detectors.'

'Then the colonel should be arrested.'

'And charged with what?'

Mr Pocock gobbled a bit, but could think of no answer to this. Mr
Calder said, 'I suppose you couldn't make some sort of gesture? Have
this bill he wants printed, and given a first reading. Since you're convinced it wouldn't get any further, no real harm would be done.'

'It would be the end of my political life.'

'If I had to make a choice between the ending of my political life and
the ending of my life, I know which alternative I would select. But then,
I'm a natural coward.'

Mr Pocock, his voice rising as it did when he was excited or alarmed,
said, 'It's a scandal. We should all be given the fullest possible protection against menaces of this sort. It's what we pay our rates and taxes for
and we're entitled to expect it.'

'Having me on your side,' said Mr Calder, 'is what you might call a
tax bonus.'

Mr Pocock was not appeased. He shook hands coldly when his visitor
left. Mr Calder, also, was silent. He was reflecting that maybe the trouble
with England was that it was run by people like Mr Pocock and not by
people like Colonel Mounteagle.

His next object was to meet the colonel. Since he could hardly march
up to the front door and introduce himself, this was a question of man-
œuvre and good luck. He was early afoot on Monday morning and
found two young men with white poles, a steel tape, and a theodolite on
the road verge just south of the manor's great gates—high columns,
each surmounted by a stone eagle poised to swoop.

As he stopped to talk to them a car swept out of the entrance. The
colonel, who was driving, spotted the men, pulled up, and got out. The
men looked apprehensive. The colonel was smiling. He said, 'Getting
ready for the great day, lads?'

'That's right, Colonel.'

'The day when the first bulldozer drives through my hedge.'

'That won't be us, Colonel. That's not our job.'

'Someone's got to drive it. Can't do it by remote control.' A thought
struck him. 'Come to think of it,' he said, 'when I was doing a similar
sort of job during the war, we *did* use remote control. But that was ships,

not bulldozers. No. As I said, someone will have to drive it.' The colonel's smile widened. 'Give him a message from me, lads. What he'll need is not police protection. He'll need insurance for his widow.'

The colonel swung round and seemed to notice Mr Calder for the first time. He said, 'Are you in charge of this mob?'

'Certainly not,' said Mr Calder. 'I just happened to be passing.'

'You don't look to me like someone who happened to be passing. You look to me like a spy. This is war. And you know what happens to spies in war.' The smile appeared again. 'They get shot.'

It was the smile that convinced Mr Calder. The colonel was neither eccentric nor in any way admirable. Whether he was mad or not was a nice point. What was certain was that he was very dangerous.

'We put a tap on both telephones,' said Mr Fortescue. 'The one from the house and the one from the factory. We picked up an interesting exchange yesterday afternoon. The colonel was speaking to a young friend of his, also ex-Army, it seems. A man called David Cairns. Cairns is assistant manager at an open-cast coal site at Petheridge, above Reading. Their coal goes down by river to the power stations at Battersea and Rotherhithe.'

'And the colonel is ordering coal?'

'He is ordering explosives. A ton of slurry explosive. Stable, but extremely powerful. It is used in open-cast mining. And in quarrying.'

'So the colonel has a legitimate reason for ordering it?'

'Certainly. And used in small quantities, under careful control, it can be perfectly safe. When I asked one of our Home Office experts what the effect would be of detonating a ton of it, he said that no one in his senses would do such a thing. When I pressed him he said it would blow a crater, roughly the size of a football field, perhaps twenty foot deep.'

Mr Calder started to say, 'Is there any reason to suppose—' but Mr Fortescue interrupted him sharply. He said, 'There were two further points. The colonel is fetching this load himself. He will take one of the barges upstream tomorrow. A run of nine to ten hours. The loading will be done when he arrives. He has also ordered a quantity of timber, which will be stowed on top of the explosive. To keep it firmly in position, he said. No doubt a wise precaution. He plans to spend the night on the boat and start back early the following morning. I think it would be a good idea if you supervised the shipment. But I confess I shall feel much happier when the whole of this particular cargo is safely stowed in the explosives store of the Clipstone Sand and Gravel Company.'

'Me, too,' said Mr Calder.

There was a jetty at Petheridge, connected by a private railway with the loading bay at the open-case colliery. A concrete track ran alongside the line. The colonel, who must have made an early start, tied up at the jetty at four o'clock. Mr Calder, who had come by road and had not needed to hurry, was ensconced in a thicket of alder and nettles at the far end of the jetty.

He awaited developments with interest.

The timber arrived first, by rail. The explosive, packed in wooden boxes, followed in a lorry, driven by a youngish man with the stamp of a cavalry officer, whom the colonel greeted as David, and whom Mr Calder assumed to be Cairns.

The wooden boxes were man-handled by the train crew and lowered into the barge. Nobody seemed unduly worried by their explosive potential, but Mr Calder noticed that they were not treated roughly. Once they were safely stowed, a small crane was brought into operation and this was used to sling on board the timber baulks, which had evidently been cut to length and which fitted snugly over the boxes.

By the time the loading was finished, evening was closing in. The train clanked off, and the colonel said something which Mr Calder was too far away to hear but which seemed to be an invitation to Cairns to come on board. He had been squatting among the nettles for three hours without achieving anything except cramp. Nothing much would happen before the barge started downstream at first light. Mr Calder's ideas turned to a drink and dinner. He got stiffly to his feet. He could see Cairns and the colonel standing in the lighted bridge house. He eased his way along the jetty in the hope that he might pick up what they were saying.

What the colonel was saying was, 'I bet you don't know what this box of tricks does.'

Cairns said, 'You lose your bet, Colonel. Almost the only interesting thing I did in the Army was the long electronics course I took at Rhyl. It's an automatic steerer. Come to think of it, that must have been the sort of thing you used when you were blowing up those submarine pens.'

'Roughly the same apparatus,' said the colonel. 'Roughly. But it was a good deal more primitive in those days.'

If Cairns had noticed the expression on the colonel's face, he might have cut short the conversation at this point. As it was, he had moved on to a second box that was beside the auto steerer and linked to it. Peering down at it he said, 'This looks like a repeater. What would you need a repeater for?'

He put out one hand to touch the dial. The colonel said, in the tone of voice he might have used to a recalcitrant subaltern, 'Don't touch that.'

Cairns's head jerked back. He seemed suddenly to realize that something was wrong.

He said, 'Do you mean that this repeater's already set? What on earth are you playing at?'

'That's none of your business.'

Cairns was getting angry too. He said, 'It is my business. You've got enough of my explosive on this craft to blow a hole in the home counties. And you've got an automatic steerer linked to a pre-set repeater. Unless you're prepared to tell me what you're playing at, I think I ought to report this to the police.'

'You'll do nothing of the sort,' said the colonel calmly. 'I'll have no Tresham here.' His hand came out of his pocket with a gun in it.

Calder was close enough by now to hear this, but not close enough to stop what followed. His feet were on the gangplank when the colonel shot Cairns through the heart, caught him as he fell, and heaved him over the side of the bridge and into the river. Hearing Mr Calder coming up the iron steps on to the bridge he swung round and shot him, once in the head and once in the body, and threw him overboard as well.

Then he put the gun back into his pocket, turned about, and descended into the cuddy. He was breathing a little faster, but otherwise showed no particular sign of emotion. His hand, as he poured himself a whisky from a bottle in the bulkhead cupboard, was steady as a rock.

The first shot had creased Mr Calder, ploughing a long furrow along the side of his head above the ear and rendering him temporarily unconscious. He had twisted as he fell, so that the second shot went into the right side of his chest, deflecting from the ribs and coming out under his right shoulder blade.

The fall into the chilly November waters of the Thames brought him round. He could use his legs, and with difficulty, his left arm. He realized that he was losing blood fast.

He let himself go with the current, kicking feebly towards the right bank, because he remembered that the towpath was on that side.

An eternity of cold and increasing pain.

Then he felt himself grounding on the gravel foreshore. Above him was a low wall of what seemed to be concrete sacks. He realized that he was incapable of climbing it and getting out on to the towpath.

He lay on his back and shouted.

The first passer-by was a young girl. She took one look down at Mr Calder and scampered away. The next one, twenty interminable minutes later, was a policeman.

Mr Behrens reached Reading Infirmary just before midnight. He was shown into a bleak reception office where he kicked his heels for ten minutes. His temper was wearing thin when a young doctor came in, accompanied by a policeman whom Mr Behrens recognized—Superintendent Farr of the Reading police.

The superintendent said, 'As soon as we knew it was Calder we got in touch with your office. They said, put the silencers on. Have you any idea what this is all about?'

'Why don't we ask Calder? He might be able to tell us.'

'He won't tell you anything,' said the doctor. Then he noted the expression on Mr Behrens' face.

'Sorry,' he said. 'I didn't mean that. He's not dead yet, and with a bit of luck we'll keep him that way. But he's lost a lot of blood. And lying about on the river bank in this weather can't have helped. I've put him under, and he'll have to stay that way for the time being.'

'How long will that be?'

'The longer the better for him,' said the doctor.

Mr Behrens recognized the finality of this. He said to Farr, 'Can *you* tell me anything? We're all of us totally in the dark. It may be important.'

'All I can tell you is that one of my men found him on the river bank, whistled up an ambulance, and got him in here. It was when they were going through his wallet that they found his "I" card with the special instructions on it, and got hold of me.'

'Did he say anything before you put him under? Anything at all?'

'Not really,' said the doctor. 'If I'd known it was going to matter I might have listened more carefully.' Men who were brought in with two bullet wounds in them and were important enough to bring the head policeman round at midnight were something new in his experience. 'He did mention two names, though—several times over. One was Cairns and the other, I think, was Tresham.'

'Tresham?' said Mr Fortescue thoughtfully, when Mr Behrens spoke to him on the telephone. 'I seem to remember a man of that name. Tresham or Trencham. He was a Norfolk fisherman. He gave a lot of help to German agents landing by submarine on the east coast.'

'And was Calder involved?'

'He was at Blenheim at the time. He could have been.'

'Then this might have nothing to do with Mounteagle. It might be a revenge killing. By Tresham's son perhaps.'

'I don't think,' said Mr Fortescue precisely, 'that this is a case in which it would be wise to jump to conclusions. What about Cairns?'

'He's a bachelor. We've telephoned his digs. No answer. The police are sending a car round.'

Mr Fortescue digested this news in silence for some seconds. Then he said, 'I'll look into the Tresham case. And I'll arrange for the police to monitor Mounteagle's barge as it goes downstream tomorrow. There's a lot to do. I suggest you go home and get some sleep. Be at the Bank by nine tomorrow morning.'

Mr Behrens went back home to the Old Rectory in the sleepy Kentish village of Lamperdown, and he lay on his bed, but he did not go to sleep. The answer to a lot of their problems was under his hand, if only he could close his fingers on it.

The deceptive light of false dawn was in the sky, and the first cocks were beginning to crow across the valley when Mr Behrens got up, pulled on his dressing gown, and made his way downstairs, walking quietly, so as not to wake his aunt, who shared the house with him and was a light sleeper.

He switched on the reading lamp in his study and searched the shelves for the book he wanted. In the end he found it among a complete set of the works of Charles Dickens.

'Are you suggesting,' said Mr Fortescue, 'that Colonel Mounteagle intends to blow up the Houses of Parliament?'

'That's right.'

'And you found this in *A Child's History of England*?'

'It was the only book I could lay my hand on quickly,' said Mr Behrens apologetically.

It was not yet six o'clock in the morning but Mr Fortescue was dressed in the pinstripe trousers and black coat appropriate to a senior bank official. Also he had shaved, which was more than Mr Behrens had done. He turned his attention to the book and read it once again.

'"*Lord Mounteagle, Tresham's brother-in-law, was certain to be in the House; and when Tresham found that he could not prevail upon the rest to devise any means of sparing their friends, he wrote a mysterious letter to this Lord and left it at his lodging in the dusk, urging him to keep away from the opening of Parliament."* So Tresham has nothing to do with our Norfolk fisherman?'

'Nothing at all. Tresham is probably something Calder heard the colonel saying when he shot Cairns.'

'Then you think Cairns is dead?'

'I'm afraid so.'

'The whole thing is unthinkable. Totally unthinkable. And yet—'

Now that he was getting used to it, Mr Fortescue seemed to be finding the idea of the wholesale destruction of the legislature more interesting than shocking. 'An outrageous idea. How would one set about it?'

'It's some sort of automatic pilot with a receiver at the other end to guide it.'

'Then has something been planted in the House?'

'I fancy the receiver will be going there tonight. In Pocock's car. That would be what the colonel was up to when Pocock heard burglars.'

'How could he be certain that Pocock would be there tonight?'

'It's the debate on Common Market finance. His pet subject. He'll be there early and stay late.'

'Well, we can soon see if you're right. We'll call on Pocock. And we'll take Brackett with us. If he finds this gadget in Pocock's car, do you know, I shall be almost inclined to believe you.'

'He could hardly have chosen a more appropriate day for it,' said Mr Behrens. The calendar on Mr Fortescue's desk had not yet been turned from the previous day. It showed November 4th.

An hour later, as the milkman and the postman were delivering their wares, three men stood in Mr Pocock's garage and watched the fourth at work. Major Brackett, who looked like a dyspeptic bloodhound and was the top electronics expert in the Ministry of Defence, was lying on his back under the car. He said, 'It's here all right. Wired on to one of the cross-members. A very neat job.'

He eased his way out, stood up, and wiped a drop of oil from his nose.

'That's all right then,' said Mr Fortescue. 'All we have to do is switch it off.' And when Brackett said nothing, 'Well, isn't it?'

'I'm afraid not,' said the Major sadly. 'Once this jigger's set and on beam, if you turn it off, or interfere with it in any way, you activate the switch at the other end, and your barge load goes up.'

'I think, Major,' said the Home Secretary, 'that if you could explain, in terms simple enough to be understood by someone like myself who knows nothing about electronics, then we might be able to see our way more clearly.'

Apart from Major Brackett, his audience consisted of the Police Commissioner, the head of the Special Branch, Commander Elfe, Chief Superintendent Baker in charge of River Division, and Mr Fortescue. Mr Behrens was sitting unobtrusively in the background.

'Well,' said the major, 'there are a number of different ways of detonating explosives at a distance.'

'As we know,' said Elfe grimly.

'The simplest is a pair of linked sets. Master and slave, we call them. The master emits an impulse which increases in strength as the two sets come together. When they are a predetermined distance apart the stronger "kills" the weaker one. This throws a switch, and the explosive goes up.'

'I'm with you so far,' said the Home Secretary.

'It can be linked to an automatic steering device. We've developed one recently, on the ranges at Bovington. It steers an old tank filled with explosive into an enemy strong point and detonates it when it gets there. In fact, if Mounteagle has managed to get hold of the latest box of tricks, there's an additional jigger which not only keeps the tank on a predetermined course but allows it to side-step obstacles. It's done with an "eye"—a photocell connected with a microprocessor that registers changes of light striking the cell and takes the appropriate action.'

'Does that mean that Mounteagle need never go on board at all? Suppose he's fixed the slave set to go off at—what? Fifty yards? That would be about the distance from the edge of the embankment to the car park under the House. Then he could leave it to steer itself downstream.'

'I doubt he'd do that,' said Baker. 'The barge would call too much attention to itself, zig-zagging down the river like a pinball. He'll surely take it down as far as he can by manual steering—at least until it's dark. Any time after that, I agree, he could leave it to its own devices.'

For a moment the men in the room were silent. They were watching a steel craft, packed with enough explosive to tear the top off a mountain, sliding downstream in the darkness, steering under bridges, avoiding other boats, obedient only to the beckoning of its master in Parliament.

The Home Secretary said, 'Where is it now?'

The Commissioner said, 'Our last report was Bell View Lock below Runnymede. The colonel was certainly on board then. He was making about four miles an hour.' He was studying a map that Baker had produced. 'Say it's dark by seven. If he keeps up that speed he'd be ten miles above Westminster by then.'

'The tide'll be against him when he gets below Teddington,' said Baker. 'He won't make more than three miles an hour after that.'

Everyone did some mental arithmetic.

Elfe said, 'Then H-hour could be either side of ten o'clock.'

'Is there any chance,' said the Home Secretary, 'of getting someone aboard *after* the colonel's left and reverting to—what did you call it?—manual steering.'

'If you tried that,' said Brackett, 'you'd almost certainly send the whole lot up. No. I'm afraid there's only one answer. Put the master set from Pocock's car into a police launch and lead the barge out to sea. Safe enough if the launch keeps two hundred yards ahead. Have an experienced man in charge.'

'I'll take it myself,' said Baker. 'That is,' he added with a grin, 'if the major will come with me in case of any—er—technical hitches.'

'I was afraid you were going to say that,' said Brackett, looking sadder than ever.

'Very well, gentlemen,' said the Home Secretary briskly. 'That seems to be the best plan. You have total authority to clear the river of craft, and take any other precautionary measures you think necessary. I assume that Mounteagle plans to bolt abroad. You'll take the usual steps to block the exits.'

The Commissioner said, 'It occurs to me, Home Secretary, that if we succeed in taking the barge out to sea and destroying it, we shall have very little real evidence left. Suppose he decides to brazen it out.'

'He'll have to brazen out one murder and one attempted murder,' said Mr Fortescue coldly. 'Calder recovered sufficiently an hour ago to tell us what happened at Petheridge.'

'When you're dealing with a madman,' said the Home Secretary, 'it's impossible to predict what he'll do.'

Mr Behrens disagreed, though he felt it was hardly his place to say so. He thought he knew exactly what the colonel was planning to do.

At ten o'clock that night Mr Behrens was sitting, alone, on a bench on a hilltop on the northern fringe of London. In front of him, and below him, a million lights twinkled through the misty darkness. There were smaller lights, which were windows and lamp standards and motorcars, and larger lights which were bonfires. The nearest was a quarter of a mile below the point where he was sitting. He could see the dark figures congregated round it like priests at a ritual burning, and he could see, lashed to a stake on top, the grotesque parody of Guy Fawkes, the first great pyrotechnic.

A rocket sailed up into the sky and burst in clusters of red and yellow lights.

Mr Behrens had chosen this particular place because he had remembered something Mr Calder had once told him and he was convinced that Colonel Mounteagle, if he avoided immediate capture, would come there too.

A bronze plaque, set in a stone pillar beside the bench, was the reason for his certainty.

'Parliament Hill Fields,' it said, 'so named because the conspirators who, in the year 1605, planned to blow up the Houses of Parliament, escaping to the north, halted their horses at this spot to observe the outcome of their device.'

With his strong sense of history, the colonel must surely come to that spot to observe the outcome of his own more powerful and sophisticated device.

Mr Behrens was wondering exactly what the colonel had planned to do, and what he would have done but for the unfortunate contretemps at Petheridge. There were several ways in which he might have escaped detection. On the supposition that the original barge would be destroyed beyond any possibility of identification, he needed only to have a duplicate ready filled with explosive, of which he had no doubt already accumulated a stock at his works, waiting for him below Tower Bridge. He could then proceed quietly on his way with this and turn a bland face of innocence to the world. Suspicion, yes. But proof would turn on a number of imponderables, such as whether they could prove the acquisition by the colonel of the self-steering device.

It was at this moment that Mr Behrens heard a car draw up and stop on the road above him. A door slammed. Footsteps came crunching down the cinder track towards the seat. Mr Behrens had never met the colonel, but he had been shown photographs of him, and in the dying light of the rocket he had no difficulty in recognizing him.

The colonel stood for a long minute, in silence, staring down at the scene below. Mr Behrens stood up, and the movement caught the colonel's eye. He turned his head.

'A magnificent spectacle, is it not?' said Mr Behrens.

The colonel grunted.

'But I fear that the main attraction has been cancelled. Owing, you might say, to a technical hitch. When it does take place, it will be some miles offshore, and with a very limited audience.'

The colonel was motionless, a black figure outlined against the night sky. When he spoke his voice sounded quite easy. He said, 'Who are you, little man?'

'I doubt if this is really a moment for introductions,' said Mr Behrens. 'I am a very old friend of one of the men you shot last night. Not Cairns, the other one.'

'The Government spy.'

'I suppose that's as good a description as any.'

'And what do you propose to do about it?'

The colonel had swung round now, but both his hands were visible, hanging idle by his side. Mr Behrens moved towards him until he was quite close, watching the colonel's hands all the time.

He said, 'It seemed to me that there was only one logical end to this matter, Colonel. You come up here to witness the success of your plan. Being disappointed in its failure—we may assume by now, I think, that it has failed—you decide to take your own life.'

So saying, Mr Behrens shot Colonel Mounteagle neatly through the heart. He had removed the silencer from his gun, being confident that the noise of the shot would arouse no interest on this particular night. He stooped over the crumpled body, pressed the muzzle against the entry point of the bullet, and fired again. Then he wiped the gun carefully and pressed it into the colonel's right hand.

A salvo of rockets soared up into the sky, and burst almost overhead with a loud crack and a shower of silver rain.

Final Demand

He was one of the growing handful of so-called 'moles' which have surfaced since Mr Le Carré gave that word a new meaning and turned it into common coinage. Like the rest, an academic gone sour; an old and pathetic would-be-spy. Years ago, the security services had identified him and, for reasons best known to themselves, implied tacit immunity from prosecution in return for what little information he'd been prepared to give concerning his fellow-traitors. Young and enthusiastic Members of Parliament, young and enthusiastic journalists had recently forced the Pandora's Box and for a few days given this wretched creature anti-hero status. I watched him and wondered why. These hounds baying at his heels hadn't even known the war; to them Hitler was little more than a sinister version of Charlie Chaplin; they'd read contemporary history, slanted this way or that, and from words penned by literate fools they claimed to 'know'.

Did ever such crass ignorance masquerade as informed information!

This man knew. The miserable, chicken-necked, wispy-haired ancient who stared from sad and puzzled eyes. *He* knew. Not the fighting war; not the tank battles or the misery of infantry warfare; not on the sea or under the sea; not in the air. This one had fought his war behind a desk and with maps; a war of reports and communiqués and the interception of enemy intelligence. He'd been privy to great secrets. At times, he'd known more about enemy troop movements than many in the German High Command. And in his own way he'd fought a good war: by his yardstick an honourable war. And now he was perplexed beyond understanding, because what he'd done had been moulded into a political shuttlecock by men whose persuasion was not too far removed from what his own had been.

'The common enemy.' His voice was high-pitched and weak with age. 'They *were* the common enemy.'

I smiled and nodded.

'Churchill said so, many times.'

'The Red Army was never part of the Allies,' I reminded him gently. 'It was a friendship of historical convenience. Nothing more.'

'More than that.' He pushed himself from the armchair. It seemed to take a great physical effort; the placing of his hands on the arms of the chair and the slow, deliberate levering of his skinny body into an upright position. As he walked to the window he said, 'It was much more than that.' Huge windows, floor to ceiling high and curtained by velvet drapes.

He raised a hand, parted the curtains, and the room lighting was subdued enough for us to see the covering of snow reflecting the frost-brightness of the full moon.

'A white Christmas,' he murmured sadly. 'It doesn't often happen.'

'The theory is,' I said, 'that in passing information to the Red Army you jeopardized the lives of Allied troops.'

'You know that isn't true.'

'That, in effect, two wars were being fought. A war waged by the Allies and a war waged by Russia.'

'I'm not a soldier,' he sighed. 'I never was. A civilian in uniform. A man blessed with certain gifts . . . no more.'

'Certain passions. Certain beliefs.'

'I was young.' He lowered his hand and allowed the curtains to fall back into place. He turned and sighed. 'God, I was young . . . once. We *all* had beliefs. Passionate beliefs. Discussions into the small hours. Arguments. Counter-arguments. We'd travelled a little. Germany. Fascism. We knew what it meant. All *we* had was Chamberlain.'

He walked slowly back towards the fire; short, shuffling steps, with the soles of his shoes making soft scuffles along the surface of the carpet's pile. He turned his back to the deep stepped, flagged hearth, and the dog grate with its spitting, blazing logs. The low lighting allowed the flames to catch the sheen of leather from the books on shelves which occupied the whole area of one wall. An old man. An old fool. Despite his near-genius in certain academic disciplines, an old fool. Communism and this. The burning beliefs of Lenin, coupled with this degree of affluence. Utterly incompatible, but he couldn't see it. He'd never been able to see it.

He placed his hands in the pockets of his jacket, thumbs hooked over the front of the pocket tops. His feet were slightly apart. Despite the hunched shoulders and the bowed head, a typical 'English gentleman'

stance. It was there. The inbred arrogance; the divine right of superiority. But the voice belied the stance. The stance was the end-product of
training and ancestry. The voice—the tone—was the result of decades
of self-doubt and indecision.

'What I did, I did well. Not for money. *You* know I didn't do it for
money. Hitler was foul. All he stood for. The whole Nazi philosophy.
Foul! He had to be stopped. Somehow he had to be stopped. We—we
in this country—*we* couldn't stop him. I believed that. In the event I
think I was mistaken, but at the time that was my genuine belief. We
needed friends. Powerful friends.'

'Russia?' I smiled.

'It seemed possible.' He raised his head and looked at me with lack-
lustre eyes. 'We speak the truth, of course?'

'We speak the truth,' I agreed.

He removed a hand from its pocket, moved it in a vague gesture, then
said, 'The isolationist lobby in America. A weighing of the pros and cons.
Russia had stopped the German advance across Poland. Stalin was
nobody's fool. Therefore . . . Russia.'

He returned the hand to its previous position in his jacket pocket.

'The beliefs?' I murmured. 'The political truths?'

'Ah, those "political truths"!' He'd lowered his head once more, and
he smiled a whimsical smile, as if sharing a secret joke with the carpet a
few feet from the toes of his shoes. 'We believed them. To us that's what
they were. Truths. As simple, as fundamental, as two and two adding up
to four. We subscribed to them. We paid homage to them. Preached them
as a new religion.' He paused and in a softer voice said, 'We even committed treason in their name.'

'And now you fault them,' I accused.

'No.' He moved his head slowly. A gentle shake. A mild reproof. 'Not
the "truths". Their application. What they led to.'

'But the truths?' I teased.

'Lenin was rather like Christ.' He seemed to rouse himself a little; to
force his scattered thoughts into something like order. There was a new,
but gentle, assurance in his tone as he continued. 'The Ten Command-
ments. A measure of perfection, but at the same time a measure of the
impossible. Lenin, too. It *should* be possible, but it discounts human
nature. Unfortunately in those days we were too young, too unworldly,
to see the flaws. We thought the impossible was attainable. We were
the new disciples. All we needed was enthusiasm and an unshakeable
belief . . .'

I eased the truth from him, admission at a time. It was unnecessary, mere curiosity on my part. I could have written the scenario without his help; there was no real deviation from the standard pattern.

A brain too active for its own good. A mind choked with high principles. Youthful enthusiasms beyond control. And, finally, a war; a common enemy; a ready-made peg upon which to drape a dream.

From Military Intelligence it had been a short step to the secret world of true espionage and counter-espionage. He'd had a mentor, but hadn't realized it. In the immediate post-war chaos it was easy enough to arrange one short trip to Vytegra, and there the facts of life had been explained. Two days in which to ensure he realized his position. In a civilized manner, of course. With subtlety. Not blackmail; nothing as crude as blackmail. Given intelligence, the victim can reach an appreciation of his own position without overt threats. His mentor did an excellent job. His mentor: in popular parlance his 'spy-master'.

Thereafter, it had been easy.

He still thought (to use his own words) 'the impossible was attainable'. He was encouraged in that belief; taught to ignore the street-corner rantings of militant reds whose loud-mouthed exaggerations do harm to the cause of International Communism. His was the gentle way. The secret way. The non-revolutionary way.

That unknowingly he lived within the ivory tower of his own stratum of society gave him ready-made immunity from suspicion. It really was ridiculously easy, and he really was ridiculously safe. Needless to say, he remained unaware of all this. It was a blind spot, recognized as such and utilized as such. The painter of miniatures rarely recognizes the skills of an interior decorator. We are all blind. The craft of the manipulator is based upon the ability to keep hidden what we already can't see.

His reputation with the British Government increased. He was promoted and, with promotion, his sphere of influence increased. His advancement as a Russian agent paralleled his growing responsibility within the British Secret Service. He was honoured by both countries. Secretly, of course. The British Government could not openly acknowledge his position in the undercover war, any more than the Kremlin could openly recognize him. To the world in general he was little more than a cypher —a near-unknown name and a man who became more and more of a recluse—but a cypher with immense power. His administrative and organizational abilities amounted to something approaching genius; the twin networks of agents—British and Russian—would have baffled and tripped a lesser mind.

That at his peak . . . until Philby unstopped the bottle and let the genie loose.

'A fool,' he sighed. 'A fool, weakened by fleshpots. He saw danger at every turn. Eventually he ran for it.'

'And allowed the investigators in.'

'Quite.'

The impression was that the talk had weakened him. He was an old man. This winter—this 'white Christmas' he'd mentioned—could end him. He had few friends. To be friends with this man after the questions in Parliament, after the newspaper revelations, after the nationwide scandal, was to be ostracized. To be excluded from so-called 'decent society'. Left, he would die alone and unmourned. I allowed myself the luxury of pitying him.

'You could have denied everything,' I said. 'Blunt and his friends were small fry.'

He moved his shoulders, took his hands from his pockets and slowly —almost creakingly—lowered himself back into the armchair.

'They couldn't have named you,' I added.

'No.' The agreement was accompanied by a slow, sad smile.

'In effect, you allowed yourself to be crucified. Why?'

'I allowed the would-be-executioners to pick up the hammer and count the nails, no more.'

'You told them . . .'

'Nothing they didn't know. Nothing they couldn't guess.' He seemed to drag a spurt of verbal energy from some hidden reserve. 'Compared with what I *could* have told them.'

'Of course.'

'What *you* could tell them.'

I nodded silent agreement.

'You,' he said with a smile, 'are of the new school. After Philby there was a great scattering . . . I don't have to tell you that. The creation of a new network, of which I was not a part.'

'It was necessary.'

'Indeed.' He even found strength enough for a gentle chuckle. 'I have often visualized it. The abandonment of this project and that. The closing of doors. The hurried destruction of cells and lines of communication. Many men must have lost many hours of sleep.'

'It was necessary,' I repeated.

'I could have told so much,' he said dreamily. 'So much more than I *did* tell. I could have told them everything.' He raised his head, and asked, 'Had I done so, what then?'

'Bigger headlines,' I suggested. 'Other than that, what has already been done.'

He moved his head as if satisfied.

'You could still tell them,' I said gently.

'What *was* . . . not what *is*.'

'The basics.' The man was a has-been; a husk of his former self. But he had once been great, therefore he deserved respect. I said, 'You have wisdom. You have experience. The basic structure can never be changed overnight. It takes years. Decades. Only the names—the individuals— can be replaced. The sleepers activated. The couriers switched. Links re- established. The foundations can never be altered. The spheres of influence remain the same.'

'Thank you.'

He moved his head. It was a strangely old-world gesture; a token bow of appreciation at my honesty. I returned the silent compliment. We were equals. Not at that moment, perhaps, but when we were both dead we would be remembered with equal affection as architects of the same cause. He linked his fingers; thin, fleshless fingers covered with translucent skin as thin and pale as fine parchment. He leaned back in the chair and closed his eyes. His voice, high-pitched and as weak as ever, droned softly as if he was talking to himself.

'I am, of course, conscious of the fact that you have visited me personally.'

'Your reputation—your past reputation—deserves nothing less.'

'Nevertheless, I thank you. A visit from a murder squad would have pained me. Would have bruised my ego . . . what I have left.'

'We're not uncivilized.'

'Of course not.'

'We honour our debts, whenever possible.'

'I would have been disappointed, had it been otherwise.' He paused, then continued, 'We have talked. You have asked me questions, and I have answered those questions. Many questions. Many answers. But as you know—as you must know from your long training—an interrogator must give in order to receive. The questions themselves have been an inverted form of answer. Informative. To be able to ask those questions is proof of personal knowledge.'

'You were always wily,' I chuckled. 'Always cunning.'

'Still am.' The eyes opened, and there was life in them which had been absent before. I felt the hardness touch my spine as he warned, 'Your hands where we can see them, please. I and my colleague—who will, I assure you, cripple you for life without hesitation should the need arise. Not kill you. We need you alive. We need your tongue.'

'Defector!' I forced myself to remain calm, but I could not rid that one-word accusation of the contempt it deserved.

'No.' He smiled a sad but triumphant smile. 'Now, *I* can be honest. Your friends are no longer waiting in the car. They are already in custody. As for defection? I never *was* your man . . . not even at the beginning. A double-agent? Yes, but for *my* country not *yours*. The façade of being "exposed". Why not use it? Why not accept the gift Philby and his friends offered?'

Expert hands tapped my pockets and removed the Luger I'd waited too long to use.

'The Russian mind.' Again the smile came and went. 'A complex thing. What I'd done—what you *thought* I'd done—deserved more than a back-alley killing. I was a danger therefore I had to go. But the manner of my elimination deserved the outward appearance of dignity. Somebody of my own status. Somebody of the status I once enjoyed. Quick, but with the final knowledge that the *coup de grâce* had been administered by an equal.' He moistened his bloodless lips. I watched his eyes more closely than before, and in the depths I glimpsed the secret of his greatness. His voice was almost bored as he said, 'Our conversation. Taped, of course. A base-line for future conversations. Sadly, you will never be part of an exchange arrangement. Accept my assurance upon that. You will disappear . . . forever. I, too, will disappear. This evening has ended my usefulness. For the rest of our lives we will continue our conversation. Months. Years, perhaps. It will be interesting . . . and informative.'

'Not for long.' My composure had returned. I could match him, calmness for calmness. 'My absence will cause immediate . . .'

'Long enough,' he interrupted. 'Road accidents. Your detention in hospital. If necessary, a report of your death. Unidentified, of course. Your masters may worry but—the nature of our unique game—they will never acknowledge your existence. It gives us time. They panic a little. We talk. They won't dismantle until they're sure. And . . .' Again the quick, almost childish chuckle. 'There are others. Like me. They, too, can be "exposed" when the time is ripe. When—what was it?—when sleepers are once more activated, when couriers have once more been switched, when other links have been established. Such work! Such activity! And in the long run all for *our* benefit.'

I allowed the two strangers to lead me from the room. I made no resistance. Pain, for the sake of pain, is no answer and I knew they would not kill me. I could feel the eyes of the old fox watching me. No matter. It was part of this most ignoble of professions; part of this never-ending game of move and counter-move. A game invented by the English during the Napoleonic Wars. Unlike the Americans—unlike my own country—unlike any other nation on earth, they have learned to play it with gentle but consummate skill.

TED ALLBEURY

The Rocking-Horse Spy

As he sat on the bench in the Science Museum watching Robbie turn the handle of one of the glass-cased models, he wondered why his day with his son never seemed to come up to his expectations. The place was full of men like him—divorced fathers with 'access' on alternate Saturdays. There was no chance of being a real father. If he asked questions about what the boy did at home it was called 'snooping', trying to find out what she was up to. And there was just a very faint element of truth in the accusation. But if you couldn't be a real father, what could you be? A pal? What eight-year-old boy wants a forty-year-old pal? He thought about him so much when he wasn't with him but, somehow, it never seemed possible to express his feelings to the boy when they were together. Access Saturdays had become a grim, arid desert of frustration and disappointment. But the small boy seemed to take it in his stride.

Patterson smiled to himself as he watched his son, one stocking down to his ankle, his face intent on the wheels of the model turning slowly. A small girl walked up and stood watching with a man who was obviously her father. There was a second handle to the model, that worked a crane, and the girl reached out to turn it. Then to his dismay his son roughly pushed aside the little girl. 'Go away,' he shouted. 'This is mine.'

He hurried over. 'Apologize at once, Robbie. Say you're sorry.'

'I'm not sorry. This is my model.'

'Say you're sorry or we shall leave right away.'

The man with the small girl smiled diffidently. 'It's OK. It doesn't matter.'

Patterson caught his son's arm, swinging him round to face the girl.

'Say it. Say you're sorry.'

For a moment there was defiance then Robbie said reluctantly, 'I'm sorry.'

Patterson turned to the man. 'I'm sorry he was rude to your little girl.'
He smiled. 'This is his favourite model but that's no excuse.'
The man smiled. 'I understand.' He shrugged. 'They are just children.'
'How about we all go to the café upstairs and have an ice-cream?'
'It's not necessary—really.'
'I'd like to.'
The man shrugged and smiled. 'OK. Let's do that.'
As they sipped their coffees Patterson looked at the girl's father. His
clothes were old-fashioned and his thin woollen tie had an untidy knot
at his throat. His face was out of some Dickens novel. Large spaniel eyes,
a full mouth; it was the face of a sad comedian.
When the children had eaten their ice-creams and were playing a guess-
ing game, the two men were having a second coffee and Patterson said,
'Are you an "access father"?'
The man frowned. 'I don't understand. What is an "access father"?'
When Patterson had explained the other man said, 'My wife was killed
in a car accident six months ago. But, like you, I think I am a poor father.'
He smiled diffidently. 'Plenty of love but no practical experience.'
'You speak very good English but you've got a slight accent.'
The man smiled. 'Part French, part Russian.'
'Have you lived here long?'
'Nearly a year now. I'm a freelance journalist. I write about electron-
ics and computers.'
'Who do you write for?'
'Magazines, newspapers.' He smiled. 'Anyone who'll take my stuff.'
'Is that why you come to the Science Museum?'
The man laughed. 'No. We generally go to the Natural History Museum
but it's closed today for building work.'
'Have you been to the zoo yet?'
'No.'
'How about we take the children to the zoo in two weeks' time? That's
when I have Robbie again.'
'Why not? Where shall we meet?'
'Let's meet at the main entrance to the zoo at one o'clock.'
'Fine. I'll look forward to that.'

There was a message for him at the security desk. He was to go imme-
diately to Logan's office.
He was surprised when he saw that it was not only Logan but also
Chester and Harris who were waiting for him.

Logan pointed to a spare chair. 'Sit down, Patterson.'

When he was seated Logan leaned forward, his elbows on his desk. 'Where were you on Saturday?'

Patterson looked surprised. 'I had my son for the day.'

'Where did you go?'

'We had a snack at a hamburger place in Kensington. We went to a museum and then I took Robbie home.'

'Which museum was it?'

'The Science Museum.'

'Why did you go to that particular place?'

Patterson shrugged. 'What the hell is all this?'

'Why did you go there?'

'We go there frequently. My boy likes it there.'

'Tell us about Malik.'

'Who the hell is Malik?'

'You talked with him for nearly an hour in the museum café.'

Patterson explained what had happened and Logan said, 'What did you talk about?'

'His daughter and my son.' He shrugged. 'Just social chit-chat.'

'Didn't his name ring a bell?'

'I didn't ask his name. Why should I?'

'His name's Malik.'

'So what?'

'He's a Russian. Suspected KGB.'

'He told me he was a technical journalist.'

'He is. That's his cover. What else did he tell you?'

'Nothing. But we're taking our kids to the zoo in a couple of weeks' time.'

'Who suggested that?'

'I did.'

'Why?'

For the first time in the interview Patterson felt a surge of anger but he said quietly, 'Because it's very difficult, and rather lonely, trying to entertain a small child for a day and doing it as a foursome with someone with the same problem makes it easier.'

'Was that the only reason?'

'For God's sake. What other reason could there be?'

Before Logan could reply, Chester intervened. Chester was the senior of the three of them.

'What were your impressions of the Russian, Mr Patterson?' Chester spoke quietly and calmly and looked as if he would value Patterson's opinion.

'He seemed a quiet sort of man. Polite. Spoke excellent English. Obviously loved his little girl.'

'Did you like him? Did you feel you could get on with him on a friendly basis?'

'I didn't think about him that way. He was just a casual acquaintance.'

'I think your meeting could be very helpful.' Chester turned to look at Logan. 'I'd like to suggest that Mr Patterson takes over the surveillance of our friend Malik. He's in an ideal position to keep a close eye on him.'

Logan obviously resented the interference of his senior but agreed without protest to the new arrangement.

Patterson sat in his own office and read the details on Malik's file. He was forty-two. Born in Moscow. Languages at Moscow University and a science degree at Leningrad. Had served for six years at their embassy in Washington. Wife died in car collision in Kiev. One child. Father Russian. Mother French. There was little else beyond the surveillance reports.

The reports showed that he had contacted a wide span of high-technology industries in the UK and France. But it was no more than any conscientious science writer would have done. But equally, they were exactly the targets that a KGB man briefed to get secret technological information would have aimed at. A casual observer would never have seen Malik as an enemy agent but Patterson had been in MI5 too long to go by appearances. They didn't have to have their eyes close together or horns growing out of their foreheads. All too often they looked like your Uncle Charlie. And after all they probably *were* somebody's Uncle Charlie. Or Ivan, or Igor. Or in Malik's case, Grigor.

It was a fine day for the visit to the zoo and the children got on well together. Malik and Patterson sat on a bench in the sunshine as the children watched the sea-lions being fed. It was Malik who seemed to want to talk.

'My name's Malik. Grigor Malik. What's yours?'

'Patterson. Joe Patterson. Joe.'

'Shall I call you Joe?'

'Of course.'

'You live in London?'

'Yes. In Chelsea. A couple of rooms. And you?'
'I live in Chiswick.' He smiled. 'I've got a girl-friend. If things work out, maybe we get married. Maria likes her very much. It's her small house where we live. She's very kind to us both.' He nodded as he smiled. 'I like her very much.' He paused. 'I'd like you to meet her.'
'I'd like that, Grigor.'
'We could go back there for tea today. I told her I might bring you and the boy back, if you agreed.'
'Fine. I'd enjoy that.'
'Do you have a new girl?'
'A few girl-friends but nothing serious.'
'You're not lonely, living alone?'
'Sometimes. But I get by.'
'How long have you been divorced?'
'Two years.'
'Is she married again?'
'Yes.'

The small terraced house in Chiswick was neat and well-kept. More or less what he had expected. But the girl-friend Kathie was a surprise. Irish, very pretty, lively and in her mid-twenties. And she obviously adored Malik and his daughter.

The children were playing in Maria's bedroom and the three of them sat around talking. Music and books.

She laughed, putting her hand on Malik's arm as she looked at Patterson. 'This one's a romantic. So it's Russian music and French novels. Proust and Flaubert with Rachmaninov and Tchaikovsky in the background.' She turned to look at Malik. 'Did you tell Joe about the rocking-horse?'

Malik smiled. 'No. You tell him.'

Kathie smiled. 'He's seen one of those beautifully carved rocking-horses and he's tempted to buy it for Maria. Do you know how much they cost? Three hundred pounds. It's crazy. He's going to borrow it from a bank.' She smiled at Malik affectionately. 'He's a big softy, this man.'

Malik smiled. 'That's what fathers are for, my love.'

The rocking-horse had been bought and the little girl's delight was obviously well-rewarding to Malik.

All through the summer Patterson had been a regular visitor to the house in Chiswick. Sometimes with Robbie and sometimes alone. In the early days he had found it disturbing to have such a close relationship with a man he was investigating. But as time went on and he was convinced that Malik was what he claimed to be—a journalist—he relaxed. He was aware that Malik had never revealed his nationality but there was no occasion when it would have been particularly appropriate. Robbie enjoyed his time with Maria and the Chiswick house had become almost a second home for both of them.

Patterson found it irksome when Logan congratulated him on his achieving such a close and useful relationship with a suspect. It made him aware of his own duplicity both to Logan and to Malik.

He had had long talks with the people who Malik had talked to at the various high-tech companies. There was no doubt that he was persuading people to give him information far beyond what was needed for genuine technical articles. And in some cases Malik had pretended to be a French national. But subterfuge and even deceit were not unknown to ordinary journalists. And he suggested this when submitting his reports to Logan. But Logan didn't share his views. For him Malik was a spy, an industrial spy maybe, but a spy all the same. Industrial espionage was part of the KGB's function in the West. They saved the Soviet Union billions of roubles in research costs, stealing from the NATO allies just as purposefully as they tried to undermine the fabric of western society.

Because of his views on Malik he was not consulted on the department's evaluation of his reports. He was shocked when he saw the piece on the front page of the *Evening Standard* which said that three suspect Russians were being held on suspicion of spying. There were grainy pictures of all of them and one was of Malik. The *Daily Mail* the next day reported that the three Russians were being expelled.

In his time in MI5 he had been responsible for the prosecution and imprisonment of many people but they had been virtual strangers. Objects of suspicion, people to be kept under surveillance from a distance. He knew little about the effect of his work on their lives. And he had always been convinced of their guilt. But Malik was different. When he talked to Logan about his doubts, it was obvious that he wasn't interested. The Russians had thrown out two diplomats from the British Embassy in Moscow and London wanted to retaliate. They didn't necessarily have to be guilty of anything substantial. Malik was just an easy and available victim.

Some instinct made him want to see the girl, Kathie, and on the second day he'd gone out to Chiswick and walked to the road of old-fashioned Victorian houses. As he approached number sixteen he saw a small group of people and then he saw the 'For Sale' notice.

He made his way through the people to the front door. It was open and there was a handwritten notice saying that the sale of goods was on the following day. He walked into the front room. There were rows of domestic bits and pieces each marked with a price. Kettles, a toaster, a box of cutlery, crockery, plants in pots, a radio and TV and a record-player. Rolled up rugs and carpets, small items of furniture. And on a table by the far wall was the rocking-horse. He looked at the card pasted to the leather saddle. It said: 'Not for sale. Deliver to Gt. Ormond St. Children's Hospital.' As he turned away she was standing at the door looking at him. Her eyes red from weeping.

She said, 'They told me I could put up the prices because they were souvenirs of a spy.'

'But these are your things, Kathie, and why are you selling the house?'

'Was it you?'

'Was what me?'

'Somebody must have been watching him. They let me see him in the police cell for ten minutes. He said they knew everything about him. Me . . .' She shrugged helplessly.

'Did he say that he thought it was me?'

'No. He said you were his only friend.' She paused. 'They don't care about people, do they?'

'Did you know he was spying?'

She laughed harshly. 'If he was a spy then you and I are spies. What lies they all tell.'

'If there's anything I can do to help you, will you let me know?'

'You mean you can find me a nice, gentle man who loves me, and spends all his savings on a rocking-horse for a small girl?'

'I'll call in next week.'

'I won't be here.'

'Where will you be?'

'I've no idea. But I won't be here.' And he saw the tears on her cheeks as he turned to leave.

The Russians were on *News at Ten* that night. At Heathrow. Photographers and reporters running alongside them. As they stopped at the air-side gate a reporter thrust a microphone up to the first Russian. 'Have you got any comment, Mr Kreski?' The big, sour-faced Russian said, 'This country stinks.' A girl reporter spoke to Malik. He was carrying one case and Maria. The little girl was white faced, one arm around her father's neck. 'How do you feel about being expelled, Mr Malik?' For a moment Malik was silent and then he said, 'I am very sad to be leaving. I had good friends here. We liked it here, my daughter and I. People were very . . .'

Patterson leaned forward and switched off the TV.

The Great Divide

When Rigby and Camilla Trefusis were peremptorily recalled from leave, both were surprised but neither was stricken. After a spell of particularly gruelling action, Denham had given Rigby a gracious little speech of thanks and two months' special leave to rest, and since Camilla had leave coming up anyway, the two old friends had gone together. Denham had insisted that their holiday be without distractions—both of them must unwind completely—and had himself arranged that they did so properly. A villa in northern Majorca would see to that.

The island was then unspoilt and, indeed, rather boring. This was as Denham had coolly intended, for he knew both women's habits perfectly: both could live without men and were sometimes glad to (when, in his experience, they did their most effective work), but sooner or later they'd feel the need of one, and that spelt the end of a peaceful unwinding. But in northern Majorca men would be hard to find. There was the Resident Great Man of Letters, but it was whispered that his tastes were unorthodox, and there was also a naval college quite close. But the cadets would be provincial and callow, quite uninteresting to experienced women, and the instructors married men with jealous wives. In any case, Dorothy spoke no Spanish, and though Camilla could get along in Castilian, enough to run the villa and order meals, that would scarcely cover a serious engagement with a man who spoke a debased Catalan. Denham had worked it all out very carefully with the result that, when he recalled them suddenly, they came with an almost unseemly alacrity.

In the days before a pleasant island had been ravaged by package tours and hourly flights, the journey had meant a sea-passage by night and then, unless you were lucky, a train. Both women were tired when they reached Victoria, but both went to Denham's office at once.

'You're looking very well,' he said. The women were looking jaded and knew it.

Camilla said, 'We've had a bit of a journey, you know. What's cooking?' She had an experienced secretary's right of plain speech.

'Enough for me to need you back badly. Enough for another job for Rigby.'

'An agreeable change from darkest Majorca.'

'Wait to say it,' Denham said, and watched her. He hadn't wished to spring bad news suddenly, and as her expression changed from zest to alarm he wondered whether she'd guessed the worst. Apparently she had, for she asked, 'Not India?'

'I'm afraid it is.'

She winced. 'So many memories,' she said, 'I vowed never to go back.'

'Sorry. May I give you the outlines?' he asked.

She nodded.

He spoke lucidly, for he had prepared his brief. The Prime Minister and his attendant progressives were determined to let India go. As Denham saw it, that was wholly inevitable. It might be held by suspending the rule of law and by heavily reinforcing the garrisons, but to suspend the rule of law was unthinkable and to keep British troops in a country they hated would bring even the best quite close to mutiny. So basically it was a question of how. The Cabinet didn't want to split India; it wanted to bequeath a single country, Hindu-dominated since that was the arithmetic of it, but with constitutional safeguards for Muslims caught in the new state. The Muslims, naturally, wouldn't wear that. They wanted partition and were fighting hard for it.

'And you're pro-Muslim?' Rigby asked.

'I am. But not for the usual reasons—far from it. There's a certain sort of old India hand who's pro-Muslim for the worst of reasons.' Denham mimicked an Indian Army voice. 'They're so much politer and so much more manly.' His voice returned to his own as he went on. 'That's prejudiced middle-class rubbish, of course. Are Gurkhas unmanly, or Mahrattas, or Dogras? My reason for wanting partition is better since it's political and therefore amoral.' Denham leant forwards in deliberate emphasis. '*The new Hindu state will turn to Russia so we do not want this state too big.*'

'I follow that, but what's the local form?'

'Our present and slightly improbable Viceroy, Veronica's bemedalled husband, would like to hand India over intact. He'd stay on as Governor-General of all of it and maybe get his marquisate thrown in. He gets on well with the Hindu Misra, who's an upper-class Brahmin, a Wykehamist too. Just the type to have His Excellency on a string.'

'And on the other side, the unfortunate Muslims?'

'There's Ali Khan, a quite different kettle. He isn't really a Khan by blood—it's just a kind of family name. He's a middle-class lawyer, hard as nails and, from what I hear, very tough to talk to. He puts his demands on the table and sticks to them, not the sort of thing a full General much likes. Most of the British officials detest him.' Denham added in a cool aside, 'From what I've seen of them that inclines me towards him. So he isn't on an easy wicket, but he does have one thing going for him. He has Veronica's ear, and some people say more.'

'I've heard rumours,' Rigby said.

'Discount them. The practical difficulties make a liaison near-impossible. But Veronica, bless her, has not been discreet. Her interest in the underdog is real. When she puts on one of those beautiful uniforms she isn't the Great Lady slumming. She gives money—God knows she has always had plenty of that—and she chivvies lethargic officials to get things done. So she let Ali show her how Muslims lived. Not being stupid, she's seen Hindu slums too but Misra didn't go with her. Oh, no. And she's been to Ali Khan's house for dinner. Naturally his wife was there and other suitable female guests. But her husband hasn't eaten with Misra.'

'It does sound something short of protocol, but why do you obviously think it's dangerous?'

'Because it could be used to smear Ali. That sort of thing in India can be even more lethal than it often is here. A little more rumour, something half-concrete, and Ali's fall is not unthinkable. And there's nobody to replace him, no first-class man, nobody whom the Muslims quite trust and nobody to hold them together. Partition would in effect be dead and Misra would scoop the all-India pool. The Prime Minister may want that but we don't. I told you why.'

'And where do I come into this?'

'Through Veronica, of course.'

'You want me to spy on her? That won't be easy.'

Denham didn't laugh often but did so now. 'Nothing so grotesque or corny. I want you to go to New Delhi and hold her hand. Particularly when it begins to get sticky. You're going to be her lady's maid.'

'Will she accept me as that?'

'She has. I suggested you be a Lady-in-Waiting, but she said that she had two already. Both dull as ditchwater—probably selected for that reason. I told her something of what you do and how you think. She said that another civilized woman was the nicest present I could possibly make her.'

'You must know her pretty well.'

'I did once.' Denham saw the two women exchange a glance and added smoothly, 'It was some time ago, as you probably realize.'

'She sounds a very nice woman.'

'She is. You'll get on together or I wouldn't be sending you.' His manner returned to the briskly businesslike. 'So any more questions?'

'Only the obvious. I take it I'll have no formal back-up, so what do I do if the going gets tough?'

'You go to Wayne Perkins if you need any heavy stuff. He's in Delhi too and I've fixed it up.' Denham raised his hand as he saw her stiffen. 'Yes, I know that you've brushed with him more than once. You don't quite trust him and nor do I. He's as passionately American as you yourself are devotedly British and if it comes to a conflict of interest he'll cross you. But in this case there isn't one—quite the reverse. America no more wants Misra all-powerful than I want an undivided India. And for exactly the same reason—Russia. For once I think you can trust him entirely.'

'What's he doing in Delhi?'

'He's at their embassy. Ostensibly as a Cultural Attaché, but in fact doing much the same as we are.'

'Then when do I start?'

'Tomorrow morning. RAF Dakota. Three stops. It won't be comfortable but you'll have interesting male company. And I'll give you a thorough brief on Veronica.'

'But I haven't any tropical clothes.'

'Then buy them in Delhi.'

Denham saw the two women smile, and flushed. He knew what they were thinking precisely . . . Men were impossible, wholly impossible, impractical, insensitive animals. But *pace* the sillier sort of feminist, they could make a woman's life much more interesting.

The journey had indeed been uncomfortable, but the company less amusing than Denham had thought. The crew of three had been polite and obliging, but the passengers resentful and surly. They were long-service soldiers, a replacement draft for India, and most of them had fought in Europe. They thought this posting unfair and said so; they talked, in fact, of nothing else, and the single young officer who nominally commanded them was clearly a very anxious man.

Rigby had had time to read her brief. A husband was part of Veronica's life, but there was surprisingly little solid about him and what there was seemed deliberately, almost cagily, neutral. The marriage had been the social event of the year: the youngest Brigadier in the army, ambitious and cosily well-connected, certain to race up the ladder to high command; and the biggest heiress of the decade. There were first-class minds who had reservations about Alfred, but then first-class minds had reservations about most things. He also liked money and didn't have any. That was all about Alfred and quite enough. Not everybody admired him slavishly, but nobody wished to make him an enemy.

On Veronica the brief was more detailed, but its essence could be put as shortly. The marriage had been one of convenience in the sense that it had pleased the worldly and by now had become, well, the best word was 'open'. But mostly with the greatest discretion. Divorce would have been unthinkable and Veronica held the purse strings firmly.

Rigby nodded contentedly. This woman she was going to serve would freewheel when she fancied, which was something they had in common. Denham had said she was a very nice woman and Rigby was inclined to think so too. It remained to be seen if she was also intelligent.

At the airport there were more senior officers to march away their near-mutinous drafts. Rigby came down last, alone, and was greeted by the station commander. She hadn't expected a guard of honour and even a Group Captain surprised her. He saluted with a certain deference and drove her in his jeep to another car. It was a Rolls but with normal plates and flew no flag. The driver wore breeches and leggings, and a chauffeur's cap. Another man had opened the door and stood waiting. He had the hard, alert air of a professional bodyguard. Inside the car a single woman sat stiffly. She was wearing a *yashmak*.

'Rupert Denham's friend?'

'I also work for him.'

'Then please get in.'

Rigby got in with Her Excellency.

'You must forgive this silly veil but it's necessary. If I go anywhere interesting the papers print it and my official social life is a screaming bore. I meet Lady Slip and Lady Gully. Lady Slip is the wife of some Commissioner somewhere and Lady Gully's man runs the police of a province. They both of them bend the knee to me, but both would pull my eyes out happily.'

'I'll bet they would.'

'You know the type? You've been in India?'

'Not for years. But I've met it elsewhere and I don't get on with it.'

'Then you're going to get on well with me.'

Something rather rare had happened: the two women had struck an instant empathy, one which lasted till the elder died. The rigid back began to relax and the Vicereine said, 'I saw you had only one bag—you'll need clothes. I'd love to come with you when you do your shopping, but it's exactly the sort of thing I can't do. I'll give you the least stupid of my various women. At least she knows which shops aren't phoney.'

'That's very kind.'

'It's only sensible. We can't have you walking about in London clothes, which brings me to a point of some delicacy. I take it you're not really a lady's maid?'

'I'm afraid I'm not.'

'It doesn't matter—you can go through the motions. Lay out the clothes I need for some rattle. There's a laundry, of course, but I don't want *dhobi's* itch. So I've an Indian woman who does my smalls. It's against her caste principles and she giggles obscenely.'

'Then how do you get her to do it?'

'Money. In this horrible country money does anything. Except provide attractive men. I'm afraid you'll have to put up with that. We can hold each other's hand when it gets too cruel. And there's one other thing you can do for me if you will. I don't sleep well alone and I take pills. Sometimes I take too many. It frightens me. So you're to give me two at night and take the bottle. If I ring in the night you're not to answer.'

They had come to the pretentious palace and Veronica led the way to her sitting-room. She mixed a drink and Rigby looked round the room. The first thing she saw was a framed photograph of Ali Khan. He wore a black astrakhan cap which suited him perfectly and his sharp-pointed beard had been neatly trimmed. He looked very handsome, undeniably male.

Rigby went to bed some hours later, but it took her several more to get to sleep.

Several hundreds of miles to the east of Delhi, in the sweltering slum they called Calcutta, the editor was saying firmly, 'We can't print this and you very well know it.'

'The Hindu papers have been hinting at it for weeks. Anything they can do to discredit Ali Khan . . .'

'It's not our business to smear Ali Khan, far less the wife of the Viceroy of India. Anyway, where did you get the story?'

'It was brought to us by a man called Gupta.'

'Who'll be a Bengali and therefore doubly tricky. He's trying to get us to splash the story, then he'll sell the hard facts to another paper. If there are any, which I do not credit. A discreet little flat in Delhi, indeed! And he with a house there, a wife and children. He's a public figure whose least movement is followed.'

'Men have done curious things for women.'

'And women for men—I grant you that.'

'Shall I put someone on it? Try to get details?'

'Certainly not. It isn't our cup of tea at all.'

It wasn't, the other man thought as he left. The editor had his CIE but he wanted to leave with a knighthood too.

Wayne had asked Rigby to dinner at his embassy, since anywhere else was out of the question. Dine at any of Delhi's hotels and the news that an American diplomat had been seen with the Vicereine's lady's maid would be gossip on every lip next morning. There were Indian restaurants and Chinese too, but Wayne didn't like Indian food and to eat Chinese was a certain tapeworm. Rigby had had one once and didn't intend to host another.

Wayne had begun by re-stating their common interest, which was to prevent a too-powerful Hindu state. Rigby had nodded agreement, but with a certain reserve. She hadn't doubted what Denham had told her—he and his kind thought the Prime Minister an innocent—but the Americans would have more than one motive. They had themselves once been a British colony and the chip on their shoulders was always visible, even on those of sophisticates like Wayne. He was Ivy League but still all-American. She didn't fault him for that; she was all-British herself. Now he was explaining smoothly, 'And there's the local side of it too— that's important. Apparently your Cabinet won't see it, but anything short of partition means civil war. Of course, if there's a split there'll be trouble, especially in the Punjab where they're all mixed up. But we don't think there need be general chaos. The Indian Army will probably divide peacefully, each regiment or company to its own people. If there isn't a clear-cut division there'll be bloody civil war.'

'Then what are you going to do?'

'Back Ali Khan for all we're worth.'

'How are you going to do that?'

'I can't tell you.'

'Since for once we're on the same side I don't see why not.'

'I put it to my Brass but they said no. They asked a very sensible question: had I ever double-crossed you? I said I had. They then asked

another: so why shouldn't you cheat on me?' He looked at her straightly.
'And would you?'
   'With pleasure.'
   Wayne managed a laugh and went on. 'Anyway, for a day or two, don't
believe what the papers tell you.'
   'I seldom do.'
   'In this case quite rightly. We can do a lot to boost our Ali, but we
can't save him from political suicide. He's a very poor negotiator. Some
of his demands are outrageous. There'll have to be two Pakistans and
there'll be nearly a thousand miles between them. Ali has asked for a con-
necting corridor. A thousand miles through the Hindu heartland! Naturally
that's out of the question. You British would have to hold it and you
couldn't. Even if you could, you wouldn't. It would mean British troops
staying on in India and that's about the last thing you'd stand for. And
Ali Khan won't get his partition on the maps he's now waving about like
flags. There'll have to be a Boundary Commission.'
   'Why are you telling me this?'
   He hesitated, but she could see it was calculated. 'I know why Denham
sent you here—in fact we talked it over before he did. And I hear that
you've been very successful. Veronica likes you and talks to you freely.
To put it another way, you have her ear. And so, it is widely believed,
does Ali Khan. If you should ever get an opening or can make one . . .'
   'I'll bear it in mind.'
   'He is dining at our embassy tonight. And be sure that he'll be seen
to leave it. A little brandy?'
   'Make it a big one.'

In Calcutta the respected editor was looking at a first pull of his paper.

MUSLIM LEADER DISAPPEARS

He nodded in approval. That was carefully neutral and therefore good.
Almost certainly, Ali Khan had been snatched and only one party had a
motive to do so. Was Misra privy? Very possibly not. He had plenty of
wild men and couldn't always control them. Either way, there was going
to be trouble, trouble with the biggest 'T' yet.

Ali Khan came to in a windowless room. There was a light in the ceiling with a steel grille covering it. His head ached and his legs were putty,
but he wasn't tied up and the sheets were clean. On a bedside table was
a telephone without a dial. He hesitated, but made up his mind. If he

didn't ring they'd come for him anyway. They'd be Hindus, of course, and they wouldn't be gentle.

To his astonishment the man who answered was the stereotype of the Muslim *khitmutgar*. He wore the long white coat of the upper servant, a coloured sash and a matching turban. He bowed deeply and said in formal Urdu, 'Will his Honour be taking tea or coffee?'

'Coffee with milk. No sugar, thank you.'

The servant returned with both on a silver tray. 'A gentleman wishes to speak with you, sir.'

'I'd prefer to receive him properly dressed.'

'That has been considered, sir.' The servant pointed to a door in the wall. 'Beyond that door is your private bathroom. You will find your clothes laid out when you return.'

The bathroom too was windowless (whoever had organized this knew his business) and fitted with every conceivable need. Ali took a shower and felt better. Back in the bedroom his clothes had been returned. His linen had been scrupulously washed, his suit pressed and his shoes shone brightly. He dressed and began to feel almost normal, for he was resilient as well as stubborn. He picked up the telephone and said simply, 'Ready'.

The man who came in was a European though he spoke with a New England accent. 'I apologize for the inconvenience.'

Ali Khan had thought it out in the bathroom; he'd been kidnapped but clearly not by Hindus. This man was an American . . .

Careful.

'How long have I been here?'

'Part of a night, a day and another night. We had to give you a pretty big shot to have time to be sure things worked as we hoped they would.' Wayne had been carrying a sheaf of newspapers; he put them on a table and said, 'The Muslim press is boiling over, accusing the Hindus of snatching you'. He had charm and was now using it consciously. Ali Khan in turn was half-way to trusting him. 'If you're meaning to help me, I don't see how you are.'

'Obvious, my dear fellow. Consider. Up to now you've been a party leader, but soon you'll be a Muslim hero and your hand will be better by two aces at least. But you mustn't overplay it, you know. You mustn't say that the Hindus snatched you and that you escaped by fighting your guards with bare hands. Just say that you're not sure who took you—that's the literal truth since you don't know my masters—and that suddenly they let you go. After brutal interrogation, of course. Your people will draw their own conclusions, and when you have time to read those papers you'll see that they already have. When we let you out in a couple of days you'll be very much more than a minority leader.'

'Why are you doing this?'

Wayne told him. 'Though I must warn you again—don't overplay it. Time isn't on your side, you see. The British are getting impatient and edgy, talking about your intransigence. I wouldn't put it past them to lose their cool. In which case they'll throw the whole thing at Misra and beat retreat. So you'll have to make a few sane concessions. That corridor, for instance—it's out. And you'll have to accept a Boundary Commission.'

'And if I don't?'

'Then God help you all.'

Her Excellency was chatting to Rigby. 'You're the only person I have to natter to. I know that's the reason Denham sent you and it's worked. So who was it who snatched Ali Khan?'

'I can truthfully say I don't know. But I can make a pretty good guess, and I have.'

'So have I, but it doesn't matter. Ali now ranks just one step below Allah. Unhappily he also knows it. He's throwing his weight about, being impossible. No concessions of any kind whatever. He wants the lot. My old man is getting distinctly tetchy and he has the power to recommend what's craven. Cut and run. I don't want that and nor do you.' Veronica drew a long breath and added, 'I'm tempted to take a hand in high politics.'

Rigby looked at the handsome framed photograph and then at the newly excited Veronica. She reflected before she asked softly, 'You might not find that disagreeable?'

'Some people think he's my lover already. He isn't since it hasn't been possible. But I find him very attractive indeed. That hard black beard all round his chin . . .' The Vicereine very slightly shivered. 'After partition is sealed and settled—on terms I'm pretty sure I could get—a bit of a scandal would hardly matter.' Veronica made an instinctive gesture with her lean and almost ringless hands. She seemed to be accepting a gift. 'You follow me, Dorothy Rigby?'

'Perfectly, and I'd do the same. But "a bit of a scandal" is pretty cool. What would your husband say if the skies fell?'

'Alfie? He'd be furious but he'd do nothing whatever. In fact there isn't a thing he could do.'

'Are you sure?'

'I'm very sure.' Veronica looked at Rigby and smiled. 'We've never had a joint bank account.'

The editor disliked the word but was euphoric under his creaking fan. For one thing he had been offered his knighthood, not in the Order he had secretly coveted, but his wife would be an authentic Lady and that would be good for domestic peace. And for another it looked like peace in India. There were going to be two Pakistans, East and West, and except by sea they'd be unconnected. And the Boundary Commission was arriving tomorrow.

'Peace for our time,' he said aloud, and an old god heard him and laughed derisively.

A Branch of the Service

I

I have been forced reluctantly to retire from a profession which I found of great interest and on a few occasions even dangerous because I have lost my appetite for food. Nowadays I can eat only in order to drink a little—before my meal a glass or two of vodka, and then a half bottle of wine: I find it quite impossible to face a menu, leave alone the heavy three- or even four-course meals in restaurants which my profession demanded.

I owed it to my father that I got the job I am now leaving, though he died before I was, as we call it, recruited. My earliest memories are the smells of a kitchen—they are happy memories even though I now find it a burden to eat. The kitchen was not one in my home: it was, as it were, an abstract kitchen which represented all the kitchens in which my father cooked—kitchens in England, Switzerland, Germany, Italy, and once I believe for a short while in Russia. He was a great chef—but he was never officially recognized. He moved from country to country. He was never out of a job, but he never kept a job long because he always knew better than his employer when it was time for him to leave.

Of my mother I remember nothing—I think she must always have been left behind on our travels. How I enjoyed eating in those days, yet I never learnt how to cook. That was my father's pride and secret. What I learnt were languages—never very well but a smattering of many. I could understand better than I spoke. The man who later recruited me understood that. I remember him saying, 'To understand is the only important thing. We don't want you to talk.'

You may wonder why it was necessary for me to eat large meals in order to keep my job. Even in a good restaurant one does not feel bound to eat more than two courses and one may always linger a long time over the wine. Yes, but I was supposed to be judging the food not the wine, even awarding stars to the food in the fashion of Michelin, but of course stars differently designed. I even had to inspect the lavatories.

In my father's eyes I would never have made a first-class cook, and he didn't wish me to spend my life as a kitchen help. Through an admirer of his English cooking in a little restaurant in St Albans where he worked for a year before quarrelling with his employer, he introduced me to a new organization which called itself International Reliable Restaurants Association, but before I had finished my first six months' training they changed the name. IRRA was a little putting off because of the Irish difficulties, and so they became instead the International Guide to Good Restaurants or the IGGR.

Their advertisements and their reputation rose together; at any rate for English customers, for they soon outbid Michelin. Michelin was too nationalist. Michelin awarded to Paris in those days five stars to eight restaurants, while to London they gave no five stars and only two four stars. The IGGR was far more generous, and that proved an advantage.

I had been an inspector for the IGGR for two years before I was re-cruited for special duties.

As I learnt during my training in these so-called duties we were not really interested in the number of stars or even in the cleanness of the lavatories. The people with whom we were concerned were unlikely to be found in very expensive restaurants, for costly eating can make the eater conspicuous.

'Rich eaters are not the main interest of this section,' my instructor told me, 'here we look out for an ordinary customer. Especially those who are more than usually ordinary—they are the likely ones.'

I found his lessons at first a little obscure, until he told me a story which explained one of my puzzling memories of Paris. He said, 'Of course in this section we are not concerned with police work, but all the same we have taken a hint from the French police. Do you remember the lottery sellers who used to come into the bistros and the small restaurants in France?'

'Yes. You never see them now.'

'And yet lottery selling is not illegal. They are gone because they had outlived their usefulness.'

'What was their usefulness?'

'The police showed them the photographs of wanted men—small fry, thieves and the like, and they would go from table to table looking at the faces. This gave us an idea for a rather more important work, a work which involves our ears more than our eyes.'

He made a long pause; he meant I think to arouse our curiosity, and curious we certainly were at having been taken away from tasting food and inspecting lavatories. But we were wrong. There was a gleam of amusement in our speaker's eyes. 'The lavatories are of particular importance,' he said.

'From the point of view of cleanness of course?' a novice (not me) asked.

I still had no idea what our instructor was talking about. 'No, no,' he said. 'Cleanness isn't our concern, but the lavatory is a private place if you want to exchange a word or a packet with a friend. Unless of course your friend is a woman, but we'll come to that possibility later.'

A lot of other possibilities came later.

'There are phrases in conversation that you hear in a restaurant which are worth attention. *Pas de problème* is less interesting in France where it is in such common use, but if one of your neighbours in a small unfashionable restaurant in Manchester (a restaurant which hasn't got even one star) says, "There's no problem" it's worth paying attention.'

I think that he felt among the novices a certain scepticism. He went on, 'A hundred chances to one, of course, nothing of interest—of obvious interest—will follow—but make a note. There remains the one chance. The lavatory too—though perhaps the chances there are a little greater. For example two men peeing beside each other and talking. Our organization fills a gap—an important gap in security. A house is watched—but that again is not our job. The telephone is tapped. Not our job. Even street meetings are in other hands. But restaurants—we are doing a great service to the state.'

A question came to my mind. 'But when once we have given a star to a restaurant we have no excuse to go on eating there?'

'You are wrong. Two stars might be gained for the next edition—or a star could be lost. A certain blackmail is sometimes necessary. You will always be welcome and given the best food.'

The best food—yes, that was my problem. A career of eating. Of course it didn't worry me at the beginning, and what attracted me was not so much being of service to the state as the hint of mystery about the whole affair. The phrase 'no problem' stayed like a tune in my ears.

II

Of course, when first sent on duty one made serious mistakes, but unlike other professions one was excused—even sometimes praised—for a mistake because it might have added a little to one's experience. My first bad mistake—which in any other profession would have ruined my career—happened to be concerned with a lavatory. But I would prefer to speak of my first lucky success which far outweighed my lavatory error, although that success too concerned a lavatory. The occasion took place in a three-starred restaurant, a smart one, but not too smart like the Ritz. In my first three years I was only told to take a watch in the Ritz once, the expense was too great and the chances too small. Waiters there were apt to notice strangers. I had been shown a photograph, but a very bad one, of a suspect who apparently had been seen at this restaurant more than once and was believed to be a foreigner. In his case they had already paid three experienced watchers—one a day—and they were almost ready to give up. His companion at table was always different.

Quite by chance—in our profession nearly everything is a chance—I happened to be sitting at the next table to a solitary man. Some instinct had made me choose the table next to him for I could see little resemblance to photographs I had been shown. However there was a foreign look about him, and perhaps (I might have imagined it) a look of impatience or anxiety, and his table was laid for two. He had ordered a glass of port (not a usual aperitif for an Englishman) and he lingered over it. I lingered too over my very dry Martini, trying to outlinger him.

At last the friend he was awaiting arrived—a woman. I write 'friend', but the greeting which he gave her struck me as very odd—'Pleased to meet you', that very antiquated English phrase, was spoken in a distinctly foreign accent.

For the rest of my meal there could no longer be any malingering. In my training I had been taught that I must always finish my meal and pay my bill while those whom I had chosen to watch were still eating. Of course I could spend quite a lot of time, after paying, with a coffee, but I must be prepared to leave my table a little before those I watched or a very little after. I had to keep in touch, at all costs, but avoid the suspicion of keeping them under observation.

This early experience of mine in the Royalty restaurant was a physically very painful one, for the pair whom I had chosen to watch had a large meal and I have always, as I have said, had a very small appetite. First they chose a mixed salad, then roast beef, then cheese and then to my horror, they ordered a dessert—this too was a foreign touch for in England we finish with cheese. It confirmed for me that the two were of different nationalities, and that 'pleased to meet you' had been an agreed signal. A momentary disagreement over cheese before dessert confirmed me in thinking that the man was French and the woman English.

Their conversation was mainly on the subject of Flaubert about whom the woman was writing a book. Of course it occurred to me that Flaubert might be the pseudonym of a third agent and Madame Bovary of yet another. They made no attempt to lower their voices.

'It's very good of you to see me,' the woman told him. 'I have used your great work on Flaubert a good deal, and it's very kind of you to allow me to quote from it.'

I knew little of Flaubert's life, but I began to learn quite a lot, and there really seemed nothing wrong with the couple.

'I'd have liked to see you once again and show you my text before it goes to the publisher, but I know how busy you are,' the woman said.

'Yes, I would like to see it, but I'm afraid I'm off by an early plane tomorrow. At 9.30.'

I made a mental note to check the time and destination, but I had really lost all suspicion and I would have called it a wasted day if it had not been for the cigarettes. After the meat course, when they were waiting for the cheese trolley, she offered him a cigarette.

He hesitated, and I thought he glanced at me.

'A Benson and Hedges Extra Mild,' she told him.

'Yes, I do like one of those, but do you mind—I only smoke one after I have finished eating. It's a habit.' However she took a cigarette and laid it by his plate.

'You don't mind if I smoke?' she asked.

'Of course not.'

He lit her cigarette and the cheese trolley arrived. She chose a Stilton and he chose a Brie. I chose the smallest bit of Gruyère that I could persuade the waiter to cut and shuddered at the thought of the dessert which was yet to come. I took an ice and after the apple tarts which they picked the woman took a coffee. I did the same. He seemed to have forgotten her cigarette, for he left it still unlit beside his plate. Perhaps a Benson and Hedges, I thought, was too mild for his taste. They continued to talk about Flaubert, but what they said was quite beyond me. At last the man asked for his bill and I quickly did the same, but theirs came first and I had no time to wait for it before I followed them from the restaurant. The man still carried his cigarette. Perhaps he had no intention of smoking it, but didn't wish to offend his companion by throwing it away.

At the door he said goodbye to her. She said, 'We haven't spoken at all of *Education Sentimentale*. If you could manage another meeting . . .'

'I'll certainly do my best,' he said. 'It has been a great pleasure meeting you.' When she had left he turned away towards the lavatory still carrying his cigarette. A tidy man, I thought, he's going to throw it into the toilet, but all the same a reasonless curiosity had settled in my brain. There was another reason too. I wanted to practise my new profession. A good cook progresses through his errors. A short pause and then I followed him walking as quietly as I could.

He was washing his hands when I entered and he had laid the cigarette to one side out of the way of the water—that eternal unsmoked cigarette. I snatched it and before he had time to turn I was out of the lavatory. There was no shout from behind me—only the sound of pursuing feet. At the hotel entrance I pushed the porter to one side and ran into the street. Luck was with me. A taxi had just deposited a customer. As I drove away I saw the customer rushing after me into the street followed by the waiter who was waving my unpaid bill. Poor man. I paid it later indirectly with interest by recommending the restaurant for a fourth star, which it certainly did not deserve.

In the taxi I looked more closely at the cigarette. There was an odd feeling in the centre—a kind of hardening of the tobacco, and at one end a kind of roughening in the packing of the cigarette. I was careful not to finger it more. It had already passed through three hands and was a little damp from its lavatory lodging—there seemed reason enough for all this. All the same I had learnt in my training to hand over any object however trivial belonging to a suspect, and this I did as soon as I reached the office of the International Guide to Good Restaurants. Then I sat down to write my report, and my instinct made me enclose with it the untidy cigarette.

III

I hadn't given in my report long when the telephone sounded. 'Scramble,' my chief's voice said, and I touched the button which would make our conversation unintelligible to anyone who might be tapping our line.

'The woman I feel pretty sure was English and the man French, I think, but they spoke to each other in English although they were both experts on Flaubert.'

'I think they wanted you to listen. They were proving, you might say, their innocence.'

'But are they guilty?'

'Guilty as hell. You've done a first-rate job. Come along in an hour and see me.'

When I went to him the cigarette lay torn in half on his desk in a small litter of flakes. 'Benson and Hedges Special Mild,' he said with a smile of satisfaction. 'Low in tar content, but certainly not low in valuable information.' He showed a little bit of wrinkled paper. 'A good way to conceal it,' he said, 'in the middle of a cigarette.'

'What's on it?' I asked.

'We'll soon know. Microdots and a code of course. You've done a good job. It was very acute of you to take the cigarette.'

Such a good job indeed that they forgave me several months later for a very bad mistake which also involved a lavatory.

IV

The cigarette had led us to a new suspect for our file, a doctor who had connections with the chemical industry. He was now placed under continuous surveillance; a whole team of us was employed night and day. His open practice was in a small country town not far from the factory which used him as a consultant when one of the employees went sick. He had been very thoroughly vetted by MI5, but our relations were closer to MI6 and there was a good deal of rivalry and even jealousy between the two establishments. The foundation of the international food guide was regarded by MI5 as an intrusion into their territory, and it was true that we had not passed on to them the information contained in the cigarette. Counter-espionage abroad certainly belonged to MI6, but our food guide was international and it would be inefficient to split the English section from the foreign. No watcher was employed more than once in two weeks and always at different mealtimes in order that the suspect would never become aware of a familiar face. Unfortunately for me the doctor was a man of inordinate appetite and after two months my turn came at the hour of dinner—the hour when his appetite was greatest. Unfortunately too I had suffered from a succession of heavy meals earlier. To award a star even to breakfasts had to be considered, and it was extraordinary how many people still preserved a pre-war appetite for what is still called an English breakfast as distinct from a continental one—eggs and bacon, or even worse sausages and bacon, sometimes even preceded by a helping of haddock.

I took over from his watcher outside a quite simple inn which was called the Star and Garter only half a mile from his own house. We were the only diners and I sat down at a table well away from his. I noticed he looked quite often at his watch, but he was obviously not expecting a friend for he had already chosen his meal. To my horror when I looked at the menu I found a set menu at a very reasonable price and he had ordered the first course which was an onion soup and my stomach cannot abide onions. If I left out the soup I would find myself well in advance of him and I would be out of touch with him when I finished the last course. Another watcher was stationed in sight of the door who would take over when he left, but I had to remain till then in sight of the doctor in case he was contacted during his meal. A doctor was always of course liable to a phone call when he was away from home, but the Star and Garter telephone would have been tapped as soon as we knew where he was in the habit of dining.

I allowed myself a glance at him every now and then when he lowered his eyes to the obnoxious soup. To me he looked a thoroughly honest man. Why would an honest man be mixed up with the man of the cigarette? Then I remembered he was a doctor. A doctor doesn't judge his patients. If he had attended the deathbed of a murderer that wouldn't have made him a murderer. If a priest appeared on our microdot file would he be reasonably a guilty man? The doctor finished his soup and ordered roast beef. Reluctantly I did the same. I had to keep in step, though I could already feel the effect of the onion soup. He was a slow eater and read a newspaper between bites. I was glad that he showed no interest in me. It confirmed my impression of his honesty. It was a cold night and I felt sorry for the watcher outside keeping his unnecessary vigil.

To my distress the doctor ordered an apple tart to follow. The only alternative on the little restaurant's menu was an ice-cream, but an ice-cream needs to be eaten with some speed before it melts, so I was forced to order the tart. My trouble was I suffer from acidity, and when the doctor followed the tart with a piece of cheese, I had to leave the table, for I felt the approach of diarrhoea. The lavatory was upstairs and as I left I ordered my bill, so as to be ready to leave on my return if the doctor didn't wait for coffee. If I found him with coffee I could spin out the time with a little difficulty over change and when he left my colleague would take over. 'And see him safely home to bed,' I thought with irritation at this unnecessary routine watch.

I won't go into the unsavoury details of my diarrhoea—it was a severe one and more than five minutes had passed before I went downstairs to the restaurant. I found that the doctor had gone, and I thought with relief, 'My job is over.' I would take something to ease my stomach when I got home.

As I paid my bill I remarked to the waiter, an elderly man, who, I found, was also the landlord, 'Not much custom tonight.'

'At night,' he told me, 'the bar trade's better. And we do more at lunchtime—passing motorists, but the doctor's a good regular and he likes simple food.'

I felt it my duty to enquire a little more about our suspect.

'Doesn't he ever dine at home?'

'No, he's a single man.'

'Not much custom for a doctor in a place this size?'

'There's always the flu. And babies. But of course his main work is up at the chemical factory. Two hundred men. Plenty of patients there. I hope you enjoyed your food, sir, and that we'll see you again. It's a small place but my own, and I keep a sharp eye on the kitchen.'

'I can tell that. Here is my card.'

'International Good Food Guide! My goodness! I never expected to see one of your fellows in my little place. So that's why you went to the lavatory?'

'Yes. We always inspect those. And I looked in on the kitchen on my way,' I lied. 'I could tell at a glance . . .'

'What?'

'Clean. Which I already knew from the food it would be.'

'It's very kind of you, sir. I do hope you'll come again.'

'Not for a year. In the meanwhile we'll give you a mention in the guide.'

'I'm very honoured, sir. Perhaps some of the big shots from the factory will read it.'

'What I advise you in the meantime is to have at least two menus. Perhaps then we could promote you to a star.'

'Never did I dream . . . When I tell the missus . . .'

'By the way what do they do in the factory?'

'All sorts of medicines, sir. Even cures for the hiccups they say. Me, I am content with a bit of Eno's. It serves most purposes.'

I bade him a warm goodbye and gave him a copy of the guide in which his restaurant would appear in the next edition. I was glad to be off because my stomach was still queasy and I had no further duties that day. I would go home and perhaps as the man had reminded me take a glass of Eno's.

I went outside and to my astonishment saw my fellow watcher pretending interest in a shop window across the road. He turned and saw me with equal astonishment.

'What the hell have you come out for?'

'What are you doing here?'

'Waiting for the doctor of course.'

'But the doctor's gone.'

'He hasn't passed that door.'

'Oh the hell. There must be a back door.'

'But why didn't you signal me as soon as you lost touch?'

'I had to go to the loo. I was only gone a few minutes and he wasn't there when I came down. He came in this way and I thought he'd gone out the same way and you'd be following him.'

'He must have had suspicions.'

'I took him for an honest man whatever the damned microdots said.'

'We've certainly messed things up this time.'

V

That was exactly what my boss said when I reported to him. 'You've badly messed things. You should never have left the restaurant before him. Even for a minute.'

'It was the onion soup and the tomatoes.'

'Onion soup and tomatoes! Is that what I have to tell the big chief?'

'I had diarrhoea. I couldn't stay and shit in my trousers.'

'You know I would have sacked you like a shot, if you hadn't made that splendid coup with the cigarette.'

'You needn't sack me. I resign. But I'd swear—microdot or not—that man was honest. He was no traitor.'

'Traitor is a silly word that journalists use. A traitor can be as honest as you or me. That chemical factory has connection with chemical warfare. A man can feel that chemical warfare is a betrayal of the world we have to live in. He could be fighting for something greater than his country. An honest spy is the most dangerous. He is not spying for money, he's spying for a cause. Look, that cigarette is more important than this mistake. One learns from mistakes, and you are a good learner. You have given me a good idea of how to use your mistake. He may have been suspicious of you. Or it may have been his regular drill. To go in by the front and go out by the back.'

I said, 'I can't go on. I'm sorry. I can't go on.'

'But why? This mistake of yours will be forgiven and forgotten.'

'But the onion soup. Tomatoes. And all the meat I have to eat. Garlic with the lamb. Cheese as well as dessert. Why do all these suspects have such a good appetite?'

'Perhaps it gives them time to observe the people around them.'

'But *they* never seem to get diarrhoea.'

'About your diarrhoea. I have an idea.' He paused and played with his pencil. 'Suppose we gave you a week's holiday.'

'I don't need a holiday except from onion soup, and tomatoes etc.'

'But I see a way of using them. Suppose you stayed a week at that little hotel and had all your meals there. The doctor would begin to accept you as a regular. You would consult him about your stomach. He might give you a treatment. Of course you would take nothing he gave you, for if he remained suspicious he might try to poison you. Any prescription he gave you would send on to us and we would have it examined. If there was anything dangerous about it our suspicions would be confirmed and we would close in on him.'

'And if they weren't?'

'We'd give him more time. He would need to have *his* suspicions confirmed too if he's a man with scruples. We would think of some way. A warning from somewhere would reach him. Or one of your own reports perhaps. We would watch his reactions very closely. All you would need to do is . . .'

'To eat,' I said. 'No. I've made up my mind. I can't make a career out of eating. No more onion soup, no more tomatoes, no more garlic. I resign.'

So it was that I abandoned the International Guide to Good Restaurants. Sometimes from curiosity I buy a copy of the latest number. At least I have done one good deed in my life. The little country restaurant remains as a 'mention' in the guide, though it has never received a star.

EDWARD D. HOCH

Waiting for Mrs Ryder

It was a continuing fascination with the Indian Ocean and the east coast of Africa that led Rand to remain in Cairo after his wife returned to her spring semester of lectures at the University of Reading. 'I want to spend a week or so on the islands off the coast,' he told Leila. 'Then I'll head back home.'

'It's the rainy season there,' she warned him. 'They call it the Long Rains.'

'I know. It comes and goes.'

'Like some husbands.'

Rand's destination was the island of Lamu off the coast of Kenya. He learned he could reach it by flying to an airstrip on Manda Island, only a couple of kilometers away, and taking a diesel-powered launch across the channel. He did exactly that on a Monday afternoon in late April, arriving in the middle of one of the Long Rains his wife had warned him about. Leila had studied archaeology in Egypt and traveled frequently in East Africa. He had wanted to bring her with him but her lecture schedule prevented it.

The motor ferry was waiting for him at the dock and by the time it had taken him and the other two passengers across the channel the rain had started to let up. 'Damned nuisance,' a stout man with a white moustache muttered. 'Been coming here for ten years and the rain's always the same in the spring.'

'Are you British?' Rand asked, though the accent didn't sound quite right to his ear.

'Australian, actually.' He held out his hand. 'James Count. I write travel books. Just now I'm updating our volume on East Africa. Lived a good bit in London, though. That's probably why you mistook me for British. You're a Brit, aren't you?'

'Yes, that's right.'

'Not many people come to Lamu in this season. You here on business?'
'No,' Rand assured him with a smile. 'I'm a retired civil servant. This
is just a holiday for me.'
'Do you have a hotel?'
'Someone back in Cairo recommended the Sunrise Guest House.'
'That's a good place,' James Count agreed, stroking his moustache.
Rand guessed him to be in his fifties. 'Especially in this humidity. The
rooms have ceiling fans and mosquito netting.'
'Sounds fine to me.'
The third passenger on the motor launch was a man in a white Muslim
cap and full-length white robe, carrying a closed umbrella against the
vagaries of the weather. He did not speak, and Rand suspected he did
not understand English. When the ferry docked on the Lamu side of the
channel he was the first one off.
'The Sunrise is at the top of this street,' James Count told Rand as
they came off the jetty. 'After you pass through customs go up to the
fort and turn right. You'll see it there.'
Rand found the place without difficulty and booked a room for three
nights. It seemed like a clean, well-run guesthouse with a good view of
the harbor. A sign in the reception area informed him that drugs and
spirits were prohibited and prostitutes and homosexuals were not allowed
in the rooms.
He turned on the overhead fan as he unpacked his single suitcase. Then,
seeing a bug in one of the bureau drawers, he decided to leave most of
his clothing in the suitcase after all. The shuttered windows opened wide
to the afternoon breeze off the Indian Ocean. It was a pleasant place despite
the bugs and the humidity. Leila would have liked it.
When it was time for dinner he went off along the ancient, narrow
lanes in search of a likely restaurant. He passed several Africans and white-
clad Muslims on the way, some leading donkeys and carts. Private motor
vehicles were not allowed on the island and donkey carts were obviously
a common form of transportation. The white-walled fort with its battle-
ments, nearly two centuries old, had been used as a prison through most
of the current century, according to a brochure Rand had picked up in
the guesthouse reception area. It was closed now while being converted
into a museum.
There were women in the narrow lanes along with the men and he
was surprised to see that they wore the traditional black wraparound garments without the usual Muslim face veil. He was even more surprised
at the cafe he chose for dining to find a pair of waitresses serving the

food. His waitress was named Onyx, a brown-skinned woman with western features, possibly in her forties. She spoke fair English, enough to understand his order.

'Bring me a bottle of beer, too,' he said after ordering his food.

'We have Tusker, a local beer.'

'That's fine.'

'Chilled or warm?' When she saw his expression of distaste she explained, 'Most Africans like it warm.'

'Not me. Chilled will be fine.'

The food was passable and the tables were mostly filled by the time Rand finished eating. He was thinking of phoning Leila back in Reading when he thought he spotted a familiar face at a corner table. Walking over there on his way out, he saw that he was correct.

'George Ryder, isn't it? I'm Jeffrey Rand. We met in London some years ago.' He kept his voice low, though the next table was empty.

Ryder was a handsome gray-haired man in his early fifties. He'd been a decade younger when Rand met him in the offices of Concealed Communications, overlooking the Thames. Rand was already retired from British Intelligence by that time, but Ryder was still quite active in the American CIA.

He looked up from his food and smiled. 'You must be mistaken. My name is Watkins.'

'Pardon me.' Rand continued on his way out of the cafe. If George Ryder was in Lamu on an assignment, he had violated a cardinal rule of espionage in calling him by his real name. Still, Ryder had never been a case agent to his knowledge. He sat at a desk in Langley, Virginia, and shuffled papers around.

Rand thought about it as he strolled around the town, taking in the waterfront and its surprising sights. One of the most unexpected was the large number of dhows, small sailing vessels used by Arab traders. Rand had seen them before on the Arabian and Indian coasts, but never in such profusion. Staring at them in the twilight as they rode at anchor close to shore, he was not aware of the white-robed Muslim until he spoke. 'The dhows are built and prepared at nearby villages. That is why there are so many here.'

Rand recognized the man who'd been on the ferry that afternoon. This time he carried no umbrella. 'Do you live here?' he asked.

The man nodded. 'I am Amin Shade. I buy and sell these boats.'

Rand introduced himself and they shook hands. 'This is an unusual place, more Arab than African.'

'It has a long history as an isle of fantasy and romance. It is both remote and unique, which is why it attracted your so-called hippies in the early nineteen seventies.'

Rand was staring out at the boats. 'I'd like to ride in a dhow,' he decided, admiring the sleek craft with their distinctive sails.

'That is easily arranged. Tomorrow morning I must sail to Matondoni, one of the villages where they are built. I would be pleased to have you as a companion.'

'That's very kind of you,' Rand murmured. 'What time do you leave?'

'Around ten o'clock,' Amin Shade replied. 'It is well to travel before the heat of the day, though the journey is brief. I will conduct my business, we will have a barbecued fish lunch, and return in the afternoon. I will meet you right here at ten. And bring an umbrella. It is sure to rain.'

Rand left him and continued along the shore. The people of the island certainly seemed friendly enough. After a time he left the shore and headed back north, the way he had come. Almost at once he heard the laughter of a young woman and somehow knew she was British. Hurrying along the street he caught up with her and saw that she was accompanied by James Count, the travel writer who'd been his other ferry companion.

'Rand, for God's sake!' Count put a heavy arm around his shoulders and Rand could smell the beer on his breath. 'Laura, this is the British chap I told you about. Laura Peters, Jeffrey Rand.'

She was much younger than Count, probably still in her twenties, with the fresh attractiveness of an outdoor person. 'Hello, Jeffrey Rand. You must come with us! I'm taking my uncle to see where I work.'

'Your uncle?'

'Don't you think we look alike?' she asked mischievously. 'If I had that moustache we'd be dead ringers!'

'Where are you two taking me?' Rand demanded with a smile.

'To something you've never seen before,' she assured him, starting down the narrow lane toward the waterfront. 'The Donkey Sanctuary!'

Even before they reached it the braying of the animals could be heard. If Rand had thought she was jesting he was proven wrong by the first sight of pens filled with injured, sick, and tired donkeys. 'What is this? Do you round them up off the streets, Miss Peters?'

'They are brought here by their owners or we find them ourselves. We offer rest and protection until they are well.'

'But whom do you work for? Who pays you for this?'

'The International Donkey Protection Trust of Sidmouth, Devon. I've been working for them the better part of a year and there's nothing like it.'

'I don't imagine there is,' Rand agreed.

She showed them around the place. The donkeys were interesting, but when Rand spotted a copy of the London *Times* in her small office he was more interested in that. 'I haven't seen one in weeks,' he admitted.

'Take it!' Laura said. 'I'm finished with it. They fly them in every week with my supplies. If you don't mind reading week-old news—'

He folded it and stuck it under his arm. 'Not at all. Thank you. Can I buy you people a beer or something?'

'A capital idea!' James Count agreed. 'I've already had a few but there's always room for one or two more.'

'Where shall we go?' his niece asked.

Count made a face. 'Only place in Lamu that serves cold beer is the Harmony Cafe. It's just a few blocks away.'

'I know it,' Rand told them. 'I ate dinner there.'

They paused at the outdoor pens while Laura petted some of her favorite donkeys, then left the Sanctuary to set off for the cafe. When they reached it Rand was pleased to see that the man who denied being George Ryder was no longer present. The owner of the place, a fat Arab named Hegad, was going over the menu with Onyx, the waitress who'd served Rand earlier. 'On Tuesday evenings we serve special Indian dishes,' he told her. 'Some traders sail up from Zanzibar for them.'

Somehow the thought of dhows docked by the jetty at Lamu like yachts on the Thames was more than Rand could imagine, but until an hour ago he'd never imagined a Donkey Sanctuary. The three of them chose a table near the door and Onyx came over to take their order. It was past the dinner hour, with only one other table occupied.

'Just beer,' Count told her. 'Three cold Tuskers.'

Onyx went off to fill the order and Rand asked about the local economy. 'What does one do for a living on Lamu?'

Laura Peters grinned. 'Tend to the donkeys. Seriously, though, there is dhow building and repairing in the villages, and fabulous tourism at the right times of the year. Shela, a village south of here, has a magnificent beach. All of that brings in money. The local police will tell you illegal currency exchange is a thriving business too, but I think they exaggerate.'

Over the second beer James Count and his niece turned their conversation to family matters and gossip about relatives in England and Australia. Rand glanced at the front page of the *Times*, skimming an article on the royal family. That was when his eye fell on an item at the bottom of the page. The headline read: *CIA Official Charged in Espionage Case*.

Rand quickly read the news report out of Washington: 'George Ryder, longtime CIA bureau chief, and his wife Martha were both indicted on multiple counts of espionage by a federal grand jury. They are assumed to have fled the country and a worldwide search is under way. It is believed that Ryder and his wife were paid more than two million dollars over the past decade to supply CIA secrets to Moscow.'

Rand lifted his eyes from the page and found himself staring at the empty table where George Ryder had been seated just a few hours earlier.

On the way back to the Sunrise Guest House Rand pondered the trick of fate that had brought him together with George Ryder at this remote outpost of civilization. They'd hardly known each other, and in truth Ryder might not even remember him. Now he was a wanted man, and Rand since his retirement was something of an unwanted man.

At the Sunrise, Rand climbed the stairs to his second-floor room and inserted the key in the lock. As he entered the darkened room he was aware of the slight swish of the ceiling fan above his head. He'd turned it off when he went out. He dropped quickly and quietly to the floor, knowing it was already too late. The red line of a laser gunsight had split the darkness and targeted the wall next to his head.

'Can't we talk about this?' Rand asked. There was a muffled sound like a dry cough and a bullet thudded into the wall above him. He slid forward under the bed, yanking off his shoe, throwing it against the side wall. The laser beam followed it, just for an instant, and Rand was out the other side of the bed, ripping the mosquito netting from its fastenings and wrapping it around the gunman before he could fire again.

He picked up the fallen gun, an awkward thing with its laser sight and silenced barrel. 'Who did you expect to kill with this, Ryder? I'm retired but I'm not crippled. How'd you find me?'

'I followed you from the ferry this afternoon.'

'One thing to remember, no matter how hot it gets you never turn on the ceiling fan when you're waiting in the dark to kill someone.'

'Give me back the gun and we'll forget about this. It was a mistake.'

'And you made it. I read your press notices in the London *Times*. I gather the Russians paid quite well.'

He sighed and glared at Rand. 'So you know what they're saying.'

'I assume it's true, since you took a shot at me. I didn't come here looking for you, Ryder. I'm retired from British Intelligence and I certainly have no connection with your CIA.'

'Then what are you doing on Lamu?'

Rand relaxed his grip on the mosquito netting but kept holding the pistol. He sat down on the edge of the bed. 'I was curious about the area. An American writer, Walter Satterthwait, called Lamu the most beautiful place he'd ever seen in his life. What are *you* doing here?'

'Waiting for my wife. She was supposed to meet me three days ago.'

'An odd place to meet, not exactly like Waterloo Bridge or the top of the Empire State Building.'

'We were here together once, years ago. Its very remoteness made it the perfect meeting place.'

'And it's on the way to Russia.'

'I doubt we'll be going there. Frankly, I don't know where we'll be going.' He turned his gaze on Rand, his face momentarily bathed in moonlight through the window. 'Are you planning to turn me in?'

'Is there any reason why I shouldn't? If the reports are correct the Russians paid you more than I earned in my entire career with Concealed Communications. How did you and your wife get into it, anyway?'

George Ryder shifted uneasily. 'If we're going to chat, I wish you'd remove this netting you've got me tangled in.'

Rand turned on the light and closed the window shutters. Then he allowed Ryder to unwrap himself. 'No tricks, or I'll see how this gun of yours works.'

'No tricks,' the CIA man promised. He sat in the room's only chair, a white wicker thing that looked uncomfortable. Rand remained seated on the bed. 'Martha and I met when we were in college,' he began. 'I was in a play and she helped with the make-up. We started going out and were married soon after graduation. I was taking a pre-law course but in my senior year I was recruited by the CIA. We moved to Washington and took up with other young couples in government service. I like to think we were popular then. People kidded us about being George and Martha, like Washington and his wife. The nineteen seventies were a glorious time. I was advancing at the company and Martha had a nice job at a travel agency. Then came the eighties.'

'What happened?' Rand asked quietly.

'I don't know. Maybe we were bored with our lives. Maybe it was simply like that spy in an Eric Ambler novel. We needed the money.'

'What were you giving them for it?'

'The names of Russian double agents. I never betrayed an American.'

'And your wife?'

'Martha used her position at the travel agency to arrange side trips for me. When I was out of the country on company business I'd hop over to a nearby city or country and meet with my Russian contact. That's how I delivered the material and how I was paid. The money went into a Swiss account in Martha's name, and she drew from it as we needed it.'

'They never suspected you?'

'Oh, sure. I was routinely questioned a few times, especially during the great mole hunt of the mid-eighties. But things always quieted down. I managed to satisfy them and even passed the polygraph tests.'

'Now you've been indicted.'

He stood up and Rand shifted his grip on the pistol. 'I'm being frank with you because we're in the same business, Rand. Or we were. Maybe you can understand how it is these days, with the Cold War over and the superpowers at peace with one another. Do you want to know how Martha and I managed to escape? The only close friend I still had in the company phoned me at a hotel two weeks ago and tipped me off. He said they'd been watching me and tapping my home phone for the past year. When I returned home Martha and I would both be arrested.'

'What did you do?'

'I sent a fax to Martha's travel agency, tipping her off in a prearranged code. She dispatched a ticket to Lamu, with a message that she'd join me here.'

'How do you think the CIA found out about you?'

'That's the damnedest part of all. My friend said my name came down a year ago from the highest level. It just took them twelve months to prove the charges were true.'

'The highest level?'

'No one will admit it. Maybe fifty years from now when the top-secret files are declassified, historians will learn about it. By that time it won't matter to anyone, especially not Martha and me. Remember what happened about a year ago? A new president of the United States met with a new president of Russia who was desperately seeking aid. The Cold War was over. Our president wanted a new beginning and the Russian president owed nothing to the former Soviet government. He owed nothing to the crumbling KGB.'

'What are you telling me?' Rand asked.

'I can't prove it, but I know what happened. They held a brief private meeting without even their advisors present. The Russian president made a final appeal for more aid, and my president asked, "What can you give me in return as a gesture of good faith?" and the Russian said, "I can give you the name of the top Soviet agent in the CIA," and he slipped a piece of paper across the table—a paper with my name on it.'

'You really think that happened?'

'It happened. The word came down to start an intensive investigation. It took them a year, but they finally nailed me. And Martha.'

'If she's not here yet she may not be coming.'

'I'll wait awhile longer. Every day when the ferry comes in from the airstrip I watch for the new arrivals. I saw you today, of course, but I hoped you wouldn't run into me, or remember me. I hoped you weren't the one sent to bring me in.'

'They'll only know where you are if they have Martha.'

'Yes. I'm betting she's still free and on her way here by some sort of roundabout route. If anyone can shake them Martha can.'

'And meanwhile you wait, and try to kill people like me. If there is an enemy here, Ryder, it could be anyone. It could be an Arab leading his donkey through the narrow lanes, or a trader sailing in on his dhow.'

'I know that.'

'You'll be running the rest of your life. That's why you're reluctant to go to Russia, isn't it? It's because you think the Russians betrayed you.'

'I'm going,' he said. 'Give me back my gun.'

Rand emptied the magazine onto the bedspread and cleared the chamber of the final round. Then he passed the weapon to George Ryder. 'You may need it, but not against me.' He returned the bullets too.

The American stuck the weapon in his belt, beneath his shirt, and left the room.

In the morning it was raining, a sudden downpour that woke Rand from a troubled sleep. He shaved and dressed and went out, borrowing one of the black umbrellas the guesthouse management kept in a stand by the front door. Although the Sunrise Guest House provided morning tea, he decided to walk to the Harmony Cafe for a full breakfast. The rain was still falling as he reached his destination and he left his umbrella inside the door. The waitress Onyx was not yet on duty but Hegad, the owner, was waiting on customers. Rand ordered banana pancakes with honey and a cup of tea. The pancakes were quite tasty but the tea was far too milky and sweet for his taste. He finally settled for a Coke.

'Has the American gentleman been around this morning?' he asked Hegad.

The fat Arab shook his head. 'No Americans today. They wait for the rain to stop.'

A few others drifted in and finally the waitress arrived, leaving her umbrella with the others. 'You are back again,' she said with a chuckle. 'Does our food deserve a second or third chance?'

'This was my first time for breakfast. Those pancakes are quite good.'

Onyx cast an eye on Hegad. 'Sometimes he lets me make them. They are even better.'

The rain was finally stopping and Rand remembered his ten o'clock appointment with Amin Shade at the dhows. He would worry about George Ryder later. He paid his bill and picked up the umbrella by the door. The humidity outside was high as the sun broke through the clouds and water vapor rose from the puddles along the lanes.

It was just before ten when he reached the mooring area for the dhows, south of the jetty. There was no sign of Shade, but he was surprised to see Laura Peters tugging on the reins of a recalcitrant donkey. She was trying, without great success, to urge him north along the shore to her Sanctuary a few hundred meters away.

'Need some help?' he asked.

'A great deal, Mr Rand. This creature just doesn't realize what I'm doing is for its own good! Could you give me a hand, push from the rear while I pull?'

He put down the umbrella and got into position. 'It's not every day I get to push donkeys.'

But it seemed to work, and the beast was soon in motion without even a parting kick. 'Thank you!' she called back to him. 'I'll give you a job any time you need one!'

He laughed and waved, turning back to the mooring area. There was still no sign of Amin Shade. Finally he asked an old man who seemed to be in charge of renting the dhows, 'Has Amin Shade been here this morning?'

The man peered at the boats bobbing on the water. 'He is out there on his vessel. He waits for you.'

The dhow he indicated was moored about fifty meters offshore. Rand could see a white-robed figure hunched over one of the two masts, but there was no rowboat riding alongside. He borrowed one from the old man and rowed himself out to meet Shade.

'Did you forget your invitation?' he asked as he pulled alongside and climbed over the railing.

The figure at the mast didn't move. It was indeed Amin Shade, but he wouldn't be traveling to Shela or anywhere else. He appeared to have been shot once in the throat. There was a great deal of blood all around, attracting flies, and Rand could see that he was dead.

Before summoning help, he looked closely at the deck in front of the sagging body. Shade had not died instantly from the neck wound. He'd lived long enough to print a half-dozen letters in his own blood. *CAMERI*, it said, or possibly the final *A* was incomplete and it was meant to read *CAMERA*.

Rand searched around for a camera but there was none on the vessel. In fact there was nothing at all that might have belonged to Amin Shade. If he'd had anything with him, the killer had taken it. Although the deck was wet from the morning rain it had not washed away the man's dying word. That meant he'd been alive during the last twenty minutes, after the rain had stopped, though the shooting could have been earlier.

Rand rowed back to shore and told the old man what he'd found. 'Amin Shade is dead. We must call the police.' The man's eyes widened. 'Did you hear a shot while you were here?'

'No, no shot! He go out to the boat with another Arab.'

'Did you see the man's face?'

A shake of the head. 'Raining. Shade covered the other with his umbrella. I went inside and did not see the other man row away.'

Presently, as word spread and a crowd gathered on the shore, the district commissioner arrived—a towering black man wearing portions of a military uniform and driving a Land Rover, the only motor vehicle allowed on the island. He listened intently to Rand's story and noted down his name and address in Lamu. 'We will talk to you further,' he promised in perfect English. 'Do not leave the island.'

That afternoon when the ferry arrived from the airstrip on the adjoining island, he found George Ryder standing in a nearby lane watching the new arrivals. Rand could see that Martha Ryder was not among them. 'Hello, Ryder,' he said. 'Do you still have the gun?'

The American looked at him distastefully. 'Are you planning a bit of blackmail, Rand?'

'No. Someone was killed today, possibly with a silenced pistol. No shot was heard. Can you imagine two silenced pistols in a place like Lamu?'

'I can imagine ten silenced pistols if I put my mind to it. I had nothing to do with any killing. I don't even know who died.'

'An Arab named Amin Shade who bought and sold dhows.'

'The name means nothing to me.'

'If you were watching yesterday's ferry, he got off with that travel writer and me. He was wearing a white robe and cap, carrying a furled umbrella.'

'I may have noticed him but I didn't know him.'

'Has there been any word from your wife?'

'None. I am beginning to fear she's been arrested. She would be here by now otherwise.' He started to turn away.

'Do you know anything about a camera?'

The American shrugged. 'Tourists and spies always carry them. Sometimes the tourists have more expensive cameras than the spies.'

Rand watched him walk away. Then he went back to the Sunrise Guest House and dug the bullet out of the wall of his room.

The district commissioner was named Captain Chegga and he remembered Rand from their morning encounter at the scene of Shade's murder. He used a small room at the post office when official business summoned him to Lamu, and in the confined space he seemed hemmed in and uncomfortable. 'It's much too humid here on the coast,' he grumbled. 'Do you have more information about the killing of Mr Shade?'

'Perhaps,' Rand answered. He took an envelope from his pocket and removed the bullet from it. 'You might try matching this with the slug that killed him. I assume it was recovered?'

'It will be. There was no exit wound. Where did this come from?'

'First tell me if it came from the same gun that killed Shade.'

The district commissioner smiled sadly. 'There are no facilities here in Lamu. The bullets must be sent to the mainland.'

'How long will that take? A few hours?'

'Ah, you Englishmen! You expect everything to happen instantly.'

'How long?'

'Twenty-four hours, at the very least. It will be morning before the bullets arrive for comparison, and afternoon before I receive a report, even by telephone.'

'I'll come back then. Meanwhile, what about Shade's background? Was he involved in anything—'

'Shady?' Captain Chegga laughed at his own humor. 'We are looking into it, never fear. Go now, Mr Rand, and enjoy your vacation. Or whatever it is that has brought you to Lamu.'

James Count was having a beer at the Harmony Cafe when Rand arrived there. 'The only place you can get a cold one,' he said, holding up his bottle of Tusker. 'Come join me.'

'How's the travel book going?' Rand asked, pulling out a chair for himself.

'Revisions, revisions. Even places like Lamu never stay quite the same. The guesthouses and cafes must be reevaluated, the prices adjusted.'

Rand told him about encountering Laura with the balky donkey that morning. 'It was just before I found that dead Arab, Amin Shade.'

'I heard about that,' the Australian said. 'Crimes against tourists are usually limited to confidence games or muggings.' He signaled to Onyx and she brought them two more cold beers. 'But then Shade was not a tourist.'

'Might he have been a smuggler?'

'Anything is possible.'

Rand saw the body again, lying in its pool of blood on the deck of the dhow. In his mind's eye he was trying to see something else, something that wasn't there—

'They say the killer was dressed like an Arab, in white robe and cap— *khanzus* and *kofia*, I guess they're called.'

'That proves nothing,' Count said.

'No, I suppose not.' Rand thought of something else. 'Is the ferry the only way onto this island?'

'Well, yes, but there are three ferries from various points on Manda Island, where the airstrip is, and another from the mainland. In addition, of course, there are always private dhows for hire.'

In the end Rand was no closer to learning anything than he'd been before. He declined Count's invitation to dinner, deciding he needed to be by himself. His long conversation with George Ryder the previous night had cut drastically into his sleeping time and he was beginning to feel the effects of it. He went back to his room and put in a call to Leila, trying not to alarm her with too much detail about the journey.

'It's beautiful here,' he said. 'A little paradise.'

'Will you be home soon?'

'I'm only booked here for three nights. We'll see what happens then.'

He thought about telling someone in London or Washington about George Ryder's presence in Lamu but decided against it. He was beginning to suspect that too many people knew about it already.

Rand spent Wednesday morning exploring the quaint little shops of the island, choosing a gift for his wife from among the native crafts and imported Asian items. In the afternoon he encountered George Ryder again, down by the ferry dock. James Count had told Rand that boats arrived

at different times of the day, but obviously it was the ferry airline connection that interested Ryder. Today the plane had brought no one at
all. The ferry carried only a man from the neighboring island with two
donkeys to sell.

'No word from her yet?' Rand asked the American.

'Nothing. If they have arrested her they will be coming for me next.'
He glanced nervously at Rand. 'You seem to be keeping an eye on me.'

'You tried to kill me two nights ago,' Rand reminded him. 'That makes
us practically brothers.'

'If they come for me, could I look to my brother for help?'

In that instant Rand almost felt sorry for the man. He didn't answer
directly, only asked, 'Where are you staying?'

'Yumbe House, a hotel at the north end of town, a few blocks inland
from the Donkey Sanctuary.'

'I'll find it.' The safest place for George Ryder might be a jail cell, but
he didn't tell him that.

After they parted Rand left the jetty and walked to the nearby post
office. Captain Chegga was in his office, relaxing beneath the slowly turning ceiling fan. 'It is Mr Rand, isn't it?'

'That's right. I came to see you yesterday. I brought you a bullet.'

'I remember.'

'Does it match the bullet that killed Amin Shade?'

'Yes, the bullets match, but it appears that the body does not match.
The real Amin Shade is alive and well on Zanzibar.'

'Then who—?'

'The dead man was an Italian ex-convict named Giacomo Verdi, a
confidence man and occasional government informer. He had been known
to indulge in blackmail in the past. He may have tried it again. Apparently
he assumed Shade's identity to help pull off some sort of swindle involv-
ing the sale of used dhows.'

'Then he wasn't an Arab at all?'

'No, no.' Captain Chegga played with the papers on his desk. 'Now if
you will please tell me where you obtained that bullet—'

'It was fired at me two nights ago by a sneak thief I discovered in my
room at the Sunrise Guest House. He escaped before I could raise the
alarm, and since he took nothing I didn't report it. That was the bullet
I dug out of the wall.'

'Interesting. The thief could have been an accomplice of Verdi's. They
may have had a falling-out.'

Suddenly the rain was back, with drops dancing against the windows of the little office. They reminded Rand of what he'd forgotten earlier. 'Did you find Shade's umbrella anywhere?'

'It was onshore. His initials were on the handle. He must have left it there when he rowed out to the dhow.'

'And now I find myself without one,' Rand said, looking out at the rain.

'It never lasts long, but you may borrow one of mine if you wish. I'm sure I'll be seeing you again, Mr Rand.' It sounded more like a threat than a promise.

The district commissioner had been right. The rain stopped within five minutes and Rand closed the borrowed umbrella. Up ahead he saw the man with the two donkeys who'd been aboard the ferry. He'd been joined now by James Count's niece from the Donkey Sanctuary, who was attempting to examine the animals.

'Need any help pushing?' Rand asked with a smile.

'No, but I'm trying to tell this man these animals are sick. I want to treat them at my place before he sells them.'

There was more talk in a language Rand did not understand, then Laura Peters seemed to end the discussion by taking a small camera from the pocket of her jeans and snapping a picture of the donkeys' heads. The trader was furious, trying to grab it from her, but Rand intervened. Finally he relented, and Laura smiled as she put away the camera and took hold of the donkeys' reins.

'Thank you for your help once again!' she told Rand. She set off toward the Sanctuary with the trader following meekly along.

Rand smiled and went on his way. He'd almost reached the Sunrise Guest House when an African man wearing a uniform similar to the district commissioner's appeared from a side lane to intercept him. 'Mr Rand, Captain Chegga wishes to see you.'

'I just saw him less than an hour ago. Is he worried about getting his umbrella back?'

The officer did not smile. 'You will come with me.'

Rand saw that he had no choice, and he fell into step beside the man. 'Where are we going? Back to the post office?'

'To Yumbe House.'

Rand recognized the name. It was the hotel where George Ryder was staying. He asked no more questions. It was a five-minute walk through the narrow lanes, and when they reached the little hotel the district commissioner's Land Rover was parked in front. They went up to the second floor where Captain Chegga was standing grim-faced with several others in the hall outside an open door.

'May I go in?' Rand asked.

The commissioner nodded. 'Touch nothing. We are waiting for the photographer.'

George Ryder was seated in a chair by the window. There was a bullet hole in his right temple and the gun was lying on the floor beneath his right hand, minus its silencer and laser scope. 'Did anyone hear the shot?' Rand asked.

'No one. The maid found him. When did you last see Mr Ryder?'

Rand knew the question was a trick. He'd never mentioned Ryder to the commissioner, but anyone might have seen them conversing at the jetty. 'Just before I stopped at your office. He was meeting the ferry from the airstrip.'

'Was there someone he knew on it?'

'No, only a trader with a pair of sick donkeys. The woman from the Sanctuary has them now.'

'Do you have any ideas about this?' Captain Chegga asked, gesturing towards the body in the chair.

'Just one. It wasn't suicide.'

'How so?'

'This place has thin walls, yet no one heard a shot. If you'll look closely at the barrel of that gun you'll see scratch marks where a silencer was attached. If he shot himself with a silenced gun, where's the silencer? Without the silencer this gun would have made more noise and left more powder burns around the wound.'

Chegga was impressed. 'You have done some detective work back in England, Mr Rand.'

'Not this sort. A bit of work with codes, but I suppose in a way it's all the same.'

'Do you know who killed him and the other one?'

'Yes.' He did know, now that it was too late.

'Will you tell me?'

'Suppose we discuss it over dinner tonight, Captain.'

'Where would you suggest?'

'The only place in Lamu that serves cold beer.'

Rand was not surprised to see James Count and his niece Laura at one of the tables when they entered the Harmony Cafe a couple of hours later. The owner, Hegad, hurried over to take their order, obviously a bit intimidated at having the district commissioner as a customer. Rand waved to Count and Laura and ordered a Tusker. Captain Chegga chose a glass of wine.

'I have spent too much time in Lamu,' the captain complained. 'There are duties on the mainland.'

'I was told nothing happens in a hurry here.'

'That is part of Lamu's charm,' Chegga agreed. 'But it can be carried too far. Will you tell me what you know?'

'All in good time.'

The beer tasted fine. Rand ordered from the chalked menu on the wall, choosing a beef dish as the safest. The captain ordered mutton. Onyx served them both in a reasonable time and Rand could see Hegad relax behind his cash register. 'Now will you tell me?' the captain asked.

Rand nodded. 'I think the time has come.'

Onyx had cleared the table of dishes and returned with the check. That was when Rand gripped her wrist and held it tight. 'What is this?' she asked.

'Captain Chegga, let me introduce you to the killer of Amin Shade and George Ryder—the elusive Mrs Ryder.'

Later, back at the little room in the post office, Rand told Captain Chegga, 'There were at least five clues pointing to Onyx as Mrs Ryder and the double killer of Shade and Ryder. For dramatic effect I might call them the clues of the borrowed gun, the wrong umbrella, the dangerous rain, the menu lesson, and the dying message.'

'I think you Englishmen sometimes read too much of Sherlock Holmes, but go on.'

'First, the borrowed gun. We established through the bullet comparison that Amin Shade, whatever his true name, was killed by George Ryder's gun. He'd tried to use it on me less than twelve hours earlier, and it was back at his side this afternoon. Conclusion: either Ryder killed Shade and then himself or he loaned the weapon to someone else. Since I'd shown that he didn't kill himself, we can conclude that he loaned the weapon to someone. Obviously that would have to be someone very close. Martha Ryder, as his co-conspirator, was the most likely person.'

The commissioner grunted. 'Except that she wasn't yet here on the island.'

'I had only his word for that, the word of a spy and traitor. He had a very good reason for keeping her presence on the island a secret. If I or someone else had come here to arrest him for extradition back to America, we'd be most likely to wait until Martha Ryder arrived too. So long as he went through the daily charade of waiting for her at the ferry dock, he was safe.'

'Go on.'

'The clue of the wrong umbrella. I had an umbrella with me yesterday morning. I left it by the door at the Harmony Cafe where I had breakfast. While I was there the waitress Onyx came in with another umbrella and left it by the door. I took an umbrella, thinking it was mine, when I left and went down to the dhow moorings to meet Amin Shade. I left the umbrella on shore to row out to his vessel and discover the body. The man who rents the dhows told me Shade was carrying an umbrella when he went out to his vessel, obscuring the face of his companion. Yet there was no umbrella on the dhow. There was nothing belonging to Shade. Obviously the killer took it as protection against the rain. You told me you found it on shore, with his initials on the handle. Had the killer left it there? No, the umbrella would have provided virtually no protection while he was rowing the boat to shore. It was taken because it was needed after landing, so it would not have been left on shore. I brought it there myself, because I picked up the wrong umbrella at the Harmony Cafe—the umbrella Onyx brought in with her.'

'But how could Onyx be Martha Ryder? Her skin color—'

'Which brings us to the clue of the dangerous rain. Why was an umbrella so necessary to the killer? Because the rain was dangerous. It would cause her body makeup to run! Ryder told me earlier he met his wife while performing in a college play for which she helped with the makeup. She used body makeup to give herself a brown skin and a perfect disguise. Onyx was not young, remember. Even in her makeup she was clearly middle-aged, with Western features. Something else—my clue of the menu lesson. Monday at the Harmony Cafe I overheard the owner explaining to Onyx that they featured special Indian dishes on Tuesday nights. The implication was that Onyx had been employed at the Harmony for less than a week.'

'She was new,' the commissioner confirmed. 'But your final clue, the dying message—'

'*CAMERI*. I thought he was trying to write *camera* until you told me that Shade wasn't Shade but an Italian confidence man named Verdi. In his dying moments he reverted to his native tongue. He was trying to write *CAMERIERA*, the Italian word for waitress. Because she was new, he didn't know the name she was using. He only knew that Martha Ryder was posing as a waitress, and when he tried to blackmail her, she took her husband's silenced pistol and shot him.'

'Why would she kill Ryder?'

'There could only be one reason. When he escaped arrest his continued freedom was too embarrassing for the governments involved.'

Rand went to the jetty a bit later when the commissioner and his Land Rover were leaving the island. He watched while Martha Ryder was led to the ferry in handcuffs. With the makeup gone she seemed simply a lonely middle-aged woman. He walked over to meet her and said, 'Tell me one thing, Mrs Ryder. Which side paid you to kill your husband?'

She stared at him for an instant before replying. 'Does it really matter? It's all politics.'

NOTES AND SOURCES

'Parker Adderson, Philosopher' by Ambrose Bierce (1842–1914?). From *Tales of Soldiers and Civilians* (New York, 1891).

Bierce was born in Ohio and fought in the American Civil War before becoming a journalist. His fiction is typically mordant in tone, often tinged with supernaturalism, and frequently turns on a surprise ending. A second collection of tales dealing with the Civil War, *Can Such Things Be?*, was published in 1895. His most celebrated work is *The Devil's Dictionary* (1911), a volume of ironic definitions.

'The Red Carnation' by Baroness [Emmuska Magdalena] Orczy (1865–1947). *Pearson's Magazine* (June 1898).

The daughter of a Hungarian aristocrat, Baroness Orczy studied painting in London where she met the artist Henry Montagu Barstow, whom she married in 1894. Besides her most famous book, *The Scarlet Pimpernel* (1905), she also wrote detective stories, including *The Old Man in the Corner* (1909, but published earlier in the *Royal Magazine*), and a historical novel about espionage, *A Spy of Napoleon* (1934). After the First World War she and her husband settled in Monte Carlo.

'The Rider in the Dawn' by Sir Arthur Quiller-Couch (1863–1944). From *Two Sides of the Face* (1903).

Quiller-Couch, a Cornishman by birth, was a prolific and accomplished writer, particularly adept at making effective fictional use of historical material. His *Astonishing History of Troy Town* (1888) was one of several novels set in the Cornish town of Fowey, where he settled in 1892. He was the original editor of *The Oxford Book of English Verse* (1900) and King Edward VII Professor of English Literature at Cambridge from 1912 to 1944.

'The Brass Butterfly' by William [Tufnell] Le Queux (1864–1927). From *Revelations of the Secret Service* (1911).

Le Queux was born in London of a French father and an English mother. He joined the staff of the *Globe* in 1891 as a parliamentary reporter but gave up journalism for fiction writing, becoming celebrated—notorious, even—for turning out sensational xenophobic fantasies warning against the German peril. These include *The Great War in England in 1897* (1894), *England's Peril* (1898), *The Invasion of 1910* (1905), and *Spies of the Kaiser* (1909). Other titles include *The Bomb-Makers* (1918) and *Bolo, the Super-Spy* (1919). Much of his success was due to the claims he made of having intimate knowledge of secret service work.

'Peiffer' by A[lfred] E[dward] W[oodley] Mason (1865–1948). From *The Four Corners of the World* (1917); published separately in the American *Metropolitan Magazine* (January 1918).

Educated at Dulwich and Trinity College, Oxford, Mason was a provincial actor before becoming Liberal MP for Coventry in 1906. During the First World War he was actively involved in intelligence work. As well as his most celebrated work, *The Four Feathers* (1902), he wrote adventure stories, historical novels, and detective fiction featuring Inspector Hanaud of the French Sûreté (e.g. *At the Villa Rose*, 1910; *The House of the Arrow*, 1924; *The Prisoner in the Opal*, 1928).

'Mr Collingrey, MP' by [Richard Horatio] Edgar Wallace (1875–1932). From *The Adventures of Heine* (1919).

Wallace overcame the apparent disadvantages of illegitimacy and self-education to become a writer whose success was nothing less than phenomenal. His output and inventiveness were prodigious. He produced novels and stories at an astonishing rate, his many bestsellers including *The Four Just Men* (1905), *Sanders of the River* (1911), and *The Mind of Mr J. G. Reeder* (1925). He died in New York working on the film script of what was to become *King Kong*.

'The Lit Chamber' by John Buchan (1875–1940). From *The Path of the King* (1920).

Buchan was the son of a Scottish Free Church minister. After being called to the Bar in 1901 he became assistant private secretary to Lord Milner in South Africa and during the First World War was a major in the Intelligence Corps. He became a Conservative MP in 1927. He wrote—journalism, fiction, history, and biography—throughout his life. The series of novels featuring Richard Hannay—*The Thirty-Nine Steps* (1915), *Greenmantle* (1916), *Mr Standfast* (1919), *The Three Hostages* (1924), and *The Island of Sheep* (1936)—influenced generations of thriller writers. He was made first Baron Tweedsmuir in 1935 and was governor-general of Canada from 1935 to 1940. The story is set in 1715, a year after the Hanoverian accession, during the first Jacobite rebellion.

'The Reckoning with Otto Schreed' by E[dward] Phillips Oppenheim (1866–1946). From *The Adventures of Mr Joseph P. Cray* (1925).

Oppenheim began his working life in the ailing family leather business, but after the appearance of his first novel, *Expiation*, published at his own expense in 1887, he became a professional thriller writer. He can have had few regrets. His name was made with *The Mysterious Mr Sabin* (1898), a typically fast-paced tale of espionage in high places, and went on to become one of the most successful genre writers of his time. Like Le Queux he warned strenuously, if less frantically and with more style, against the German menace.

'Giulia Lazzari' by W[illiam] Somerset Maugham (1874–1965). From *Ashenden; or, The British Secret Agent* (1928).

Born in Paris, the son of a lawyer attached to the British embassy, Maugham published his first novel, *Liza of Lambeth*, in 1897. From 1914 he travelled extensively in Europe, Asia, and elsewhere with his secretary and companion Gerald Haxton and in 1926 settled at Cap Ferrat on the French Riviera. His best-known novel, *Of Human Bondage* (1915), is strongly autobiographical. He was a master of the short-story form, his collections including *The Trembling of a Leaf* (1921) and *Six Stories in the First Person Singular* (1931).

'Judith' by C[harles] E[dward] Montague (1867–1928). From *Action and other stories* (1928).

Montague, educated at Balliol College, Oxford, joined the staff of the *Manchester Guardian* in 1890 and later became assistant editor. He was a well-known critic and reviewer and also wrote several novels, including *A Hind Let Loose* (1910), *Rough Justice* (1926), and *Right off the Map* (1927). *Disenchantment* (1922) is a bitter account of his experiences as a soldier during the First World War.

'The Pigeon Man' by [George] Valentine Williams (1883–1946). From *The Knife Behind the Curtain* (1930).

Educated at Downside, Williams joined Reuters (as Ian Fleming was later to do), eventually becoming Berlin correspondent, a post which provided him with plenty of material for his fiction. During the First World War he was commissioned in the Irish Guards, was wounded in action, and was awarded the MC. He also served in the Second World War, this time on intelligence assignments and as a member of the Political Warfare Executive based at Woburn Abbey. He scored an immediate success with his first novel, *The Man With the Club Foot* (1918), about a sinister German secret agent, Dr Adolph Grundt. This was followed by other Clubfoot novels, including *The Return of Clubfoot* (1922) and *Clubfoot the Avenger* (1924).

'Jumbo's Wife' by Frank O'Connor [Michael Francis O'Donovan] (1903–66). From *Guests of the Nation* (1931).

O'Donovan was born in Cork, the son of a soldier. He is best known as a short-story writer, though he also wrote literary criticism and produced translations from the Irish. His collections include *The Saint and Mary Kate* (1932), *Bones of Contention* (1936), *Three Old Brothers* (1937), *Crab Apple Jelly* (1944), and *Domestic Relations* (1957).

'Affaire de Cœur' by W[illiam] E[arle] Johns (1893–1968). From *The Camels Are Coming* (1932).

Johns, forever remembered as the creator of Biggles, enlisted in the Norfolk Yeomanry and served in Gallipoli and Salonika from 1916 to 1917, in which year he transferred to the Royal Flying Corps. In the last year of the war he was shot down and taken prisoner. He was the founder-editor of *Popular Flying* (1932). As well as the first Biggles stories collected in *The Camels Are Coming*, Johns produced over ninety books featuring his flying hero.

'Flood on the Goodwins' by A[rthur] D[urham] Divine (1904–87). First published in 1933; reprinted in the Faber anthology *My Best Spy Story* (1938).

Divine, born and educated in South Africa, was war and defence correspondent for the *Sunday Times* until 1975. He wrote several thrillers, as well as works of non-fiction, with a naval or maritime background.

'How Ryan Got Out of Russia' by Lord Dunsany [Edward John Moreton Drax Plunkett, 18th Baron] (1878–1957). From *Mr Jorkens Remembers Africa* (1934). Fantasist, dramatist, poet, Irish revivalist, and friend of Yeats, Gogarty, and Lady Gregory, Dunsany occupies a unique place in Anglo-Irish literature. His first book, *The Gods of Pegana* (1905), was a collection of non-Celtic mythological tales illustrated by the *fin-de-siècle* artist S. H. Sime, who also illustrated succeeding volumes such as *The Book of Wonder* (1912) and *The Blessing of Pan* (1927). His popular series of Jorkens books began with *The Travel Tales of Mr Joseph Jorkens* (1931).

'A Patriot' by John Galsworthy (1867–1933). Written in 1927 but first published posthumously in *Forsytes, Pendyces and Others* (1935), a collection of miscellaneous pieces assembled by his wife, Ada Galsworthy.

Galsworthy, educated at Harrow and New College, Oxford, trained for the law but turned to professional writing under the influence of his wife and with the assistance of Edward Garnett. His first volume of stories, *From the Four Winds*, appeared in 1897, the first of his Forsyte novels, *The Man of Property*, in 1906 (though the family made its first appearance in one of the stories in *Man of Devon*, 1901). He was awarded the Nobel Prize for Literature in 1932.

'A Double Double-Cross' by Peter Cheyney [Reginald Evelyn Peter Southouse Cheyney] (1896–1951). From *You Can't Hit a Woman and other stories* (1937).

One of the most popular thriller writers of the inter-war years, Cheyney did not achieve success until he was 40 with *This Man is Dangerous* (1936), featuring his private detective Lemmie Caution. Though he achieved his popularity largely through his crime and detective novels, some of his best work was in the espionage genre, in such novels as *Dark Duet* (1942), *The Stars Are Dark* (1943), and *Dark Hero* (1946).

'The Army of the Shadows' by Eric Ambler (b. 1909). From *The Queen's Book of the Red Cross* (1939); reprinted in *The Story So Far: Memories and Other Fictions* (1993).

Ambler's career began as an advertising copy writer. His first novel, *The Dark Frontier* (1936), was a chillingly prophetic story about a small Eastern European state that succeeds in making an atomic bomb. This was quickly followed by *Uncommon Danger* (1937), *Epitaph for a Spy* (1938), *Cause for Alarm* (1938), and, in 1939, *The Mask of Dimitrios*, perhaps his best novel. In these novels, and the many others that came after them, Ambler established himself as a major writer of intelligent, realistic thriller fiction that looked forward to, and has continued to influence, later writers such as John Le Carré.

'Citizen in Space' by Robert Sheckley (b. 1928). From *Citizen in Space* (1955).

Sheckley, born in New York, is a leading American writer of science fiction who also works in the crime and mystery field. He was the fiction editor of *Omni* from 1980 to 1982. His publications in the suspense genre include *Dead Run* (1961), *The Game of X* (1965), and *Time Limit* (1967). He has also published several collections of science fiction short stories.

'Risico' by Ian [Lancaster] Fleming (1908–64). From *For Your Eyes Only: Five Secret Occasions in the Life of James Bond* (1960).

Educated at Eton and Sandhurst, Fleming joined Reuters in 1931 and from 1933 to 1939 worked as a banker and stockbroker in London. During the Second World War he was the assistant to the director of Naval Intelligence. His iconic creation James Bond burst upon a receptive world in *Casino Royale* in 1953 and continued his exploits in *Dr No* (1958), *Moonraker* (1958), *Goldfinger* (1959), *The Spy Who Loved Me* (1962), *On Her Majesty's Secret Service* (1963), *You Only Live Twice* (1964), and *The Man With the Golden Gun* (posthumously published in 1965). He was also the author of a series of children's stories, published together as *Chitty-Chitty-Bang-Bang* (1964) and subsequently filmed (with a screenplay by Roald Dahl).

'Keep Walking' by Geoffrey [Edward West] Household (1900–88). First published in 1968; reprinted (as 'The Instinct of the Hunted') in *Ellery Queen's Mystery Magazine* (August 1972).

Household was educated at Clifton and Magdalen College, Oxford. After working as a banker in Romania and as a travelling salesman he began to contribute stories to the *Atlantic Monthly*, publishing his first novel, *The Third Hour*, in 1937. He is best known for his superb Buchanesque thriller *Rogue Male* (1939), about the consequences of a failed attempt to assassinate Hitler. It was filmed in 1941 as *Man Hunt*. A sequel, *Rogue Justice*, was published in 1982. Other novels include *A Rough Shoot* (1951), *Watcher in the Shadows* (1960), and *The Last Two Weeks of Georges Rivac* (1978). He also wrote books for children.

'Paper Casualty' by Len [Leonard Cyril] Deighton (b. 1929). From *Declarations of War* (1971).

Deighton is one of the giants of contemporary thriller writers. He was educated at Marylebone Grammar School and at the Royal College of Art. For a time he worked as an illustrator and was art director of an advertising agency. His first book, *The Ipcress File* (1962, filmed in 1965), was an instant success. The main character, who is nameless, is a wise-cracking working-class hero—the complete antithesis of the Buchanesque tradition. The success of this creation, combined with Deighton's terse and compressed style, and the use of apparently hard fact concerning the mechanics of espionage, gave the book landmark status in its genre. His other novels include *Funeral in Berlin* (1964, filmed 1967), and the sequence featuring his cynical hero Bernard Samson: *Berlin Game* (1983), *Mexico Set* (1984), and *London Match* (1985).

'Signal Tresham' by Michael [Francis] Gilbert (b. 1912). From *Mr Calder and Mr Behrens* (1982), but first published in *Ellery Queen's Mystery Magazine*.

Michael Gilbert served in North Africa and Italy during the Second World War and was mentioned in dispatches. A founder-member of the Crime Writers Association, he has combined a successful career as a crime writer with that of a practising solicitor. His first novel, *Close Quarters*, was published in 1947. Other volumes include *Be Shot for Sixpence* (1956), *The Tichborne Claimant* (1957), *Game Without Rules* (stories, 1967), *The Etruscan Net* (1969), *Petrella at Q* (stories, 1977), *Death of a Favourite Girl* (1980), and *The Black Seraphim* (1983). He was awarded the CBE in 1980 and edited *The Oxford Book of Legal Anecdotes* in 1986. His two MI6 agents, Daniel John Calder and Samuel Behrens (along with their Persian deerhound Rasselas), are amongst his most successful creations.

'Final Demand' by John Wainwright (b. 1921). From *Winter's Crimes 14* edited by Hilary Watson (1982).

Born in Leeds, John Wainwright served as an aircrew gunner in the Royal Air Force during the Second World War and as a policeman in West Yorkshire from 1947 to 1969. He writes mainly in the crime and mystery field. His many novels include *Death in a Sleeping City* (his first, 1965), *Kill the Girls and Make Them Cry* (1974), *Heroes No More* (1983), and *Portrait in Shadows* (1986). He also writes as Jack Ripley.

'The Rocking-Horse Spy' by Ted Allbeury [Theodore Edward le Bouthiller Allbeury] (b. 1917). First published in *Woman's Own* (1986); reprinted in *Other Kinds of Treason* (1990).

Born in Stockport, Lancashire, and educated in Birmingham, Allbeury served in the Army Intelligence Corps from 1940 to 1947. After the war he worked in advertising and public relations and did not become a full-time writer until the early 1970s, when he was 54. His first novel, *A Choice of Enemies* (1973) is partly autobiographical and tells the story of a man who is blackmailed back into intelligence work. Amongst his other works, many of which have become best-sellers, are *Moscow Quadrille* (1976), *The Alpha List* (1979), *The Judas Factor* (1984), and *The Seeds of Treason* (1986). He also writes as Richard Butler and Patrick Kelly.

'The Great Divide' by William Haggard [Richard Henry Michael Clayton] (1907–93). From *The Rigby File*, ed. Tim Heald (1989).

Haggard was born in Croydon, the son of a clergyman. The source of his pseudonym was H. Rider Haggard, a distant relative of his mother. Educated at Lancing and Christ Church, Oxford, he entered the Indian Civil Service in 1931, becoming a magistrate and sessions judge. He gained direct experience of intelligence work in the Indian Army during the Second World War. His first novel, *Slow Burner*, was published in 1959 and introduced his main character, Colonel Charles Russell, head of the Security Executive. In many ways Haggard's political thrillers hark back to the world of Buchan and Richard Hannay; but at the same time they have a realistic edge that looks forward to the darker fictions of Deighton and Le Carré. They include *Venetian Blind* (1959), *The Arena* (1961), *The Antagonists* (1964), and *Yesterday's Enemy* (1976). The volume from which this story is taken is a collection of reminiscences, by several hands, of the celebrated (though fictitious) secret agent Dorothy Mayotte Rigby and her friend Camilla Trefusis.

'A Branch of the Service' by [Henry] Graham Greene (1904–91). From *The Last Word and other stories* (1990).

Greene was educated at Berkhamsted School, where his father was headmaster, then at Balliol College, Oxford. He joined the Roman Catholic Church in 1926. His unique brand of superior thriller writing, what he called 'entertainments', was hugely influential and can be seen at its best in novels such as *Stamboul Train* (1932), *The Confidential Agent* (1939), *Our Man in Havana* (1958), *The Third Man* (1950), and *The Human Factor* (1978). Greene had the all too rare ability to invest popular genres such as the thriller and the detective story with authentic moral seriousness.

'Waiting for Mrs Ryder' by Edward D. Hoch (b. 1930). *Ellery Queen's Mystery Magazine* (November 1994).

Ed Hoch is one of America's most prolific writers of espionage and detective fiction and a leading anthologist. His work has featured prominently in *EQMM* over several decades. The story is Hoch's version of what might have happened after a case like the Aldrich Ames CIA revelations.

PUBLISHER'S ACKNOWLEDGEMENTS

The editor and publisher are grateful for permission to include the following copyright material:

Ted Allbeury, 'The Rocking-Horse Spy' from *Other Kinds of Treason* (New English Library, 1990; Coronet/Hodder & Stoughton, 1993). Reprinted by permission of Hodder Headline PLC.

Eric Ambler, 'The Army of the Shadows' from *The Queen's Book of the Red Cross* (1939). Reprinted by permission of Campbell, Thompson & McLaughlin.

Peter Cheyney, 'A Double Double-Cross' from *You Can't Hit a Woman* (Collins, 1937). Reprinted by permission of Toby Eady Associates Ltd.

Len Deighton, 'Paper Casualty' from *Declarations of War* (Jonathan Cape, 1971). Reprinted by permission of Random House UK Ltd.

A. D. Divine, 'Flood on the Goodwins' from *My Best Spy Story* (Faber & Faber Ltd., 1938). Reprinted by permission of David Higham Associates Ltd.

Lord Dunsany, 'How Ryan Got Out of Russia' from *Mr Jorkens Remembers Africa* (William Heinemann, 1934).

Ian Fleming, 'Risico' from *For Your Eyes Only* (Jonathan Cape, 1960). Copyright © Glidrose Productions Ltd., 1960. Reprinted by permission of Glidrose Publications Ltd.

Michael Gilbert, 'Signal Tresham' from *Mr Calder and Mr Behrens* (Hodder & Stoughton, 1982). Copyright © Michael Gilbert 1982. Reprinted by permission of Curtis Brown Ltd. on behalf of the author.

Graham Greene, 'A Branch of the Service' from *The Last Word and Other Stories* (Penguin Books Ltd., 1990). Reprinted by permission of David Higham Associates Ltd.

William Haggard, 'The Great Divide' from *The Rigby File* (Hodder & Stoughton, 1989).

356 · Publisher's Acknowledgements

Edward D. Hoch, 'Waiting for Mr Ryder' from *Ellery Queen's Mystery Magazine*, Nov. 1994. Reprinted by permission of the author.

Geoffrey Household, 'Keep Walking' from *Ellery Queen's Mystery Magazine*, Aug. 1972. Copyright © Geoffrey Household. Reprinted by permission of A. H. Heath & Co. Ltd.

W. E. Johns, 'Affaire du Coeur' from *The Camels are Coming*. Reprinted by permission of A. P. Watt Ltd. on behalf of W. E. Johns (Publications) Ltd.

A. E. W. Mason, 'Peiffer' from *The Four Corners of the World* (Hodder & Stoughton, 1917). Reprinted by the permission of A. P. Watt Ltd. on behalf of Trinity College, Oxford.

W. Somerset Maugham, 'Giulia Lazzaro' from *Ashenden* (William Heinemann, 1928). Reprinted by permission of Reed Consumer Books and A. P. Watt Ltd. on behalf of the Royal Literary Fund.

Frank O'Connor, 'Jumbo's Wife' from *Guests of the Nation* (Poolbeg Press, Dublin). Reprinted by permission of the Peters Fraser & Dunlop Group Ltd.

E. Phillips Oppenheim, 'The Reckoning with Otto Schreed' from *The Adventures of Mr Joseph P. Cray* (Hodder & Stoughton, 1925).

Baroness Orczy, 'The Red Carnation'. Reprinted by permission of A. P. Watt Ltd. on behalf of Sara Orczy-Barstow Brown.

Robert Sheckley, 'Citizen in Space' from *Citizen in Space*. Copyright © 1955. Reprinted by permission of Sheil Land Associates Ltd.

John Wainwright, 'Final Demand' from *Winter Crimes 14* (Macmillan, 1982).

Valentine Williams, 'The Pigeon Man' from *The Knife Behind the Curtain* (Hodder & Stoughton, 1930).

Any errors or omissions in the above list are entirely unintentional. If notified the publisher will be pleased to make any necessary corrections at the earliest opportunity.